Bluebell's Christmas Magic

Bluebell's Christmas Magic

Marie Laval

Where heroes are like chocolate – irresistible!

Copyright © 2021 Marie Laval

Published 2021 by Choc Lit Limited
Penrose House, Crawley Drive, Camberley, Surrey GU15 2AB, UK
www.choc-lit.com

The right of Marie Laval to be identified as the Author of this Work
has been asserted by her in accordance with the Copyright, Designs and
Patents Act 1988

A CIP catalogue record for this book is available
from the British Library

ISBN 978-1-78189-446-0

Printed and bound in Great Britain by Clays Ltd, Elcograf S.p.A.

Acknowledgements

I would like to thank my son Nicolas and daughter Clémence for providing me with a steady supply of very silly Christmas jokes, and all the friends who responded to my call for Christmas cracker jokes: Alison Creig, Jackie Ladbury, Helena Fairfax, Karen Aminadra, Sue McDonagh, Melody Winter, Kirsty Ferry, Tanja Celia and Marcia Woolf. I may not have used all your jokes but I am very grateful for your suggestions and the inspiration you gave me. Several of the jokes in the story are actually some I made up all by myself … but if I am very proud of them, I can reassure my children that I will not embarrass them any further by taking up stand up comedy!

I would also like to thank my Authors on the Edge friends, and especially Helena Fairfax for her encouragements.

Finally, I would like to thank the Choc Lit Panel for believing in *Bluebell's Christmas Magic*: Dimi E, Emily S, Bee M, Gillian C, Haley E, Jo O, Janice B, Carol D, Gill L, Joy S, Ruth N, Alma H, Joy B, Sharon W and Naomi Mc. Thanks also to Choc Lit for publishing the story and my brilliant editor for her great advice and suggestions, and to the Choc Lit graphic designers for giving me yet another beautiful and very festive cover.

Merci beaucoup!

Chapter One

'There's nothing to worry about. Nothing at all.' Cassie repeated the words through gritted teeth as she drove up the lane, but it did nothing to quieten the thudding of her heart or loosen the knot squeezing her stomach into a tight fist. The keys that she had stuffed into the front pocket of her dungarees weighed cold and heavy against her chest, an unpleasant reminder of where she was heading. Belthorn Manor. The name alone was enough to make her shudder...

The jagged outline of the mountains disappeared in low clouds and mist descended on the patchwork of snow, dead bracken and pine forests covering the hills. Belthorn wasn't even in sight and already the landscape filled her with gloom. She couldn't feel any further from the cheerful fairy riding a feather duster that was painted on the side of her van, under the catchphrase *'Don't let dust and grime get to you, call Bluebell to the rescue!'* Today, Cassie was the one who needed rescuing...

The van skidded as she negotiated yet another bend in the road, narrowly avoiding bumping into the back of a Range Rover parked at a weird angle near the Sanctuary Stone. Another rambler who had ignored the 'Private Road' sign at the bottom of the hill, no doubt. She changed gears and the van lurched ahead.

Belthorn's distinctive round chimneys soon poked out of the mist. Cassie drove past the rhododendron bushes and the pine trees that shielded the house from harsh winds, and scanned the grounds. No shadow crept across the vast expanse of lawn; no ghostly silhouette lurked in the ruined abbey nearby or shivered on Wolf Tarn's pebbly shores. The only ominous shapes were the spiky branches of the monkey puzzle tree reaching out to the sky like a giant stick insect.

The fist in her stomach loosened, and she felt her body relax for the first time that afternoon. Perhaps there really *was* nothing to worry about. She would open up the house, get the job done and go home. Two hours max, that's all it would take to dust, vacuum and tidy the main rooms. Of course, she would have to come back when Belthorn's new resident arrived in a week's time, but she would worry about that later.

She took the bag with her cleaning gear out of the van and pulled the keys out of her pocket to examine them. She hadn't been there for a while. Which was the right one?

She was about to insert the biggest key in the lock when the door was yanked open and a brute of a man stood in front of her, his broad shoulders filling the doorway.

In the blink of an eye she took in his strong, square jaw covered with stubble, the fine scars that ran across his cheeks and forehead, the misshapen nose which was bent to one side, as if it had been broken several times, and his slightly dishevelled brown hair that reached down to the collar of his shirt. But it was his eyes – hazel and gold, fierce and cold – that made her take a step back and scream in terror...

A burglar! A huge brute of a burglar! Adrenaline shot through her. Still screaming, she stumbled backwards, grabbed the first thing she found in her bag, and held the feather duster in front of her like a sword.

He frowned and took a step forward. 'What's going on?' His voice was very deep and very rough.

'Don't move!' She screamed at the top of her voice and took another step back, one hand still poking the air in front of her with the feather duster, the other frantically searching her dungarees' pockets for the keys to the van. Which one had she put them in? For the first time in years, she wondered if wearing dungarees with so many pockets was such a good idea.

Not looking in the least impressed, the man strode outside,

glanced at the van then at her. 'Listen, miss... *euh*... Bluebell. There's no need to call the police. My name is Lambert – Stefan Lambert. I'm a friend of Charlie Ashville's. He invited me to stay.'

He pulled a bunch of keys out of his jeans pocket and dangled them in front of her. 'See? I have the keys. I can show you my passport if you'd like, as well as Charlie's email giving me directions to this place.'

She tilted her head up and frowned. '*You* are Stefan Lambert?'

He looked down and nodded.

'But... You were supposed to be here next week.'

'There's been a change of plan.'

Now her heartbeat had slowed and the blood had stopped pounding in her ears, she could detect the slightest hint of a French accent in his deep, gruff voice. Heaving a sigh of relief, she lowered the feather duster. 'You scared me. I thought you were a burglar.'

'If it's any consolation, you scared me too. You have a very... ahem... strong voice.'

'That's because I used to sing in a band.'

A smile flickered on his face and warmed his golden hazel eyes. 'I don't know about your singing, but your screams must have frightened all the wildlife in a three-mile radius.'

For a second, he didn't look as cold and intimidating and she smiled back. 'If that's the way you feel, then I promise I'll refrain from singing in your presence.' She walked towards him, and extended her hand. 'Shall we start again? Good afternoon. My name is Cassie Bell, and I am delighted to meet you.'

And that was the truth. At least Lambert was a man of flesh and blood, and not one of the shadows that still haunted her nightmares...

She walked closer, filling his senses with a fresh, feminine citrus scent. She had a surprisingly strong handshake for such a small woman, and her smile seemed genuine. Yet, he had seen the terror in her eyes when she'd first seen him, and it was no wonder. The accident had left him with scars and broken bones, and a face that could at best be described as rugged, and at worst as hideous – at least that was what a couple of women had said the last time he ventured into a restaurant in Paris. The sooner she left him alone, the better.

She looked around and frowned. 'How did you get here? Did you take a taxi?'

He released her hand and stepped back. 'I walked.'

Her eyes widened in surprise. 'You walked? All the way from Red Moss?'

His heart grew cold. 'No... I... I had a problem with my car about two miles down the road. Something flew in front of my windscreen – a bird, I think. It was icy. The car skidded and ended up in a ditch. I wasn't able to get it out.'

There was no way he would tell her that he'd had some kind of hallucination. She would run away screaming again, perhaps even poke him with that ridiculous feather duster of hers.

'The black Range Rover near the Sanctuary Stone...' she whispered, before giving him a worried glance. 'Are you all right? You're not injured or anything? Perhaps I should take you to the GP's surgery for a check-up before they close for the weekend.'

She looked at him with such concern that he almost blurted out that he'd never be all right again, and that it wasn't just his body that was a broken mess but his mind too – no, make it his whole life.

'I'm fine,' he snapped, 'but I need to phone a garage and arrange for the car to be towed out of the ditch.'

'If you weren't planning on going out again today, your car will be quite safe on the lane overnight. I'll let Mason know first thing in the morning. He owns the garage in the village and will sort it for you.'

'Can't you phone him now?'

She shook her head and her blonde fringe fell into her eyes. She flicked it aside. 'There's no landline at Belthorn, no mobile phone signal either… and no television or Wi-Fi here. The only concessions to modern life are the electricity and the central heating, although neither is very reliable. The previous Lord Ashville wasn't interested in modernising Belthorn. He used this place as a retreat from his busy London life, and his son hasn't made any changes either.'

She cocked her head to one side and her fringe fell into her eyes again. 'You said you were a friend of Charles Ashville's. Have you known him long?'

'We have worked together on and off for years.'

'So you're a doctor too?' Another smile lit her heart-shaped face, and dimples appeared on her cheeks. He couldn't help but notice that she had a very nice smile. Her pale grey eyes, the colour of misty mornings, and her mop of blonde hair tied back with a red bandana were rather nice too.

She was looking at him, waiting for his answer.

'No. I am…' He shrugged, trying to ignore the pain in his back and shoulders, and corrected, 'I *was* a helicopter pilot in the French army but often worked with Inter Medics on rescue missions, most recently in Mali.'

'That's interesting. Are you here on holidays?'

'Sort of.' It wasn't really a lie.

'If it's quiet you're after, then Belthorn is perfect. As you have seen, the house is very isolated.'

'That's fine by me.' Silence, oblivion, forgetting about the world, and the world forgetting about him, was what he craved, especially with Christmas coming up.

'Won't you mind being alone here?' She pulled a face as she looked at the manor house's stone façade and mullioned windows, and the strange round chimneys rising from the roof.

Suddenly, exhaustion made his body ache all over and his

mind yearn for silence and sleep. 'Right now, being alone is my idea of heaven. Listen, I don't mean to be rude but I've had a long journey. I'm tired and—'

'And you need a cup of tea, of course! What was I thinking of?' She turned away, picked up her bag and strode into the house before he could say he didn't like tea and what he needed was for her to climb back into her van, with her feather duster and over-cheerful personality, and leave him alone.

Instead, he followed her into the house and closed the heavy oak door behind him.

Chapter Two

'Have you explored the house yet?' She took off her red duffle coat and hung it on the old-fashioned stand in the corridor.

'No. I'd only just got here when you arrived.' He gestured to the large khaki holdall that he had dropped at the foot of the stairs.

She flashed him a smile. 'Then why don't you take a look while I make you that hot drink? I'll call you when it's ready.'

She turned away and strode down the uneven stone-flagged corridor in her baggy dungarees and Doc Martens boots, the bright red bandana scarf tied in her blonde hair making a splash of colour in the winter afternoon's dim light.

He might as well do as she said. It didn't look as if he had much choice anyway... With a resigned sigh, he pushed the first door to his right and entered a spacious drawing room dominated by a stone fireplace. A large leather armchair stood next to it. A sofa covered with faded chintz fabric, a couple of antique looking glass-fronted cabinets displaying trinkets, and paintings of misty landscapes and a ruined castle – or was it a ruined abbey, like the one that stood on the grounds of the manor house? – completed the old-fashioned décor.

Not what he was used to, certainly, Stefan thought with a grim smile, recalling the spartan interiors of the successive army barracks where he had spent most of the past twenty years, or the barely-furnished Paris apartment where he crashed when he was on leave, and where he had spent the last few weeks since coming out of hospital.

The next room down the corridor was a huge, dark oak-panelled dining room with equally dark and dismal furniture. He grimaced, closed the door and carried on. Further along was a music room with a grand piano that cast a large, menacing shadow on the wall. The last door he tried opened into a library, with floor-to-ceiling bookshelves, a massive desk and an art deco cupboard he immediately recognised as a drinks cabinet.

Flipping the top open he took out a crystal tumbler and a decanter filled with amber liquor. This was more like it. Brandy. Better than tea any time. He poured some in a glass and drank it all in one gulp before walking to one of the patio doors framed by thick brown curtains. Blue grey mist bathed the garden where rhododendron bushes ran wild and the outline of the mountains now disappeared in the shadows.

All he could hear was silence.

Charlie was right. This place was perfect.

'Tea's ready!' the woman called.

Or it would be once he was alone.

He would give Cassie Bell five minutes to show him around then he would ask her to leave. He had done enough socialising for one day. No, make that a month.

'How do you like your tea?' she asked when he came into the kitchen.

'I don't.'

She gave him a puzzled look. On the table were two mugs of steaming hot tea, a jug of milk, a bowl of sugar, and a plate with an assortment of biscuits.

'I usually drink coffee,' he explained.

'You should have said. There's some instant coffee too.' She turned to open a cupboard.

'Leave it. It's all right. I'll drink the tea... Thank you,' he added in a softer tone, attempting the impossible task of making his voice sound less raw.

She sat down, took a small pad and a pen out of one her dungarees' many pockets, and looked at him. 'My colleague – make that former colleague, since she just resigned...' annoyance flashed in her eyes and she tapped her pen on the cover of her notebook '... well, Sophie used to come here twice a month to keep the place clean, but with you arriving early, I need to do a big shop in the supermarket in Keswick tomorrow, so we should make a list. I'll take care of your Christmas shopping too.'

She flipped her notebook open and looked at him. 'What would you like?'

He blinked. 'Christmas shopping?'

Her grey eyes sparkled. 'I promise I shall do my best to help you have a good Christmas. I do love Christmas, don't you?'

His whole body stiffened, and he gripped the handle of his mug so tightly his knuckles became white. How could he tell her that the mere mention of Christmas made him want to punch the wall? That it reminded him of what he had done – and who he had failed.

'My granddad often says I must be an elf in disguise,' Cassie Bell carried on. 'He even bought me a hat so I can look like one. Anyway, you'll need a tree, of course. Christmas isn't really Christmas without a tree, don't you think?'

What was this nonsense about elves and hats and Christmas trees, and did the woman have to talk so much, and so fast? Did she not need to breathe once in a while?

He raised a hand to stem the flow of words. 'Hang on a minute, Miss Bell...' Or was it Mrs? There was no wedding ring on her finger, but that didn't mean anything.

'Please call me Cassie. After all, we are going to see quite a lot of each other over the next few weeks.'

He blinked again. 'We are?'

She nodded. 'I shall come here every day to clean, tidy up and do your laundry. I will also take care of your shopping and do my best to provide good, hearty meals, but I must warn you that cooking isn't my forte, so please don't expect any Michelin cuisine from me.'

He frowned. 'I don't understand what you're talking about. I don't need anyone to clean, shop or cook for me. And by the way, I came here to forget all about Christmas, so don't

9

bother getting a tree or whatever else you were planning to buy. In fact, don't bother coming back at all.'

The woman's smile frosted over and her dimples faded away. 'There seems to be a misunderstanding. I have instructions from your friend Charles to come here every day. Think of me as your housekeeping fairy, rescuing you from all boring household chores.'

A fairy wearing dungarees and riding a feather duster… that was the picture painted at the side of her red van. He stared at the woman in front of him, and sighed. Bloody Charlie. Was he so afraid he'd do something daft that he'd hired a babysitter to watch over him?

'I'll take care of Charlie,' he said, his voice even more raspy than usual. 'I came here to be alone, not to be rescued by anyone, even less by an overzealous cleaning lady…'

She slapped her pen and notebook onto the table.

'I am sorry if that's the way you feel, but I'm being paid to do a job, and I intend to do it unless I get confirmation from Charles Ashville that my services are no longer required.'

She narrowed her eyes and tilted her chin. 'And if you don't mind me saying, this house would benefit from a little Christmas cheer… and you certainly would too, as well as from a good dose of good manners.' She crossed her arms, and two red spots appeared on her cheeks.

Touché. Stefan almost smiled. It looked like this cleaning fairy may be riding a feather duster instead of a broom but she could turn into a bit of a witch if provoked, and she wasn't all sugar, smiles and dimples.

He held his hands up. 'Message received loud and clear. You can come to Belthorn and do whatever you have to do until I get in touch with Charlie…'

Last he'd heard, Charlie was working in a field hospital in a very remote and very dangerous part of Mali. His friend didn't need to worry about him on top of everything else he had to contend with over there.

'But I object to you doing my laundry,' he added. 'I will take care of my socks and underpants myself.'

If he was hoping to make her smile, he'd failed miserably. She gave him a hard grey stare, flipped the cover of her notebook open and took hold of her pen again. 'That's fine with me... So, would it be *overzealous* to ask a few questions about your dietary requirements?'

The hurt in her tone made him feel a little guilty. After all, she was only doing what Charlie had asked. It wasn't her fault his friend was being overprotective. 'Not at all. Fire away.'

'Are you a vegan or vegetarian?'

He shook his head.

'Any allergies or food preferences I should know about?'

'None.'

She scribbled something in her notebook, then slipped it back into the pocket of her dungarees. 'Good. I will get some supplies tomorrow, enough to tide you over for the weekend. Now I will show you the fuse box, how to work the heating and where to find the instruction booklets for all the appliances.'

He nodded and rose to his feet. His back screamed in protest but he tightened his fists in his pockets against the pain. He'd give her five minutes – ten at the most – and then he would do what he craved to do. Take his painkillers. Lie down and slide into oblivion.

Chapter Three

He was a bear, Cassie decided as the van rumbled down the lane. No, make that a rude, grouchy and disgruntled bear, and he had no excuse for being so obnoxious when she was only doing her job and trying to be helpful.

Lambert had more or less shown her the door the moment she had finished explaining how to use the oven range, where to find the fuse box and the stopcock, and how to start the boiler should it fail. He hadn't even glanced at the various manuals for the appliances. In fact, thinking back to the cold, harsh glare in his hazel eyes and the nervous twitch that had appeared by the side of his mouth when she said she had to give the house a thorough vacuum, clean the bathrooms and make his bed, she was surprised she had lasted that long.

He had retorted in that deep, rough voice of his that the vacuuming could wait and that he'd make his own bed, and had hardly given her the time to put her coat on and gather her bags before shutting the door in her face.

He made it very clear that he wanted nothing to do with her. 'Well, *Monsieur* Lambert,' she muttered to herself, 'I don't want anything to do with you either!'

The problem was that she couldn't leave him alone, however much she wanted to, without paying back the money Charles Ashville had already transferred to cover her housekeeping costs, and waving goodbye to the bonus he had promised to pay her if his friend was satisfied with her services. Business was scarce in winter and she needed every penny.

The lane was slippery, and she slowed to a crawling pace as she approached the Sanctuary Stone and Lambert's car. He may not look like a man who would be easily spooked, but something had scared him, enough for him to skid and crash the car. What had he seen? Her throat dried up, and her fingers gripped the wheel more tightly. What if it was the ghost of the Grey Friar who haunted the ruined abbey, and her nightmares? She let out a slow breath. Better not think about the Grey Friar. People claimed that thinking about him was enough to conjure him up...

Her breathing only steadied once she had driven over the cattle grid at the bottom of the lane and she was back on the main road. She could forget about Belthorn until the following day. What she couldn't get out of her mind, however, was Stefan Lambert's hazel eyes and the sound of his broken voice. However unpleasant he was, the man shouldn't be alone at night in that big, gloomy manor house. No one should.

She had hardly parked in front of Bluebell Cottage when her grandfather opened the front door. He must have been standing at the window, watching out for her.

'What took you so long, Trifle?' he asked, using the nickname she had been given as a child, and never managed to lose. 'I've been waiting for my tea. Did you forget it was Friday night?'

Cassie took her bags from the back of the van and walked up the path leading to the door. 'Sorry, Granddad, but I've been busy.'

'Busy doing what? Only this morning you were complaining that there wasn't much work.'

She hung her coat on the peg in the hallway, and dropped her bags to the floor. 'I had to go to Belthorn. Sophie resigned today, just like that! She's going to live with her boyfriend and work as a waitress in Manchester, can you believe it?'

'Can I believe what? That you went to Belthorn although you hate the place, or that scatterbrain friend of yours left Red Moss?'

'Both.'

Her granddad followed her into the kitchen. He was dressed for going out, his white hair freshly washed and combed back. Cassie's nose twitched. It smelled like he'd splashed on the aftershave she'd bought him for his birthday too.

It didn't matter what time of year it was, or what the weather was like, Friday night was pub night for Joseph Bell and his friends, just like Tuesday night was dance night and Thursday afternoon bingo, dominoes and card games at the community centre. At seventy-seven, her granddad had a social life she could only envy.

'You look very dapper in your chequered shirt,' she remarked, with a smile.

'Thank you, love.' He smoothed an imaginary crease along his left arm. She knew it was imaginary because she had ironed the shirt that very morning.

She took some butter, milk and half a dozen eggs out of the fridge, and a mixing bowl from the cupboard. 'Scrambled eggs on toast all right for you?'

'Aye, that'll be fine, love. What were you saying about young Sophie?'

Sophie was twenty-eight like Cassie, but for her granddad, anybody under the age of fifty was a child. While she whisked the eggs in a bowl with a little milk, a pinch of salt and some black pepper, Cassie told him about Sophie's sudden departure for Manchester.

'Bah. Young Sophie is in love,' he said.

'But she's only known John for five minutes – well, for a few months – whereas we've been friends forever!' Cassie huffed. 'We were at primary school together; we sang in that eighties tribute band, Bandanamama, in all the pubs in the area…' And had so much fun doing so, even if, as Stefan Lambert had said, her voice had enough volume to scare the wildlife away.

'Sophie has worked with me ever since I took over from Mum and started Bluebell Cleaning. How can she leave everything for that boyfriend, just like that? What if it all goes wrong and she finds out they are not suited at all and it was a great big mistake?'

'Then she'll come back. It's no big deal. Red Moss will still be here, as will her family… and you.'

Cassie stopped whisking the egg mixture and drew in a breath. Would she always be there, like the hills and the fells and the tarns? Would she stay at Red Moss until she grew old, having never experienced life away from the village and never achieved her dreams?

'I cannot fathom why folks would rather live in a crowded city, and breathe car fumes rather than the clean, fresh air of our fells and valleys,' her granddad said. 'At least you don't believe all that nonsense about life being better in a big town, do you, Trifle?'

Aware that he was looking at her, she shook her head, added milk, whisked the eggs again and whispered, 'Of course not, Granddad.'

How could she tell him that part of her wished she could be as free – and brave – as Sophie?

Her grandfather let out a loud sigh. 'Sophie will be back, with or without her Romeo, you'll see. Shall I butter the bread?'

'Please.' She poured the mixture into the frying pan and scrambled the eggs whilst he set the table. A few minutes later, they sat down to eat.

'Bon appétit,' she said without thinking, and was immediately reminded of Stefan Lambert, and the way his eyes had darkened when she had mentioned Christmas. What had happened to make him hate Christmas so much? She let out a frustrated growl and put her fork down.

Her granddad looked at her. 'What's the matter, Trifle?'

'I was thinking about the new guest at Belthorn. I'm worried about him, all alone up there. Did I tell you he was French?'

Her granddad frowned. 'French? What's he doing at Belthorn?'

'I don't know. He's a friend of Charles Ashville's. He said he was a helicopter pilot. I think he was injured in combat or something.' Her throat tightened at the memory of the fine scars criss-crossing Lambert's forehead and cheeks, and the way his face had twisted in pain when he sat down.

She was expecting her granddad to come up with some silly joke about Frenchmen and onions, frogs or snails, but he only stared at her.

'A Frenchman convalescing at Belthorn…' he said in a slow, thoughtful voice. He put his fork down. 'Do you remember your great-great-aunt Ruth Merriweather's story?'

She shrugged, impatient. 'Of course. Everybody knows that story.'

'No, they don't. Not the full story, anyhow. I'll give you something to read before I go out.'

He leaned across the table. 'By the way, I have a new joke for you. What do French people like to sing at Christmas?'

Her grandfather was practising for the forthcoming Comedy Night at the village pub. 'Hmm… I'm not sure. What is it?'

He tutted. 'You're not trying very hard, Trifle. It's "Jingle Snails", of course!' And he burst out laughing.

'Oh, Granddad,' she groaned.

His blue eyes sparkled. He looked so pleased with himself she didn't have the heart to tell him that this may not be his best joke. Then again, it wasn't his worst one either.

The silence was deep and absolute. Not even the faintest sliver of moon lit the night sky. No star pricked the thick, velvety blackness. Never had he felt so alone and cut off from everything and everyone else.

No one except Charlie knew where he was – and Cassie Bell, of course – and that was exactly what he wanted. He had scribbled a note for his mother, asking her not to worry, claiming that he was staying with friends over Christmas and promising to be in touch sometime in the New Year. She would be relieved to be rid of him for a while, and not have to tiptoe around his black moods whenever she felt obliged to visit. She would also be glad not to have to stand between Stefan and his father, who had practically disowned him for letting the family name down.

A retired army officer, his father had been disgusted by Stefan's 'fiasco', as he called it. If he was to be believed, Stefan was the first Lambert ever to go on sick leave and 'soft in the head', as he referred to Stefan's breakdown.

Stefan drew the curtains and turned back into the drawing room. What should he do now? He could read the paper he'd bought at a service station on the way, the thrillers he had packed before leaving Paris, or the training manual for a long-range tactical transport helicopter he'd been asked to rewrite. There was also a walking guidebook to the Lakes that Charlie's sister had given him when he'd collected the keys to the manor house from her London flat.

Thrillers didn't appeal much tonight. He wasn't in the mood to plan a walk. As for the training guide, he had the next few weeks to get to grips with it. This was probably his last ever army job, since he'd better face the truth that he'd probably never fly again.

He wandered into the library and stopped in front of one of the tall bookcases lining the wall. His finger lingered over the spine of the books. He pulled out a couple that looked interesting then slotted them back into place again. Nothing took his fancy. Perhaps he should just pour himself a brandy and go to bed early.

He was about to turn away when he spotted a handful of books about aviation and the First World War on the bottom shelf. Among them was a leather-bound book with a small insignia etched on the spine. Curious, he bent down to pick it up and stared at it in wonder.

'*La Cigogne*?' He would recognise that insignia anywhere.

It was the legendary downstroke stork of the SPA 3 – the elite French aviation escadrille of the First World War.

He opened the book, flicked through the thin, yellowing pages, and got his second surprise. It wasn't a book but a journal, written in French in faded blue ink. There was a name on the first page – André Vaillant, with the mention SPA 3 *pilote*.

How had that journal ended up in the library of an old manor house in the North of England? Stefan poured himself a brandy and walked back into the drawing room with his glass and the book. Settling into the battered armchair next to the fireplace, he slid a cushion behind his back. A fire would be more homely, not to mention more efficient than the antiquated radiator, but he had left it too late to get wood from the shed.

Never mind. He could always make a fire the following day, after sorting out his car... and apologising to Cassie Bell.

The memory of the startled expression on the young woman's face as he more or less pushed her out of the house made him flinch. He had been rude, and there had been no call for it. It wasn't her fault if Charlie was being his usual overprotective self and hired her to keep an eye on him.

The funny thing was, he had been in a hurry to get rid of her because he wanted to take his painkillers and go to bed, but his backache had eased the moment she had left.

He drank a sip of brandy, enjoying the subtle but fiery taste, and opened the diary. Immediately a musty smell rose from the yellowing pages. Narrowing his eyes to decipher the spidery writing, he read the first entry dated 1st August 1919.

1.8.1919, Belthorn Manor.
I never thought that I would one day consign my thoughts into a journal. I was never a prolific or particularly gifted letter writer, but Aurelia gave me this journal for my birthday and

made me promise to record my adventures in the wilderness of the North of England, as she put it.

So here is the first, and very dull, instalment. Perhaps I should name this diary *Journal of an Ill-tempered Cripple*, but it would make me sound bitter and ungrateful and, despite everything, I am neither.

My arrival at Belthorn today was a bit of a shambles, my fault I hasten to say. I left Paris a couple of days earlier than planned because Mother's constant fussing, although well intentioned, was driving me insane. The journey from Dover, then London and Lancaster was uneventful. I arrived early in the evening and found a room at the Toll House Inn, not far from the station. The dining room was almost empty when I got there, but soon filled up with a dozen or more men drinking and smoking and exchanging harrowing memories and grisly war anecdotes.

I only lasted a few minutes before getting up and limping back to my room. I don't need to listen to anybody else's nightmares. I have enough with my own.

The train was delayed in Lancaster this morning and was two hours late pulling in at Foxfield Station. As I wasn't supposed to arrive today, the carriage Ashville said would collect me wasn't there, but I secured a place on a farmer's cart, which took me to the small village of Coniston where I stopped for a late lunch at the Sun Inn. A boy was sent to warn William Merriweather, Ashville's caretaker, of my arrival. The man arrived within the hour, twisting his cap in his hands and apologising profusely for getting the day of my arrival wrong. I reassured him that it was I who had travelled early, and we set off in his cart.

As we travelled to Belthorn Manor he only spoke to point out the odd farm or hamlet on the way, but it didn't matter because I was too busy looking at the rocky peaks and deep green valleys dotted with white and grey sheep – Herdwick breed, Merriweather informed me – gushing waterfalls and *lakes mirroring the grey sky. I can honestly say that I have never seen such a breathtaking landscape. I wish I could see it from the sky, but I know my flying days are over...*

Belthorn is a small manor house with three gables, turrets at both ends and the most unusual chimneys I have ever seen – tall and round, they rise from the roof like the masts of a ship. The hall is set in vast grounds that must have once belonged to an abbey, judging from the nearby ruins half-covered in brambles and overgrown vegetation. It even has its own lake – 'Wolf Tarn'.

Intrigued, Stefan turned the page over. Why had André Vaillant ended up at Belthorn Manor in the summer of 1919?

The house is staffed by two housemaids and a cook. There is also a gardener, although I only caught a glimpse of him. Everybody was very kind and polite. They didn't stare when I struggled to get out of the cart, limped my way along the corridor and hobbled up the stairs but I sensed they were curious and uneasy towards me.

The younger maid, a comely girl called Ruth, showed me to a large, airy room overlooking the back of the house and the fells. Two paintings hang on the wall opposite my bed – the portrait of a rather sad young woman, and a painting of a woodland cottage and a swan gliding on a lake. Intrigued, I asked the maid about it, and she said it was called The Hunchback and the Swan.

Stefan frowned. How odd... The very same paintings hung on the wall of the bedroom he'd chosen.

Now the house staff have retired for the night, I am alone in the parlour. The silence is swallowing me, cocooning me and I feel I can breathe again. Will this be the place where I forget the tumult and the horror of the past few years, and where I learn to live again?

Stefan closed his eyes and shut the book. Vaillant's thoughts and experiences seemed to mirror his own, but he was too exhausted to read on. What had happened to him and did he find the peace and solace he was looking for at Belthorn?

Chapter Four

Cassie's grandfather wrapped his woollen scarf around his neck and slipped his coat on.

'You won't be late back, will you?' she asked.

He winked. 'Are you afraid in case Doris from across the road lures me into her house to have her wicked way with me? The woman is forever knocking on the door to ask me if I've seen her cat, but who knows, perhaps it's an excuse and she secretly fancies me.'

She laughed. 'I don't think Doris has any romantic interest in you, Granddad.'

Her granddad made a pretend shocked face. 'Don't dismiss me so quickly, young lady. I'll have you know that I was quite the heartthrob in my youth and can still cause a stir among all the lovely ladies of the community centre.'

'I'm sure you can, especially when you bring them cakes from Salomé's bakery or regale them with your risqué jokes. Unfortunately, Doris only loves her cat and sees you as the villain who is trying to steal it away from her.'

'It's not my fault if that darn cat prefers Bluebell Cottage to his own home!'

'No, it's not... Anyhow, you know I can't sleep until you're home and tucked up in bed, so please don't let Big Jim talk you into a lock-in tonight.'

'Don't worry, Trifle, I shall come straight home at closing time.' He looked in the hallway mirror to adjust his favourite tweed cap – the cap he had been looking for since the beginning of the week.

Cassie pointed to it. 'You found your cap. Where was it?'

The happy twinkle faded from his eyes. 'In the cupboard under the stairs. I have no idea how it got there.'

Her chest tightened but she forced a smile. Her granddad's

memory seemed to be failing lately. He kept misplacing his keys, his medication, even his bank card, but there was no point remarking on it. It would only upset him.

'What matters is that you found it,' she said.

He nodded. 'Are you sure you don't want to come to the pub with me?'

'Positive. I'm tired, and I want to read the letters you gave me.'

Once alone, Cassie tidied up the kitchen, did the washing-up and made herself another mug of tea that she took into the living room. She picked up the bundle of letters her grandfather had given her, and untied the faded blue ribbon that bound them together.

There were only six, all addressed to Ruth Merriweather at Patterdale Farm, Red Moss. Patterdale was the farm her maternal great-great-grandparents, William and Mary Merriweather, had tenanted before their landlord – Thomas Ashville – sold it to them after the First World War. It had passed down to their children, grandchildren and their descendants, and now belonged to her cousin Tim, his wife Rachel, and their three children.

Life was hard on the farm for William and Mary's family, so in order to make ends meet they were forced to seek other sources of income. William worked as part-time caretaker to Belthorn Manor, and occasionally at the slate quarry too. His two daughters, Ruth and Betty – Betty being her great-grandmother – filled in as housemaids when the Ashvilles were in residence, or when there were guests. It was ironic that a century later Cassie should carry on with the family tradition, and look after another Ashville guest at Belthorn.

Cassie knew all about Ruth, her great-grandmother's sister. One could not live in Red Moss and ignore the young woman's tragic story, which was repeated to children and teenagers as a warning not to go anywhere near Wolf Tarn's treacherous waters.

No one, however, had ever mentioned any letters before now. Her grandmother must have had them for years, yet she had never disclosed them to Cassie, and her granddad had only chosen to hand them over after she'd told him about Stefan Lambert.

Cassie flicked through the envelopes. They all bore a faded red stamp featuring a woman wearing a funny hat and a flimsy Grecian dress, with the words *'République Française'* printed in white and a faded blue circular postmark. The writing on four of the envelopes was the same, hurried, spidery and hard to read, whereas the writing on the last two envelopes was more elegant. Probably a woman's handwriting, Cassie decided.

She pulled out the first letter, dated October 1st 1919, and started reading. Thankfully, it was in English or she wouldn't have been able to understand very much. French hadn't been her best subject at school.

My darling girl,
After a dreary but uneventful journey I arrived back in Paris yesterday to find my mother desperately ill. Even though Aurelia had warned me in her letter urging me to come home, it was still a shock to find my mother so weak. The doctor visited this morning and didn't offer much hope of her recovering. He said that the infection had reached her lungs and that the fever was now putting too much strain on her heart. It was something he had seen too many times already this year. The Spanish Flu, as he called it, has caused ravages all around the world, our poor mother was now its latest victim.

Aurelia and I are taking turns to sit at her bedside. The house is dark and gloomy, and filled with an ominous silence, as if death had already crept in and lay in waiting.

Thinking of your beautiful smile and of the day when I can hold you in my arms again is the only thing that keeps me

sane at this sad time. I hope you are keeping safe and well.
Please take care, my love.

   Yours forever,
   André

So Ruth had a French sweetheart, and what's more they had met at Belthorn! That was something nobody had ever mentioned before. She pulled out the next letter, dated one week later. This time André was writing about his mother's funeral that had taken place in the pouring rain. He had caught a chill – unless it was the dreaded influenza – and was unable to sort out his mother's papers as quickly as he would have wished. He was, however, hopeful to come back to Belthorn before Christmas. *'And then we will get married and I will take you back to Paris. You'll love it here.'*

   He wrote again in early November. He had been very ill, presumably with the Spanish Flu.

If only you could see me, my love, coughing and wheezing, too ill to get out of bed and my hand shaking so much I can hardly hold a pen. I am a pitiful sight indeed, but I force myself to eat broth and swallow the tonic the doctor prescribed, even if it tastes vile. Aurelia is looking after me, but I have made arrangements for her to stay with relatives in the country outside Reims when I come back for you. I told her about you, my darling Ruth, and she cannot wait to meet you. I hope you are keeping well and all is well at Patterdale Farm.

He finished with tender words and promises of a life filled with love and happiness. His next letter a couple of weeks later had a very different tone – a very cold tone. André mentioned feeling weak and having to postpone his journey back to England once more, but there were no burning declarations of love, no 'darling Ruth' or mention of their forthcoming wedding. Her fingers were shaking as Cassie pulled out the next letter. It wasn't André who had written, but his sister Aurelia. Cassie held her breath as she read the short, heartbreaking message. Aurelia wrote that André would not be going back to Belthorn. That he had realised Ruth and he were not suited after all and their marriage would be a grave mistake and only result in unhappiness for both of them. He was releasing her from the engagement and wished her well for the future. It was pointless for Ruth to write again because André would return her letters unopened.

Only one envelope remained. It had Aurelia's handwriting again, but it was quite bulky this time, and no wonder since it contained a letter Ruth had written to André, and that he was returning, unopened, like his sister said he would. She lifted the envelope with Ruth's childish handwriting and imagined her applying herself as she wrote the French address, hoping that André would read her words, and come back to her. But he hadn't even bothered to open it.

Cassie's heart lurched in her chest and her fingers stroked the envelope that nobody had ever opened. Should she do it? Would it be disrespectful to read Ruth's letter now, a hundred years after she posted it to her French lover?

Surely it would be far more disrespectful *not* to read it! A young woman had probably poured her heart into a letter that no one had ever read...

She got up to retrieve a knife from the kitchen drawer and carefully slid the blade along the top of the envelope to cut it open, before lifting a thin sheet of yellowish paper, covered with faded blue handwriting and marked with brown creases where it had been folded for so long.

My André, my darling,
This is the third letter I am writing since your sister returned the previous two, and I dare hope that you will read this and reply to me this time. Why are you being so cruel? What have

I done wrong that made you change your mind – change your heart – about me? Are you ashamed of me because I am only a housemaid and my father is a farmer? Every night I dream that you are back, but then every morning I realise that you are still far away and do not love me any more. Please, my darling, answer me. Come back to your Ruth. My heart is breaking.

Cassie examined the date the French post office had stamped on Aurelia's envelope – December 19th 1919. It had been delivered to Patterdale Farm just a few days before Ruth had drowned in Wolf Tarn...

Perhaps it would have been better if she hadn't opened the letter after all, Cassie thought, as she folded Ruth's letter and slipped it back into the envelope.

For a few moments, she stared at the room without really seeing the twinkling lights on the fake tree, the faded beige wallpaper that peeled off in places and the pedestal lamp with its mustard coloured shade and bedraggled tassels her granddad refused to throw away because his darling Elsie – her grandma – had bought it when they were newly-weds, some fifty years earlier.

For once, as her gaze swept over the old-fashioned gas fire with its blue and white patterned tiles and fake coals that didn't glow any longer, Cassie didn't cringe at the overwhelming 1950s décor, and her fingers didn't itch to rip the carpet and fussy wallpaper off and give the room, and the whole cottage, a fresh new look.

Her granddad had been right. The letters hinted at a story she hadn't suspected – a story that was more tragic that she could ever imagine.

She jumped to her feet. Her granddad had been right about something else, she thought, as she slipped on her duffle coat and grabbed her handbag. She did fancy some company after all.

The pre-Christmas lull wasn't something Red Moss's only pub was familiar with. In fact, in the run up to Christmas, the Eagle and Child was usually busier than usual. Tonight, it was so packed people had to brave the cold to drink outside, even though, unlike trendy bars in Ambleside, Keswick or Windermere, it didn't boast any fire pits or outdoor heaters.

Cassie stopped to say hello to a couple of friends before pushing the door open. The bright lights made her blink and a disorientating wave of heat, noise, beer and food smells hit her senses.

Tinsel and baubles sparkled from the Christmas tree standing in a corner. Fairy lights in the shape of snowflakes dangled from the ceiling's wooden beams, and a Christmas song played on the music system. Behind the bar Sadie sported sparkling earrings and a bright red top. Even Big Jim, the landlord, usually in jeans and faded rock bands T-shirts, wore a colourful Christmas sweater that stretched over his ample belly. Cassie couldn't identify if the animal frolicking at the front of Big Jim's jumper was a reindeer or a fox.

'Hey, Cassie!' a man's voice called as she pushed her way across the crowded room.

Her body tensed but she greeted the tall, stocky blond man standing in her path with a smile. 'Hi, Piers. How are you?'

'All the better for seeing you, gorgeous.' Before she could move out of the way, Piers bent down, slid his arm around her waist and kissed her cheek, dangerously close to her mouth. His lips were warm and moist, and she tried to repress a gasp as she caught the whiff of beer, musky aftershave and sweaty socks that always seemed to cling to him.

Still holding her tightly, he smiled. 'Fancy a drink, darling?'

'No, thanks. I only came in to have a word with my granddad.'

His smile faded. 'We haven't had a proper chat for ages. Come on, it's the season of goodwill. Don't you think you owe me at least one drink? It's in your interest to keep me sweet. I'm your boss, after all, as well as your landlord, so to speak. We could enjoy a drink or two and talk about work, life... and love.'

She stiffened. 'Perhaps next time.'

Piers often liked to remind her that as Charles Ashville's property manager, he had given her the contract for the holiday lets on the Ashville estate without which her small cleaning company couldn't survive, and bring up the fact that Bluebell Cottage was an Ashville property that her granddad rented for a very advantageous rent that hadn't changed much since the 1970s. However, she had no intention of keeping Piers sweet, at least not in the way he implied. She was well aware of his reputation as a ladies' man, but as far as she was concerned he was her boss, as well as her granddad's landlord, and she would maintain a professional relationship with him.

'Make sure it's soon.' He released her, and she wiped her cheek discreetly as she pushed her way through the crowd towards the quieter back room where her granddad and his friends usually retreated.

Sure enough, he was sitting at a table with David Fern and Tom Hays, both of whom had worked with him at the slate mine in the next valley. From the number of empty glasses on the table and the men's red cheeks and animated discussion, it was safe to assume that they were finishing their second pint, exchanging puns and jokes, and complaining once again that things were better 'in the olden days'. It was over fifteen years since they had retired from the slate mines, and loved nothing better than to moan about the 'circus' that the mines had become since Matt Jamieson had taken over from his father and created an adventure park to boost the mines' income.

Sighing inwardly because she liked Matt and admired what he was trying to do to keep his business going, Cassie walked over to them and pulled a chair out.

'Do you mind if I join you, gentlemen?'

Her granddad arched his eyebrows in surprise when he saw her. 'Trifle! You changed your mind.'

She nodded, said hello to David and Tom and sat down. 'I read the letters.'

'I knew you'd be intrigued. You were always going on about poor Ruth when you were growing up. I had to tell your grandma to stop stuffing your head with nonsense.'

It wasn't nonsense, but she didn't protest. 'Did you ask her not to mention the letters to me?'

'I sure did. It wasn't a good tale for a girl with too much imagination like you.' He drank the last of his beer and put his pint down.

'Then why give them to me tonight?'

'I had a funny feeling when you mentioned that Frenchman who just arrived at Belthorn Manor.'

'A tourist at the manor house at this time of year?' David Fern looked at her, curiosity shining in his eyes. 'What's he doing up there?'

'Resting, I suppose,' she answered.

'You said he'd been in an accident, didn't you?' her granddad asked.

She shrugged. 'I think he has, but I didn't ask him for his life story.' And even if she had, she doubted Stefan Lambert would have answered. 'He seems a very private person,' she added. Private was one way of putting it. Rude was another, more accurate one...

'Well, he'll be private enough up there for sure. He'll only have the sheep to talk to, and the Grey Friar, of course.' Tom Hays laughed and gestured towards the empty pint glasses and got up. 'It's my round. Same again, lads?'

The other two men nodded.

'What about you, Cassie?' he asked.

'I'll have half a cider, thanks.'

'I'll give you a hand,' David Fern said as he got up and the two men walked to the bar.

As soon as they were out of earshot, Cassie leaned over the table towards her granddad. 'What can you tell me about the letters?'

'There isn't much to tell. You read them, so you know who wrote them and what's in them, and now you understand that what happened to Ruth wasn't an accident.'

Cassie shuddered. 'You think she deliberately walked into Wolf Tarn and drowned.'

He nodded. 'Her lover had deserted her. Her family had disowned her. She lost her reputation, and nobody in the village would talk to her or give her employment, apart from the vicar, that is. The poor girl had nothing left.'

'That's not what Grandma told me. She said there was some evil involved in Ruth's death, and that people were reluctant to talk about her for a long time after she died, as if her name was cursed.'

'I think it's more likely that her parents were ashamed. She had broken off a very advantageous engagement to gallivant around with that French airman who had come to convalesce at Belthorn... and you know the rest.'

'Ruth was engaged? I didn't know that.'

'She was betrothed to Gideon Hardy, a rich farmer from Coniston. He was a very good match for her, much better than the Merriweathers could ever have hoped for. No wonder they were very angry when she broke up with him.'

'Hardy? Was he a relation of Piers, by any chance?'

He nodded. 'He was his great-grandfather. The family have been landowners around here for generations.'

Her grandfather's friends came back with the drinks, and the conversation rolled on to the preparations for the Christmas Fair in a few weeks' time, and the problems the organisers faced to staff Santa's grotto that year. Nobody, it seemed, wanted to be Santa.

'Why don't any of you volunteer?' Cassie suggested.

'We're getting too old for dealing with overexcited children all day,' her granddad replied. 'Last time I dressed up as Santa, I got so warm in my costume with that fat pillow on my belly I almost passed out, and I'm not even mentioning the fake beard that gave me a rash for days afterwards.'

'I fell asleep in the grotto and my snoring scared the children away,' David Fern added, laughing.

Cassie's granddad laughed. 'You had supped too much ale at lunchtime, that's why you fell asleep, you scoundrel.'

'I may have to volunteer myself,' Big Jim remarked as he came round to collect empty glasses.

'You sure have the belly for it,' Joseph Bell said and his friends burst out laughing. 'You won't need a pillow.'

Big Jim patted his belly with his free hand and smiled. 'I'll help if no one else wants to do it. It always brings in good money for the Mountain Rescue Service.'

'It's a shame the fair is so late this year,' David complained.

Big Jim shrugged. 'It was agreed that the local villages shouldn't compete too much between one another and have Christmas events on the same days. Our village got the last date in the draw at the council meeting. Last year, our Christmas Fair was one of the first in the area, this year we're the last. It's just the luck of the draw.'

As the men talked about the latest village news, Cassie felt a prickly and unpleasant sensation between her shoulder blades, as if a line of ants was crawling up her spine.

She turned round, and caught Darren Morse staring at her from his table in the far corner of the room. He nodded, lifted his pint glass in mock salute, and went back to checking his mobile phone.

As usual the man made her uneasy, even if he spent a lot of time at Bluebell Cottage these days, doing odd DIY jobs for her granddad.

She drained her cider and got up. 'Gentlemen, I'll be off now.'

'Wait a minute, pet, I'll go to the bar with you. It's my round,' her grandfather said, patting his jacket's breast pocket. He frowned, and looked at her and at his friends. 'I don't believe it. I've left my wallet at home.'

Not again, Cassie thought. It was the second time that week that he had gone out without any money.

'Pull the other one, Joseph,' one his friends said. 'You're an old miser, and you're only trying to get out of buying us a round.'

'No, no… I'm sure I put it in my pocket earlier.'

Cassie's heart tightened. He was getting more forgetful with every passing day. Perhaps she should make an appointment with the GP for him – not that he would ever agree to go.

She took her purse out of her handbag and pulled out a twenty-pound note. 'Here you are, Granddad,' she said, handing him the note.

'Thank you, Trifle. I don't understand where that wallet can be,' he muttered to himself as he walked to the bar.

It would be rude to ignore Darren on her way out, all the more so when he stood up as she walked past. 'Hi, Cassie,' he said in his soft and quiet voice.

She smiled. 'Hi, Darren. How are you? And how are things at the campsite?' She tilted her head up to look into his dark brown eyes, which were as usual cold and unfathomable.

He scratched his wispy beard. 'Quiet now that we're closed for the winter. There are no annoying kids kicking footballs and trampling all over the bushes, no drunken lads messing up the toilet block, or posh couples complaining that there's no Wi-Fi or air conditioning in their yurt or that their pod is too small.'

She smiled. 'You don't sound like you're enjoying your job very much.'

'It's a job.' He shrugged and glanced towards the counter where her granddad was buying drinks. 'By the way, your grandfather mentioned earlier that he needed help fixing a new lock to your back door. Would you like me to call at the cottage tomorrow and take a look at it?'

She frowned. 'He hasn't told me anything about it.' Then again she'd been busy all day, and tonight her mind had been on Belthorn's new guest and Ruth's old letters.

What's more, it wasn't the first time her granddad forgot to mention a meeting he had arranged or an appointment at the dentist or the doctor. Poor Granddad, she thought as love and worry welled in her chest, he'd always been so witty and sharp-minded. It looked like his memory was failing him.

'He's at the bar. Why don't you go over and make arrangements with him?' she suggested before saying goodbye and making her escape.

Luckily Piers was busy talking to his rugby pals at the bar. She kept her head down so he wouldn't see her and heaved a relieved sigh once she was out of the pub.

Chapter Five

At the peak of the tourist season, Saturday meant rushing around, organising her part-time, seasonal staff like a military operation to make sure everybody was at the right place at the right time, kept to the schedule and got through the cleaning of two dozen holiday cottages between ten in the morning and four in the afternoon.

In the wintertime, things were a lot quieter and the reduced workload was easily divided between herself and Sophie. The only problem now, of course, was that Sophie had left and Cassie was on her own. Hiring new permanent help was something she would have to consider when the season picked up at Easter. By then, who knows, Sophie may have grown disillusioned with life in Manchester and come back to Red Moss... And Cassie may have dyed her hair pink like her fashionista friend Cecilia, who ran the village trendy art and clothing shop!

Still in her flannelette pyjamas and dressing gown, Cassie made a pot of tea, slid a couple of slices of bread into the toaster, and checked her notebook to make sure she wasn't missing anything. She only had one holiday cottage to see to that morning before driving to the Old Gatehouse where Nadine Hartley, the very glamorous wife of a local solicitor and one of her regular clients, had asked her to do a last minute tidy up before the cocktail party she was hosting in the evening. After that, she would go shopping for Stefan Lambert and drive to Belthorn.

It was altogether a rather quiet day, which was lucky as she couldn't stop yawning and rubbing her eyes. Ruth's tragic love story, and even more tragic death, had preyed on her mind and kept her awake for a long time. When she'd finally fallen asleep she had dreamt about Belthorn, but a very different

Belthorn. In her dream the abbey was still standing, and the sound of bells ringing echoed in the night and bounced against the hills, a slow and solemn call – a warning, perhaps. Someone, or something, was waiting, and watching, on the shore, whilst on the surface of Wolf Tarn a shadow spread until the whole lake was as smooth and black as a pool of ink.

She had woken up shaking, with her heart beating hard and the sheets tangled around her body. It had been a while since she'd dreamt about Belthorn – and about *that* night…

Falling asleep again was out of the question, so she had switched on her bedside lamp, retrieved her sewing basket and finished a new cushion cover for Mason's living room. It didn't take long, so she looked through her fabrics bag and selected strips of red and green felt to make another cushion, for Belthorn this time. Stefan Lambert may not want any Christmas decorations, but he hadn't said anything about new cushions.

Of course, it would take a lot more than new soft furnishings to cheer the old hall up and bring a smile to Lambert's lips. It would take a whole makeover for the hall… and possibly a personality transplant for the Frenchman.

When she finally put her handiwork away and tried to fall asleep again, it wasn't only her nightmare or Ruth's letters she was trying to forget. Someone else had been on her mind. Someone with broad shoulders and a rotten temper, and with eyes like burnished gold and a voice so deep the memory alone was enough to give her goosebumps.

And that morning too, as she spread a thick layer of strawberry jam onto her toast, she still couldn't help thinking about Stefan Lambert. Had his first night at Belthorn been comfortable? Had he enjoyed the peace and quiet or had he felt lonely? How would he react when she saw him later on that afternoon?

One thing was certain. She wouldn't put up with any more

rudeness. She would keep out of his way if that's what he wanted, but she had a job to do, whether he liked it or not.

She finished her breakfast, washed up, and went up to her room to shower and get dressed. It didn't take long since she wore the same sensible clothes day in, day out. She put on a long-sleeved grey T-shirt, denim dungarees and gave her shoulder-length hair a quick brush through before twisting it into a bun that she secured with a bandana scarf – a blue one, today. Her friends and family jokingly said that she'd been stuck in a time warp since her Bandanamama days, but there was nothing wrong in being faithful to a look, especially when it was practical for her work, was there? Just like there was nothing wrong with being faithful to her family, her job, her clients...

She was about to run downstairs when she caught a glimpse of her reflection in the mirror. A little make-up would hide her pale cheeks and the dark circles under her eyes. She reached out for her make-up bag, and applied a coat of mascara, some blusher and pink lip gloss.

Her granddad was pottering about in the kitchen when she came down. He pointed at her face. 'Why are you wearing make-up to go cleaning houses?'

Cassie let out a sigh. His memory may be faltering, but there was nothing wrong with his eyesight.

'Are you meeting some young man you haven't told me about?'

'Of course not. And it's not really make-up, only a little lip gloss.'

'Where did you say you were going today?'

She told him her schedule for the day.

'So you're going to Belthorn again,' he said.

'I told you, I have to go there every day. I'll drive up there in the afternoon after shopping at SuperSaver in Keswick. Charles Ashville's guest needs food. Perhaps that will make him less grouchy.'

'Get him some real coffee, not that instant rubbish. French people love their coffee, don't they? And buy some smelly cheese, some of those baguette bread sticks, and plenty of good red wine, of course.'

Cassie laughed. 'Coffee, cheese and wine? That's not proper food!'

Her granddad nodded. 'It's a start.' He scratched his head and broke into a smile. 'Why don't you make him your steak pie? If he doesn't like it, you can always bring it home for me. You know it's my favourite.'

She bent down to kiss his cheek, breathing his comforting scent of pine soap and shaving foam. 'I'll make a pie just for you as soon as I have a bit of time, I promise, Granddad.'

She took her keys from the key rack and was about to leave when she remembered what Darren Morse had told her in the pub the night before.

'By the way, what's wrong with the back door?'

Her granddad shrugged and looked at her with a puzzled expression. 'Nothing's wrong with it. Why do you ask?'

'Darren mentioned that you'd asked him to fix a new lock or something.'

His blue eyes took on the vague, slightly lost stare she had noticed more and more these past few weeks. 'I don't recall asking him anything, unless...' His lips relaxed into a smile. 'Ah yes... He said something about the back door sticking when he came yesterday to fix the leak in the radiator upstairs.'

'Is it leaking again? I thought he mended it last week.'

Her granddad nodded. 'That radiator is giving him trouble. Anyway, he came through the back door because he didn't want to put muck all over the hall, and that's when he realised that the latch was catching. Is he coming today then?'

'I'm not sure. He was in the pub last night. Didn't he talk to you after I left?'

He shook his head. 'I was with the lads. He probably didn't want to disturb us. I think he's a bit shy.'

'Shy or not, he seems to be around here fixing something or other every other day. And when I say fixing, I'm being kind. The television aerial is still playing up, the bath taps drip constantly and the radiator in the back room is still leaking. I'm going to have to call a proper plumber.'

'Don't be so harsh on the lad. It's good of him to come round to old folks' houses and give them a hand with repairs and stuff. Apparently Doris Pearson is so chuffed with him she recommended him to all her friends at the community centre.'

'Doris as in *"the angry cat woman from across the road"*?'

Her granddad laughed. 'Now you're being mean. She may be a bit obsessed with her Fluffy, but that's because she's lonely. Anyway, she is full of praise for young Darren.'

'Maybe he does a better job at her house than he does here. I must dash. See you tonight.'

'Fasten up your coat, and don't forget your hat. You don't want to catch a cold.' Her grandfather handed her the red and green pom-poms hat she had deliberately left on the hallway peg.

She repressed a grumpy reply. How old did he think she was telling her what to wear, and why did he force her to wear that ridiculous hat? But she immediately felt mean and petty. He was only looking out for her. So what if she looked like a crazy, jumbo-sized elf?

She said nothing and put the hat on. She took the bag in which she had stuffed her new cushions, waved him goodbye and walked out into the cold, grey morning. The chilly wind stung her cheeks, and the air smelled of wood fire, coal smoke and snow as she walked to Salomé's bakery.

The bell above the door chimed as she walked in, and delicious cinnamon, ginger and hot chocolate fragrances immediately enveloped her. She took a deep breath and smiled at her friend who was piling up sugar-coated buns on the counter, next to a tray of *churros*.

'I'm in cake heaven,' Cassie declared. 'The best – no, the only – place I want to be.'

Salomé wiped her hands on her white pinny. 'I'd rather be in man heaven. At least I wouldn't be putting any weight on. I always lose my appetite around attractive men.'

Cassie put her hand on her heart. 'No man, however attractive, will ever put me off your cakes, and that's a fact.'

Salomé laughed and rolled her chocolate-brown eyes. 'That's because you haven't met the right one yet. What can I get you today?'

Cassie ordered iced buns for Mason, and for his office manager and surrogate mother, Brenda.

Salomé wrapped the cakes in a pretty pink paper bag. 'I put an extra one in for you too – on the house,' she said.

Cassie thanked her and hurried out of the bakery and down the main street to Mason's garage at the far end of the village. This time it wasn't scents of hot chocolate, ginger and cinnamon that made her smile as she pushed open the door to the reception area, but the smells of grease, leather seats and petrol fumes. They always reminded her of her father, who had co-owned the garage with Mason's dad for years. If her father's voice and features had almost completely faded away from her memory, one second in the garage was enough to recall the elusive sensations of her childhood, and what it felt like to climb on his knees and snuggle in his arms when he came back from work at the end of the day.

Cassie shook her head, and opened her eyes. As usual, the small, cramped and untidy office was far too hot, since Brenda insisted that the fan heater be switched on full all the time.

Mason was sorting through paperwork. He looked up and pointed at her hat. 'You need bells on that!'

She pulled the hat off. 'It's ridiculous, isn't it? Granddad bought it for me and insists I wear it. Mason, I need your help.'

'What can I do for you? Don't tell me there's something wrong with your van again.'

'No, it's not the van.'

'Then you finally agree to come for a ride on my motorbike.'

She shook her head. 'That will never happen. I'm far too scared.'

'Even with me?'

'Even with you, champion!' She gestured to the photos of Mason hanging on the office walls, and showing him astride large motorbikes or lifting race trophies. One of them featured him next to a 500cc blue and white motorbike, wearing matching leathers with a beaming smile on his lips, and his bright blue eyes twinkling as he radiated happiness. In fact, Cassie had never seen him look that happy since. That was the year he won the MotoGP World Championship, and the year he surprised everybody when he stopped racing and took over his father's garage.

'Too bad. What is it, then?'

She told him about Stefan Lambert's Range Rover being stuck in a ditch on the way to Belthorn and he promised to go there later that morning. She almost warned him about the Frenchman's grumpy temper, but decided against it. Mason would find out soon enough.

'By the way,' she said as she put two of Salomé's paper bags on Mason's desk, 'I bought you and Brenda a couple of Salomé's pastries, and…'

She lifted one of the cushions from her tote bag and held it up for Mason to see. 'I made you a new cushion! I thought it would go well with the paint we picked for your lounge and with your new sofa. If you like the colours, I'll make you more in the same style. I have lots of fabric left.'

Mason smiled and reached out for the cushion. 'I don't know what it is with women and cushions… but thanks, Cassie. It looks good, and I appreciate your determination to turn me from a colour-and-style-blind mechanic from the back of beyond into a sophisticated male, even if I'm a lost cause.'

Despite the smile on his face, his eyes remained sad.

'I'm not trying to turn you into anything,' she said, her heart tightening. 'You are wonderful just as you are... and what would the village do with a mechanic too stylish to put grease on his manicured hands and his designer overall?'

This time the sadness disappeared and he laughed good-heartedly. 'True. You're a good pal, Cassie.'

'You're welcome. See you later.'

The holiday cottage took about an hour to clean. She always left a bouquet for holidaymakers – fresh flowers in the spring and summer and whatever she could find in the winter. There were holly, mistletoe and winter berry bushes at the front of the cottage so she cut a few branches, which she arranged in a vase on the kitchen table, together with one of her granddad's jokes for the holidaymakers who were due to arrive later in the day.

When she had taken over her mother's cleaning business and re-launched it as Bluebell Cleaning, her granddad had suggested she give her clients jokes too. 'People won't mind opening their wallets if you make them laugh,' he had said, and he had since then contributed to her small business with a weekly supply of jokes and puns.

Cassie checked the visitors' book and smiled as she read the latest comments. *'Great cottage, clean and welcoming. We loved the biscuits and the joke! We have a joke for you too: How do you communicate with a fish? Drop him a line. Merry Christmas!'*

Her granddad would like that, she thought as she sprayed some of her favourite lemon essential oil to freshen up the air. What the cottage needed, however, was more than a pretty bouquet and a fresh scent. It was a complete change. The furniture was outdated, the curtains too flowery and the carpet bore the marks of many muddy footprints and spilled glasses of red wine, however much she scrubbed it.

It was the same for all the holiday cottages, but Piers categorically refused to make any improvements, saying it would cost too much. When she had pushed her design book into his hands and timidly suggested she do the redecorations on a tight budget, he had looked at her as if she had lost her mind and burst out laughing. 'What do *you* know about design? Forget it, Cassie. If Charlie ever decides to modernise the cottages, he'll hire a proper designer.' But I am a proper designer, she wanted to say – at least she had the diploma... But what would have been the point? He hadn't even glanced at her sketchbook.

Her next stop was The Old Gatehouse where Nadine Hartley welcomed her with a panicked expression and a long list of instructions issued in her usual husky, breathless voice. 'Go easy on the lemon spray. It clashes with my Givenchy,' she finished before driving away in her gleaming silver Mercedes Coupé to have her hair and nails done at a nearby luxury hotel spa.

Two hours later, Cassie peeled off her rubber gloves and tidied the cleaning products under the sink. Even though Nadine never smiled at her granddad's jokes, she took one out of her bag and left it on the black granite kitchen island...

Stefan had left the curtains open all night, and the first thing he saw when he opened his eyes were grey smudges in the sky above the outline of the mountains. He checked his watch, and blinked in surprise. It was late.

He hadn't slept well. But then again he never did, and at Belthorn there were the added factors of a lumpy mattress, creaking floorboards and rumbling pipes coupled with the deep silence outside. His back had played up again, and as he tossed and turned the memories, guilt and remorse had kicked in. It had taken two doses of painkillers before he had managed to drop off, sometime after four in the morning.

He pulled the sheets and the duvet down, and repressed a groan as he stood up. The physio assured him that he was on the mend, but there were mornings when the pain clawing at his back was enough to make him howl – that's if he was able to howl. Given the state of his vocal cords, he was more likely to croak.

The heating didn't appear to be working much and his breath steamed in the freezing cold bedroom as he cursed his way through his stretching exercises. Fully awake now, but with his back and shoulders aching like hell, he grabbed his towel and walked to the bathroom. He wasn't expecting a hot shower from the antiquated appliance above the bath, and he didn't get one, but at least the tepid water washed away the remnants of the night, and he was ready to face his first day at Belthorn Manor.

After donning a pair of jeans and a jumper over his shirt, he laced up his army walking boots, and went down to the kitchen. A quick search of the cupboards uncovered a packet of biscuits and a tin of soup. That would do for a late breakfast. He made some coffee, and ate whilst watching the dark grey clouds race against one another above the rugged, snow-tipped mountains.

He had just finished washing-up when he heard an engine outside. It was followed by a loud knock on the front door that echoed through the house. The housekeeper was back, even though he had done his best to put her off. Remembering his intention to apologise for being short-tempered the day before, he fixed a smile on his face and went to open the door.

It wasn't Cassie standing at the door but a dark-haired man in a high-vis orange anorak, oil-stained jeans and thick biker boots. Behind him was a roadside rescue truck. 'Stefan Lambert?'

Without waiting for his answer, the man smiled. 'I'm Mason Austin. I run the garage in Red Moss. Cassie said you needed a hand with your Range Rover.'

Stefan nodded. 'That's right. Thanks for coming. You're saving me a long walk to the village. Let me get my coat and my keys.'

Mason gave him a lift to the Sanctuary Stone. Together they hooked a cable onto the tow bar at the back of the Range Rover. Mason climbed back into his truck to action the pulley, and the car was back on the lane in no time.

'Do you want me to check it over?' he asked after Stefan started the engine and revved it a few times.

'It sounds all right to me.' He didn't mention that he was a skilled mechanic himself and could service and repair a whole range of engines, from mopeds to water pumps and generators, to light aircraft and helicopters. Instead he asked how much he owed for putting the Range Rover back on the road.

Mason shook his head. 'You can buy me a pint at the pub this evening.'

Stefan frowned. 'Are you sure?'

The mechanic smiled. 'Positive. I am usually there by eight on a Saturday night.'

'Then I'll see you tonight.'

He turned to look at the standing stone by the side of the lane, and lifted a hand to touch the grooves carved on its cold, rough surface.

'That stone looks old,' he remarked.

'It's the abbey's Sanctuary Stone,' Mason Austin said. 'I believe there were several of them in the old days.'

Stefan traced the patterns with his finger. 'What's a Sanctuary Stone?'

'They marked the boundaries of the abbey where criminals could be granted asylum... or at least that's what Miss Parker, our primary school head teacher used to tell us. She's retired now, but if you're interested in the history of the village, I'm sure she'd be happy to talk to you.'

'I may very well do that.'

The men shook hands, and drove away in their respective vehicles. Back at Belthorn, Stefan set off to explore the manor house's surroundings. His friend had warned him about the dangers of the fells. There were abandoned mine shafts, hidden pits, boggy terrain and ghylls – long, narrow ravines. And of course there was the weather, which could change in the blink of an eye from sunshine into a hellish snow blizzard or blinding white fog.

He zipped up his coat, wrapped a thick scarf around his neck and set off on the rocky path that snaked from the back of the house to the top of the hill. He would try to make it to the top. Failing that, the fresh air and physical effort would tire him out, and perhaps help him sleep instead of twisting and turning in bed, agonising about the past, with guilt and remorse festering inside him like an infected wound.

Charlie said that he would heal in time. How could he tell his friend that most days he didn't think he *deserved* to heal? Days when he couldn't breathe, and didn't want to breathe?

Coming here might be the easy option – the coward's option, his father had sneered. All Stefan wanted was a place to hide, push the memories away, if only for a while, and forget about Christmas.

Climbing that hill would be a start.

Chapter Six

By two o'clock, Cassie was loading the van with groceries, fruit and vegetables, packs of coffee and bottles of wine, bread rolls and baguettes.

'Hi, Cassie. Do you need a hand?' Darren's voice said behind her.

Startled, she swung round too fast and bumped her head against the door.

'Ouch!' She rubbed her forehead. 'Thanks, but I have finished now. What are you doing here?'

'Shopping, like you. You bought a lot of stuff.'

She loaded the last two bags into the van and slammed the boot shut. 'It's not for me. It's for Belthorn Manor.'

'Ah yes, your grandfather mentioned that someone was staying there. Some French guy, he said. Belthorn is such a big house. How will you cope on your own now that Sophie has left?'

She frowned. How did he know that Sophie had gone to Manchester? 'I'll be fine.'

'I can help.'

The words were on her lips before she realised. 'No, thank you.'

He stared down at her, his brown eyes expressionless. 'If you change your mind, you know where to find me. By the way, I'm on my way to buy a new lock for your back door. I'll fit it tomorrow morning, since your granddad said you were going to a birthday party at your cousin's farm in the afternoon.'

Her granddad seemed to be discussing their private life with Darren an awful lot lately, and she wasn't sure she liked it.

'Tomorrow is Sunday. Won't you have better things to do than fix our lock?'

He shrugged. 'Not really, and I'm always happy to help.'

It was true. Darren was generous with his time, and she should be more grateful. She forced a smile. 'All right, then. See you tomorrow morning. Thank you.'

He put his hand on her trolley. 'I'll put it back for you.'

'Thanks.' She walked to the driver's side and climbed behind the wheel.

What a strange young man... As she drove to Belthorn she recalled what she knew about him, which was almost nothing. She had first seen him around the village at the beginning of the summer when he got the caretaker job at the lakeside campsite. He lived in one of the mobile homes, didn't seem to have made any friends – at least he was always alone when she saw him – but had made himself indispensable with many older residents of the village, and if her granddad was to be believed, even her grumpy neighbour Doris was a fan. And yet she couldn't help it. There was something about him that made her uneasy.

It was snowing by the time she drove over the cattle grid and climbed the lane up to Belthorn. Her fingers tightened around the steering wheel, and the usual knot hardened in her stomach as images from her nightmare flashed into her mind, mixing with the images from *that* night, ten years before...

It was only to be expected if she was nervous. After all, this was only the second time she'd been to Belthorn on her own. Her mother had always been with her when Charles Ashville's father was still alive, and when her mother had retired and Cassie had taken over her small housekeeping business, it was Sophie who had taken on the twice-monthly visits. Cassie would get used to coming there alone – she had to...

Mason had been true to his word. Lambert's Range Rover was no longer near the Sanctuary Stone but parked in front of the manor house. Her spirits lifted a little. Lambert may not be the most agreeable of men, but at least she wouldn't be alone in the old house.

Even though she had keys, Cassie rang the bell, and unloaded the shopping as she waited for Lambert to come to the door.

There was no answer so she let herself in.

'Hello!' she called a few times, but her voice was met with deep silence, and her heart sank. The Frenchman must have gone for a walk, and she was alone after all...

'It's fine. It's fine. Everything's fine,' she whispered to herself in a singsong voice even though she felt anything but fine.

Her footsteps echoed on the stone-flagged floor as she walked down the corridor, opening doors and flicking old-fashioned light switches on in a bid to banish any lingering shadows.

In the kitchen the only clues that Lambert had been there were the mug, soup bowl, spoon and saucepan washed and arranged neatly by the side of the sink. It was probably his way of telling her that he could clean after himself and didn't need her.

She put the shopping away and made the steak pie for Lambert's evening meal, before tackling the housework she should have done the day before, trying not to jump every time the floorboards creaked, the pipes gurgled or the wind tapped on the window panes.

It was no wonder Charles Ashville and his sister Gabrielle rarely spent any time there since their father's death. And yet, Cassie thought as she surveyed the drawing room's faded wallpaper, the oak beams criss-crossing the ceiling and the dark oak furniture... With a colourful throw or two on the sofa, plenty of soft cushions, some fairy lights along the mantelpiece to soften the lighting, and a fire in the fireplace, the room could look almost cosy and welcoming.

She would start the transformations straight away. She slipped her coat back on, extracted a pair of secateurs from her bag and went in the snowy garden to cut sprigs of pine and spiky branches dripping with pretty red berries from the holly bushes growing near the gates. She walked back into the house, shook the snow from her coat and spent time arranging the foliage in bouquets in the hallway and the drawing room.

His heart pumped hard, his breath grew ragged and his legs ached. He tilted his head up and thick snowflakes touched his face. The weather was turning and it was getting dark. He may not make it to the top of the hill, but he hadn't felt this alive for a long time.

He turned round and started on the way back at a good pace. The house soon appeared at the turn of the path. From his vantage point high up on the fell, the ruins of the abbey seemed a lot more extensive, and closer to the manor house, than he'd thought. For the first time he noticed that both the abbey and the manor house appeared to be built from similar stonework. It might be interesting to dig up some facts about the place and learn about the history of Belthorn Abbey and its links to Charlie's family. Perhaps he would pay Miss Parker a visit, and ask her if she knew anything about André Vaillant too…

As he proceeded further down the hill, he spotted Cassie Bell's bright red van on the drive. He let out a resigned sigh. His own personal dust buster fairy was back.

He reached the small mountain lake, marked on the map as Wolf Tarn. Round and grey, with a smooth, glassy surface, it looked like a giant eye staring back at the sky. Snowflakes floated down like feathers and dissolved as they touched the water.

As he followed the path around the tarn, he saw a white car drive slowly up the lane and stop at the gates. A tall, gangly man got out, the hood of his anorak pulled down over his face and his shoulders hunched against the snow and the cold wind, and walked to Cassie's van. He bent down as if checking the tyres, then straightened up and stalked to the kitchen door.

Stefan's skin prickled at the back of his neck.

It was probably nothing. Cassie could have called someone to service her van or make a delivery, but he didn't like the man's furtive manner. He didn't like it at all. Instinct kicked in, and he started running.

The kitchen door squeaked open, and Cassie let out a relieved sigh. At last Stefan Lambert was back. She tidied the vacuum cleaner away, hurried to the kitchen... and stopped dead. Darren stood in the kitchen, flicking through the notebook she had left on the kitchen table.

Her mouth opened in shock. 'Darren... What are you doing here?'

He flipped the notebook shut and looked at her. 'I knocked but there was no answer, so I came in.'

She hadn't heard any knocking. Then again, she had been dusting and vacuuming.

He unzipped his anorak, and pulled a bottle of wine out of his inside pocket. 'You forgot this in your shopping trolley, so I thought I'd bring it over.' He put the bottle on the table.

Cassie frowned. 'Did I? I'm sure I put away four bottles.'

'There was a bottle left,' Darren insisted. He gave the kitchen an appraising look. 'Wow! This is a massive kitchen. I could fit my entire mobile home in here.'

She forced a smile. 'Yes, it's really big. Listen, Darren, it was kind of you to drive all this way and bring the wine, but you can't just walk in here.'

'I said I knocked.' Even though he spoke quietly, his voice had taken a stubborn edge. 'Where's the French guy who's staying here?'

'I think he went out for a walk.' She sighed as worry gnawed at her again. Where had Lambert gone? What if he got lost as night fell?

'Good. Then you can give me a tour of the house. I've wondered what Belthorn Manor was like inside for ages.' He took off his anorak and draped it on the back of a chair.

She swallowed hard. 'No. Sorry, I can't do that. It's not my house.'

He shrugged. 'Who's to know? After all, the owner isn't here, and you just said that the guest is out. I meant it, you know, when I said I wanted to help. It's an old house and there must be lots of things going wrong. I am always happy to fix things.'

He may be happy to fix things but it didn't mean he was any good at it, a little voice whispered in her head. Immediately she chastised herself for that uncharitable thought.

'We'll see…'

'Any chance of a cup of tea? It's freezing today and the heating in my car isn't working. I got really cold driving up here.'

He rubbed his hands together, and she felt guilty again. After all, a cup of tea was the least she could offer him when he'd driven all this way to bring her the bottle she had forgotten.

'Sure.' She filled the kettle and reached out for cups on the dresser's top shelf.

'Wait. I'll get them for you,' he said from behind her.

His body brushed against her, and she swirled round with a gasp. There was nothing threatening on his face, and his eyes were just as impassive as always, yet her instinctive reaction was to step back.

She bumped against the dresser, making the plates, cups and saucers rattle. At the same time the kitchen door crashed open and banged against the wall. Darren swung round, dropped his hand, and Cassie swiftly stepped aside.

Stefan Lambert, his face red from the cold, his hair and coat covered with snow, strode in. Forget lions or bears. Today, he looked like the abominable snowman. His eyes glowed, hot and hard, and even from where she was standing she felt the threat that radiated from him.

He looked straight at her. 'Are you all right?' His voice sounded even rougher than she remembered.

She nodded and opened her mouth to reply, but Darren was quicker.

'You must be the French guest. Your accent gave you away.'

He smiled but Stefan only gave him a cold, appraising look.

'I'm a friend of Cassie's,' Darren carried on. 'We were just about to have a cup of tea before Cassie showed me around.'

Cassie opened her mouth in protest, but how could she object that it wasn't at all what had happened, and that she had never agreed to show Darren the house without calling him a liar?

Stefan frowned as he looked at her, and suddenly her face was burning. Now he must think that Darren was her boyfriend, and she was taking advantage of her job to sneak him into Belthorn.

She picked up Darren's anorak from the back of the chair and held it out. 'Thanks again for bringing the bottle, Darren.'

'No problem. I'll call round at the cottage tomorrow morning as agreed. We can always have that cup of tea another day.' He slipped his coat on, nodded to Lambert and walked out.

Chapter Seven

The adrenaline rush had vanished, leaving his heart pounding and his body aching all over. Taking his coat off would require a superhuman effort so he dragged the zip down and collapsed into a chair. That served him right for running down a mountain path to rescue a damsel in distress.

He would do well to remember that he was no knight in shining armour, and it transpired that Cassie Bell was no damsel in distress after all, but had been entertaining a friend – or boyfriend. So much for his infallible instinct... He should have saved himself the bother, and the aches and pain.

'It's not what you think.'

Cassie Bell stood in front of him, two pink spots on her cheeks and her fingers toying with a strand of blonde hair that had slipped down from her messy chignon. She had pulled up the sleeves of her grey top, uncovering slender forearms. Her dungarees swamped her slight frame, and the front pockets filled with tissues, pink rubber gloves, a packet of wipes, pens and scissors and heaven knows what else, made her look a little like a mummy kangaroo.

He cast a weary look in her direction. 'And what do I think?'

She bit her lip and her face took on a deeper shade of red. 'That I asked Darren to come here... that he is my boyfriend. I know what it must have looked like, but the truth is I hardly know him. He's not even local. He's only lived in Red Moss for the past six months or so.'

The corners of his lips twitched, and he couldn't help but smile. 'Is Red Moss one of these places where people have to live for two generations before they are considered locals?'

'Three generations actually, according to my granddad, although there are exceptions,' she replied with a lopsided smile.

The fist in his chest loosened and he breathed more easily, although there was absolutely no reason why he should feel relieved that the tall, lanky man wasn't Cassie Bell's boyfriend. She was only his housekeeper – babysitter, more like – and who she went out with was none of his business, but he hadn't liked the look of the man and the cold, calculating expression in his eyes. Most of all he hadn't liked the way he had stood so close to the young woman, crowding her.

'I met Darren when I was shopping and he was kind enough to bring me a bottle I had left in my trolley.' She frowned, and whispered, 'Although, now I think about it, I am sure I unpacked all four of them.' Still frowning, she opened a cupboard, and counted up to four. 'Yes, I did have them all! How odd... Darren must have made a mistake.'

Or he had been looking for an excuse to come to Belthorn, Stefan finished silently.

Cassie turned round, and buried her hands in her dungarees' enormous side pockets. 'By the way, I did a big shop. The cupboards were bare and Charles Ashville transferred money to cover your grocery expenses. You said yesterday that you weren't fussy with food, and I do hope you'll like what I bought.'

Worry flickered in her grey eyes, and he cursed himself for his short-temper the day before. She was only doing what Charlie had instructed after all. It wasn't her fault that his friend was being overprotective and didn't trust him to take care of himself.

'Thank you. I'm sure it'll be great, but I will pay the shopping bills from now on. Don't worry,' he added quickly when he saw she was about to object, 'I'll sort everything out with Charlie when I get in touch with him.'

Remembering his resolve to be more approachable, he glanced at the oven and breathed in heart-warming scents of cooking meat and vegetables. 'It smells nice.'

Her face lit up. 'It's a steak pie, with potatoes and vegetables. I made some gravy too.'

'Sounds good. Leave the oven on. I'll eat later, after you've left.' He stood up and immediately repressed a groan as a spasm seized his spine, knocking his breath out. The run down the hill hadn't done his back any favours. Now the pain had returned with a vengeance and it was taking more strength than he possessed to hide it.

Gripping the back of the chair so hard his knuckles turned white, he squeezed his eyes shut, forced a few deep breaths down and focussed on remaining on his feet. There was no way he was making a spectacle of himself by rolling about on the floor, crying like a baby in front of the young woman, even if it was what he felt like doing right now. With luck the spasms would ease before she noticed he was in agony.

Luck wasn't on his side.

'What's wrong?' Cassie Bell asked. 'You look dreadful. Are you hurt?'

Still holding on to the back of the chair, he flicked his eyes open and met Cassie's soft grey gaze, filled with something he had seen too many times these past few months to not recognise it. Compassion. Concern. But most of all, pity.

'I'm fine. You can go home now.'

She shook her head. 'I'm not leaving until you've eaten and I'm sure you're all right.'

'I'm giving you the evening off,' he growled. 'Take it.'

She crossed her arms. 'The only person who can give me time off is Charles Ashville. Until I hear from him, I have to do the job he appointed me for.'

Another spasm clenched his back in a tight grip, robbing him of the strength to argue. 'Suit yourself,' he muttered between clenched teeth. 'I'm going to lie down for a while.'

Mustering what little strength he had left, he walked woodenly to the door, pausing to rest his hand against the wall in the hall and catch his breath, once he was sure she couldn't see him. He made it up the stairs after much cursing, and once in his room popped a couple of his strongest painkillers into his mouth.

When he no longer felt that he was in danger of passing out, he lowered himself like an old man onto the bed to take his boots off, his breath short and sweat pearling on his forehead from the sheer effort of it. Closing his eyes, he reclined onto the bedcovers and prayed for the pills to take effect. Fast.

'Dinner's ready!' Cassie called from the bottom of the stairs.

It was her second attempt at waking Lambert up, but, like the first half an hour before, it appeared unsuccessful. She couldn't leave dinner much later. The pie would be dry, the vegetables mushy. She was getting hungry, having only eaten a banana and Salomé's iced bun for lunch, and her granddad would be waiting for her – and worrying.

She climbed to the top of the stairs, called again and held her breath to listen, but there was no reply. She tiptoed along the corridor, careful not to trip on the folds of the dark red carpet, which was pinned to the uneven floorboards. What if he had fainted, or was too weak to reply or to get up? Of course, the man could also have decided to ignore her completely in the hope that she would go away.

Having done some cleaning upstairs that afternoon, she knew that he had chosen one of the rooms overlooking the hillside at the back of the house. For some reason, it hadn't surprised her. He didn't seem the kind of man who would enjoy the master bedroom's four-poster bed, flowery silk wallpaper and Persian rugs... unless it was the view of the ruined abbey emerging from the mist like a ghost ship that had put him off.

She walked to Stefan's room, listening to the sounds of his breathing, and called from the threshold. He still didn't wake up.

Perhaps she should leave him to rest and go home, but he had looked in pain earlier, and it might be dangerous to abandon him alone at Belthorn. On the other hand, she couldn't stay there all evening.

Feeling shy and awkward, she walked into the room and around the bed. He had left his bedside light on, and the glow made his features softer, smoother, and his skin golden. She watched his powerful chest rise and fall with every breath, and something stirred insider her. He said he'd been in Mali with Charles Ashville. Piers had told her that Charles had almost died in an ambush a few months before... perhaps it was where he had been injured too, why he sought solace at Belthorn, and why he wanted to spend Christmas alone?

Suddenly he moved in his sleep, his breathing quickened, and his face contracted, as if in pain. She'd better wake him instead of staring at him whilst he slept.

She walked to his side of the bed and put a hand on his shoulder and gave it a tap. 'Stefan. Wake up. Dinner's read—' she started.

She didn't have time to finish. His fingers encircled her wrist like a steel manacle and pulled her down. Her knees buckled and she fell forward on top of him. 'Hey, what...?' Her face rubbing against his shirt, she felt the pounding of his heart, breathed in his clean, soapy scent mixed with the smells of snow and wind, and wriggled to break free from his grasp.

He was still holding her wrist, but her other hand was free, so she pressed it, palm down on his chest, to push her body up until she was level with his face. 'Stefan!' she shouted.

He opened his eyes. The irises were a warm, shimmering gold. 'Cassie?'

Immediately, his fingers loosened their grip on her wrist. She jumped to her feet and stepped well back, her heart pounding and her body burning. The whole thing has taken two, three seconds, but she could still feel the imprint of his hard, muscular body and the thudding of his heart resonated inside her.

'I only wanted to wake you up to tell you that dinner's ready,' she said weakly.

He sat on the side of the bed, and raked his fingers in his brown hair. 'I hope you don't think I was trying to...' He blew a long, shaky breath, and looked at her, his eyes filled with anguish. 'I wasn't trying to assault you or anything... I was just... dreaming.'

He gestured to the box of medicine on the bedside table. 'These are pretty strong painkillers. I am sorry... It happens, sometimes. I dream I'm still over there. In Mali. It was pretty tough, and...'

His voice faltered, and her heart filled with sadness and compassion. 'Don't worry about it,' she said quickly. 'I suppose it's my fault for sneaking up on you while you were sleeping, but I have been calling for ages and you didn't wake up. So much for my loud voice scaring all the wildlife away...'

She smiled.

He didn't smile back. 'Give me a few minutes and I'll come down.'

Chapter Eight

He walked to the bathroom, and splashed cold water on his face. Gripping the sides of the sink, he looked at the grim reflection in the mirror. Droplets of water slid down the hair he hadn't had cut for months, got caught in the stubble he didn't bother to shave any more.

Never mind his scarred face, his backache, and the broken voice caused by the damage to his vocal chords. He was a mess. He was losing it. Again. The doctor at the military Val-de-Grâce Hospital had warned that the dreams would reoccur. Pushing the memories away and refusing to talk about what had happened wouldn't help, he had said. Stefan knew he was right. He knew he needed to talk. But he couldn't. Every time he started, his throat closed up, and the words wouldn't come... So he told the doctor all he needed to get better was to be left alone for a few weeks.

It looked like he was wrong.

He grabbed a towel, dried his face, and combed his damp hair back with his fingers. He had scared Cassie, and no wonder. She must have thought he was going to hurt her, and God knows what else.

His back was still stiff but the painkillers had dulled the throbbing to a bearable ache, and he made his way downstairs.

'How are you feeling?' Cassie asked as he walked into the kitchen.

'Better, thanks.' He was well enough to notice that she made a charming picture, her face pink and dewy from the heat of the stove and framed by curly tendrils of blonde hair. Heat flashed through him as he remembered the sensations her soft body pressed against him had aroused, and how small and delicate her wrist had felt in his hand.

He cleared his throat. 'Listen, Cassie... You don't mind if I call you Cassie?'

She shook her head. 'Not at all.'

'You should call me Stefan, since it appears we are going to see a lot of each other,' he suggested.

'All right... Stefan.'

'I am really sorry about earlier.'

She raised her hand to stop him, and looked at him, her grey eyes serious and kind. 'You already apologised. It wasn't your fault. Let's talk no more about it.'

She gestured to the table where she had already set a plate, some cutlery and a wine glass. 'Please sit down. It won't be long.'

A napkin was folded on the plate and on top were two blue Post-it notes. He picked them up and looked at her. 'What are these?'

She smiled. 'Jokes I give my customers to cheer them up, courtesy of my granddad. Since you didn't get one yesterday, you're having a double helping today.'

'You give your clients jokes?'

She winked. 'Don't forget that I'm the good mood fairy. I offer an all-round rescue service – rescue from dirt, dust and gloom too!'

He nodded, even though rescuing him from his gloom would take more than a few jokes, and read the first Post-it. 'What did Father Christmas say to the elves when they visited the honey factory? Be Hive yourself.'

He put it down and read the other one. 'What did the Zombie get when he bit the snowman? Brain Freeze.'

He looked up and she gave him a sheepish smile. 'You don't have to say anything. I know they're a bit corny.'

He smiled back. 'I like them.'

Her face lit up. 'Really?'

'I don't usually say things I don't mean.' Glancing at the table, he asked, 'Why is there only one plate? Are you not eating with me?'

She shook her head. 'I'm here to make your meals and clean the house, not to eat. What's more, my granddad is waiting for me at home. Please sit down.'

If the nap and the painkillers had done him good, he felt even better after a slice of Cassie's steak pie and a small glass of red wine, even if the woman's non-stop chattering made him a little dizzy. She was a whirlwind of activity, dashing around the kitchen to wipe the worktops, tidy up and put utensils away, and talking all the time.

He lost count of the questions she asked, her first being why was his English so good? He told her about his uncle marrying an Englishwoman and the holidays he had spent with them and his cousins in their house in Kent. Cassie then wanted to know if it was his first visit to the Lakes, and how long he intended to stay. More questions followed. Did he enjoy hiking? Sailing? Rock climbing? Eating out? What was his favourite dish, and his least favourite dish?

'I need to make sure I cook what you like,' she said.

'You don't need to worry. I'm not fussy.'

She laughed. 'Please don't say that... You don't know what horrors I am capable of!'

She asked him about Christmas in Paris. Did the Eiffel Tower really sparkle at night? And what about the fireworks, were they as spectacular as on television?

She didn't seem to notice that his replies had become monosyllabic, then barely civil grunts. Suddenly, he'd had enough. He put his knife and fork down and glanced out of the window. Night had fallen and it was still snowing.

'You should go home before the weather gets worse,' he said, interrupting her flow of words.

She turned to look at him, shook her head and carried on scraping the pie dish, sending washing-up foam everywhere. 'I have to finish this first.'

'Leave it. I'll do it later.'

She scrubbed harder. 'No you won't. It's my job.'

There was a steely edge to her voice that told him there was no point arguing. The woman was as stubborn as she was chatty.

He could be stubborn too. He stood up and put his plate, glass and his cutlery into the sink. 'Then I'll follow you to the village as soon as you've finished. I don't want you risking an accident in that old van of yours.'

This time a mischievous glint appeared in her eyes. 'My Bluebell van may be old but it's perfectly safe.'

'The road is slippery and dangerous. I'd rather be with you, just in case...'

She arched her eyebrows. 'I'm used to driving in the snow and had special tyres fitted. Beside, I'm not the one who drove my car into a ditch.'

Her quick retort almost made him smile. 'Actually, there's another reason I want to follow you to Red Moss. I arranged to meet Mason Austin in the pub. I owe him a pint for helping me out this morning. I don't want to get lost and I need you to point me into the right direction.'

That was the best excuse he could think of.

This time she nodded. 'Ah... all right. You'll have a great evening. The Eagle and Child is a friendly pub, and Mason is a great guy.'

She may be right... Here at Red Moss there was no risk of bumping into anyone he knew and having to answer endless questions about the accident, deal with sympathetic comments about his injuries, or lie about how he was coping with civilian life.

Chapter Nine

Cassie may not want to admit it, but she was glad Lambert was following her to the village in his Range Rover. Even with the snow tyres Mason had fitted at the beginning of winter, the van kept skidding and the Range Rover's headlights shining in her rear-view mirror were a reassuring presence.

She wasn't fooled by his excuse. There was only one pub in Red Moss, and it was in the centre of the village. He couldn't have missed it. The truth was that he was worried about her and wanted to make sure she got home safely... and that gave her a warm, fuzzy feeling inside.

She slowed down when she reached the Eagle and Child, beeped her horn and waved him goodbye. As she parked in front of Bluebell Cottage, she couldn't help but wonder what the locals would make of the Frenchman's surly temper, of his rough voice and battle-scarred face.

Long-legged Sadie would no doubt find him very intriguing. She would also notice his broad shoulders and moody eyes, and probably waste no time in fluttering her eyelashes at him.

'I'm back!' She hung her coat on the rack and popped her head into the living room. Her grandfather sat in his favourite armchair next to the gas fire, his legs stretched out in front of him, his feet encased in his carpet slippers.

He lifted his eyes from his paper and smiled. 'Hello, love. You look shattered. Was it a hard day?'

'It wasn't too bad. Sorry I'm a bit late. I've been to Belthorn.'

He frowned. 'What was it like to be back up there, and was that Frenchman still cantankerous today?'

She pulled a face. 'I'll get used to it – and to him. Eventually. Actually Lambert insisted on following me back to the village. He said he was meeting Mason at the pub, but I think he was worried about me driving back on my own in the snow.'

'That was good of him.'

'Yes, it was.' She thought back at the determined look in Stefan's eyes when he had marched into the kitchen and saved her from Darren's unwanted attentions, at the mix of pride and vulnerability etched on his face when he refused to admit he was in pain... at the heat of his body when she tried to wake him up and he yanked her to him. The memory alone was enough to make her dizzy.

But she'd better get on with making the tea rather than reminisce about Stefan Lambert's hard chest and strong arms. She took the bags of frozen chips, peas and fish fingers out of the freezer and switched the grill on.

'What did you do today, Granddad?'

Her grandfather immediately proceeded to recount the events of his day. The newspaper had been delivered late and he had complained at the newsagent's.

'While I was there, I picked up your magazine – the one you like, about fancy houses and expensive wallpaper. Where did I put it? I swear it was on the worktop earlier.' He fumbled through the piles of letters and papers, getting agitated and muttering to himself.

Her heart sank at his new memory lapse. 'Don't worry about it. It will turn up. Tell me what else happened today.'

'Not much.' He scratched his head, leaving his white hair all fluffed up. 'Except that there has been another burglary in the village – that's the fourth in as many weeks.'

Cassie sighed. 'Who was it this time?'

'Sylvia Gasby. All her jewellery, and the money she keeps for emergencies in her underwear drawer, was stolen.'

Sylvia was an energetic septuagenarian, a pillar of the community centre where she volunteered most days, and another of Cassie's regular clients. So far, all four victims of the spate of burglaries were clients of hers.

'The police said she must have left a door unlocked

or a window open as there was no sign of a break-in,' her grandfather added.

'Poor Sylvia... I'll call round tomorrow morning and take her cakes from Salomé's to cheer her up. She must be very scared and very upset.'

Cassie switched the oven on. 'By the way, I met Darren in Keswick this afternoon. He was buying a new lock for the back door.'

'That's right. I gave him twenty pounds for it.'

'You found your wallet, then?'

He sighed. 'It was in my coat all along, but in another pocket. I'll go to the cash machine tomorrow to pay you back. I gave Darren my last note for the lock.'

'Don't be daft, Granddad. I'm glad you found it. Why do you say you have no money left? Didn't you get your pension from the post office yesterday?'

He smoothed his hair back with trembling fingers, and his eyes took on the vague and slightly lost gaze he adopted more and more often these days. 'I must have dropped it on my way home yesterday. All I had left was twenty pounds and a few coins.'

He looked so puzzled she didn't have the heart to scold him for his carelessness.

'He's a nice lad, is Darren,' her granddad carried on, 'and he likes to chat – about you, mostly. He's interested in everything you do and everywhere you go. I think you may have an admirer there.'

'Hmm... I'm not sure. There's something about him...'

But her granddad wasn't listening. 'It's time for my game show. Call me when tea's ready.' And he tottered back into the living room.

Whilst the fish fillets and chips were under the grill, Cassie hunted around the kitchen for her magazine. It was the only link to the wild and crazy dream she had once cherished of becoming an interior designer. A dream that started when fresh out of school she started working for her mother, and rearranged people's interiors in her head as she cleaned. A dream that had blossomed when she had met Nathan.

Nathan... The memory of the handsome and talented interior designer whose offices she had cleaned for several years was as usual enough to make her pause and catch her breath. How many times had she gaped admiringly at him as he sat at his drawing board, looking sexy and inspired, with his shirt sleeves rolled over his tanned forearms and his hair dark and ruffled under the bright light of his architect's lamp? He'd had no idea how instrumental he had been in her decision to enrol at college to study for an A-Level in art then spend all her wages on a long-distance course in interior design.

To him, she was the timid cleaner he occasionally chatted to about the weather or the new veggie café in town. But to her Nathan was everything. Her first proper crush and the man she wanted to impress more than anyone else in the world.

She was far too shy to talk to him about her course. She didn't even tell him when she passed with flying colours. But when he entered a competition to refurbish a boutique hotel in London, she secretly worked on her own proposal. At last, she thought, he would realise that she was more than a cleaner. She was even naïve enough to dream that he might offer her an internship, or even see her as a woman, not just the cleaner wearing dungarees and rubber gloves.

It was almost too painful to remember the stunned expression on his face the day she had mustered the courage to show him her portfolio. Silent, his dark eyebrows knitted in concentration, he had flicked through her proposal, his surprise quickly followed by a pitying smile as he pushed the drawings back into the folder. He had asked if she had shown them to anyone, and when she had said he was the first, he had promised to take another look at them and give her detailed feedback.

In the meantime, he'd said, she should focus on giving the

office a thorough clean. He was thinking of relocating to London and an estate agent was coming to value the premises the following day.

She had no idea how she managed to finish cleaning his offices that evening, her heart breaking from the news he was moving away, and from the lukewarm reaction to the designs she had poured so much of herself into.

She had waited a couple of days before asking for more feedback, and then wished she hadn't. He had been kind, but brutally honest. Her work showed promise, but the colour schemes, the shapes and concepts were amateurish and lacked originality. If she was serious about working as a designer, she should do a 'proper' degree at university. For her own sake, and because he didn't want her to be laughed at, he asked her not to show the drawings to anyone else. In fact, she should leave them with him.

She had burst into tears. He had handed her a Kleenex, put his arm around her shoulders and let her sob all over his tailored blue shirt, and given her the evening off. A few days later the 'For Sale' sign had gone up, Nathan had moved to London shortly afterwards, and she had never heard from him again.

Cassie's grandfather laughing in the living room brought her back sharply to the present. Perhaps it was no bad thing the magazine was nowhere to be found. It did no good to reminisce about the past and dream about what could have been. She may still sketch designs and ideas, but the only interior design she did these days was for her close friends, and much of it only involved choosing new colour schemes and making cushions.

She took two plates and put them on the table, and was reaching into the cutlery drawer for knives and forks when her phone rang.

'Cassie, thank goodness you're home!' Nadine Hartley sounded even more panicked and breathless than usual. 'The waitress the caterer hired for the party tonight has cancelled. I don't have anybody to help and my guests are about to arrive. It's a disaster. You must come over right now.'

'But I know nothing about waitressing!'

'There's nothing to it. All you'll have to do is serve the champagne and the canapés. I'll make it worth your while,' Nadine insisted. 'I'll pay twice the cleaning rate, and it'll be over by ten o'clock, I promise.'

Cassie sighed. She could do with the extra money, and she needed to keep Nadine Hartley happy. 'I suppose I could help out.'

'And you'll tidy up afterwards? You're so good at tidying up. It will take you no time at all.'

'Well…'

'That's settled, then. You need to come straight away, and do wear something nice for a change, not those awful dungarees.' Nadine ended the call, and Cassie put the phone down, cursing her lack of backbone.

'Granddad, I have to go out.'

He frowned. 'Now?'

'Nadine Hartley is having a party, her waitress let her down and she is in a complete panic. I have to go.'

'That woman is always in a panic.' He glanced at the window. 'It's still snowing, Trifle. You'll have to be careful.'

'I will. Don't worry. The fish and chips are ready. You can eat while I get changed.'

After a quick shower, she pulled a long-sleeved black dress with a pretty low-cut collar – the only smart dress she owned – and a pair of tights out of her wardrobe. She would wear pumps inside Nadine's house, but slipped on her snow boots to drive there and back. She slapped on some make-up, tied her hair in a neat ponytail and ran down the stairs.

'You didn't even have any tea,' her granddad complained.

'I'll eat something there. There should be plenty.'

'Don't forget your hat!'

Sighing, she grabbed her hat and her coat, pecked a kiss on her granddad's cheek, and rushed out.

Chapter Ten

Stefan pushed open the door to the Eagle and Child and froze as his eyes struggled to take in the Christmas extravaganza in front of him.

Decorations dangled from the ceiling. A huge tree stood in a corner, disappearing under baubles and tinsel, and fairy lights blinked and twinkled along the walls, along the beams, and along the counter. This was Christmas gone mad.

'Are you going in or not?' a man asked behind him.

'Sorry.' This really wasn't the kind of place he wanted to spend an evening, or even an hour, but he owed Mason Austin a pint, and he was a man of his word. Gritting his teeth, he walked into the pub, bending down slightly to avoid the paper snowflakes dangling from the ceiling.

He was an hour and a half early for his meeting with Mason Austin so he bought half-a-pint of bitter and found an empty spot at the far end of the counter from where he could both watch the football on the giant television screen and observe the locals. People stared, but that was only to be expected, so he nodded to those closest to him, ignored the others, and drank his beer as he focussed on the match as he waited for Mason.

One of the bar staff walked over and plucked a few empty glasses from the counter.

'Hi there. I'm Sadie.' She smiled and flicked her long blonde hair over her shoulder. 'I don't think I've seen you around.'

'I arrived yesterday.' Hopefully his curt reply would discourage her from asking any more questions. The last thing he wanted was to be dragged into a conversation. He'd had enough with Cassie's chatting.

Her eyes opened wide. 'You're French! Am I right?'

He nodded and she put a hand on her heart. 'I do love a

man with a French accent. If you need help finding things to do in the area, give me a shout. I'll be happy to show you around.'

'Sadie, leave the punters alone and scoot back over here,' a big man wearing a Christmas jumper with some kind of dog pattern – or was it a squirrel? – shouted from the other end of the counter. 'There are glasses to be collected over here, in case you haven't noticed.'

The girl sighed. 'Big Jim is a slave driver. I'll come back for a chat later, when he's not looking.' She winked and walked away.

'There aren't many new faces around here in the winter,' an elderly gentleman said appearing next to him. 'It's only normal young Sadie should be curious.' The man smiled. 'You must be that Frenchman who's staying at Belthorn.'

Without waiting for his answer he added, 'I'm Joseph – Joseph Bell. It's my granddaughter who's looking after you.'

Stefan narrowed his eyes. 'Cassie?'

'That's the one. Tell me, young man, how do you find Belthorn? A bit remote, I guess.'

'It suits me.'

The man removed his cap and coat and hung them on the old-fashioned coat stand next to the counter.

'I wanted to thank you for looking after Cassie tonight and making sure she got home all right.'

Stefan frowned. 'I didn't do anything. I only drove down to the village behind her.'

'Still, it was nice of you. I do worry about her driving that old van in the snow, even if she claims that it's safe. You'll keep an eye on her, won't you, my lad?'

Was Joseph Bell asking him to look after his granddaughter? If he knew how Stefan had failed the people in his care, he wouldn't want him anywhere near a member of his family.

'Of course,' Joseph Bell carried on before Stefan could find a suitable reply, 'you mustn't tell her. She wouldn't like that,

71

since she thinks it's *her* job to look after folks. You would think she'd have enough work with cleaning houses, but no... she brings folks flowers and cakes, sprays perfume everywhere because she says it improves people's mood, and buys yards of fabrics to make cushions for everybody. I mean... how many cushions do people need?

'Cassie is far too soft-hearted,' he added. 'Take tonight. One of her regular clients asked her to waitress at a party and she didn't like to refuse so she went out again without having anything to eat. She said she would have something later, but I bet that Hartley woman won't give her a minute to sit down.'

He gestured towards Stefan's glass. 'Can I get you another beer, son?'

Stefan shook his head. 'I'm fine for now, thanks.'

Cassie's grandfather ordered a pint and Darren Morse walked into the pub. He smiled at Joseph and nodded at Stefan.

Joseph cast him a surprised glance. 'Do you know young Darren?'

'I met him this afternoon at Belthorn,' Stefan replied in a non-committal voice. 'Cassie forgot something at the supermarket, and he brought it over.'

Joseph nodded. 'That was nice of him. Then again, he is always very helpful. He does lots of jobs for us at the cottage. He's a good lad but he's a bit shy, and between you and me I think he's in love with Cassie. He's always asking about her.'

Stefan frowned. Morse was in love with Cassie? Yes, that could explain the way he had behaved with her in Belthorn's kitchen and the story Stefan was sure he had made up about the bottle of wine...

The pub was filling up fast. Joseph Bell introduced Stefan to a couple of his friends, two elderly gentlemen he said he used to work with at the local quarry, and Mason Austin walked in soon after.

'How's the car?' he asked.

72

'Good. Thanks again for your help this morning. We agreed I owed you a pint. What are you drinking?'

Mason said he'd have a pint of Jennings and the two men talked about cars and motorbikes. When Stefan mentioned he'd been a helicopter pilot in the French army, the conversation immediately veered onto the Lake District mountain rescue team and their new S-92 helicopters.

Mason was easy to listen to, and even easier to talk to, and he seemed fascinated by the helicopters Stefan had piloted. 'You mean you actually piloted both assault and transport helicopters?'

'Gazelle, Tiger and Cougar, among others.'

'No wonder you didn't need me to look at your car engine this morning. I bet you can fix just about anything.'

Stefan smiled. 'I manage.'

Perhaps it was the warm, friendly atmosphere that put him at ease, or the mechanic's sympathetic questions, but Stefan talked more about himself than he'd ever intended to. He mentioned his career spanning over fifteen years, and hinted at a couple of missions he'd taken part in.

'You were with Charles Ashville over there, weren't you?' Mason asked. 'We heard that he was almost killed.'

Stefan's voice was rougher than usual when he answered. 'Yeah, it was a close call.'

Mason cast a sympathetic glance towards him, but didn't make any comment. All the time Stefan kept an eye on Darren Morse who had crept closer to Cassie's grandfather and appeared to be listening to the lively discussion he was having with his two friends.

Mason pointed to the elderly men and laughed. 'They must be bickering about Comedy Night again.' Seeing Stefan's quizzical look, he explained, 'It's an amateur stand-up contest organised by the pub in aid of the Mountain Rescue Service. Joseph has won it for the past fifteen years.'

Sadie came over to collect their empty glasses. 'Can I tempt you into another beer, gentlemen?' Her husky voice implied that she would like to tempt them into something infinitely naughtier than a drink.

Stefan shook his head. 'Not for me, thanks.'

He bought Mason another pint, and the conversation rolled over other charity events planned in aid of the Mountain Rescue Service over the Christmas period. When Stefan next glanced towards the bar and the television screen, Morse had left.

He couldn't explain the feeling of dread suddenly tugging at the pit of his stomach. 'Excuse me a moment,' he told Mason before walking up to Joseph Bell.

'Where did you say Cassie was tonight?' he asked.

Chapter Eleven

If Nadine asked her one more time if she had vacuumed the living room carpet, wiped the kitchen worktops, and washed, dried and put away the crystal flutes, and put all the leftovers in the bin, she was going to explode and say something she would definitely regret!

It was almost eleven. Her feet ached from standing, her cheeks hurt from smiling, and the cramps tightening her stomach were a sore reminder that she hadn't eaten anything, not even one of the fancy canapés she had served all evening. The last guests had left an hour before and Nadine's husband had retreated into his study with a cognac and a sour face.

'I am exhausted!' Nadine strolled barefoot into the kitchen, her bright coral-painted toenails a splash of colour on the dark granite floor tiles. A champagne glass in one hand, she dangled her black slingback shoes from the fingers of the other.

'It was a great party, wasn't it?' she declared in a slightly slurred voice, 'even though I had to do practically everything on my own.'

Cassie bit back a retort. Nadine had done nothing but flutter between her guests, nibble at the finger food, drink champagne and boss her around, which, of course, was her prerogative as the party's hostess.

'Isn't Piers Hardy a dream?' Nadine sat on a breakfast bar stool and drank a sip of champagne. 'The man has such charm and charisma, it's no wonder women are queuing up to fall into his arms.'

Not this woman, Cassie thought. Piers's attentions left her cold, even if he didn't seem to notice.

Nadine put her flute down. 'Let's put it this way. I wouldn't push him away if he tried it on. John only ever thinks about work. He never looks at me, never pays me any compliments, and always looks miserable.'

Complaining about her husband was one of Nadine's favourite pastimes, along with shopping and treatments at expensive spas, but Cassie knew she wasn't expected to comment, so she carried on scrubbing the worktops.

'Now, Piers is different,' Nadine continued. 'He noticed I'd had my hair and nails done. He told me I looked nice in my new dress, and he could hardly keep his eyes off me all evening – or his hands, for that matter.'

Cassie scrubbed harder. Nadine wasn't the only woman Piers had pursued all evening. He had brushed against her every time he walked past, touching her arm or shoulder to ask for another drink, watching her constantly as she poured more champagne into flutes or walked to the kitchen and back to replenish the trays with nibbles.

Her breath caught in her throat as she recalled how he had blocked her way in the corridor. 'You should dress like that more often,' he had said, his gaze fixed on her chest, and trailing down to the white frilly pinny Nadine had insisted she wear.

Embarrassed by his hot stare, Cassie had stepped back, but he had come closer. 'What are you doing tomorrow night? We could go out – not to the Eagle and Child, somewhere more private.'

Nadine calling her had saved her from having to reply, and she had made her escape.

'John said that Piers's estate management business is doing really well,' Nadine remarked. 'So not only is he a hunk but he's making loads of money too. You're lucky to be working for him.'

Not that lucky, Cassie thought. It was exhausting trying to put him off. It was only a question of time before he asked her out again, and the prospect tightened her stomach into a knot and made her want to be sick.

She opened the cupboard under the sink to store the cleaning products, peeled off her rubber gloves and stacked the sponges by the side of the huge granite sink. 'I've finished now, Nadine. I'm going home.'

Nadine's eyes were slightly unfocussed as she glanced around. 'Already? Are you sure you tidied everything away? I don't want to find crumbs all over the carpet or a messy loo tomorrow morning. I need to pay you, I suppose. Now, where's my purse? I hope I have enough change.'

Cassie tightened her lips. Nadine owed her more than just a few coins since she had promised her double her cleaning rate for her waitressing that evening.

'Don't worry about it,' she said calmly, even though the woman was starting to annoy her very much. 'I'll bring you an invoice next week, together with my monthly cleaning bill.' She changed into her boots, put her coat on and slipped out before the woman could ask her to do anything else.

The drive had been full of cars when she'd arrived, so she had parked on the road a short distance away. It was never a busy road, but at this time it was dark and deserted, and so quiet sounds of her breathing and her boots crushing the frozen snow echoed in the night.

Her van's dark shape loomed ahead, and she clicked her key fob to unlock the door. Something wasn't right. The van stood lopsided, with the driver side much lower than the passenger side. She opened the door, grabbed the torch in the glove compartment, and shone the light on the tyres.

Both tyres on the driver's side were flat. Great... Just great, she groaned. Now what? It wasn't worth phoning a taxi. On Saturday night, the few taxis serving the area would be busy, and she would be home by the time it took a cab to pick her up. There was nothing else to do but to walk.

With a weary sigh, she looped her handbag around her shoulder, locked the van again and set off in the direction of Red Moss.

She had been walking for less than five minutes when the sound of an engine hummed behind her and headlights swept the road. Even though the car drove slowly, she stepped aside and left plenty of space for it to go past, but instead of overtaking, the car stopped. Nervous, she gripped the torch more tightly. The window slid down, and Darren Morse smiled at her.

Cassie's heart sank. Of all the people who could drive by, why did it have to be *him*?

'Hey,' he said. 'I almost didn't recognise you in the dark. What's up?'

She forced a smile. 'I'm walking home. My van has two flat tyres.'

He whistled between his teeth. 'Two flats. That's really bad luck. Hop in and I'll give you a lift home.'

Cassie shifted from one foot to the other. What should she do? She was cold and exhausted and he would save her a long walk, and she couldn't think of a single good reason to refuse. What's more, she didn't want to upset Darren. He might make her uncomfortable but her granddad liked him.

'Thank you.' She walked around the car and was opening the passenger door to get into the car when a Range Rover drove round the bend and came to a screeching halt. The driver door swung open and a man jumped down, his tall silhouette standing against the glare of the car's powerful headlights. She didn't need to see his face to recognise him.

Stefan Lambert. What was he doing there? This wasn't the way back to Belthorn!

He strode over, and looked down at her. 'Is everything all right?'

She nodded. 'My van has two flat tyres, and Darren was kindly offering me a lift back.'

'Was he now...?' he muttered.

'Lucky for me, he was driving past and—'

Without letting her finish her sentence, Stefan leant down

to talk to Darren through the open door. 'It's all right. You can go. I'll drive Cassie home.'

Frowning at Stefan for his abrupt dismissal, she smiled at Darren. 'I'll see you at the cottage tomorrow morning. Good night.'

'Sure. No worries.' Darren nodded. Cassie pushed the door shut and he drove off.

'Are you truly all right?' Stefan asked, now towering over her.

She glanced up. 'Why wouldn't I be?'

He didn't answer but gestured towards the Range Rover, which was still sitting in the middle of the road with the engine running. 'Let's get in the car so I can take you home.'

He opened the passenger door and pushed a map off the seat for her to sit down. He started driving down the lane in silence. He was frowning and clenched his jaw as if he was annoyed, although what about she had no idea.

'Did you have a nice time at the pub?' she asked to diffuse the tension.

He let out a grunt, which could mean anything.

'Did Mason come?'

He nodded, but still didn't say a word. She sighed in frustration. Lord, the man was hard work.

'Did you meet anybody else?' she insisted.

'I had a chat with your granddad, actually.'

'You met my granddad?' How strange. Her grandfather didn't mention he was going out...

'Yes. We... ahem... talked,' he said, eyes focussed on the dark, windy road. 'Morse was in the pub too. I'm pretty sure he was listening when your grandfather told his friends where you were working tonight. When I realised that he had left, I had a bad feeling, and one thing they teach you in the army is never to ignore a bad feeling.' He clenched his jaw, and added, 'It looks like I was right.'

'Well, I did have a problem with my van, so in that respect

your instinct was right,' she conceded, 'but Darren was going to give me a lift, so I wasn't completely stranded. It was indeed very lucky he happened to drive by or I would have had a long walk home.'

'Perhaps it wasn't a coincidence.'

She looked at him. 'I don't understand.'

He sighed, as if she was being particularly dense. 'Perhaps he had something to do with your flat tyres.'

'Don't be ridiculous!'

He shrugged. 'Where does he live?'

'At the campsite.'

'Where is that?'

'At the other end of the village, on the lake's south shore.'

'So he had no reason to be on this stretch of road at this time of night.'

'He could have been visiting someone.' She paused. That was unlikely, since most houses on that stretch of road were expensive detached ones, farmhouse conversions, or luxury holiday lets – hardly the kind of people Darren would be mixing with. 'Or he could have been going for a drive.'

He glanced at her and arched his eyebrows. 'At this time of night, and in this weather?'

She pulled a face. 'It's stopped snowing.' But it was unlikely, it was true.

'How long did you say he's lived here?'

'About six months. He arrived at the start of the summer season.'

'What do you know about him?'

She took a deep breath. 'Listen... Mr Lambert.' Or should she call him *Sergeant Major* or whatever rank he'd reached in the French army, because right now he sounded like an army officer interrogating a particularly stupid recruit.

'I thought we were on first-name terms.'

She sighed. 'All right. Stefan.' Her voice caught in her throat as she said his name. It sounded intimate – too intimate

– even though there was nothing intimate about the way he was barking questions at her.

'Are you implying that Darren is stalking me?'

'That's exactly what I'm implying, yes.'

She let out a derisive laugh and pointed at her pom-poms hat, her shapeless duffle coat and snow boots. 'Do I look like the type of woman who gets stalked?'

This time his eyes were hard when he turned to her. 'Don't be naïve. Looks have nothing to do with it. Any woman can be the victim of a stalker, whatever she looks like.'

She gasped. At least now she knew what he thought about her. Not only was she dim – another word for 'naïve' – but she was ugly too. More compliments to add to 'overzealous', no doubt.

She counted up to ten to make sure her voice was steady. 'Darren would never do anything so...' she racked her brain for a suitable word, 'weird.'

'It's not just weird. It's criminal. You must report him to the police.'

This time, she bristled. In fact, she was getting downright annoyed at the bossy and condescending tone of his voice. She shook her head, and the pom-poms swung around her face. No wonder he didn't take her seriously with that silly hat! She pulled it off and placed it in her lap.

'Listen... Stefan. I am grateful for the lift home. However, I am sure there's a perfectly innocent explanation for my van having flat tyres and Darren driving by tonight. There must have been nails or broken glass on the road, or I drove through potholes – heaven knows the roads are bad enough around here. I see absolutely no reason to accuse Darren of vandalising my van and cause him to be in trouble with the police.'

Stefan stopped at a crossroads. Despite the absence of road signs, he didn't hesitate but took the first road to the left. His sense of direction must come from being in the army, like his short temper and his lack of conversational skills.

'I didn't tell you before because I didn't want to worry you,' Stefan said after a couple of minutes, 'but I was walking down the hill this afternoon when Morse arrived at Belthorn. After parking his car, he appeared to be checking the tyres on your van.'

She shrugged. 'Why would he do that? No, don't answer. I really don't want to talk about Darren any longer.'

'Didn't you say that he lied this afternoon when he claimed you forgot a bottle of wine at the supermarket?'

She blew a frustrated sigh. 'No. I said he was mistaken.'

'Ignoring a problem doesn't make it go away.'

'Who said there was a problem?'

'Your grandfather said that the man has a crush on you.'

She let out a frustrated sigh and shook her head. 'I don't believe Darren has a crush on me at all, but even if – and that's a very big *if* – that was the case, having a crush on someone isn't a crime, or else half the world would be behind bars at some point.'

She gestured towards the crossroads at the centre of the village. 'Take a left here, please. Bluebell Cottage is at the end of the street.'

He followed her instructions, and she turned to him as soon as he'd stopped the car in front of the house.

'Thank you very much for the lift. I shall see you in the morning.'

'How will you get to Belthorn now your van is out of order?'

'Mason will lend me one of his old cars if he can't fit new tyres on my van tomorrow.'

She pulled her hat on, bent forward to retrieve her bag and the torch at her feet just as he leant forward too. His shoulder brushed against her cheek. Their fingers met on the torch. His face was only a couple of inches away, so close she felt the warmth of his breath on her face.

He looked at her. The light from the lamppost in the street

reflected in his eyes, made shadows on his face and outlined the contour of his mouth. The air seemed to crackle and sizzle around them. Frissons danced on her skin, and the same warm, tingly feeling she'd experienced earlier when he'd pulled her on top of him hummed inside her, making her heart beat faster. He didn't move, didn't speak, and for a moment they just stared at each other, until a cat meowing nearby broke the spell.

Stefan reached out for the torch and handed it to her. 'Here it is,' he said in his rough voice as they both straightened up.

'Thanks.' She slipped the torch inside her bag, opened the door and climbed down. 'I'll see you in the morning.'

She hurried up the short path and opened the front door.

'Why are you so late, Trifle, and where is your van?' her grandfather said from inside.

Cassie watched the Range Rover drive off and closed the door. 'I'll tell you all about it over a cup of tea. I need to put my feet up. It's been a long evening.'

There were, however, two things she would keep to herself: Stefan's ridiculous statement about Darren Morse stalking her, and the no less ridiculous pull of attraction she was feeling towards him.

Chapter Twelve

The manor house loomed at the end of the track, its chimneys rising like masts against the night. He drove slowly, but the slippery lane wasn't the reason why his fingers gripped the steering wheel so tightly and his shoulders tensed up.

Cassie Bell was, and the way she had brushed off his suggestion that Morse may be stalking her. It couldn't be a coincidence that the man had checked her wheels in the afternoon then happened to drive past late at night to offer her a lift home when she had flat tyres. What were the odds of having two flat tyres at once?

He shook his head and let out a long breath. Why did he care so much anyway? After all, he had come to Belthorn to be alone, not to take an interest in anybody else's problems, or worry about the woman Charlie had hired to babysit him. It didn't help of course that Cassie's grandfather had more or less entrusted her to him, and that for some unexplained reason he now felt responsible for her. He didn't need a shrink to tell him he was overcompensating for his past failings, but there was something more – something that was a very, very bad idea...

He was attracted to her.

It had taken all his self-control not to wrench her away from Morse's car earlier, and hold her in his arms to keep her safe. But that was nothing compared to what he had felt as he pulled up in front of Bluebell Cottage. The urge to kiss her, and feel her soft lips under his, had been almost too strong to resist. Thank goodness for that stray cat that had shaken him back to his senses.

He unlocked the front door and stomped his boots onto the mat to get the snow off before hanging his coat on the rack and pushing open the door to the drawing room. What had happened there?

The room looked different, felt different. It even smelled different. And yet, nothing much had changed... The furniture had been rearranged. Pine sprigs, holly and red winter berries made a splash of colour on the mantelpiece. Several boxes of chocolates were piled up on the coffee table next to Vaillant's diary, and a huge cushion in festive colours sat on the sofa – probably Cassie's handiwork, if her grandfather was to be believed. As he breathed in the fresh scent of pine mingling with Cassie's lemon fragrance, the tension in his shoulders ebbed away, and he couldn't help the smile forming on his lips.

Not only did Cassie clean and cook for him, but she struck a bit of her Bluebell fairy magic to make Belthorn a nicer, more comfortable place... He pictured her grey eyes, in turn sparkly or limpid, the dimples that appeared on her cheeks every time she smiled, and her hair the colour of sunshine, and his chest tightened.

Being attracted to Cassie was a very bad idea, and he'd do well to keep away from her as much as possible...

He made some coffee, picked up André Vaillant's diary and went up to bed where he read until the writing blurred and danced on the page and he couldn't focus any longer. For the first time in weeks, he fell asleep straight away and didn't dream of anything until the grey light of dawn filtered through the curtains and woke him up the following morning.

He made a couple of ham and cheese sandwiches, filled a bottle of water, grabbed a banana and a handful of chocolates and stuffed everything in a rucksack. It looked cold so he zipped his parka up, wrapped his scarf tightly around his neck and pulled down his woolly hat before locking the door.

Taking a deep breath of crisp, clean air, he glanced up at the soft blue sky. A faint crescent of moon and a few stars still shone over the ragged peaks to his right, but the snowy fells already sparkled under the pale morning sunshine that peeped over the summit. A ribbon of mist captured the sun's golden rays and floated halfway up the mountains. Trees stood still and fluffy with frost. It was a picture of beauty, peace and serenity.

Charlie once told him that some valleys were so narrow they didn't get any sunshine at all during winter months. The thought made him shudder. He couldn't imagine spending months trapped in the shadows...

He started on the steep path behind Belthorn Manor. He had worked out a circular route that would take him to Patterdale in the next valley then back to Belthorn Manor. He hadn't chosen the walk at random. He wanted to see the farm André Vaillant mentioned in his journal, if it still existed. It was the farm Charlie's great-grandfather had owned and tenanted to Ruth Merriweather's family and where young Ruth had taken André one sunny summer's day.

Because of André's injuries, the couple had walked on the path that meandered at the bottom of the dale. He, on the other hand, would try to ascend the fell and walk down into the next valley.

As he started on the trail, Stefan recalled the words the convalescing pilot had written after his first visit to Patterdale – words of hope that were etched into his mind.

I feel like a man again, a man who dares to hope that he has a future. Today was a dream come true, not only thanks to the beauty of the valley, the scents of the meadows, the sunshine that warmed my skin and brought brightness to my soul, but because I was with Ruth.

The path to Patterdale followed a chirping, fast-flowing beck. Wild flowers covered the vast expanse of pastures like a colourful carpet, or hid like tiny secrets in the glades or the cracks in mossy stone walls. Ruth named them as we walked. There were white Wild Angelica, yellow Adder's-tongue, Spearwort, vivid blue Harebells, cup-shaped brownish Water Avens and many others.

Ruth... whispering her name brings back the sunshine of

that wonderful day. She slipped her small hand in mine to help me through the rough terrain, and left it there until we reached the farm. And when we set off on our way home after having tea and scones with her mother, it was I who reached out for her hand, and she didn't snatch it away.

Dare I hope that Ruth's timid smile, her kindness and the warmth I read in her eyes are not caused by pity for a lonely, crippled man far from his loved ones at home? Dare I hope that my life is not over as I feared, but merely at a crossroads?

Stefan dislodged loose stones as he climbed up, and the sounds they made as they rolled down the fell echoed in the morning's silence. He soon got into a rhythm and found that he walked faster and with less difficulty than the day before. He reached a beck singing between snowy banks, its crystal clear waters trickling down the hillside, and looked back.

If it weren't for the manor house below, he could easily believe he was in a forgotten world that had lain hidden and untouched since the beginning of time. Today, Wolf Tarn made a circle of perfect blue in the landscape. Yet, even in the glorious sunny morning, he couldn't help thinking that there was something almost sinister about it.

The sun turned warmer as the morning wore on, the mist burned out and the snow covering the hillside started to melt. He was alone except for a few sheep. Their bleating echoed across the valley and accompanied him all the way to the top of the fell. At last he reached the cairn marking the summit. Out of breath and his muscles burning, he found a boulder to sit down on and have his lunch and savour the view and the silence.

He could see for miles, all the way to the flat, golden shores of the Irish Sea. Coniston and Monks Water Lake were long blue shapes in the distance, and the landscape was a succession of rocky crags, barren fell tops, vertiginous drops and narrow ridges.

He finished his sandwich, drank half his bottle of water,

and spread his map flat on the boulder to check his route. If he followed the ridge to another cairn he could just about spot in the distance, he should find a path to his right, go down via a disused quarry road, and end up in Patterdale.

It felt good to walk, climb, and scramble down the crag and onto a narrow sheep trail, and not to think about anything else than the next step, the next foothold.

The quarry was an ugly grey scar on the hillside. It was fenced off and signs to keep out had been nailed to an old gate. Rusty cables as thick as his thigh snaked across the path or sprung from the ground, whilst man-made mounds of broken slate scattered the surroundings. A couple of old wagons lay tipped on their side next to a derelict stone hut.

It may be a ghost town these days, yet men had carried out noisy and dangerous work there in the past, and Stefan tried to imagine what it must have been like to work this high up in the mountain, in the cutting wind and pouring rain, the freezing cold and the stifling heat.

He was about to carry on when he heard a voice singing. It sounded like a child. Stefan looked at the gate and the fencing around the quarry. It looked sturdy enough to keep people out, especially a child. And yet, someone had ventured inside.

'Hello? Who is there?' he called.

Immediately a boy with pale blond hair appeared at the window of the ruined hut. He looked to be about eight or nine years old and wore a bright red anorak.

'Hello,' the boy replied.

'What are you doing in there? It's not safe.' Even though he wanted to climb over the fence and yank the child into a safer place, Stefan forced a smile. He must take care not to scare the little boy.

The child showed him the toy he was holding. 'I'm trying my new metal detector. I got it for my birthday. I want to find treasure, so I can buy toys. My dad said I've been naughty and won't get anything from Santa this year.'

'You won't find any treasure in there, just old rusty tools and machinery. Where are your parents?'

'At the farm.'

'I'll take you back,' Stefan decided. He looked at the gate and the fence. They looked secure. 'How did you get in?'

The boy walked to the far end of the fencing, crouched down and lifted a piece of loose mesh wire. He thrust his metal detector through first then twisted his little body and made it to the other side. He grabbed hold of his metal detector then ran towards Stefan.

'Do you often come here?' Stefan asked.

The boy nodded. 'All the time.'

Stefan frowned. 'It's dangerous. You could get hurt and nobody would know where you are.'

The boy didn't reply but stared at him. 'What's wrong with your face? Have you been in the war?'

Stefan looked at the snowy peaks and the bright blue sky and nodded. 'Yeah, you could say that.'

'Where was it?'

'A long way from here.'

'Your voice is weird too. What happened to you?'

'None of your business. Come on, now.'

The boy shook his head. 'I'll only come if you tell me.'

Stefan sighed. Damn, that child was stubborn. 'All right. I'll tell you as we walk. Is this the way home?'

The boy nodded.

'I'm Stefan, by the way. What's your name?'

'Louis Merriweather.'

Stefan frowned. 'Merriweather?' That was Ruth's family name.

'Now tell me what happened to your face. You promised.'

As they walked, and in a few brief sentences, Stefan told him about his former job carrying supplies and people in his helicopter – soldiers, doctors and nurses, people who'd been hurt.

'I was in Mali last year. Do you know where Mali is?'

The boy shook his head.

'It's in Africa,' Stefan explained.

'Where they have lions, and elephants and camels?'

Stefan laughed at the boy's excited voice. 'Yes. They have all that, especially camels.'

'Did your helicopter crash?'

Stefan nodded. 'My co-pilot and I were trying to evacuate a clinic – doctors and nurses and people who were very sick and their families – and…'

They were shot at as he was taking off. He lost control. The helicopter started spinning and fell to the ground, and when he crash-landed they were shot at again. He managed to pull a couple of children and an elderly woman out of the craft, shouting out all the time for Charlie and Isa to get out. He ran back into the helicopter to find Isa slumped against the cockpit, her eyes open but glassy and blood soaking her flight suit. From the odd angle of her neck he had known straight away that she was beyond help. Charlie was unconscious but breathing, so he dragged him out and was about to go back when there was a second of deadly silence as if the whole world was sucked into a void… then the craft exploded.

He pushed away the memories of carnage and mayhem, the sounds of crying and screaming, the stench of blood and death that so often came back to haunt him. If only he had been faster and could have rescued more people before the helicopter exploded. If only…

Aware of the boy staring at him, he finished. 'There was an accident, and I got injured.'

'Was your face all smashed up?'

He nodded.

'Did you cry?'

'A little.'

'I would cry a lot if my face was all broken like yours.'

'When you're in pain, you have to focus on other things. They teach you stuff like that in the army.'

'I want to know all about it.' He stretched his hand in front of Stefan. A grubby plaster was wrapped around his thumb. 'I cut my finger the other day and it hurt so much I couldn't stop crying. My dad got annoyed with me and told me to man up but it didn't work.'

Stefan couldn't help but smile in front of the boy's indignant face.

They walked down the path in companionable silence for a while, then the boy spoke again. 'Did everybody die in the crash?'

Images flitted in Stefan's mind – images of death and destruction that were imprinted into his brain, into his soul.

'No,' he lied. He looked at the boy and forced a smile. 'Everybody was fine.'

'That was lucky. You must be very brave, and very clever, to have saved everybody. I want to be brave and clever like you when I grow up.'

Stefan swallowed a denial. He was neither brave nor clever. There were too many people he hadn't saved that day.

They followed the path down towards the dale where copses of fir trees painted splashes of dark green against the snow, and smoke billowed out of the chimney of a long farm building. From the top of the path he saw a tractor, several cars and a quad bike.

'That's my farm,' the boy announced. 'It's called Patterdale. It's my birthday today. You have to come in and eat some cake. Mum made a huge chocolate cake. It's very good.'

Patterdale? So this was what used to be Ruth Merriweather's farm, and in all probability it was still in the Merriweather family.

Louis ran ahead, climbed over the ladder stile and carried on into the farmyard and Stefan followed. Two sheepdogs barked furiously and jumped at him as he made his way towards the farmhouse. He gave them a pat on the head, and followed the boy to the front door. He had to speak to Louis's parents, tell them where he'd found him. The quarry was too dangerous a playground for a little boy.

Louis pushed open the door to the farmhouse and gestured for him to come in. He wiped the snow and mud off the soles of his boots on the doormat. A woman was laughing in a nearby room. As he walked through the hallway cluttered with dirty boots, coats and toys, he realised with a bump to the heart that he knew exactly who the woman was.

Chapter Thirteen

'Mum! Dad! I found a man who pilots helicopters in Africa and I told him he could have some of my chocolate cake,' Louis announced at the top of his voice as he ran into the dining room.

Cassie looked up just as Stefan Lambert walked into the room, bending down to avoid banging his head against the door lintel.

Her first thought was that she was glad she had discarded her dungarees and changed into the top she'd recently bought from Cecilia's studio. Her second was that Stefan didn't seem in the least happy to see her.

'By heck, Lambert! What are you doing here?' her granddad exclaimed. He turned to Rachel and her husband Tim. 'That's the man I was telling you about, the Frenchman our Cassie is looking after at Belthorn Manor.'

Rachel and Tim jumped to their feet, a welcoming smile on their faces as he hesitated on the doorstep. 'Come in. Please.'

Stefan looked at the bottle of Prosecco, the plates and cakes on the table, and put a hand on Louis's shoulder. 'I didn't mean to interrupt a family celebration. I found this young man in the quarry and wanted to return him home safe and sound.'

He narrowed his eyes as he looked at Cassie, and added, 'I had no idea you would be here. The boy said his name was Merriweather, not Bell.' He sounded almost reproachful, as if he'd been lured into a trap and it was all her fault.

'That's because he's my cousin Tim's son,' she explained, 'and Tim is a Merriweather, from my grandmother's side of the family.'

Rachel gave her son a stern look and wagged her index finger at him. 'You went to the quarry again, even though we forbade you to. You're grounded, young man. Go to your room right away.'

Louis's lower lip started trembling. He turned to his father, but Tim said in a stern voice, 'You heard your mother. Give me your metal detector. You can't have it until I'm sure I can trust you.'

The boy cast Stefan an accusing glance as he brushed past him on his way out. There were stomping noises on the stairs, and a door slammed shut on the first floor.

'I'm sorry I upset him.' Stefan pulled off his woolly hat and raked his fingers in his brown hair, leaving it all spiked up.

'What do you have to feel sorry for?' Rachel asked. 'You were kind enough to bring him home. He knows he isn't allowed in the quarry.'

Gesturing to the table, she added, 'Please make yourself at home. You must have a drink and some cake too.'

He shook his head. 'Thank you, but I must go back.'

'Come on, son,' Cassie's grandfather called out. 'You can't refuse our Rachel's hospitality. And if you don't mind me saying, you look as if you could do with a rest.'

Stefan looked about to protest again, and shrugged. 'If you're sure I'm not imposing. Thank you.'

Suddenly everybody was fussing around him. Rachel took his parka and his rucksack. Tim asked him if he wanted tea, coffee or wine, or something a bit stronger. 'I have an excellent brandy, if you're interested.'

Stefan said he was, and Cassie's grandfather invited him to sit down.

'Let's give the man some cake. It's a long walk from Belthorn. He must be famished.' Turning to Stefan, he added, 'By the way, it seems I must thank you for looking after our Cassie again and driving her home last night. Two flat tyres at once... who ever heard of such bad luck?'

'I'm glad I could help.' Stefan sent her a pointed look, but thankfully said nothing about Darren. The last thing she wanted was for him to start accusing him of stalking her and interfering with her tyres in front of her family.

'Sit down, Lambert.' Her granddad gestured to the empty chair next to her. 'She's one of a kind, our Cassie – a hard worker with a heart of gold. She'll make a terrific wife to a lucky man one day.'

'Granddad!' Cassie hissed in shock. What was he playing at?

Ignoring her, he leant towards Stefan and winked. 'She's a real softie, you know, that's why we nicknamed her—'

'Don't you dare!' Her face heating up, she cast her grandfather a warning glance, but he carried on, 'We call her Trifle.'

Stefan looked at her and arched his eyebrows. 'Trifle?'

'It's a pudding,' her granddad explained. 'Layers of sponge soaked in sherry, custard cream, jelly and whipped cream. It's pretty, soft, and sweet, like our Cassie.'

Cassie's face now burnt so much it hurt. What was wrong with her grandfather today? Why was he hell-bent on humiliating her in front of their guest?

'Oh. Hmm… Right. I know what it is, but I can't say I've ever eaten any.' Stefan Lambert's expression was unfathomable.

While everybody was busy fussing, getting him a plate, a glass and some cutlery, he turned to her and asked in a low voice, 'What did Mason say about the tyres?'

'That I had been very unlucky and promised to order new ones tomorrow. In the meantime he lent me his old Land Rover.'

Stefan looked puzzled. 'Bad luck had nothing to do with it. Didn't you tell him it was Darren Morse who—'

'I know that's what you think.' She remembered that he had called her naïve the night before – but she knew he meant 'stupid'. 'But you're wrong about Darren. I didn't tell Mason anything. I didn't tell my granddad either, so please don't mention it. He would only worry.'

Stefan's eyes turned dark and stormy, but before he could speak, Tim placed a glass of brandy in front of him, Rachel put a large slab of cake onto his plate, and her granddad asked him if he had enjoyed his walk.

'Very much so,' he replied. 'The paths from Belthorn are in good condition, and well signposted.'

That sparked a general conversation about the erosion of tracks, the unpredictability of the weather, and dangers run by ill-equipped walkers who set off in flimsy clothes and flip-flops to climb the fells, or relied on apps on their mobile phones to find their way instead of planning their walk using 'good, old-fashioned common sense,' Tim said, shaking his head.

'You wouldn't believe the number of folks who call here, weak and exhausted because they misjudged the distance or the terrain, didn't look at the weather forecast, and don't even have a map or a compass.'

He turned to Stefan and smiled. 'I bet you set off well prepared for your walk this morning.'

'Charlie's sister gave me several maps of the area when I picked up the keys to Belthorn Manor at Charlie's London flat.'

'You know the family well, then?' Rachel asked.

Stefan nodded. 'I can't say I know Gabrielle very well, but Charlie's a good friend.'

'Gabrielle Ashville always thought she was too good for us lowly peasants,' Rachel remarked with a shrug, 'but Charles is nice. Cassie said you worked with him in Africa.'

Something flashed in his eyes – regret or pain, it was hard to tell – but his face remained stony. 'That's right.'

Cassie burned to ask him what exactly had happened, but the tone of his voice didn't invite any questions.

'It's a shame he rarely comes here,' Tim remarked. 'It would be good to see a member of the Ashville family at Belthorn Manor from time to time. At the very least, it would stop Piers Hardy behaving like he owns the estate. That man is a bully and it's high time he was put down a peg or two.' He clenched his fingers around his glass and shook his head.

'Last time we saw Charles and his sister was at their father's funeral,' Rachel said. 'They both looked as if they couldn't wait to get away, which is understandable given the circumstances, I suppose. And of course there is the small matter of the curse.'

Stefan frowned. 'What curse?'

Cassie turned to Rachel and rolled her eyes. 'Please don't start with this old story.'

But Rachel ignored her and said in a gloomy voice, 'The curse of the Grey Friar pursuing his terrible revenge on the Ashville family.'

She turned to Cassie. 'You saw the Grey Friar, didn't you? You should tell us about your nightmare Christmas party. It's a long time since I heard the tale.'

Cassie's throat tightened. 'I don't want to talk about it. Not now. Not ever.'

'Come on, Cassie. It's a good story, and surely you want Stefan to know about the strange things that may happen while he is all alone at Belthorn?' Rachel's cheeks were flushed, probably because of the three glasses of sparkly wine she had enjoyed at lunchtime.

'No, I don't want to talk about it,' Cassie warned, but her cousin only giggled and turned to Stefan. 'Cassie and her friends made a campfire near Wolf Tarn, and while the others were enjoying themselves Cassie wandered off and some horrible spectre of doom appeared on the—'

'Rachel, please,' Cassie cried out. Why was everyone in her family trying to annoy her and make her look stupid today?

Rachel glanced at her and shrugged. 'As you wish, but it's a good story.'

'It wasn't a story. It was real.'

Rachel shrugged. 'You may say so, but the police didn't find anything.'

'Cassie always had way too much imagination where Belthorn was concerned,' her grandfather cut in. 'Cassie's grandma – my Elsie – was exactly the same. She was always claiming some lost spirit or other was talking to her. When it wasn't her aunt Ruth, it was some long-forgotten Ashville lass pining away for her sweetheart, or that grey-cloaked friar that lurks in the ruined abbey to cause mischief.'

Cassie noticed that Stefan frowned when her granddad mentioned Ruth, as if he recognised the name, but she immediately dismissed the thought. How could he know about Ruth Merriweather?

Her granddad sighed and a wistful smile stretched his lips. 'My Elsie sure kept me awake many a night with her silly tales.'

'They weren't all silly tales, Granddad,' Cassie protested. 'Grandma used to say places keep imprints of the past, and I for one believe she was right. I don't care if you all think I'm crazy, or stupid, or both. I know what I saw, heard and felt that night. And before you say anything, no, I didn't have too much to drink.'

Her granddad raised his hands in a calming gesture. 'Don't get yourself all upset, pet. Nobody is calling you crazy.'

He yawned and rubbed his eyes. He looked old and tired suddenly.

'Are you not feeling well?' Cassie asked, concern replacing her bad mood.

He yawned again. 'I'm a little sleepy, that's all. It must be Rachel's good food and that sparkly wine I drank at lunchtime.'

'Then why don't you have a rest while Rachel and I make some coffee?' Cassie stood up, picked up a cushion from the sofa and put it on the armchair near the fireplace. 'Come and sit here, you'll be nice and warm.'

Rachel grumbled that she'd rather have another glass of Prosecco than coffee but dutifully got up and went into the kitchen to make a pot, and Cassie followed to help as soon as her grandfather was settled in his armchair.

'I'm sorry I upset you before,' Rachel said after she closed the door. 'I don't know what came over me.'

Cassie sighed. 'It's all right, but I don't want you to ever mention that night again, especially in front of guests.'

Rachel measured scoops of ground coffee for the coffee machine. 'Talking about guests, once you get used to the scars on his face, I find Stefan Lambert very attractive, in a rough and rugged kind of way.'

'You think so too?' Cassie said without thinking, and immediately her cheeks started burning.

Rachel wagged her index finger at her. 'Oh, oh! I see... You fancy him, don't you?'

Cassie's cheeks burned harder. 'What are you talking about?'

'I'm talking about you acting all coy around our guest, and now turning red like a tomato when I mentioned that he is a bit of a hunk.' Rachel lowered her voice. 'I also noticed his gorgeous hazel eyes – or are they golden brown? And by the way, he looks at you like he'd rather gobble *you* up instead of my chocolate cake.'

'You've got it all wrong, he thinks I'm ugly and stupid, he said as much yesterday.'

'I may be a little tipsy, but I know what I see.'

Cassie couldn't help it. She couldn't understand it, and certainly didn't want to feel that way, but she loved the thought that Stefan might find her pretty. It was utterly ridiculous since she'd only just met the man and he wasn't even nice to her. What's more, he wasn't her type at all. She preferred trendy, dark-haired and moody interior designers... didn't she?

Rachel pointed at Cassie's new top. 'That top really suits you, you know. It clings to all your good bits. You should wear things like that more often, instead of your baggy dungarees. It's no wonder you've ended up an old spinster.'

Cassie finished slotting dirty plates in the dishwasher and curled her fists on her hips. 'I'm not that old! I'm only twenty-eight. And I can hardly wear nice clothes to clean houses, can I?'

She paused, and lowered her voice. 'But seriously, do you really think that Stefan finds me attractive?' It was like being sixteen all over again, and whispering about boys from the local college or the farm hands Rachel's father used to hire for the summer. Rachel may be a few years older but she had been her friend long before she married Cassie's cousin Tim. In fact, she was the one who had asked Cassie to sing backup vocals in the Bananarama tribute band she and two other friends had formed. Why Bananarama, Cassie had never understood. There were more up-to-date bands they could have copied from, but the tribute band had been a laugh, if not a success.

'I wouldn't have said so if I thought otherwise.' Rachel laughed and pecked a kiss on Cassie's cheek. 'Now go back there and charm him with your witty conversation, your lovely smile and sexy cleavage while I make the coffee and finish tidying up in here.'

Cassie went back to the dining room to find that Louis's two younger brothers had come back indoors after playing with the new metal detector. Their cheeks were bright red with the cold and their fine blond hair crackled with static electricity as they pulled their woolly scarves and hats off.

'We didn't find any gold,' Ollie complained, 'only a few coins and some old bolts and nails. We'll have to look somewhere else if we want real treasure.'

'The quarry is out of bounds, is that clear?' Tim warned. 'It's a dangerous place, and if I ever find out you've been there, you will be grounded, like your brother. It was lucky Mr Lambert brought him home or he might have been seriously injured.'

The boys stared at Stefan, and William, the youngest, said, 'Who is he? He looks weird.'

His brother elbowed him in the ribs. 'Shut up. You're being rude.'

Will elbowed him back and said in a loud whisper. 'Why? It's the truth. He has scars on his face, and his nose is all bent. Maybe he's a wrestler like on the telly, or a boxer.'

Tim stood up, a stern look on his face. 'That's enough, you two. Go up and wash your hands.'

'Sorry about that,' he told Stefan when the boys had disappeared upstairs.

'Don't worry about it. Children are always curious about strangers,' Stefan replied, 'especially ones who look like me.'

'Still, they should know better than to be rude to a guest. I'll go and check on them before they flood the bathroom,' Tim said and left the room.

Stefan looked at Cassie, then at the window. 'I'd better make a move.'

He winced as he rose to his feet. He may not like to admit it, but he was probably in pain, like the day before.

'I'll drive you back after we've had some coffee,' Cassie decided.

He frowned. 'Thanks, but that's not necessary. Besides, it looks like your grandfather won't be ready to leave for some time.' He gestured towards the rocking chair where her granddad was asleep and snoring softly, his feet resting on the padded stool in front of the fire.

'Don't worry about him. He's staying here for a few days. He claims he wants to help out at the farm, but what he really wants is to spend time with the children. He dotes on the boys.'

Evening shadows now filled the lounge, so Cassie switched on a couple of lamps. A layer of frost already coated the outside edges of the windows, drawing delicate lace-like patterns on the glass. Inside the farmhouse, however, it felt warm and cosy, as always. It wasn't just because of the flames dancing in the fireplace and reflecting on the polished copper plates on the walls; the mismatched plates on the dresser; or the maroon sofa and chairs that seemed to have been there forever. It was the warmth from Rachel's family, and the love that was woven into the very fabric of the house. Perhaps one day she too would have a house filled with joy and children's laughter.

Stefan Lambert was looking at her. The flames from the fireplace cast trembling shadows on his face and reflected into his eyes, giving them the depth and the colour of summer dusk. Any coherent thought immediately evaporated from her mind like mist under the sun. It was the same pull of attraction as the night before in the Range Rover, only ten times stronger.

They didn't move, didn't talk. The only sounds in the room were the tick-tock of the clock, the crackling of the fire, her granddad's snoring, and the pounding of her heart.

Chapter Fourteen

'Sorry it took so long.' Rachel walked in, carrying a tray with steaming cups of coffee, a jug of milk and a pot filled with sugar. 'Where is Tim?'

Cassie turned to her cousin, with soft, faraway eyes. 'He went upstairs with the boys to make sure they washed their hands.'

In need of a few seconds to catch his breath, Stefan grabbed hold of the poker and bent down to stab it at the logs. Ribbons of red sparks flew up into the chimney like fireflies.

What had just happened?

It had been different from the dizzy rush of attraction of the previous night. This time it had felt as if Cassie and he were alone in the same dream, and he had seen something in her eyes, something like...

He clenched his fingers around the poker. No, he wouldn't go down that route. It was crazy to imagine, even for one second, that Cassie could be attracted to him, and have feelings for him. They had only just met. She didn't know anything about him or his past, didn't know what he had done, or hadn't done, and what he was capable – or incapable – of...

He put the poker back and straightened up, clenching his jaw against the worsening ache in his back and shoulders. He was tired from his walk, the brandy had gone to his head, and the warmth of the farmhouse had done the rest, mellowing him and blurring the distinction between reality and wishful thinking.

And, of course, he was drawn to her. How could he not be when her lips were smooth and pink, and always ready to stretch into a smile, and her grey eyes sparkled with kindness and intelligence? He wanted to kiss the adorable dimples in her soft, round cheeks, nuzzle the side of her neck, savour the taste of her skin and breathe in her fresh, feminine scent. He wanted to touch her, linger on the curves on her hips and pull her against him, and…

This was madness! He couldn't even remember when he had last been that attracted to a woman. He'd better pull himself together. At least the walk back in the freezing cold would take care of the fiery need in his body even if it would do nothing to cool the arousing images his feverish imagination kept conjuring.

Tim came back downstairs, Cassie's grandfather woke up from his nap, and suddenly everybody was talking about someone's forthcoming wedding. Stefan tore himself from his heated thoughts, sat at the table with the others and tried to focus on the conversation.

'Kerry is driving us crazy,' Rachel said. 'Only last week she was happy with a no-fuss reception at the campsite with only a few friends and family and asked that guests give money to an orangutans sanctuary in Malaysia in lieu of wedding presents, and now she's complaining that it's going to be a disaster and has us all tearing our hair out.'

'But the wedding is in a fortnight's time. Surely it's too late to organise anything,' Cassie's grandfather objected.

Rachel shook her head. 'Try telling her that.'

Tim patted his wife's shoulder. 'I'm glad you weren't as fussy as your sister.' He looked at Stefan and explained, 'We got married at the church in the village and had our reception at the Eagle and Child.'

'Then we came back here, got changed and put in a few hours' work,' Rachel interrupted, her eyes twinkling with laughter. 'I had to feed the animals and shovel muck on my wedding night.'

'Your Kerry isn't marrying a farmer, but a solicitor from John Hartley's firm,' Tim remarked. 'Mind you, Alastair is so work-obsessed I wouldn't be surprised if he didn't get her to type a few reports on his wedding night.'

'That's a lot of fuss for what should be a happy day,' Joseph Bell said. 'You should tell Kerry that what matters isn't the fancy reception but the life she's going to make with her young man afterwards.'

'She's worried Alastair's London friends and family find her rough and uneducated, and think we're all peasants,' Rachel said.

'But we are peasants, my love,' Tim told his wife.

She elbowed him in the ribs. 'Speak for yourself. I am a part-time secretary at the village school! But seriously, I feel for my sister. I know she's a pain, but most of Alastair's relatives and friends are quite posh and snooty, and she is desperate to impress them.'

Rachel and Tim carried on talking, but Cassie didn't join in the conversation. She sipped her coffee, her fingers fiddling restlessly with her spoon, and seemed to take great pains to avoid looking at him. It wasn't surprising. She must be terribly embarrassed and perhaps a little scared of him after the way he had stared at her – like a starving man at a feast…

'By the way, Joseph,' Tim said, 'I hope you have a few new jokes for Comedy Night. Not long to go now.'

The elderly man stirred a spoonful of sugar into his coffee. 'I have indeed been working on my new repertoire, although I still intend to perform some of my old classics or else people will be disappointed.'

Tim and Rachel laughed. 'Disappointed? Relieved, more like.'

Joseph tutted and turned to Stefan. 'As a matter of fact, I just made up a new riddle, and you shall be the first to hear it. "What did the policeman say to the naughty Christmas pudding?"'

Stefan frowned. 'Sorry?'

Joseph slapped his hand to his forehead. 'You probably don't know what a Christmas pudding is, being French. It's a round cake made with fruit soaked in brandy that we eat with cream or brandy sauce. So, what do you think the policeman said to the naughty Christmas pudding?'

Stefan had no idea. 'Hmm... Since there's alcohol involved, could he say that the pudding was over the limit?'

'Not bad, but not the right answer.'

'That it was rolling down the hill too fast?' Stefan suggested.

'Still not right... I'll put you out of your misery. The policeman said: "I'm taking you into custardy!"'

Ignoring the chorus of groans from Tim, Rachel and Cassie, Joseph Bell burst out laughing and slapped his thighs with the palm of his hands. 'It's good, isn't it?'

Cassie got up, muttered that she was going to check on the boys and left the room, still without looking at him. She must be regretting her offer of a lift back to Belthorn.

'I think I'll walk after all,' he said when she had gone upstairs.

Joseph Bell frowned. 'But it's a long way, and it's dark now.'

'I'll be all right. I have a torch, and I'm used to walking long distances in all kinds of weather.' There was no need to add that the days when he used to run twenty kilometres in full army gear and with a thirty kilos rucksack on his back were long gone.

He thanked Rachel and Tim for their hospitality, retrieved his bag, zipped up his coat and walked out into the night. The dogs barked at him again as he strode across the muddy courtyard, fastened the gate behind him and started on the track down the hill.

The cold stung his cheeks, and made his breath steam and his eyes water. As he walked away from the farm, the silence, troubled only by the distant barking of dogs, covered the mountains like a thick blanket. It couldn't be more different than Mali, and yet it was the same sky, the same moon and the same stars. The same feeling of complete solitude.

In the desert the silence was sharp and pure as crystal. The friendships intense, the stories shared around the campfire magical and the music poignant. There was something in the desert at night that made you feel at once very small and insignificant, and indestructible... But nobody was indestructible. His throat tightened and he looked at the moon shadows on the snowy fields.

He had only walked a few hundred yards when a car rattled down the lane behind him and headlights swept over the path. A battered Land Rover rattled to a stop next to him. He stopped at the side of the lane as Cassie wound the window down. She was wrapped up in her red coat and a thick red scarf, and with the pom-poms dangling from her woolly hat and framing her face, she looked like a creature straight out of a Christmas story.

'I said I would drive you back home. Why didn't you wait?' She sounded annoyed.

'You were busy.'

She shrugged and pushed the door open. 'I only wanted to kiss the boys goodbye. Get in.'

He frowned. 'Are you sure?'

'Of course, I'm sure.'

He climbed into the car and they set off down the bumpy farm track. It took fifteen minutes of uncomfortable silence to reach the bottom of the lane leading to Belthorn Manor. The Land Rover skidded on the main road several times, so it was only fair to think that the lane to the manor house would be even more treacherous. There was no need for Cassie to risk an accident for his sake.

'Leave me here,' he said. 'I'll walk the rest of the way.'

She shook her head. 'No, I'll drive you back.'

'It's only three or four miles at the most from here. I'll walk.'

She slowed down as they approached the turn for Belthorn. 'But, it's cold and dark, and you're not...'

Pride punched his stomach. 'Not fit enough. Is that what you were going to say?'

She sighed. 'I couldn't help but notice that you seemed in pain earlier.'

'I feel much better now,' he lied. 'In fact, the walk will do me good, and it will clear my head too.'

She bit her lip. 'Are you sure?'

'Positive.'

She brought the Land Rover to a halt. 'It's a shame I missed you when I called at Belthorn this morning. There's some steak pie and vegetables left in the oven, and I put enough logs in the drawing room so you can make a fire tonight.'

'You shouldn't have.'

'It's all right. It's—'

'It's all part of your job. I know.'

She smiled. 'I'll see you in the morning.'

'Sure,' he replied, even though he had no intention of being at Belthorn when she came. The woman brought far too many temptations.

He let himself out and stood watching as she drove off. Soon, the tail lights of the Land Rover disappeared and he was alone, with only the silver glow of the stars and the moon to light the way.

He had lied when he said that he was feeling better. If anything, his body ached even more after the bumpy car journey. He stumbled on lumps of icy snow, the rucksack hanging from his shoulder weighed like a ton of bricks, and it hurt just to breathe. Thank goodness there was nobody around to watch him amble his way up the lane like an old man.

Walking past the Sanctuary Stone at last, he calculated that he only had another two miles to go – another hour's walk, at the snail pace he was going – and distracted himself by dreaming about a steaming cup of coffee, a slice of Cassie's steak pie, and memories of the young woman's sunny smile and sparkling grey eyes.

The walk up the lane took so long that he lost track of time but at long last the dark shapes of Belthorn and the abbey emerged against the starry night sky. He wasn't easily spooked but he had to admit that there was a certain atmosphere about the place. It was no wonder it had given rise to scary stories.

What had Cassie experienced there that was so terrifying that years later she was still reluctant to talk about it? Was it anything to do with that ghostly Grey Friar Rachel talked about? Charlie had never mentioned any weird story about the place, but then again his friend hardly ever talked about Belthorn…

He fished his keys from his pocket with fingers numb with cold despite the gloves, unlocked the front door and with a sigh of relief made his way to the kitchen to warm up that steak pie he had been dreaming about during his long trek back.

Later in the evening, he poured a dash of brandy into a mug of hot coffee and brought the drink to the drawing room. Cassie must have been sewing again, because there was a new cushion on the armchair, this time with a colourful patchwork design.

A blue Post-it stuck to the mantelpiece attracted his attention. Another joke, no doubt.

'What is Father Christmas's cat called?' He turned the note over, and couldn't repress a smile. 'Santa's Paws.'

Shoving the note into his trouser pocket, he looked around. Cassie had filled a wicker basket with logs, newspapers and kindle. It would be a shame not to make a fire when she had gone to so much trouble.

Kneeling down in front of the fireplace, he scrunched up sheets of newspaper in the grate, snapped a few twigs and added a couple of logs before lighting the fire. Soon, flames danced, hissed and crackled, warming him and soothing his body and soul.

He sat down in the armchair with André Vaillant's diary on his knees.

How uncanny that Ruth Merriweather should be Cassie's great-great-aunt, and that Patterdale Farm belonged to her family… What must it be to have roots that went so deep, to live and work on a piece of land your family had owned for generations?

His family had lived on military bases around the country as he was growing up, and for the past twenty years he had himself moved around a lot. His Paris flat had been meant as an investment and wasn't somewhere he really wanted to return to. Perhaps he should sell it, and find something else.

He still had time to consider his options, but whatever he chose would probably be a complete change from the life he'd known so far, and that scared the hell out of him.

Ever since he was a child, being a helicopter pilot for the army was all he'd ever dreamt of, and nothing had deterred him from his goal. Not the fact that only ten per cent of applicants were successful, or the physical demands of the gruelling four year training, followed by a further two year course as a Puma, Cougar and Caracal helicopter pilot.

He would never forget the thrill of his first rescue mission… and the horror of his last.

He looked away from the fire and opened Vaillant's diary. What had become of him? Had he found happiness with sweet Ruth Merriweather or had he returned to France alone? Perhaps he could ask Cassie. She might know the full story.

Stefan turned the pages until he found the last entry he had read.

Chapter Fifteen

Cassie checked the time and switched on her laptop to Skype her mother. It was the second time that week, which immediately prompted her mother to ask her if everything was all right.

Cassie forced a smile. 'I'm fine, Mum, but with Granddad at Patterdale Farm the cottage is very quiet.'

'Why don't you fly over for Christmas? It would be lovely to have you here with us.'

'Granddad will never leave Red Moss during the festive season, not when he has the Comedy Night to look forward to. It's his last one too.'

'You could always come on your own.'

Cassie shook her head. 'I can't let my regular customers down. It's not just the cleaning, Mum. My elderly ladies look forward to my visits. We have a cup of tea and a chat, not to mention Granddad's jokes, which always cheer them up. The festive season can be really hard on those who have no family around. Besides, some of them feel scared and vulnerable because of the recent burglaries in the village, and me calling on them reassures them.'

'But, my darling, you're a cleaner, not a miracle worker! You're not responsible for other people's happiness. Actually, what about making me happy for a change? I haven't seen you in months.'

Cassie sighed. 'I know, Mum. I'm sorry, but besides my elderly clients, I also have the holiday cottages to look after too and the bookings are picking up now for Christmas and the New Year. And, of course, there's Charles Ashville's guest at Belthorn.'

Her mother pulled a face. 'I had forgotten about him. How are you getting on? I know how much you hate it there.'

'I'm slowly getting used to it.'

'And what about the guest? Has his mood improved at all?'

Cassie looked away from the screen. The picture on the screen might be a little blurry but she couldn't take the risk of her mother noticing that the mere mention of Stefan was enough to make her blush.

'He is still grumpy, and he still doesn't like Christmas,' she replied, trying to keep her voice casual. 'To tell the truth, I've hardly seen him this week. He either goes out as soon as I arrive at Belthorn, or he shuts himself in the library to work.'

'What does he work on?'

'A training guide for helicopter pilots, I believe.'

The man was avoiding her, no doubt because of that awkward moment at Patterdale Farm when she had gawked at him like an enamoured teenager. She cringed every time she recalled it, which was often, and yet she still could do nothing to stop her heart from racing or stop her face from burning when she bumped into him at Belthorn.

'Don't worry, love, your hard work and lovely smile will win him round in the end,' her mother said, 'and Granddad's jokes are sure to improve his mood. It can't be pleasant for him being alone at Belthorn.'

Cassie nodded. 'I made lots of new cushions, rearranged the furniture a bit, and bought a few new things to cheer the place up, and I even started sketching a few ideas.'

'Darling, please don't get carried away,' her mother interrupted. 'Remember what happened last time... and even if your drawings are good – which I'm sure they are,' she added quickly, 'you know very well that what Piers told you is true. If ever Charles and Gabrielle want to update the place, they will ask a proper designer, not—'

'Not the local cleaning lady, is that what you mean?' She couldn't help the bitterness in her voice.

Her mother had the grace to look embarrassed on the screen. 'Don't say it like that. There's nothing wrong with being a cleaner. I was a cleaner all my life and built up a nice little business that I passed onto you.'

'I know, Mum, and I'm very grateful. I love running Bluebell Cleaning and I love helping people out.' There was no point telling her mother that she would love being an interior designer even more.

After saying goodbye and switching off her laptop, Cassie warmed up some soup, cut a piece of bread, and sat down to eat whilst flicking through her notebook and the menus she had planned for Stefan. She was no great cook, and devising varied and tasty meals stretched her imagination to the limit. Perhaps she shouldn't bother. It wasn't as if Lambert had commented about her food over the last week, or about her cleaning, or any of the changes she had made to Belthorn for that matter...

She finished her tea and glanced at the clock on the kitchen wall. Only half past seven. The prospect of another evening alone made her want to cry. On an impulse, she reached out for her mobile and texted Salomé. Fancy a drink at the pub? The answer came back almost immediately. *Good idea! I'll text Cecilia. See you there. xxx*

Feeling considerably more cheerful, she washed up, took the bin out through the back door, muttering when her key got jammed in the new lock Darren had fitted. Was the man actually able to fix anything at all?

She managed to pull her key free, and ran upstairs to shower and change into her new top and a pair of black jeans.

Her mobile rang as she was going out.

'Cassie, you just have to help us!' Rachel cried out.

'What happened? Is it the boys... or Granddad?'

'No, it's our Kerry.'

Cassie drew in breath. 'What has she done now?'

'She saw photos of a Tarzan and Jane wedding in a bridal magazine at the dentist's this morning, and now she wants one,' Rachel said.

Cassie burst out laughing. 'Are you kidding me?'

'I wish I was. She wants to turn the campsite clubhouse into a jungle, with drum beats and fake monkeys.'

'Why doesn't she fly to that orangutan sanctuary she is sponsoring? There'll be plenty of real monkeys there.'

'You know she's only keen on that charity because she thinks it will make her look good with Alastair's trendy friends. She doesn't really like monkeys. In fact, she would probably complain they look horrid and smell disgusting!' Rachel paused. 'Oh and by the way, she wants vines too.'

'Whatever for? Alastair never wears anything but smart suits. I can't imagine him swinging from the trees with nothing else but a loincloth. What's more, it's the middle of winter. Couldn't Kerry pick a Narnia- or *Frozen*-themed wedding instead?' Or an *Alice in Wonderland* wedding, she carried on silently, so that with a bit of luck she and her stuffy fiancé could disappear down the rabbit hole forever.

'Stop laughing. It's not funny. So, are you going to help? You'll know what to do. After all, you're an interior designer.'

'No, I'm a cleaner.'

'But you have your diploma, and you've done bit of decorating for people – Mason, Salomé, even Cecilia at The Studio. If someone can turn the clubhouse into a pretend jungle, it's you. And before you ask, we did try to tell Kerry it was too late, but she threatened to cancel the wedding. Mum keeps crying and my dad locked himself in the barn with a bottle of whisky and is refusing to come out.'

That sounded like Rachel's sister all right. The girl had a gift for creating havoc... and getting her own way in the end.

She sighed. It looked like she had no choice. 'What's your budget?'

Rachel stated a ridiculously low sum.

'You must be joking. I couldn't even buy paper napkins with that!'

'I wish I was. Mum and Dad have already paid for the

catering, the flowers, the dress and most of the honeymoon in Barbados, as well as a six-month sponsorship of the orangutan sanctuary. That's all they can spare. So are you going to help?'

Cassie took a deep breath. However annoying Kerry could be, she was, in a roundabout way, family. 'I'm not promising any miracles, or even any monkeys – real or fake – but I'll see what I can do.'

'Thank you. You're the best!' Rachel screeched. Cassie could almost imagine her jumping up and down.

'Don't get too excited. I said I wasn't promising any miracles. By the way, how do you find my granddad?'

She hadn't told anyone, not even Rachel, about her grandfather's increasingly frequent memory lapses.

'He's great, as usual.'

'Does he seem distracted and forgetful to you?'

'Not that I've noticed. He's been helping Louis with his history homework, and Ollie with his maths, and there was nothing wrong with his dates or his timetables. Why do you ask?'

Cassie blew a relieved breath. 'No particular reason. I'm glad he's having a good time with the boys.'

'Actually, we would like him to stay over until after the wedding. Tim and I haven't had a night out alone together in ages and he offered to babysit. Would you mind?'

Although she didn't relish the prospect of being alone for another week or so, Cassie could find no reason to object.

'Great. So I'll see you tomorrow night at the pub for our Kerry's hen do at six o'clock sharp. I booked the taxi for eight, which will leave us plenty of time for a few drinks before we go to the restaurant. Remember to wear dungarees, a stripy top, and a bandana in your hair. The Bandanamama girls are back!'

Cassie moaned. 'I see you haven't given up on that silly idea of a reunion sing-along.'

'It will be a laugh, you'll see.'

'It'll be a disaster! We haven't rehearsed anything. I'm not even sure I can remember any of the songs.'

'The words will be on the screen, and we could never sing that well anyway, so it will be just like the old days. Oh, I nearly forgot... Bring your feather duster too.'

'Whatever for? So I can do a spot of cleaning in the pub between songs?'

'You'll need it to tickle people. You're the good mood fairy after all.'

'Tickling random people as they eat and drink will make them choke, not laugh.'

'Just do as I say, will you? Wait a sec, your granddad wants to talk to you. I'll put him on.'

There were muffled sounds as Rachel put the phone down then her granddad's voice bellowed down the phone. 'Hello! Is that you, Trifle? Can you hear me?'

Cassie grimaced and pulled the phone away from her ear. 'Yes, Granddad, you don't need to shout.'

He explained that he needed fresh clothes, his smart suit and shoes for the wedding. 'Can you also take some money from the cash machine? My card and the pin number are in their usual place in the filing cabinet upstairs.'

She sighed. How many times had she told him not to keep his bank details together? 'Anything else?'

'Rachel wants you to invite Lambert to Kerry's wedding reception. One of the groom's guests cancelled and they're a man short at the table. Apparently, it's upsetting the balance or something like that.'

Cassie gasped. 'Can Rachel not find anyone else to replace the missing guest?'

Her grandfather chuckled. 'You don't sound too keen, pet, and yet I had the impression you liked him.'

'Well, you got the wrong impression, and he feels the same about me. Most of the time, he grabs hold of his coat and his car keys as soon as I arrive, as if he can't wait to get out of my way.'

'That's because he's shy. Ask him please. We're counting on you.'

Cassie reluctantly promised, and arranged to drive up to the farm with her grandfather's clothes and money the following day.

Like every Friday night, the pub was heaving. A crowd of men cheered in front of the giant TV screen where a rugby match was in full swing. Cecilia and Salomé were already at the bar, and Cassie started towards them.

'If that isn't the sexiest cleaner in the whole of Cumbria.' Piers's voice behind her stopped her in her tracks.

Her spirits sank. She should have realised Piers would be with his rugby pals tonight. Forcing a smile, she swung round. 'Good evening, Piers.'

Immediately, he wrapped one arm around her waist and bent down to kiss her cheek, his lips straying dangerously close to her mouth yet again. 'Hmm. You smell nice, as usual.'

And you smell of beer and sweaty rugby socks, as usual, she wanted to reply. She tightened her lips and said nothing.

'What can I get you to drink?' he asked.

'I can't stop, sorry. I'm meeting my friends.' She gestured towards the bar where Cecilia, Salomé and Sadie were giggling as they read the cocktail menu. She tried to slide out of his grip but his arm tightened around her waist.

'Have a drink with me, Cassie.'

'Sorry, but I'm already late.'

He let go of her at last and she took a step back, away from his wandering hands.

'Never mind, I'll take you for lunch when you come to my office for your performance review next week.'

'What performance review?' Cassie stared at him, puzzled.

'The review meeting when you show me your paperwork, I audit your invoices, and we look at the comments in the guestbooks in the holiday cottages.' He was still smiling but his pale blue eyes had grown cold, and there was now an edge to his voice.

She frowned. 'We've never had a performance review before, and you know I only ever get nice comments about my work.'

'Charlie's sister emailed me. She wants detailed reports about the estate. I have no idea why. Charlie's father used to trust me with everything, but now apparently Gabrielle is taking an interest... As if she knows what she's talking about. She's an actress, or a singer, or whatever, not an accountant. She doesn't have a bloody clue about running the estate.' He sounded annoyed and his face had turned bright red.

'By the way, how are things with the French guy at Belthorn? I heard Sophie left you in the lurch. Are you managing all right on your own?'

'I'm fine. Lambert is fine. Everything's fine,' she answered more sharply than she'd intended.

'Good. Don't forget Charles promised you a bonus if Lambert gives you a good report. You have to keep him happy.'

'I'm doing my best.' With a last, forced smile, she made a quick escape and joined Salomé and Cecilia at the bar.

'Look who has a big jingly hat!' Salomé laughed, pointing her finger at her pom-pom hat. 'It's Miss Santa Claus!'

Sadie waved her hand towards her friends in a dismissive gesture. 'Don't mind them. They've had a couple of Big Jim's festive cocktails already.'

As usual, the barmaid looked very glamorous, dressed in a tight black top and leggings, her make-up perfect, her eyelashes impossibly long and thick, and her hair smooth and shiny. She handed Cassie a drinks menu. 'All the cocktails are half price tonight. Would you like one?'

Cassie took her coat off and turned to Salomé and Cecilia. 'Why not? What do you recommend, girls?'

Salomé raised her glass half-filled with a red and yellow drink. Pomegranate seeds trapped in ice cubes floated on the surface.

'So far, I tried a Red Spanker and an Angel Titsel, and they're all... hic... delicious!'

Cassie laughed at the silly names and pointed at her friend's drink. 'What is this one called?'

'Rudolph's Snot. I know. Revolting name, but it's actually really nice. Here, have a sip. And it's red, so it'll match your coat.'

'I'll have that one, then, Sadie.'

'Let's hope for a successful festive season!' Cecilia said when Sadie brought Cassie's cocktail.

'I'll drink to that,' Salomé said, and the three women clinked their cocktail glasses together.

'Remember... we must look into one another's eyes and take care not to cross our glasses,' Cassie said. 'We don't want seven years of bad luck.'

'I thought it was seven years of bad sex?' Cecilia said.

Salomé shrugged. 'Pff! I don't care if I never have sex again. Sex is awfully overrated, if you want my opinion.'

Cecilia pointed to Cassie's new top. 'It really suits you. I'm glad you bought it.'

Cassie always felt frumpy next to her friends – fabulously exotic Salomé, with her chocolate-brown eyes and long dark hair, and petite Cecilia, with her bobbed, candyfloss-pink hair, who was always arty and stylish, even in jeans, baggy pullover and wellies.

'I received some new stock this week,' Cecilia added. 'You should pop in some time.'

'I may do just that. I wouldn't mind a new dress for Kerry's wedding.' It had nothing to do with the fact that Stefan Lambert might be there, of course...

'I hope there's a wide choice of sexy bachelors.' Cecilia sighed. 'Don't get me wrong, I don't mind dancing with your granddad or his friends, but apart from Mason Austin and Matt Jamieson, all the attractive men around here are either married or retired – or both!'

Just then, there was a choir of loud expletives from the rugby club members. Salomé slid Cassie a sideways look. 'At least *you*'ll have someone to dance with next Saturday. You seem very friendly with Piers Hardy.'

Cassie pulled a face. 'I have to be. He's my boss, in a manner of speaking, since he manages Charles Ashville's estate.'

'He's quite good looking, and he looks as if he fancies you,' Cecilia remarked, cocking her head to one side.

'He fancies any woman the wind blows his way.'

'You don't sound too keen on the guy.'

Cassie sighed. 'I've had enough of him groping me at every opportunity.'

'Why don't you tell him to get lost?'

Because she needed the Ashville contract to keep Bluebell Cleaning afloat. She also needed Piers to carry on letting Bluebell Cottage to her granddad. Of course, she couldn't say that aloud because it made her feel weak and pathetic, so she drank a sip of her cocktail and said with more assurance than she felt, 'I can cope with Piers.'

Salomé frowned and pointed with her chin to the other end of the counter. 'The guy from the campsite has been staring at us – or at you, rather – for the past ten minutes.'

Cassie followed her gaze. Darren Morse smiled at her. She nodded back.

'You don't look too keen on him either,' Cecilia remarked.

Salomé shuddered. 'I don't care if all the grannies and granddads of Red Moss sing his praises, he gives me the creeps.'

'Same here,' Sadie remarked as she whisked the empty glasses off the counter. 'The one I'd like to see more of is that sexy Frenchman who is staying at Belthorn.'

Salomé and Cecilia looked at Cassie, their eyes shining

with curiosity. 'You can tell us all about him. What's he like? What's he doing at Belthorn? Is he really a helicopter pilot? And does he know when we're finally going to see the elusive Charles Ashville?'

Cassie laughed and raised her hands. 'Girls! One question at a time, please.'

Answering her friends didn't take long, because there wasn't much she could tell them about Stefan.

'As for Charlie Ashville,' she finished, 'I have no idea when he's planning to come here, if ever. The only communications I have with him are infrequent emails, either directly or through Piers's office. Stefan said he was working somewhere in Mali.'

Cecilia sighed. 'I was told he is a very good doctor and that he's very clever, very handsome and very—'

'Very arrogant, rude and disagreeable,' Salomé finished, narrowing her eyes. 'I had the misfortune to meet him when he came for his father's funeral, and I for one would be happy never to see him again.' As if to make her point, she slammed her empty cocktail glass down on the counter.

Cecilia added, 'I heard he doesn't like it here. Someone even mentioned some kind of curse on the family. What's that all about?'

It was no wonder her friends didn't know much about the Grey Friar's curse, being relative newcomers. Salomé had bought the bakery two years before, and Cecilia had moved from London at around the same time.

'It's a long story,' Cassie started reluctantly.

'Then let's get another drink and you can tell us all about it.' Cecilia ordered more cocktails and bags of crisps and the three women settled at a table in the back room.

Chapter Sixteen

Cassie sipped her cocktail. 'You both know Belthorn Abbey, or what's left of it, don't you?'

'George…' Salomé paused. 'I mean, Lord Ashville, gave me a tour once.'

Cassie looked at her friend in surprise. 'Did he?'

Salomé smiled. 'I was delivering some cakes he'd ordered for a party and he offered to show me round. He invited me back on several occasions to give me tours of the manor house… among other things.' She sighed and added in a wistful voice, 'He was a charming and fascinating guide.'

Charles Ashville's father had enjoyed a fearsome reputation as a ladies' man. He probably wouldn't have been able to resist trying to add Salomé to his long list of conquests, and what better than a private tour of the grounds and a few old family ghost stories to impress the young woman… From Salomé's dreamy voice and the faraway look in her eyes, it seemed he had succeeded.

'You were lucky to be given a tour,' Cecilia remarked. 'I only ever saw the ruins from the path when I was hiking up the fell.'

'That's because the Ashvilles never opened Belthorn Abbey to the public,' Cassie explained.

'So what is the curse people are talking about?' Cecilia asked.

'Well, a long time before the manor house was built, Belthorn was a small but wealthy abbey belonging to the Cistercian order.'

'George said they were called the grey friars,' Salomé remarked.

Cassie nodded. 'That's right. When Henry VIII dissolved the monasteries in the North of England, he sent one of his trusted men, Sir Thomas Ashville, to close down the abbey and confiscate their assets. Rumour has it that Thomas kept much of the abbey's gold and valuables for himself, and set about destroying the place with more enthusiasm than was needed. There were accounts of terrible atrocities committed by him and his men.'

Salomé pulled a face. 'With ancestors such as these, it's no wonder Charles is such a horrid bully. It must be in his genes.'

Cassie cocked her head to one side to look at her friend. Charles shared the same genes with his father, whom Salomé seemed to have been rather fond of. What on earth had Charles Ashville done to make friendly Salomé so angry?

'The king gave the Belthorn estate to Sir Thomas,' she carried on.

Cecilia picked up one of the pomegranate seeds floating in her glass and crunched it between her teeth. 'Why do people talk of the Grey Friar's curse?'

'Well, Thomas Ashville died shortly after the manor house was built. He broke his neck when his horse threw him. People said that it was spooked by the figure of a grey friar... but all friars had been either massacred or driven away, so it could only be—'

'A ghost!' Cecilia exclaimed.

Cassie nodded. 'It was said that it was the ghost of the abbey's last abbot, seeking revenge for the murder of his monks. Over the centuries, people have claimed that the Grey Friar always appeared before a member of the Ashville family died, hence the legend about a curse.'

'George did mention something about it, I recall, but he laughed it off,' Salomé said, toying with her straw.

Cecilia shivered. 'He fell down a shaft in one of the disused quarries up the hill, didn't he? I wonder if he saw the ghost too before he died.'

She looked at Cassie. 'What about you? Have you ever seen that Grey Friar?'

Cassie's heart grew heavy. She looked down and stirred her straw in what was left of her cocktail. 'I saw something once, but I'm not sure what it was. All I know is that it was very scary.'

As if sensing her reluctance, Salomé glanced at her and shrugged. 'Well, I for one don't believe in silly old ghosts, so let's talk about something else.'

Cassie breathed a sigh of relief. 'Good idea! Actually I may need some input from you two.' She told them about the Tarzan and Jane themed wedding she had now promised to arrange for the following Saturday, and both her friends laughed so much they almost spat their drinks out.

'I think I have just what you need,' Cecilia said. 'I just received a flamingo made of recycled flip-flops from a Kenyan artist.'

'Never mind the fake wildlife… What about Tarzan?' Salomé asked. 'You need a man who can look good in trunks, and from what I have seen of Kerry's fiancé, I don't think that's him.'

Cassie pulled a face. 'You're right. Finding Tarzan is going to prove difficult.'

'I can think of a few men who would fill a loincloth nicely,' Salomé remarked, toying with her cocktail's paper umbrella, 'starting with Piers over there.'

'Mason Austin and Matt Jamieson would do too,' Cecilia added.

'I think Stefan Lambert would make the best Tarzan,' Cassie declared.

'Oh yes?' Salomé smirked. 'And why would that be?'

'He has the eyes for it,' Cassie answered in a dreamy voice, 'tawny like a lion's, fearless like a warrior's, but full of shadows and vulnerability.'

Cecilia whistled between her teeth. 'Wordsworth, eat your heart out.'

Salomé poked Cassie with the tip of her paper umbrella. 'It looks like this Jane has found her Tarzan.'

'And this monkey has found her banana,' Cecilia joked.

Cassie's face caught fire under her friends' mocking gaze. 'Don't be silly. I was just... Oh, and forget about Tarzan. Help me make a list of the things I need to turn the campsite clubhouse into a jungle instead!'

It was nearly closing time when Cassie parted company with her friends, who lived close to each other and were walking home together.

Still smiling, and a little giddy from the cocktails and the thought of Stefan Lambert clad only in a loincloth swinging from a vine and wrestling a crocodile with his bare hands – Johnny Weissmuller style – Cassie dug her hands inside the pockets of her coat and returned to Bluebell Cottage, taking care not to slip on the pavement covered with icy, compacted snow.

She unlocked her front door, took a few steps in the corridor and froze.

The light was on in the kitchen. But she was sure she had switched it off before leaving. Was her grandfather back from Patterdale Farm?

'Granddad?' she called. 'Are you here?'

Her voice echoed throughout the house but no one answered. What if someone had sneaked in? Red Moss was usually safe, but there had been those burglaries in recent weeks...

The thought sobered her up immediately. Her heart racing, her fingers gripping the strap of her handbag, she took a few hesitant steps, and peered into the kitchen.

It was empty.

Of course, it was empty! What had she expected to see, the ghost of the Grey Friar sitting at the table, having a cup of tea and munching on one of her granddad's custard creams?

Shaking her head she filled the kettle, opened the cupboard to get a mug and a tea bag. And stepped into a puddle of water... Her heartbeat picked up pace again. Why was the floor wet? Her gaze followed a trail of splashes to the back door.

Then she remembered that she had taken the bin out earlier. The backyard was covered with snow, some must have stuck to her shoes, and it had melted. She relaxed once again. She should calm down and stop imagining things. It wasn't good for her heart or her blood pressure!

She should have a hot drink and go straight to bed.

She poured hot water into her mug, stirred in some milk and was reaching into the cupboard for a packet of biscuits when something crashed down upstairs, the noise as loud as thunder in the silent house.

She cried out. The biscuits fell to the floor. And she stared at the kitchen ceiling, her heart thumping hard. What had made that noise? What – or who – was up there? Rooted to the spot, she held her breath, but all she could hear now was the clock and her own heartbeat drumming twice as fast.

Seconds ticked by. She slowly released the breath she had been holding and bent down to pick up the biscuits from the floor. She had to do something. She couldn't stay in the kitchen all night. Should she be brave and go upstairs and check if anyone was hiding up there, or be a coward, go out and ask one of the male neighbours to investigate the source of the noise?

She wasn't feeling brave at all right now and the second option seemed the most attractive. She retreated back into the corridor, opened the front door ... And a ball of ginger fur flew down the stairs with a loud meowing, slid between her legs, almost tripping her over, and ran out into the street.

Doris Pearson's cat! It must have sneaked in when she took the bin out. What a fool to get so worked up over a cat!

Cassie held her hand to her thumping heart and let out a long sigh.

'Oh, Fluffy, you naughty, naughty cat!' she whispered, even though the cat had melted into the shadows. Weak with relief, and her fingers shaking, she closed the door again and locked it.

Saturday didn't get off to a good start. She slept through her alarm and woke up after nine. In a panic, and her head thumping from drinking too many of Big Jim's Christmas concoctions, she rolled out of bed, showered and dressed in her usual work attire. As she fumbled with the dungarees' metallic clasps, she groaned at the thought of the hen party that evening.

Why did Rachel insist on a Bandanamama karaoke? It was bound to be a disaster, they would look ridiculous, and Kerry might not even like their impromptu performance.

Her first job that morning was at Barbara Carlton's house at the end of the street. She didn't usually clean Barbara's house on a Saturday, but she had asked Cassie to swap her days.

'Come in, love,' Barbara said as she showed her into her cottage and tottered down the corridor in her slippers.

Cassie put her bag down and took her coat off. 'I'm sorry I'm late. I was a bit under the weather this morning, but I'll make up the time.' There was no need to explain that Big Jim's cocktails were to blame.

'Will you have a cup of tea before you start?' The elderly lady flicked the switch on the kettle without even waiting for an answer. Cassie had long since understood that the tea and biscuits ritual was for Barbara and her other elderly clients as – if not more – important as cleaning the house.

'Please.' Cassie sat down, and looked around, and pointed at the muddy floor and the collection of tools on the worktop. 'What happened there? Are you having some work done again?'

Barbara smiled and put a steaming cup of tea in front of Cassie. 'It's that nice boy. Darren. He's fixing a new lock on my back door.'

Cassie frowned. 'Is he?' How very odd... Darren had just fixed the back door at Bluebell Cottage too. 'Is he here? I didn't see his car outside.'

'He just popped out for some screws from the hardware shop. He won't be long. I wanted to give him some money for the petrol but he said he didn't want it. He is such a nice, helpful young man, don't you think?'

'Hmm...' Cassie blew on her cup of tea and drank a sip. 'Does he come here often?'

Barbara broke into a smile. 'Once or twice a week. There's always something or other to fix in these old houses. I suspect it's the same at Bluebell Cottage. It's lucky there are people like him, or I would have to pay a fortune in plumbers, electricians or general handymen.'

'Yes. My granddad finds him very resourceful too. Oops, talking about my granddad, I almost forgot to give you your joke of the day.'

She dug out his latest joke from her handbag and handed it to Barbara. The old lady slipped her reading glasses on and chuckled to herself as she read aloud. '"What did Mrs Mouse say when Mr Mouse came back from the shop with a big lump of cheese?"... "Grate!" Oh dear... where does he find these jokes?'

There was the sound of the front door opening and a man's voice called. 'I'm back.'

Barbara put the paper on the table. 'Here is Darren,' she said. 'I gave him my key so that he wouldn't have to ring when he came back and disturb me in case I was having a nap. I seem to fall asleep at the drop of a hat these days. Getting old really is no fun.'

She toyed with the ring on her finger. The morning sunlight caught the ruby, making it sparkle.

Cassie smiled. 'That's what my granddad says too. I hope you're getting plenty of rest.'

The old lady repressed a yawn. 'I'm taking too much

rest, love. I'm so tired some days I don't even make it to the community centre.'

'Then perhaps you should go to the doctor.'

'Oh no. I wouldn't dream of annoying the doctor with my little complaints. It's just old age.'

Darren strolled into the kitchen. His eyes widened and his mouth tightened when he saw Cassie. Was it her imagination or didn't he look pleased to see her? She hadn't spoken to him since she had rejected his offer of a lift after Nadine Hartley's party. Perhaps he was still nursing a grudge.

'Hi, Darren.' Feeling awkward, as she couldn't forget Stefan's ridiculous claims that Darren was stalking her, she gave him what she hoped was a friendly smile.

'Hi.' He nodded stiffly in return before turning to Barbara. 'You didn't say you had visitors. I can come back another time.'

'Oh no, love. It's all right. I'd rather you fixed my door today. I don't want to have a dodgy lock and get burgled. It's worrying what's going on in the village.'

He took a packet of screws and bolts out of his pocket and put them on the worktop. There were long, red scratches on the back of his right hand, all the way to the wrist.

'What happened to your hand?' Cassie asked. 'It looks really sore.'

Darren immediately put his hand back into his pocket, and answered without turning round. 'It's nothing. Just a stupid cat.'

'I hope you put some disinfectant on those scratches. You don't want them to get infected.'

She got up and gave Barbara a worried glance. The old lady kept yawning and rubbing her eyes. 'I'll get on with the cleaning now. Why don't you lie down for a while?'

'I think I will, love, if you don't mind.'

Barbara mustn't have had the strength to do much housework in her house lately because the place was a mess, and Cassie spent the next two hours tidying up and giving the cottage a thorough clean. She tackled a pile of ironing even though that wasn't strictly speaking included in her list of chores, leaving the kitchen until last in the hope that Darren had finished whatever he was doing. Who would have thought that changing a lock would take so long and require so much banging and clanking?

At last, the noise stopped. The front door opened and closed, and there was the sound of an engine starting in the street. Cassie went downstairs to tackle the kitchen and to mop the muddy prints off the floor.

'All done!' she called a short while later, popping into the living room where Barbara was dozing, her head resting on a cushion Cassie had made for her a few weeks back, with her reading glasses perched on the tip of her nose and a book in her lap. The elderly lady looked at her with the same befuddled look her granddad had sometimes, and muttered a sleepy goodbye.

The rest of the morning went fast. Cassie took care of a couple of holiday cottages, and drove up to Patterdale Farm to bring her grandfather some fresh clothes and the money he had asked her for. She didn't mention Fluffy giving her a fright the night before, but she did say she was worried about Barbara.

'The woman is as tough as old boots,' he said with a dismissive gesture. 'All she needs is vitamins. Rachel bought me some this week, and I already feel much better.' And it was true that he did look much better too.

Last on her list for the day was Belthorn. The manor house was empty once again. As usual, the kitchen was spotless. No dirty cup, plate or cutlery was left in the sink. Did the man even eat or drink? The living room was tidy, and Stefan had once again swept the ashes out in the fireplace. As for his room, it hardly looked lived in.

There was nothing for her to do but a bit of dusting

and vacuum cleaning, make an inventory of the fridge and cupboards, prepare lasagne for the man's evening meal, and leave his daily joke on the kitchen table. Joseph had clearly been inspired by Kerry's latest whim…

'What does Tarzan like to do at Christmas? Juggle Bells!' It made Cassie smile, but whether or not the Frenchman would smile too was doubtful. He said he liked Joseph's jokes, but he was probably only being polite.

Night was falling when she locked Belthorn's door and drove back to the village. She had to get ready for Kerry's hen do. Cecilia had promised to do her hair and make-up, but it was rather pointless since she wasn't dressing up but wearing dungarees, a stripy top and a bandana scarf in her hair… and a feather duster.

Chapter Seventeen

Stefan hadn't planned to go to the pub that evening, but even he could get sick of his own company. At Belthorn the silence was only broken by the crackling of the fire in the fireplace, the pipes gurgling, the floorboards creaking, and the odd gust of wind pressing against the windows that made the old building groan like a ship in a storm. After spending the day at Allonby, the prospect of an evening alone stretched in front of him as long and dreary as the deserted beach he had trudged on. He would stop at the Eagle and Child, get a drink and something to eat, and watch a match of football or rugby on the television before going back.

He pushed the door open and winced at the noise hitting his eardrums. It seemed he had stumbled on a party – a very raucous party. Three women were singing very loudly a hit from the eighties he vaguely recognised, and a dozen other women of all ages danced, clapped and cheered around a girl dressed in a skimpy leopard print dress, and with a bunch of bananas tied to her waist. What was all that about?

He was about to turn right round and get out when Mason waved and called him from the bar, and he reluctantly made his way across the pub, trying to avoid bumping into the revellers.

'What are you drinking?' Mason asked.

'I'll have half a bitter. Thanks.' Stefan frowned and scanned the room. 'What's going on?'

'It's a hen party and Bandanamama, Red Moss's answer to Bananarama,' Mason replied with a grin. 'Do you recognise any of the singers?'

Stefan looked at the three women properly this time. They were all wearing dungarees and stripy tops, and bandana scarves. He recognised Rachel, the tallest of the three. He had never before seen the red-haired woman who was jumping around so energetically she seemed to be on springs. The third, in the far right, almost hidden by the Christmas tree and holding a blue feather duster was…

'Cassie?'

How had he not seen her straight away? Her blonde hair gleamed, piled up on top of her head in a messy bun. Her red lipstick emphasised her rosebud lips, her flawless skin glowed under the spotlights. Her red bandana was tied around her slim neck. He swallowed hard. She looked pretty and fun, and so sexy she didn't need to be singing about Venus, flames and desires for his heart to do a little flip and his body to grow hard. What bad luck! He had spent most of the last week trying to avoid the woman and fight the pointless attraction he felt for her, only to run into her tonight.

He swallowed a mouthful of beer, and cleared his throat. 'What's with the feather duster?'

Mason laughed. 'No idea, but I hope they stop soon. My ears can't take much more.'

Both men flinched as Rachel's voice hit a very high-pitched note. 'I see what you mean,' Stefan said. He ordered steak and chips at the counter, and Mason found them a free table in the back room where most of the elderly customers seemed to have retreated. If the singing was still loud, at least they could talk. More importantly, he couldn't see Cassie and could forget the lustful thoughts she awakened inside him – feather duster or not.

The music stopped as the barmaid brought his meal over.

'I hope you don't mind if I eat,' Stefan said, picking his fork up.

'Not at all. Actually, I'm feeling a bit peckish myself,' Mason answered as Stefan tucked into his chips. 'I'll order something at the bar too, and get us more drinks.'

The seaside air and the long walk along the beach at Allonby had made Stefan ravenous and he wolfed down his meal in ten minutes. He was putting his knife and fork back onto his empty plate when Cassie's voice resounded behind him.

'Stefan! Mason said you were here.'

His shoulders tensed. He would have to talk to her after all…

He pushed his chair back, stood up and turned to face her.

She looked even more tempting close up. Her eyes were huge and moody and her skin smooth and flawless. She glanced at the table, pointed to his empty plate with her feather duster, and pursed her lips – her perfect, kissable lips.

'If I had known you'd rather have chips at the pub, I wouldn't have spent an hour making lasagne for your tea.'

'Ah. Sorry. Stopping here was a spur-of-the-moment decision.'

She shrugged. 'Never mind. It'll keep until tomorrow.'

He nodded again, stuck for something to say. 'The singing was… interesting,' he said, cursing himself for sounding so dense.

Her cheeks coloured. 'You don't have to pretend. I know what you think of my voice… It was awful.'

'Your friends seemed to like it.'

She laughed. 'After a few of Big Jim's cocktails, they would sing and dance to anything.'

They stood in front of each other without speaking for what felt like a long, awkward minute, so to break the silence, he asked, 'What's with the feather duster?'

She ruffled the blue feathers with her fingers and smiled. 'That's another of Rachel's brilliant ideas. She wants me to tickle people to make them laugh and put them in a good mood. Personally, I don't think it'll work. Perhaps you could be my first guinea pig.' A mischievous smile appeared on her lips, and dug dimples so cute in her round cheeks a flash of pure lust coursed through him.

'What are you doing?' he asked in a voice even more croaky than usual.

'Testing Rachel's theory.'

The tip of the feather duster caressed his face, his throat. His whole body tensed and hardened, but he resisted taking a step back.

'You're wasting your time. I'm not ticklish.'

She lowered the feather duster and shrugged. 'Too bad... Ah well, the night is young and I'm sure there will be plenty of ticklish people around I can cheer up.'

Mason walked back into the room, a plate of chips in his hand. 'Sorry I was so long. The girls are looking for you, Cassie. The minibus has arrived to take you to the restaurant.'

'Very well. Gentlemen, I wish you a pleasant evening.' Turning to Stefan, she added, 'It's going to be a long night, so I'll come to Belthorn in the afternoon, if that's all right with you.'

He clenched his jaw. 'I already told you that you don't need to come every day and I can—'

'Manage perfectly well on your own,' she finished with a tutting sound. 'Yes, you said that before, and I said that I had a job to do.'

She winked, and with a last flourish of her feather duster, turned round and walked out, swaying her hips in the most enticing manner. He swallowed hard. Who would have known that dungarees could be so sexy?

'I don't know about you,' Mason remarked as he sat down, 'but I'd rather stay away from Cassie and her feather duster tonight. I don't want to disgrace myself and fall about in fits of giggles if she tickles me.'

Stefan nodded but it wasn't giggling helplessly he was worried about if Cassie tickled him again with her feather duster – it was not being able to resist the urge to yank her to him and to kiss her.

The thunder of machine gunfire hit the plane. The wind burned his face. He tasted the smoke billowing from the engine, and terror gripped his insides as the plane spiralled through the clouds and the ground loomed closer. He was going to die. He was already dead...

He woke up with a start and sat up so fast he banged his head against the headboard. Sweat stuck his T-shirt to his chest, his heart galloped hard and fast and panic dried his throat. As his eyes gradually became accustomed to the darkness, he made out the outlines of the furniture, the curtains and the paintings on the wall opposite, and fear loosened its iron grip. He wasn't in a SPA 3 plane falling to his death. He was at Belthorn, safe in bed.

He rubbed his face hard and drew in a deep breath. It wasn't the familiar nightmare that forced him to relive over and over again the trauma of his helicopter bursting into flames in front of him, but it was almost as harrowing. That was what André Vaillant and his comrades must have experienced day in, day out, as they flew their planes over the battlefields of Northern France over a hundred years before.

Vaillant... Why was he unable to stop thinking about the man?

He got up, dragged on his jogging pants over his boxer shorts, put on a fresh T-shirt and a sweatshirt and, his breath steaming in the freezing cold house, he went downstairs to make coffee and light a fire.

He drew the drawing room curtains onto the greying dawn. Once the fire got going and gave out both light and warmth, he sat down in the old armchair. Cassie had made yet another cushion – this time one with green and red tassels that reminded him of the pom-poms on her hat. He shook his head. The woman was obsessed with making cushions. There were new ones everywhere – in his bedroom, in the library and even the dreary dining room where he never ate, and of course, in the drawing room. Not that he complained, far from it. At least they smelled nice, were soft and colourful, and supported his back when he sat down to read.

She had also draped fancy fabrics on the sofa, pulled a string of fairy lights along the mantelpiece, and put up more holly, winter berries and sprigs of pine arrangements everywhere. Belthorn was transformed, touch by touch, like by magic...

He wedged the plump reindeer cushion behind him, put the steaming mug on the coffee table, and opened Vaillant's diary.

5th September 1919

I kissed her. I kissed my sweet Ruth.

I was reading in the garden this afternoon when she came looking for me to ask if I wanted a cup of tea. She looked so pretty with the autumn sunlight dancing on her skin and turning her hair golden, that I couldn't help it. I stood up, drew her to me, and kissed her. She didn't push me back, didn't run away. My heart close to bursting, I held her tight. For a too short moment, we were alone in the sunshine, with the birds singing and the breeze rustling the trees. It felt wonderful.

Then she stiffened, shook free of my embrace and ran away. I haven't seen her since. Her mother later said that she had been taken ill and gone back to the farm.

What if Ruth never wants to see me again, what if I have ruined everything? How can I convince her that my feelings for her are genuine, that I'm not just a crippled, good-for-nothing ex-pilot but mean to marry and take care of her?

Ashville may not like Belthorn very much but I have found peace, beauty and love here. I don't dream of flying every night like I used to. I have almost forgotten the tat-tat-tat of machine guns; the stink of burning oil; the impotent rage when a comrade's plane was shot down. Almost forgotten too the abject fear that twisted my guts before every mission.

During all those weeks in hospital, surrounded by men crying out, the stench of death and rotting bodies, and the pervading smell of disinfectant, the only moments of relief were Ashville's visits. To pass the time he told me old stories about Belthorn – the Grey Friar who haunts the abbey, the lady who mourns the death of her lover, and the felon who was refused sanctuary by the abbot and whose shadow hovers near the stone.

Stefan looked up from the diary, and gazed at the flames that danced in the fireplace as he thought back to the day he had arrived and the shape that had floated in front of his windscreen near the Sanctuary Stone, forcing him to crash the car. It was lucky he didn't believe in ghosts.

The stories amused me, intrigued me, and made me forget my predicament, at least for a few hours. When Ashville said Belthorn would help me heal, I laughed aloud. Nothing would ever help me. I was finished and couldn't see what I could do with the rest of my life. I didn't even know if there could be a rest of my life.

Stefan's fingers rested on the brittle, yellowed page for a moment, and traced the faded contours of Vaillant's last words. How uncanny that the man's experiences, his thoughts and feelings should almost echo his own a century later – minus kissing a girl, of course.

What would Cassie do if he tried? Would she stare at him in horror and run away like Ruth had, or would she nestle in his arms and let him savour the sensations of having her soft body pressed against him?

He snapped the diary shut. It was a moot point, since he had no intention of ever being foolish enough to try and find out...

He rose to his feet with a grimace of pain and walked stiffly to the mantelpiece where he had left his phone the night before. After coming back from the pub he had felt compelled to look at some photos, for the first time in months. Photos of a trip to Mount Hombori with Charlie; of a blood coloured sunrise over the sand dunes during his last hike in the desert – probably his last ever; of friends and colleagues at a birthday party someone had thrown for one of his mechanics at the base...

The last photo had sent knife-stabbing pains into his chest. It was Isa, smiling as she stood in front of the plastic Christmas tree she had decorated at the base, the previous year. She loved Christmas, and had been ecstatic to learn that her leave request had been granted at last and that she would be spending Christmas with her family back home for the first time in three years... That's where she would be now if he hadn't insisted they flew to Charlie's dispensary despite the terrorist threats. If he hadn't messed up and caused her death.

Isa, whose parents kept sending him texts and emails he never read because he could too easily guess what they contained. They were angry, grieving, lost, no doubt... Whatever they had to say or write, he told himself a hundred times every day, they couldn't hate him more than he already hated himself.

He put the phone down again, and walked to the kitchen to make another coffee. His eyes swept over the table and Cassie's latest sticky note. 'What did the aliens from the cheese planet say when they landed on Earth?' He flipped the note over. 'Gratings!' Despite his grim mood, a smile tugged at the corner of his lips and he added the Post-it to the pile on the dresser, on top of the joke she had left two days before – something about 'raindeers' being the wettest animals in the world...

Cassie... He could smell her citrus fragrance everywhere in the house, and it conjured pictures in his mind – pictures of her laughing and of him doing all the tickling with her feather duster. It was crazy to feel so attracted to someone he had only just met, but he couldn't help it. Perhaps it was that syndrome psychiatrists talked about, the one when a patient fell for their nurse or doctor.

He made himself another coffee and returned to the drawing room. There was still time to read a few more pages before Cassie's daily visit.

15th September 1919,

Ten days without seeing Ruth, and I was going mad. Ten days torturing myself thinking that if she hadn't returned to Belthorn, it was because she wanted nothing to do with me. I had to see her, talk to her, and ask her if she would give me a chance to prove myself to her and her family, so I set off for Patterdale Farm yesterday after breakfast.

It was pouring with rain, and by the time I got there I was drenched and exhausted, and my clothes splattered with mud. As I knocked on the door I heard voices inside. One was a man's – harsh and aggressive. The other was Ruth's, and she was crying.

I didn't hesitate but pushed the door open, in time to see a great brute of a man wrap his arms around her waist and yank her to him.

'Get your hands off her,' I shouted, anger surging inside me. I rushed in, my aches and pains all but forgotten.

Ruth's eyes were wide with fear. The man's mouth twisted into a sneer and he shoved Ruth aside. 'You're that French cripple who's staying at Belthorn, aren't you? Ruth is as good as my wife. You've no right to meddle in our affairs. Now crawl back where you came from and leave us alone.'

He was much bigger than me, but love and desperation gave me speed and strength. I rushed forward, curled my fist tight and punched him squarely in the face. He stumbled back with a grunt, blood pouring out of his nose.

My triumph didn't last long. The brute charged towards me in the manner of a bull, so fast I didn't have time to step away. He head butted me in the stomach, pushed me all the way against the wall. I smacked the back of my head. A white light flashed inside my skull and I passed out.

The next think I knew, I was lying face down in the mud outside the farmhouse.

'André, wake up!' Ruth's voice pierced through the pain. There were other voices too, among them Ruth's father.

'I'll fetch the doctor,' he said. 'What a mess you've put us in, girl. What will Lord Ashville say when he finds out that his friend received a beating because of you? What if he turns us out of the farm?'

'I did nothing wrong,' Ruth whimpered.

'Your mother said you encouraged him instead of telling him you were spoken for.'

'That's not true! I never encouraged him. We're... friends. And I don't want to marry Gideon. You know he's a bully.'

'Marrying Hardy is the best thing that can happen to you, and to us as a family, so you'll do as you're told. I don't want to hear any more nonsense about the Frenchman. This is real life, not one of your penny novels... or that silly folk story you like so much – The Hunchback and the Swan.'

As I passed out again, an image flashed in my memory. This was the painting in my bedroom, a man looking out of his window at a swan gliding on the pond, its feathers white as snow. When I next woke up someone was probing my skull, my arms, my legs.

'Nothing appears to be broken,' the man decreed.

'Are you sure he'll be all right, doctor?' Ruth's father asked. 'He got a bump on the head and he's been out of it for a while now.'

My head hurt like hell and my mouth was parched but this time I opened my eyes and looked at Ruth's father. 'Tell Ruth... that I'll look after her. Please...'

Merriweather gave me a black look, but it was the doctor who spoke next. 'Don't agitate yourself, young man. You need to rest, but first we must get you out of those wet clothes.' He asked Ruth's father to bring a shirt and a pair of long johns for me to change into.

I managed to undress and put on William Merriweather's clothes before lying down again. How weak and pitiful I was. No wonder Ruth's family considered me unsuitable for their daughter.

'I shall come back to check on you tomorrow morning and if you feel better William will take you back to Belthorn. For now, you should drink this. It'll help you sleep.'

Whatever he gave me made me fall into a deep slumber. The doctor came back as promised the day after and pronounced me fit to travel. Ruth's mother gave me back my clothes. She had dried them and brushed the mud off so they were reasonably clean. I climbed onto William's cart with considerable difficulty, but I was damned if I'd ask for a helping hand. A man has to hang on to whatever pride he has left even when he was beaten up and humiliated in front of the woman he loves.

I had hoped to see Ruth but she wasn't there, and fearful of causing any more trouble between her and her parents, I didn't ask after her. As we set off on the road to Belthorn, I was however determined to find out more about the brute she seemed destined to marry, even if she appeared against the match... even if I dared to hope that she had tender feelings for me. It was now up to me to prove that I was worthy of her.

Stefan closed the diary and put it down on the table. He needed a break from Vaillant, from the account of his hopes and broken dreams that in so many ways mirrored his own...

Chapter Eighteen

'I'm so glad the van is ready at last. What took you so long?'

Mason looked up from the engine he was fixing and pulled a face. 'First the supplier couldn't get hold of any snow tyres, and then they sent me the wrong ones. In the end it turned out to be a total waste of time.' He sighed. 'I only wished I'd checked your old tyres before ordering new ones.'

'Why is that?'

'The tyres weren't punctured but had faulty valves. I could have fixed them straight away had I realised... The thing is, I was so busy that week I got Shaz to tow your van back and take the tyres off without asking him to check what was wrong with them. I just took your word for it that they both had a puncture. Shaz assumed I knew the valves were faulty. I only realised my mistake yesterday.'

He shook his head and sighed. 'Of course, since it's my fault I didn't charge you for the new tyres.'

'Thanks... but does this valve problem happen very often?'

Mason shrugged. 'It's not uncommon, but it was really bad luck both failed at the same time.'

Cassie frowned. Stefan would probably insist that luck had nothing to do with it and her flat tyres were Darren Morse's doing. Something the Frenchman had said came back to her. Darren had looked as if he was inspecting her tyres the day he came to Belthorn... what if he had been fiddling with the air valves instead? Now she was being paranoid too!

'Thanks, Mason. I owe you one. Is Brenda in?'

'She's in the office,' he replied before grabbing hold of a spanner and bending down over the engine of an old Fiesta.

Cassie pushed the door to the office, and immediately took off her hat and unbuttoned her coat.

'Good morning, Brenda. I don't know how you can stand having the heating on so high. Aren't you roasting in here?'

Brenda laughed and patted her tight brown curls. 'Nothing is ever too hot for me, darling – and that goes for radiators, curry... and men. Talking of hot men, I bumped into your *Mushier* Lambert in the pub the other night.'

Cassie rolled her eyes. 'He's not my *Mushier* Lambert,' she said, mimicking Brenda's terrible French accent. 'It's *Monsieur* Lambert, and there's nothing "mushy" about him.'

'I agree with you there. He may be no oil painting, but there is something very attractive, very hard, and very male about him. And those wonderful tawny eyes of his do strange things to my system.' Brenda let out a dreamy sigh.

'He has a short temper and a grouchy disposition,' Cassie said.

'There was nothing grouchy about him the other night,' Brenda protested. 'Sadie and I had a long chat with him. In fact, Sadie got along so well with him she was practically sitting in his lap by the end of the evening.'

Cassie felt a nip of jealousy in her chest. 'Is that so?'

So, Stefan could be charming and communicate with words and sentences as well as grunts or monosyllables. It must be only around her that he reverted to being a caveman. That's because he found her stupid and irritating, not to mention that he resented her for coming to Belthorn every day. He had hardly been able to hide his dislike at the pub on Saturday night. Mind you, it had been silly of her to try to tickle him with her feather duster. Even after a couple of Big Jim's cocktails, she should have known that it wouldn't cheer him up. She seriously wondered if anything could... Between the feather duster incident and her awful Bandanamama singing, he no doubt found her even more irritating now, if that was possible.

Brenda chuckled. 'Well, not literally, of course, but young Sadie seemed very keen on him.' She handed Cassie a piece of paper. 'Here is your guarantee for the tyres. Sorry for the mix up. Mason has been a bit distracted lately, poor boy.'

'What's up? Is he not well? Between the garage and doing up his house, he works too hard. He was complaining the other day that he didn't have time to undertake all the changes I suggested. I can help with the painting and decorating. In the meantime, I'll make a few new cushions for his living room.'

'I don't think paint or cushions are going to help, love.' Brenda's eyes hardened. 'But it's nothing we can't handle. He'll be all right, eventually. I'll make sure of it.'

None the wiser about what was the matter with her friend, Cassie bid Brenda goodbye, and spent an hour doing her admin at Bluebell Cottage. She made a cup of tea and studied her diary.

The only item that stuck out was the review meeting with Piers the following Friday, which she had scribbled in big red letters, and she spent the following hour searching through her files for the relevant timesheets to cover the past few months, cursing when some were missing – Sophie had probably forgotten to file them before she left for Manchester – and organising those she had in chronological order. She would have to visit every cottage before Friday to take photos of the comments in the guestbooks with her phone, in case Piers's secretary hadn't taken care of that herself.

She could only hope Piers wouldn't try to renegotiate her contract to bring her fee down. Why was this review even necessary, and why should her work matter to Gabrielle Ashville, even if she was suddenly taking an interest in the running of the estate?

She dropped the papers on the kitchen table and blew out a loud breath. Of course! She should have put two and two together before. Mason must have heard that Gabrielle was coming back... Poor Mason. No wonder he was distracted.

She checked her watch. Salomé's must be open by now. She

would buy some buns for Stefan's breakfast before driving to Belthorn.

Half an hour later, her red van bumped along the road towards Wolf Pass Road. It was good to have it back at last. Mason – or perhaps Shaz – had even given it a valeting. The wooden dashboard gleamed, the carpets were grit and mud free and a fresh scent lingered in the cab, mixing with the blissful smell of fresh cinnamon buns.

Belthorn Manor's chimneys appeared on the line of the horizon, dark grey against the overcast sky. Although her fear had lost its sharp edges in the past weeks, the place still made her uneasy, especially in the run up to Christmas and the anniversary of the most horrible night of her life…

Lambert's Range Rover stood in the drive and lights shone from a couple of windows both downstairs and upstairs. Stefan was in, but the odds were that as usual he would hibernate in the library and only make one brief appearance to make himself some coffee, or he would grab his coat and his keys as soon as she arrived after grunting a vague greeting – and that's if he was in a good mood. He obviously reserved his charm and witty conversation for long-legged Sadie…

She rang the bell, waited for a minute or two, and then let herself in. She put her shopping bags down and took her hat and her coat off.

'Hello? Is anyone home?' she called.

Stefan appeared at the top of the stairs, barefoot and wearing grey sweatpants and a khaki T-shirt. He looked out of breath, as if he'd been working out. Cassie's pulse started racing and her heart skipped another beat as she tried not to gawp at his broad shoulders, or his tanned, muscled arms.

'I wasn't expecting you so early,' he said in lieu of greeting.

'And a good morning to you too,' she muttered. No matter what Brenda said, the man was crabby and unpleasant, and right now she couldn't think of any reason why just being close to him should turn her into this hot, clumsy, breathless mess.

She lifted the shopping bag with Salomé's bakery logo on. 'I thought I would surprise you with breakfast to celebrate getting my van back at last, and I bought cinnamon buns from Salomé's. I'll put the shopping away and make you some coffee.'

He walked slowly down the stairs and stopped halfway. The grey morning light filtered through the stained glass insert on the front door and shone directly on his face, turning his eyes a bright, and very cold, gold.

'Leave the bags. I'll sort out the shopping later, and don't bother locking the front door behind you. I'm going out soon.'

He turned round and walked back up, leaving her holding the bag of pastries, and feeling thoroughly dismissed, and a complete fool.

Chapter Nineteen

He wasn't sure how long he could stand so he gritted his teeth against the pain and attempted to walk back up the stairs. It had been stupid to push his body so hard these past few days. He may have wanted to banish the ghost of Vaillant's hopelessness and despair – and his own ghosts and inadequacies too, but he was paying the price now.

He fully expected Cassie to slam the door as she left. That was why he had been so rude after all.

Instead her voice rang behind him. 'I'm not going anywhere until I have tidied the house, done the dusting and vacuum cleaning and prepared a hot meal for you. If you don't want any breakfast, then I won't make you any coffee and I'll leave the buns in the kitchen for you to eat later.'

Why couldn't she leave him alone?

Very slowly because his back was killing him, he turned to face her. 'The house doesn't need tidying every day, and you can forget about the cooking because I'm planning to eat out again today,' he lied.

She still didn't move, but stared at him, frowning. He clearly hadn't been obnoxious enough. 'Damn it, Cassie, surely it's not that hard to understand that I want to be on my own and don't need you buzzing around with your cleaning spray and your feather duster every bloody day.'

Suddenly his back seized up and the pain was too much to bear. With a gasp, he grabbed hold of the banister, gripped the wooden handrail hard and slowly lowered himself onto a step.

Cassie leapt up the stairs, knelt down in front of him, and put a hand on his knee. 'Stefan... What's wrong? Do you need a doctor? Is it your back again? Wait... I'll get a cushion for you to lean against.'

It reminded him of the way she had fluttered around

her grandfather and pushed a cushion behind his back at Patterdale Farm.

'I don't need a bloody cushion. I must have pulled a muscle when I was training, that's all.' He tried to sound dismissive but his voice came out weak and hoarse.

She moved up one step to sit right next to him. Her hand slid up and down his thigh as if he was a child who needed comforting. But he wasn't a child and far from comforting him, her caresses were having an altogether different effect. Did she even realise what she was doing? Perhaps he should be glad. At least focussing on keeping his body in check took his mind off the pain clawing at his back.

'Can I help? Tell me where it hurts,' she said in a soothing voice, rubbing and patting his thigh in turns.

'It's not my leg but my back that's the problem,' he muttered between clenched teeth.

She leant closer, so close her lemony fragrance filled his senses, wisps of silky blonde hair tickled his cheek and her breasts pushed against his arm. He pulled away slightly to gaze into her limpid grey eyes. Today they were the colour of rain clouds.

The pain bit into him again and he drew in a sharp breath. How long was she going to sit next to him, stroking him and her face a picture of kindness and concern? As if it wasn't embarrassing enough that he couldn't even stand, he started shivering. The only burning sensations in his body were those triggered by the pain and by the rubbing and stroking of her hand on his thigh.

He leant away but she shuffled close again. 'Tell me what I can do to make you feel better.'

That was easy, he almost replied. She could leave her hand exactly where it was, or move it a tad higher. It was proving a great distraction against the pain... He ground his teeth. 'If you really want to make yourself useful, bring me my painkillers. They're on the bedside table in my room.'

'Sure.' She jumped to her feet and ran upstairs, and was back in no time with the box of extra strong painkillers he kept for emergencies and a glass of water.

He gulped two tablets down. A long minute passed then a couple more. The spasms in his back subsided at last, and the pain was down to a manageable level.

'I'm all right now,' he said at last.

She let out a sigh of relief, and put her hand against her heart. 'Good. You gave me such a fright. You were so pale I thought you were going to pass out. Now let me help you into the drawing room. You can lie on the sofa and put your feet up whilst I make you some coffee.'

She slipped her hand under his elbow to help him stand up.

'There's no need to fuss. I said I was all right.' He disentangled himself from her grasp, walked down the rest of the stairs and picked up her shopping bags. He'd be damned if he let her carry them to the kitchen. He hated having her do jobs for him.

She, however, had other ideas, and tried to snatch one bag from him. He stepped back, out of her reach.

'You shouldn't lift or carry anything or you'll hurt your back again,' she protested.

'A few bags aren't going to make much difference.' He took the bags to the kitchen, put them on the table and proceeded to take the shopping out. Now that his backache had eased off, he had to do something – anything – to cool the fire her caresses had inadvertently started in another part of his anatomy.

He held out a couple of tins. 'Where do you want these?'

This time he wasn't quick enough, and she managed to wrestle a tin of baked beans from his hands.

'I'll do it. Now do as I say and sit down, or...' Her tone was fierce, and her eyes even fiercer. Even though the top of her head only reached up to his shoulder she held the tin of beans up in the air like a weapon.

Tension suddenly uncoiled and loosened inside him. He had to see the comic side of the situation. This five foot one – five foot two at most – woman was prepared to beat him up with a tin of beans if he didn't do as she said.

'Or what?' He smiled and pointed at the tin she was still gripping tightly. 'Will you smash it against my skull? That would be a way to help me forget my backache.'

Her cheeks blushed deep pink and she dropped the tin down on the table. 'Sorry... I don't want you to be in pain again, that's all. Why don't you sit down while I unpack?'

He crossed his arms on his chest. 'Only if you have breakfast with me. I'm not used to being waited on. And don't tell me you're only doing your job.'

She sighed. 'All right, then. I haven't had any breakfast, and I would have to be mad to turn down one of Salomé's pastries.'

As soon as she had put away the tins, jars and various items of groceries she had brought, Cassie switched the oven on and made the coffee while he sat there watching and feeling pretty useless. By the time the coffee had percolated, and she took the cinnamon buns out of the oven, the pain in his back had died down and he felt ravenous. She poured two cups and handed him one whilst he slathered butter on two of the cinnamon buns and started eating.

'They're good.' He poured another cup of coffee and cradled the mug in his hands as he reclined in his chair.

Cassie licked the sugar off her fingers. 'Salomé won a competition on the television three years ago, you know, and bought the little bakery in the village a few months later with some of her prize money.'

She sighed. 'Poor Salomé. I've always wondered why she chose to settle here. She could have gone back to Spain where she came from, or settled in the South of England. She still isn't used to the snow and the rain. Two years on, she still wears scarves and thermal underwear even in summer!'

'Is she Spanish?'

'She's English, but was brought up in Spain where her parents own a restaurant. Everybody in the village loves her.'

He arched his eyebrows. 'What about that "three-generation rule" you told me about?'

She laughed. 'It doesn't apply to her. I grant you, people were a bit unsure of her exotic ways at first, but she soon won them over with her lovely personality and delicious cakes… all but one, that is.'

'Who is that?'

'Your friend, Charles. Salomé complained that he was terribly unpleasant to her when he came for his father's funeral last year. Having said that, the poor man probably had a lot on his mind. His father had just died in that freak accident, and he must have been upset, even if…' She glanced up at him and bit her lip.

'Even if…?'

'Well, people say that the two men weren't close.'

Stefan drank his coffee. It probably wouldn't be too much of a betrayal of his friend's confidence to explain the rift between Charlie and his father.

'Charlie has devoted his life to Inter Medics, but his father believed that charity work wasn't in keeping with the family's standing in society. Now that I'm here, I can understand why.' He looked around. 'This house. The old abbey. The land. I knew Charlie's family was well off, but I had no idea they owned all this. He used to describe Belthorn as a decrepit old family house in the middle of nowhere.'

She smiled. 'Personally, I would agree. I've always found this place gloomy and horrid.'

Perhaps this was his chance to satisfy his curiosity and find out why she seemed so scared of the place. 'What happened to make you dislike Belthorn so much?'

Cassie's smiled vanished. It was as if the sunshine had been sucked out of the kitchen window and a black cloud had crept inside. She pushed her chair back so abruptly it scraped against the tiled floor as she got up to collect the empty plates and cups and piled them up into the sink.

'I'll tell you some other time, perhaps.' But her tone implied that she had no intention of ever talking about it. Turning the hot water tap on, she squirted some washing-up liquid into the water and proceeded to wash-up.

'I haven't had my joke today,' he said, trying to lighten the mood.

She turned round, dried her hands and rummaged inside her handbag. 'Sorry. There you are,' she said, handing him a Post-it note. 'It's another winter joke, courtesy of my granddad. Perhaps not his best one, but I'll let you be the judge.'

Their fingers brushed as she handed him the note. 'What did the policeman say to the ice lolly thief?' he read. He turned the paper over. 'Freeze!' He smiled. 'That's funny.'

She smiled back, and the cute dimples reappeared on her cheeks. 'If you think so then you'll have to come to Comedy Night at the Eagle and Child on the Friday before Christmas. I have the feeling the competition is going to be a lot tougher for my granddad this year, and that people may be getting tired of his old-fashioned jokes.'

He remembered what Mason had said. Comedy Night was in aid of a good cause – a cause close to his heart, since all proceeds went to the Mountain Rescue and the Air Ambulance teams.

'All right. I'll come.'

'Really? That's great!' She sounded surprised but sincere, although why she should be happy about him coming was a mystery to him. He must be her most disagreeable client – not to mention her ugliest one.

She walked to the fridge, opened the door and started pulling some meat and vegetables out. 'I'll prepare a casserole that you can warm up for your tea tonight. Where are you going today?'

He'd only said he was going out because he didn't want Cassie to stick around and see him in pain, but the truth was that he was fed up with driving around aimlessly, even if the area was breathtakingly beautiful.

He shrugged. 'I'm not sure. I'll see where the road takes me.'

She hesitated. 'If you have nothing special planned, perhaps you would like to come with me to Keswick. I have to pick up some props to transform the campsite clubhouse into a jungle for Rachel's sister's wedding reception on Saturday, and I could do with a hand.'

He frowned. 'A jungle?'

She let out a sigh. 'I know. It's crazy, isn't it, but after months of insisting she didn't want anything special, Kerry is now set on a Tarzan and Jane wedding... and whatever Kerry wants, Kerry must get. She's always been a little spoilt.'

She paused and her cheeks coloured. 'By the way, you're invited to the reception.'

'Invited? But I don't know anybody.'

'You know me and my granddad. You know Rachel, Tim and the boys too.'

'Well, I don't think...'

She cocked her head to one side and her eyes sparkled with mischief. 'If you're worried about what to wear, let me put your mind at rest. I ordered a batch of loincloths for the groom and gentlemen guests. It's incredible what you can buy online these days.'

He swallowed hard. 'Loincloths?'

She nodded. 'To be in keeping with the Tarzan theme, of course... I'll make sure the clubhouse's heating is turned on full, so you won't catch a cold.' A smile played on her lips and her eyes twinkled again.

His mind went blank and all he could say was, 'No way!'

She burst out laughing. 'I'm only joking. I can't believe you fell for it... although you are of course free to act up a childhood fantasy, wear a loincloth and swing from a vine ululating like Tarzan if that's what you want. The guests might enjoy a bit of a show.'

His body hardened, and his blood pulsed in his veins. Suddenly he could think of a couple of fantasies – very much adult ones – he would like to act out with Cassie Bell right now, be it in a jungle or on a kitchen table.

'So, are you coming – both to the wedding and to Keswick with me today?'

She was still looking at him, waiting for him to reply. He gave himself a mental shake. 'Why not?'

He might say that he wanted to be alone, but the prospect of another drive out with only the car radio and his dark thoughts for company wasn't inspiring. As for the wedding, he should make an effort. It would be polite to show his face, since he had been invited. He didn't have to stay long.

Right now, however, he was going to take a very long, very cold, shower.

Chapter Twenty

'I thought we could stop at Castlerigg before picking up my order from the crafts warehouse,' Cassie said as she climbed onto the passenger seat of the Range Rover. 'Are you sure you want to drive?'

'Positive. What's Castlerigg?'

She replied that it was an ancient stone circle – one of the largest in England. He realised he would have agreed to go anywhere she suggested, even a shopping centre, and the thought made him frown. Was he so desperate for company – or was it only Cassie's company he craved? He brushed the uncomfortable thought aside and focussed on driving down the lane without the car skidding into the ditch.

Cassie's phone beeped as they approached Red Moss. She took it out of her bag, and read the message on the screen.

'Not again!'

He glanced at her. 'Any problems?'

'It's Fluffy, my neighbour's cat.'

He arched his eyebrows. 'Don't tell me… He's hungry and wants you to buy a tin of sardines for his lunch.'

She laughed. 'It's not the cat texting me, but my next door neighbour. Apparently Fluffy sneaked into my house, and his owner is on the warpath and demands I release it straight away or she'll call the police, the firemen *and* the RSPCA to break our door down and arrest me for pet kidnapping – shouldn't that be catnapping?'

She gave him an apologetic smile. 'Would you mind stopping at Bluebell Cottage so I can let him out and avoid being thrown into jail?'

'Sure.' He parked outside the cottage, and turned the engine off.

'This shouldn't take long,' she said, 'but you're welcome to come in rather than wait in the car.' Glancing at the other side of the street, she added, 'Oh dear. Doris is coming, and she looks angry.'

A grey-haired lady wearing a thick brown fleece and a rather scary scowl on her face strode towards them, stomping her walking stick onto the road. Cassie's cat problems were none of his business, and the last thing he wanted was to get involved in a neighbourly dispute, but the woman did look angry, and Cassie had gone very pale, and a surge of protectiveness washed over him.

'I'll come with you.'

She looked relieved. 'Thank you.'

The old woman hardly waited for them to get out of the car before shouting at Cassie. 'You took your time, young lady. My Fluffy has been locked up in your house for hours.'

'It's hardly been that long, and I only just got the message.' Cassie smiled but the woman scowled harder.

'I know what you and your granddad are up to,' she said, 'and I have a mind to report you to the RSPCA and the police for cat stealing.' She had raised her voice and punctuated every word with a whack of her walking stick against the cottage's gate.

Cassie let out a sigh. 'How many times must we tell you that we are not trying to steal your cat? I don't understand how Fluffy managed to sneak in again, but I'll let him out straight away, don't worry.'

The woman narrowed her eyes and tapped her stick on the ground. 'Get on with it then.'

Cassie produced a set of keys from her handbag, but in her haste to open the front door she dropped them and they clattered onto the stone flags. Stefan bent down quickly to pick them up and handed them to Cassie, who mouthed a 'thank you'.

The woman gave him a suspicious look. 'Who are you?'

'A friend.' He wanted to say a lot more. That her cat was

hardly going to come to any harm at Bluebell Cottage, even if he was locked in for a few hours. That perhaps he had found a better, friendlier place to hang out. And that she need not be so unpleasant to Cassie... But that wouldn't help the situation so he kept his mouth shut.

Cassie opened the front door. Immediately, a large ginger cat shot out of the house and curled around the old woman's legs with loud meows.

'My poor Fluffy darling.' The woman bent down to stroke the cat but it lashed out at her hand and darted across the street before disappearing between two houses. She stared at the red scratches on the back of her hand and cast Cassie a reproachful glance before marching back to her cottage, muttering and waving her stick.

Cassie pulled a face. 'Doris is really mad at me now. Let's hope her cat comes back soon.'

'I'm not sure I would if I were him,' he remarked. 'She is one scary lady.'

'She's lonely, that's all. Her husband died years ago, and her children rarely visit. Fluffy is all she's got.' Her eyes, her voice, were sad. Did she really not mind that the old woman had just been rude to her and threatened her with the police?

'I hope Fluffy hasn't made too much of a mess. Last time he sneaked in, he broke my bedside lamp, messed up all the fabrics and threads in my sewing basket, and scattered paperwork all over the floor in the back room upstairs – not to mention almost gave me a heart attack.'

He followed Cassie into the kitchen, and she gestured to a chair. 'Please sit down,' she said. 'I'll run upstairs and check the windows are shut properly. I don't want Fluffy sneaking in again.'

A sketchpad and boxes of artist's pencils and crayons were spread out on the kitchen table. Curious, he pulled the sketchpad towards him and lifted the cover. The first sketch made him catch his breath. It was Belthorn's drawing room, but not as it was now. In fact, the only recognisable features were the fireplace, the elaborate ceiling and cornices and the tall windows. Cassie had given the walls rich cream and mushroom shades, and the sofa and armchairs a re-upholstered look in striking plum and lime green. Curtains in similar colours framed the windows, and interior shutters let sunlight filter into the room.

He flicked through the pages, each depicting various rooms at Belthorn. He knew nothing about interior design, but Cassie's ideas were at the same time quirky and elegant, and full of sensitivity to the manor house's character. Gabrielle and Charlie would love them.

Why was the woman wasting her time cleaning houses and babysitting him when she could do something infinitely more creative and rewarding, not to mention better paid?

He recalled his conversations with Sadie and Brenda at the village pub on Saturday night. Neither woman had needed much prompting to talk about Cassie.

'She's hardly done anything with her interior design diploma,' Brenda had said.

'That's because she's been too busy running Bluebell Cleaning,' Sadie had added.

'And looking after her granddad,' Brenda had added. 'Don't get me wrong, Joseph is a lovely man, but he does rely on Cassie far too much.'

Brenda had explained that Cassie's father – Joseph's son – had died when Cassie was a toddler. Her mother had remarried when Cassie finished high school. 'When Keith retired from the police two years ago, they sold their house and bought an apartment in Tenerife. Cassie took over Bluebell Cleaning and moved in with Joseph to keep an eye on him. She hasn't had much time to herself since, poor love.'

Stefan had steered the conversation onto Morse but unfortunately, neither Sadie nor Brenda had been able to tell him much. Morse rarely spoke to anyone at the pub, never drank more than a couple of pints, and generally kept himself to himself. 'Having said that, he is popular with the village's elderly folks,' Sadie had added. 'He does odd jobs for them, so I guess he must be a nice guy.'

Stefan's mobile pinged as he was thinking about the best way to find out information about Morse whilst still flicking through the sketchbook. He did what he had carefully avoided doing for weeks. He took the phone out of his pocket, and opened the message without looking at the sender's details.

He stared at the screen, and it felt like there was not enough air to breathe. A photo of Isa and himself standing in front of a Cougar helicopter filled the screen. He remembered the day perfectly. It was her first mission as co-pilot, two and half years before. After a short flight to survey the area surrounding the base, they had spent time in the control room working on flight plans for the following days before having lunch and a game of table football with other personnel in the canteen. They had clicked from that very first day, had worked together on more missions than he could remember and had become friends as well as colleagues. She had told him about her family, her hopes for the future, and about the terrible times she'd been through when as a young recruit she had been the victim of a vicious, manipulative stalker and had almost resigned from the army...

He read a few words before the lines blurred on the screen. 'We know how highly Isa thought of you. She would want you to have this.' He scrolled down to the name at the bottom of the email. Carole Bertier. Isa's mother.

He put the phone on the table, closed his eyes and tried to catch his breath. Isa had trusted him with her life and he had let her down.

'The cat didn't make too much of a mess this time, but I still have no idea how he got in...' Cassie said as she came back into the kitchen.

He opened his eyes to find her staring at him, then at the photo on his phone.

'Are you all right? Did you have bad news or something?'

He slipped the phone back into his pocket. 'I'm fine. Just fine.' He blinked. 'What were you saying about the cat?'

She frowned as if she didn't believe him, but didn't insist. 'All the windows upstairs are shut. Fluffy must have sneaked past me as I went out this morning. I swear that cat must have an invisibility cloak! I am really sorry for dragging you here, and for that unpleasant exchange with Doris.'

'Don't worry about it.'

She fastened her coat and picked up her handbag. Only then did she notice the sketchbook open on the table, and her eyes widened in shock. 'You looked at my drawings?'

He didn't bother apologising. 'I like your sketches of Belthorn. More to the point, I think Charlie would like them too.'

'Do you really believe that?'

He nodded. Her eyes sparkled, the dimples on her cheeks deepened, and a soft, mellow sensation spread through his chest. He could get used to Cassie looking at him this way. After the shock of receiving the photo and the email from Isa's mother it was like a warm, soothing balm on his aching heart.

Cassie's smile died down almost immediately and she let out a deep sigh. 'I have no intention of showing Charlie, or anyone, my designs. I don't want to hear again that I should stick to what I do best – cleaning.'

Her shoulders sagged, her eyes misted and she closed the sketchbook and placed the boxes of pencils on top. It wasn't like her to be so defeated. He hated seeing her so sad. He hated even more the urge to reach out and cradle her in his arms to comfort her.

'Perhaps you should try anyway,' he said in a gruff voice, stuffing his hands into his coat pockets.

She slung her handbag on her shoulder. 'Forget it. Shall we go?'

There was no point insisting, so he followed her out. 'By the way, have you seen any more of Morse?'

She nodded. 'He was at a client's house last Saturday, but you are wrong about him having... feelings... for me. He didn't look happy to see me at all. One thing is certain. I won't be asking him to mend anything around here ever again.'

He arched his eyebrows. 'Why is that?'

'Nothing he fixes ever works. Sometimes I wonder how he got the caretaker job at the campsite. He certainly is rubbish at maintenance.' She frowned as if trying to remember something and muttered. 'His hands... there's something about his hands...' She shrugged and locked the door. 'Never mind. I can't remember.'

On the road to Keswick, Cassie hardly paused for breath as she pointed to local landmarks and told him about the villages they drove through, and the fells rising around them like benevolent giants, snow caps gleaming in the bright sunshine. A few weeks ago, he would have been irritated by her constant chatter, but not today. Today she made him smile, and her stories were a distraction from his usual brooding thoughts.

'Castlerigg is always crowded in summer, but it should be quiet today,' Cassie said as he drove up the hill, and followed the brown tourist signs to the stone circle.

She was right. The Range Rover was the only car in the car park. Cassie put her pom-pom hat on and slipped her hands into her gloves. The sun may be shining but it was exposed up on the hill, and the icy wind pricked his skin and made his eyes water.

He pushed the wooden gate open onto a field where snow-tipped stones formed a circle in the frozen landscape. His boots bit into the snow and his breath steamed in front of him as he strode across the field. The air was so pure and sharp he could taste the frost on his lips.

Cassie pointed to mountains in the distance. 'That's Skiddaw over there, the highest fell in the Lakes. And this is Blencathra.'

'This is amazing.' He stood at the centre of the circle and turned slowly to take in his surroundings.

'There are thirty-eight big stones and four smaller ones,' Cassie carried on, her cheeks now as red as her coat.

'When I was a little girl, my grandma told me that the stones were the ancient people's tool to communicate with their gods and loved ones – a bit like a telephone or a walkie-talkie, if you like.'

Her pink lips stretched in a wistful smile. 'I loved the idea that my father could hear me if I whispered very close to that stone, over there.'

She pointed at one of the bigger stones at the far side of the circle. 'He died when I was little and I don't remember him much. Of course, I realised later it was all nonsense, but I still came back over and over again to whisper my worries to the stone, and I always felt better afterwards. People say that talking is part of the healing process when you go through sad or traumatic times and...'

She left her sentence unfinished and gave him a searching look.

'You looked upset earlier about the photo on your phone. I want you to know that you can talk to me if you like...'

His heart thumped in his chest. He looked down. 'Talk to you? About what, exactly?'

She put her gloved hand on his forearm. 'About your friend in the photo, or about whatever troubles you.'

'Why should you care?' He couldn't help the bite in his tone.

Her cheeks turned a deeper pink. 'I know it's none of my business, but it's obvious you have been through terrible times, and if you feel like talking, you can trust me. I will listen and not say a word. In fact, I will be as silent as the standing stones.'

In this glorious setting, with the winter sun sparkling on the snow, the hills and the stones standing all around them like silent witnesses, the memories of the crash and the bloodbath he had caused were like gruesome, nightmarish ghouls. Worst of all was the pity in Cassie's eyes.

His mouth twisted into a sarcastic smile. 'You really take your job to heart, don't you?'

'My job?'

'Bluebell to the Rescue... Dirt, gloom and bad memories – you think you can make them all vanish with your Christmas jokes and your feather duster, but there are things that nobody – and not even you – can sort out.'

Her eyes widened in shock. 'It's got nothing to do with my job. I just want to help.'

'Thanks for the offer of a counselling session. I'll bear it in mind.'

He looked down at her, and felt even more rubbish when he saw her lips tremble and tears glisten in her eyes. It had only taken a few bad-tempered words to kill her smile.

She pulled a tissue from her coat pocket and blew her nose. They resumed their walk but didn't talk any more. He should apologise, of course. In fact, he should apologise for the way he'd been ever since he'd arrived – for being rude and bad-tempered, when she only offered kindness and support, and never mind if it was only because it was in her job description.

He opened his mouth to speak but she beat him to it.

'I'd like a few minutes alone, if you don't mind,' she said without looking at him.

He nodded and went back to the car. From behind the wheel he watched her touch the large stone she had pointed to before, and his heart did that funny thing again. Was she thinking about her father and telling him what a miserable brute Stefan was for making her cry?

Suddenly there was no more bitterness, no more hurt pride, self-pity or anger, only overwhelming tenderness for the young woman who believed that her dead father was listening to her troubles and would make everything better...

Chapter Twenty-One

'The edges of the lake are frozen,' Stefan remarked as they reached the end of the path and stood side by side looking at the island at the centre of Derwent Water.

These were the first words he'd spoken since they had left Castelrigg. Cassie slipped her hands into the pockets of her coat to keep them warm. She had left her gloves in the car – an oversight she sorely regretted now.

It wasn't the only thing she regretted. She shouldn't have been so pushy earlier. Whatever ailed Stefan beside the physical pain must be linked to the woman in the photo. She wore a military boiler suit and stood in front of a helicopter. It was fair to assume that she must have worked with him.

It had been insensitive to ask him to talk when it was obvious the photo had brought back painful memories, and he had every right to be annoyed with her. She was no psychologist or counsellor. She wasn't even a friend.

There was only one thing to do. She had to apologise. Taking a deep breath, she turned to face him, only to find that he was looking at her.

'Listen, Cassie...' he started.

'I'm so sorry,' she blurted out at the same time.

A half-smile stretched his lips. 'Sorry? What for? I'm the one who needs to apologise. I was rude... again, and there was no need for it. I know you mean well, and it's nothing personal, but there are things I don't want to talk about – ever.'

'No, I'm the one who's sorry. I shouldn't have tried to interfere. I promise never to pry or ask awkward questions again. Friends?'

She extended her hand. He looked down, winter sunlight caught his eyes, turning them pale amber. She could stare into his eyes for hours, and still find different shades of gold, brown and green. She held her breath. Would he rebuff her and tell her to mind her own business, or would he accept her offer of peace?

'Of course.' He took her hand.

A freezing gust of wind blew from the lake and rattled the bare branches in a nearby clump of trees, and she shivered. Stefan released her hand. 'Let's go into town and find somewhere to have lunch.'

Half an hour later they walked into a cosy pub in the town centre. It was packed with office workers enjoying an early Christmas dinner, and they were lucky to find a table close to the fireplace.

'Busy place,' Stefan remarked, pulling a chair out for her.

He sat opposite and handed her a menu whilst he studied the chalkboard where daily specials were displayed. 'I'll have the steak pie, although I'm sure it won't be as good as yours,' he said after a few seconds.

Heat spread over her cheeks. She lifted the menu to hide her face and pretended to study it, although she had no idea why she should be so flustered. Praising her steak pie wasn't exactly a sexy compliment, and from what he had said before, she knew he didn't have a very high opinion of her intellect or her physique.

'I'll have the Cumberland sausage and mash,' she said, putting the menu down.

He asked what she wanted to drink, and got up to place their order at the bar and she relaxed against the back of her chair. A fire crackled in the fireplace nearby and catchy music played in the background. The people sitting at the next table had had too much to drink already, judging from their loud voices and raucous laughter as they pulled crackers and read out the silly riddles inside. Had he been there, her granddad would have probably joined in with a few jokes of his own.

Worry knotted her stomach again, like every time she

thought about her grandfather these days. There was definitely something wrong with him. Before withdrawing money as he requested, she had checked his bank balance and found it surprisingly low. What had he done with his money? He must have bought expensive Christmas presents for the whole family this year – not a good idea, considering how small his pension was.

A man's hand fell heavily onto her shoulder, making her cry out in shock. She looked up and met Piers's smirking face.

'Hello, darling. Fancy seeing you here all alone.'

She repressed a groan and forced a smile. 'Hi, Piers. This is a surprise. Are you having lunch here too?'

'I was with a client and we just finished. Why didn't you tell me you were coming to Keswick today? We could have met up.'

'It wasn't planned. Stefan Lambert invited me.' She pointed at the bar where Stefan stood head and shoulders above the other patrons ordering drinks.

'Is that him over there?' Piers pulled a face. 'Poor chap... He does look rather... battered. What happened to him, do you know?'

'I really couldn't say. Didn't Charles write to you about him?' It was odd that Piers knew nothing about Stefan Lambert when he and Charles Ashville were such close friends.

Piers shook his head. 'Not a word apart from the original email I forwarded to you.'

Stefan walked back towards the table, half a pint of bitter in one hand and a glass of lemonade for her in the other. His gaze went from Piers's hand on her shoulder to her face, and his eyebrows gathered in an imperceptible frown.

'Hi there. I'm Piers Hardy, Charles's oldest buddy and estate manager.' Piers removed his hand from her shoulder at last, and she shuffled her chair away from him.

Stefan put the glasses down and introduced himself.

The two men shook hands, and Piers chuckled. 'Did you catch a cold walking on the hills? You sound terribly croaky. You should ask Cassie to work her magic on you and prepare you a hot toddy.'

Stefan's face remained impassive. 'Neither magic nor hot drinks will help, I'm afraid. My croaky voice is one of my battle wounds.'

'Ah. Sorry.' A red flush suffused Piers's already florid cheeks. 'I must buy you a drink some time so we can compare notes about Charlie. Is he still planning on wasting the best years of his life working for peanuts for a charity in that godforsaken country?'

Stefan's eyes turned icy. 'You'll have to ask him, although I'm not sure he would appreciate you calling his work at Inter Medics a waste of time.'

'That's not what I meant... not really...' Piers's colour deepened, and he shifted on his feet. He glanced down at Cassie.

'I hope you won't forget our date on Friday. I'll take you somewhere nice for lunch after our meeting.' His hand found her shoulder again and gave it another squeeze.

She squirmed under his touch. 'There's no need for that.'

'I insist.'

She stiffened as Piers's hand slid down her back and he bent down to kiss her cheek before finally taking his leave. Stefan watched him walk out of the pub and sat down.

'You don't like him much,' he remarked.

She gave him a tight smile. 'Is it that obvious?' She let out a long sigh. 'Piers is all right, really. He's been good to my family. He allowed my granddad to keep renting Bluebell Cottage for next to nothing if he takes care of minor repairs, and he gave me the Ashville holiday cottages contract after my mum retired. I owe him a lot.'

'And he knows it.'

Her fingers tightened around her glass of lemonade. That

was true. Piers did take advantage of his position of power and the worst thing was that she was so afraid of making him angry that she let him.

'He's been a good friend of Charles Ashville since they were both boarders at a private school in Windermere,' she remarked to shift the focus away from herself and her lack of backbone.

Stefan pulled a face. 'I find it hard to believe that he and Charlie have anything in common.'

'I believe they are very close. They used to do everything together, apparently, and Piers took over the management of the Ashville Estate from his own father.'

Stefan looked thoughtful. 'Is Hardy a common name around here?'

'Not really. Piers's family has been here for generations, like mine… In fact, I recently discovered that his great-grandfather had once been engaged to my great-great-aunt Ruth.'

A waitress approached with two steaming hot plates.

'Who's having the steak pie?' she asked, staring down at the plates as if she was afraid to drop them.

Stefan said that he was. The young woman looked up. Her eyes widened, and her hands shook so much she almost tipped the contents of his plate all over the table.

'I'm sorry.' Her chin wobbled as if she was going to cry.

'No worries,' he replied, but his face paled and his eyes turned a darker, harder gold.

The girl placed Cassie's plate in front of her so quickly that it clanked against the salt and pepper dispensers, knocking them over. 'Oh. No. I'm so sorry,' she stammered again before hurrying away.

'Poor kid,' he whispered when she had left. 'Sometimes I forget…'

'Forget what?'

He focussed his serious gaze on her. 'That not everybody is as good at hiding their feelings as you are.'

Her heart jumped and her face caught fire. Had he guessed that she was attracted to him? 'What feelings?' she stammered.

He shrugged. 'You know. Fear, disgust, pity. That poor girl must be wondering how you can eat with an ugly brute like me. She's probably going to have nightmares for weeks.'

'Nonsense!' How could he think, even for one second, that his appearance was so revolting that it could give a woman nightmares – and worse still, seem to accept it?

Yes, he had scars, and his nose was broken in two, if not three places. Yes, his voice was hoarse, harsh and raw, and he might not be in the top physical shape he had been before his accident. But he was still strong and incredibly attractive, and one look from his tawny eyes and her heart did somersaults, her skin prickled all over and her thoughts took a decidedly hot and naughty turn. She wasn't the only one feeling that way either. Brenda and gorgeous Sadie fancied him too – not that she could tell him.

'The waitress was clumsy, that's all and—' she started, but Stefan stopped her with a hard look.

'It's all right, Cassie, you don't need to make excuses for the girl. I don't resent her for being put off by me, honest… She isn't the first, and she won't be the last.'

He looked at his plate, ate a few mouthfuls of steak pie and put his fork down. 'Just what I thought… It's good, but not as good as yours.' He looked up. 'Are you not hungry?'

'Yes. Yes, of course.' She cut a piece of sausage, but her appetite had vanished.

'By the way, what were you saying earlier about your great-great-aunt Ruth and Hardy's relative?'

She doubted he really was interested, but it might help him forget the unpleasant episode with the waitress.

'I recently found out that they were once engaged,' she replied.

'Did they ever marry?'

She shook her head. 'Ruth broke up with him before drowning at Wolf Tarn during the winter of 1919.'

'She drowned?' His face seemed paler. It didn't make sense. Why should he care about one of her ancestors?

'On Christmas Eve, actually. Everybody believed it was an accident,' she carried on, 'but I think she committed suicide.'

He put his knife and fork down. 'Why would she do that?'

'She was desperate. Her family had disowned her when the man she loved – a French pilot who was convalescing at Belthorn – abandoned her. I recently got hold of some letters that led me to believe that they had become lovers and planned to elope together. Unfortunately, he returned to Paris to care for his mother who was poorly with the flu. She died, and he too fell ill. The last letter Ruth received was from his sister, who asked her not to write again because André didn't wish to pursue the relationship. She wrote that André would return her letters unopened… and that's exactly what he did.'

She shook her head in disgust. 'The cruel, despicable man seduced her and didn't even have the courage to break off their liaison himself but asked his sister to do it for him. It must have been devastating for Ruth to receive all the letters she had poured her heart out in and he hadn't even opened, let alone read. Her body was recovered from Wolf Tarn on Christmas Day, a hundred years ago exactly this year.'

She stopped. It seemed incongruous to talk about Ruth's death with happy Christmas music playing and people laughing in the background.

Stefan frowned. 'I think you're wrong. Vaillant was a good man. Something must have happened that prevented him from coming back to Red Moss.'

She let out a startled laugh. 'How do you know that? And how do you even know his name?'

'I found his journal at Belthorn, and from what I've been reading, he did mean to marry Ruth. He was planning to come back to Belthorn, that's why he left his diary behind.'

The diary must be the brown leather-bound book she had seen in the drawing room. 'How very peculiar that it should fall into your hands,' she said. 'Will you let me read it?'

'Of course, but it's in French, so I'll have to translate it for you.'

'Yes, please, and I'll show you Ruth's letters. That way perhaps between the both of us, we can figure out what really happened. It will be like putting together a puzzle.'

'Talking about puzzles,' Stefan said, 'what is the "Guess the Santa" contest everybody is talking about?'

'It's a village charity event in aid of the Mountain Rescue Team, like Comedy Night. Someone dresses up as Santa and people put a bet on to guess their identity. If nobody gets it right, all the money collected goes to the mountain rescue charity. Otherwise they split the money.'

'It sounds like a good plan.'

'Except that nobody wants to be Santa this year. Mason even suggested that I do it. He said nobody would ever guess it was me.'

Stefan shook his head. 'I would.'

'Really? How?'

'Your perfume. Lemon. Clean. Fresh. Summery. It would be a dead giveaway.'

Her heart sank. 'Oh. I see. You think I smell of cleaning products.'

He arched his eyebrows. 'Is that what it is? I like it. Beats expensive French perfume any day.'

He was making fun of her... Her chest tightening, she heaved a shaky sigh and looked down to glance at her watch ostensibly. Better not show that she was upset. After all, she knew what he thought of her. She shouldn't be surprised that he thought she smelled like a bottle of ecological disinfectant.

'We'd better have coffee before collecting the props from the warehouse,' she said, glancing back up.

Stefan reclined against the back of his chair and grinned. 'Ah yes, the props for the infamous Tarzan and Jane wedding…'

It was a real smile, and the first time he'd looked carefree and unguarded, and she had a glimpse of the man he must have been before his accident. She held her breath as a thousand feelings assailed her. The tips of her fingers tingled with the need to follow the line of his face, run through his brown hair, and rest on his shoulders. She longed to snuggle against his chest, feel the strength of his arms closing around her and the heat of his skin, and hear the beating of his heart… like that time, when she had woken him up and he had pulled her to him.

A sudden thought took her breath away. This physical attraction was confusing, burning, maddening, and felt very much like… infatuation.

She swallowed hard. Was she falling in love with Stefan Lambert?

She glanced up. He was looking at her. His eyes reflected the soft, golden glow of the fire, and a smile still played on his lips. She'd better pull herself together, or he would see right through her, and how mortifying would that be?

'About Kerry's wedding on Saturday,' she started, scrambling through her heated thoughts for something suitable – anything – to say. 'Don't worry if you can't come. It wasn't fair of me to put you on the spot earlier. You may have other things planned already.'

'I said I would come… as long as I can keep my shirt and trousers on, and you don't expect me to perform the Tarzan jungle call, and rescue Jane from the tree tops.'

The image made her sigh. What wouldn't she give to be Jane and be rescued by Stefan?

Chapter Twenty-Two

It was late afternoon by the time they arrived back at the campsite, but it was so dark by then it could have been the middle of the night. With only a few static caravans and chalets rented out and nearby Monks Water Lake looking like an abyss under the starless sky, the campsite had the look and feel of a ghost town. The pebbly beach and the jetty were deserted, and the tarpaulin covering the rental kayaks flapped noisily in the cold wind. The restaurant was shut for the winter, and only a handful of lights from houses dotted the shoreline.

'Are you sure you should carry all those into the clubhouse?' Cassie pointed at the boxes piled on top of one another in the boot of the Range Rover.

'We had that very same discussion in Keswick when I loaded them into the car, and I told you I was all right then.' What kind of man would he be if he couldn't lift a few boxes? he grumbled inwardly. He did his best to ignore the twinges in his back, and when he bent down to put the boxes on the floor in the clubhouse, he turned away so that Cassie wouldn't see him catch his breath.

When he'd lined all the boxes up against the wall, Cassie stood in the middle of the room and twirled on herself. 'In three days, this place will be unrecognisable,' she declared, flashing a smile in his direction.

He smiled back, not wanting to appear pessimistic but it was difficult to imagine how the uninspiring reception room, with its cream walls and tartan carpet, the bar at one end and wooden dance floor at the other, could be made to look even remotely like a rainforest fit for Tarzan and Jane and their pet monkey... or was it a pet elephant – or both? He couldn't quite remember.

'What do you mean, unrecognisable?' the campsite manager asked as he walked in.

Cassie gave the man a friendly smile. 'Hi, Patrick! I'm going to transform the clubhouse into a fake jungle.'

The man recoiled. 'A jungle? Nobody mentioned a jungle before. I thought this was going to be a normal, straightforward wedding reception.'

'Don't worry. The décor will be fun but tasteful,' Cassie said and she proceeded to explain her vision, getting more and more animated as she described the fake foliage on the walls, the multicoloured paper flowers and animal cardboard placemats she would design and cut out.

'I will hide animal masks among the foliage too so that they look as if they're peeping out of the leaves, and there will be yellow fairy lights all around the room. Do you think the bar staff would agree to wear grass skirts and flower necklaces?' She stopped to catch her breath and looked at the manager, who had grown very still and, Stefan thought, rather pale.

'So, you see,' Cassie finished, 'I have everything planned, and you have nothing to worry about.'

Patrick looked at her and scratched his head. 'That's a massive amount of work and you only have three days. Who is going to help you?'

Cassie looked surprised. 'No one... I'm doing everything myself.'

'There's no way you can possibly do all that alone. The place will end up looking a mess. The clubhouse has been hired out for a business meeting on Monday morning,' Patrick said. 'I can't see how you can tidy everything up on your own. I'm sorry, Cassie, but I have to put my foot down and veto the whole jungle idea.'

'I *can* do the whole room by myself in three days,' Cassie insisted, 'and I can tidy everything up for the meeting on Monday. I'm a cleaner. I'm used to clearing up mess!'

Patrick shook his head. 'No, love, it won't work. You

can put fairy lights up and make paper flower necklaces, of course, but that's all.'

'I've bought everything now, and Kerry is counting on me for her jungle. She'll be dreadfully disappointed.'

Cassie's voice wobbled, and her smile disappeared, but Patrick remained unmoved. 'You should have asked me before. I'm sorry.'

'It's not your fault,' Cassie said, shaking her head.

It was seeing the tears glisten in her eyes that did it. Stefan forgot all about his resolutions of living a quiet life and keeping as far as possible from the young woman.

'What if I helped Cassie set everything up and tidy the room up for Monday?'

Patrick frowned, looking unconvinced. 'You would help?'

Stefan nodded. 'I am in the army, so I'm used to organising things so that they run like clockwork.' He had no idea why it was suddenly so important to see the young woman smile again.

'And you're sure you can tidy up for Monday morning?' Patrick insisted.

'Positive.'

Patrick sighed and smiled at Cassie. 'In that case... I suppose you can go ahead.'

'Thank you, Patrick, you won't regret it!' Cassie clapped, ran up to him and gave him a resounding kiss on the cheek.

'Steady on, girl,' Patrick said but his grin belied the stern tone of his voice. 'I have one condition... No monkey business!'

He laughed at his own joke, and added, 'I'll leave you two to it, and I'll see you bright and early tomorrow morning.'

As soon as he had left Cassie looked at Stefan. 'Thank *you*.'

The happy smile she gave him was the best reward he could have hoped for. 'Don't mention it,' he grunted, but inside he felt absurdly pleased with himself.

He shoved his hands into his coat pockets, and cleared his

throat. 'I hope you know what you're doing, because the man was right. This is going to be a challenge, not to mention the fact that I may know about flying and fixing helicopters but I'm pretty useless at making paper flowers – not that I ever tried, mind you.'

Cassie laughed. 'Don't worry. I have everything planned. As for making paper flowers, there's nothing to it.'

He had his doubts, but he said nothing.

The following morning, Stefan met Cassie at the campsite at eight thirty. She issued him with a list of instructions before leaving for her cleaning jobs around the village, but popped back at regular intervals during the day to survey his progress, give him encouragement, and bring flasks of coffee, sandwiches and cakes from the village bakery.

After the umpteenth cream bun, he remarked that he would soon be too heavy to climb on a ladder, but she only laughed. 'The least I can do in return for all your hard work is feed you well. I'm sure Tarzan didn't complain if his Jane fed him too much when he was building their tree hut... he knew that he needed to keep his strength up, like you!'

Surprisingly, as he emptied bags and boxes, affixed netting and fake foliage to the walls, and even got to grips with the templates for the giant paper flowers, he found that he was enjoying himself. Perhaps not *really* enjoying himself, but at least he felt useful – more useful than he had in days, when he was just driving around aimlessly or brooding alone at Belthorn.

He tried not to think about what the guys at the base would say if they could see him cut and stick crepe paper to make paper flowers or exotic fruit under the direction of a woman with tousled blonde hair tied with a bright red bandana scarf and dressed in dungarees far too big for her, but whose smile lit up the room and the grey winter day.

'We have made great progress today,' she said, surveying

the room at the end of the first day. 'You are the best assistant I've ever had – not that I have had any. Thank you!' She stepped towards him until she was within touching distance, and for a second he thought she was going to kiss him, like she had kissed Patrick the day before. His body tensed, his mouth dried up, his breath hitched in his throat. Time stood still...

She didn't kiss him. Instead, she lifted a hand to the side of his face and brushed his cheek with her fingers. A piece of pink paper spiralled to the ground. She took a step back and smiled. 'That's better. We can't have you walking around with pink paper stuck to your beard, can we? That would spoil your manly demeanour.'

She turned round and busied herself with tidying the scissors, the balls of string and ribbons, the glue and the sticky tape, and he stood there with his heart drumming too fast. He was an idiot. Of course, she was never going to kiss him.

The following two days were more or less the same, with Cassie feeding him, fussing and giving instructions, tweaking the design or completely changing her mind about where she wanted the lights, the masks, the balloons...

She never stopped talking as she cut, glued, and made intricate paper flowers. She chatted about the village, about her grandfather, or about her work.

'The worst are the people who talk to me very slowly as if I am stupid; the couples who spend thousands of pounds on luxury holidays abroad but quibble my invoice every single month; the women who talk about their marital problems and their husbands' quirky bedchamber habits, or those who fantasise aloud about having an affair with the postman, the gardener or their gym instructor – or the three of them at once – and then blank me when I meet them in the village.'

She looked at the flower necklace he had just made and frowned. 'There's too much pink in that one... Anyway,' she added, 'thankfully most of my regular clients are lovely – my elderly ladies especially. We always have a chat and a cup of tea before I start work. I am worried about a couple of them who seem constantly sleepy and forgetful at the moment... a bit like my granddad, actually.'

Silence and Cassie didn't go hand in hand, but he soon worked out that she didn't expect him to venture an opinion or even answer with anything else other than a grunt or a mumble.

Being at the campsite gave Stefan the opportunity to keep an eye on Morse, who seemed busy shovelling snow, gritting paths, or carrying tools and equipment.

'He's all right for basic stuff like moving things around and cleaning,' Patrick said when Stefan asked for his opinion about Darren, 'but he's not much good at anything else. It's a wonder he managed to get a caretaker job at a posh retirement complex in Manchester, or at some of the top campsites in the country like Wizard's Point in Devon or King's Forest in Yorkshire.'

On Thursday afternoon, Cassie arrived with yet more cakes from Salomé's. 'Wow, it looks wonderful!' she exclaimed, looking at him as if he had completed a heroic feat when all he'd done was inflate some banana shaped balloons and affix them to the foliage. Nevertheless, his chest puffed with pride so much he had to give himself a mental shake.

Damn. He had it bad. Real bad.

'There isn't much left to do now, and it's all thanks to you,' she added, blowing a strand of hair off her face. She knotted her red bandana scarf as a headband, and flicked open the notebook in which she had drawn her plans and written her lists. 'We just need to put up the lights and we're ready, one day ahead of schedule!'

For the following couple of hours, they hung lights around the room, interweaving them with the netting that supported the foliage and the giant colourful flowers he had made. When the last box was empty, Cassie declared that they should pack up for the day.

'Kerry had better give you an extra large piece of wedding cake on Saturday. I could never have done all this without you.'

'I'm glad I could help,' he said as she locked up the clubhouse. 'You're good at this, especially considering the short time and the limited budget you had to work with. It's a shame you don't want to show your sketches to Charlie's sister.'

'I would never dare,' she said, pensive as they made their way to their respective vehicles in the deserted car park. The sky had darkened and a blue grey line ran along the ridge of the snowy peaks.

'Why not?'

'I don't want her to laugh at me and tell me to stick to mopping floors and scrubbing bathrooms.'

'Gabrielle would never say anything of the sort.'

She shrugged. 'Yes she would. You said you didn't know her very well, but she isn't a very nice person. I am flattered that you like my ideas but I enjoy being a cleaner and it's what I'm good at.'

Her phone rang from the depth of her handbag. She fished it out and put it against her ear. 'Rachel? What's up?' She gasped. 'No... when did that happen? Oh no. Poor Louis... how is he? What...?'

She glanced at Stefan and frowned. 'I'm on my way. Don't worry. I'll be there as soon as I can.'

She put her phone back into her bag. 'Louis broke his arm in PE this afternoon. He is at Kendal Royal Infirmary with Rachel and they need a lift home. Tim is in Carlisle and my granddad is babysitting Will and Ollie, so I'll have to go and get them.'

'Poor kid. Is he in much pain?'

'Rachel said he was being very brave. I am sorry to leave you in the lurch, but I promise I'll come by later.'

He frowned. 'Don't even think about it.' He couldn't help

his abrupt tone of voice. No matter how many times he told her he could take care of himself, the woman insisted on treating him like an invalid.

'In that case, I'll make it up to you tomorrow.' She unlocked the van, slid the back door open and started fumbling with the back seat, which was folded to one side. 'Oh, bother! I've had that seat folded for so long it's stuck.'

'Let me have a look.'

He tried to manoeuvre the seat back into position, but it wouldn't budge. After ten minutes, he had to admit defeat. 'I can't move it either.'

'What am I going to do? I can't have Louis and Rachel both sitting in the front with me, it wouldn't be safe.'

'Why don't I take you to the hospital in the Range Rover and drive Louis and Rachel back to the farm afterwards?'

She looked at him. 'Are you sure you don't mind?'

'Of course, I'm sure.'

'Then, I accept. Thanks.' Her lips stretched into a tentative smile, and she added, 'It seems that I've had a lot to thank you for these past few days. How can I ever repay you for all your help?'

He opened the passenger door of the Range Rover for her. 'Make me another of your steak pies and we'll call it quits.'

She laughed. 'It's a deal!'

The traffic was so bad it took over an hour to reach the hospital. He found a parking space and they hurried to the reception desk where Cassie gave the clerk on duty her cousin's name. The woman typed the name on her computer, and looked up.

'He's in the treatment room.' She smiled and gestured to the waiting area. 'You can make yourselves comfortable over there.'

Cassie sat on one of the brightly coloured plastic chairs, took her phone out and typed a message. 'I'll let Rachel know that we're here.'

Looking around, he spotted a newsagent and a coffee bar. 'Tea or coffee?' he asked.

'You don't have to get me anything.'

'I want a coffee, so I might as well get something for you.'

'Then I'll have a coffee too, please.'

He ordered two coffees and a blueberry muffin for Cassie, and scanned the shelves at the newsagent's for a magazine she would like. Celebrity gossip. Golf. Women's fashion. Gardening. An interior design magazine caught his eye. He bought it and made his way back to the waiting area.

'I hope we don't have to wait too long, and most of all I hope that Louis is all right. He acts tough but he's only a little boy, and Rachel sounded dreadfully upset.' Cassie's voice trembled as if she was about to cry herself.

He ripped the sachets of sugar and poured the sugar into her coffee and stirred it in, then handed the cup over together with the muffin.

She smiled at him, and whispered a thank you.

Time seemed to stand still. People were coming in and out – patients and their families, paramedics, nurses – and still there was no sign of Rachel or Louis. When they finished their coffee, he showed her the magazine he'd bought. 'Why don't you read this? It may help the time pass more quickly.'

'I love that magazine,' she said, reaching out for it. 'My granddad buys it for me every month, but he lost the latest issue.'

She put the magazine on her knees and started flicking through it.

Suddenly she stiffened, let out a gasp, and brought the pages closer to her face. 'I don't believe this!'

Chapter Twenty-Three

Cassie stared in disbelief at the photos of a bedroom with walls painted in sunny yellow with white and pale lavender stripes and furniture consisting of a Provençal style chest of drawers, a tall wardrobe and a cherry wood double bed covered with a white quilt and cushions matching the wallpaper.

Her fingers clasped the magazine more tightly as she examined every detail. It was no wonder she recognised the room. It was almost identical to the sketches she had presented to Nathan two years before, down to the embroidered counterpane, the delicate lace curtains that created enchanting patterns on the wooden floor as sunlight streamed into the room, and the bouquet of lavender sprigs standing in the clear glass vase on the bedside table.

According to the captions they featured a bedroom in the five star London boutique Maritel Hotel. How could this be possible?

Her throat tight and her brain fuzzy, she read the interview with Maritel Hotels' director, then read it again.

'*Nathan Hardman's delightful Provence-inspired designs for our London hotel won him the commission for the refurbishment of the whole of Maritel's UK hotel chain. We want him to replicate what he achieved in our flagship London hotel. His ideas are the mark of his incredible talent. He has managed to capture the very essence of our brand and the comfort, luxury and escapism that we want to offer to our guests.*'

Alongside the article was a photo of Nathan standing next to his drawing board, looking his usual sharp and handsome self in a navy three-piece suit, crisp white shirt and dark plum silk tie, his dark hair artfully ruffled, and his dark brown eyes moody and thoughtful.

'*The best ideas are often the simplest,*' he was quoted as saying. '*Provence will never be out of fashion, because it represents the ultimate nostalgia – a dream, a fantasy, of sharing simple, delicious food in the sunshine with friends and family, listening to the woody call of cicadas in the heat of a lazy summer afternoon, breathing in the scent of aniseed and lavender drifting in the air, and drinking a glass of chilled rosé wine or homemade lemonade.*' That was beautifully put – a lot better than she could ever have described the concept behind her designs, but then again Nathan was better educated and had been in the business for years.

According to the article, the hotel refurbishment had been completed a couple of months before and Nathan had travelled extensively to France then the US. Was that the reason why he hadn't been in touch to tell her he had used her ideas? Did he want to surprise her with the finished project before telling people that the whole Provence concept was originally hers?

A queasy feeling spread in the pit of her stomach. What if he had presented the Provençal scheme as his own and had no intention of giving her any credit for it? She dropped the magazine on her knees. No! Nathan would never do anything so dishonest... Then why had he not contacted her?

'This reminds me of a farmhouse in the South of France I once stayed in as a child,' Stefan said, pointing at one of the photos. He glanced at her, looking puzzled. 'What's the matter? Don't you like the photos?'

'I do. It's just that...' She might as well tell him. 'These were actually my designs – or at least, they very much look like my designs. I had no idea they had been used. Last time I saw them, Nathan... that's him, there... he told me they weren't good enough, but now, it seems he used them anyway.'

'Without asking you?'

'There must be an explanation. He is a very creative person, a wonderfully talented and innovative designer, but always very busy – too busy to get in touch with me, no doubt.'

'How well do you know the guy?'

'I cleaned his office in Ambleside for years. He inspired me to study for a diploma in interior design.' Her voice mellowed as she recalled the charming, seductive man she used to have a terrible crush on... Not any longer. He was still terribly handsome, and stylish, and he looked as moody and brooding as ever, but all she felt now as she peered at Nathan's photo was confusion.

'I see.' Stefan lifted his cup to his lips to drink, but must have tipped it too fast, and some of his coffee spilled onto his pullover and his trousers. He muttered something in French and took a paper napkin from the table to pat the stains dry.

'Cassie!' Rachel called from the doorway to the waiting room. She looked pale and worn out. Her handbag and Louis's rucksack hung from her shoulder, and she carried her son's anorak and school sweatshirt on top of her own bulky coat.

Next to her, Louis toddled in, sporting a bright blue and red splint on his arm. 'Look, Cassie. I have a spit on my arm,' he shrieked.

'It's called a splint,' Rachel corrected, almost stumbling under the weight of the coats and the bags, 'and remember what the doctor said. You're not supposed to mess with it and you have to keep it still.'

Cassie forgot all about Nathan and Maritel Hotels and jumped to her feet, followed by Stefan. Hurrying to Louis's side she gave him an awkward bear hug, taking care not to touch his arm. 'How are you, darling?'

Louis nodded. 'I'm all right now, but I'll have to come back for another test.' Turning to Stefan, he added, 'I was scared and I cried at first, but then I thought about you and how much you must have hurt when you broke your face, and I decided to be brave.'

'Crying is allowed, even when you're brave,' Stefan said, crouching in front of Louis and ruffling his hair. 'I cried too when I... broke my face.'

Rising to his feet, he reached out for the coats and Louis's rucksack Rachel was carrying. 'Let me take those for you.'

Rachel let out a sigh of relief as she unburdened herself of the coats and bag. 'Thank you, and thanks for coming too. I'm sorry I dragged you all the way here, but I didn't know who else to call.'

'Don't be. It's no problem.' He draped Louis's anorak on his shoulders, and made a show of pulling a face as he lifted his rucksack. 'What do you have in there? It weighs a ton – it's almost as heavy as my army bag.'

Louis looked up. 'Really? What do you have in your bag? Weapons?'

'No weapons, only tools and radio equipment, which are much more cool.' Stefan let out a low, rumbling laugh that gave Cassie shivers all over.

'I wonder what they are talking about,' Cassie mused as man and boy walked towards the exit, talking and laughing.

Rachel linked arms with her and tilted her chin towards Stefan's back. 'He's really nice, not at all the Grinch you've made him out to be.'

'He can be very short-tempered, believe me, but he has been brilliant this week. I could never have finished the clubhouse for Kerry's wedding without his help.'

Stefan had been more than brilliant. He had been kind, attentive and patient, following her instructions to the letter, and not getting frustrated if she asked him to take something down and put it up somewhere else in the room, then changed her mind again. Her heart had almost melted when earlier on at the clubhouse he had showed her the last of the paper flowers he had stuck to the walls and the banana balloons he had inflated, looking very pleased with himself.

Rachel gave her a nudge. 'So is he going to dress up – or down – as Tarzan to make the jungle décor more authentic?'

Cassie made a pretend gasp. 'Rachel Merriweather, you are incredible! Your son just broke his arm, you've spent hours in hospital, and all you can think about—'

'Is the body of the fit man my favourite cousin has taken a shine to,' Rachel finished. 'Tell me, has Tarzan tasted your lovely *trifle* yet?' She laughed and nudged Cassie again.

'Sshh now,' Cassie scolded, her face burning, as they reached Stefan's car. Rachel seemed bent on embarrassing her. Thankfully, Stefan was walking ahead with Louis so he hadn't heard her.

He lifted Louis into the back seat and strapped him in. Rachel winked at Cassie and sat next to her son, and Stefan held the passenger door open for Cassie.

Louis fell asleep almost as soon as they started on the road to Red Moss, and nobody spoke much during the drive back to Patterdale Farm, except for Rachel checking her phone and giving regular updates on Tim's journey back from Carlisle.

Stefan decided to drive straight to the farm. Cassie could always pick up her van from the campsite later. It was very late and snowing by the time they arrived at Patterdale. Stefan carried a sleepy Louis out of the car and into the farmhouse. Rachel asked him to take the boy straight to his bedroom so that she could put him to bed and led the way to the first floor, picking disregarded socks and toys off the stairs.

Cassie took off her duffle coat and hung it up in the hallway. The farmhouse was quiet, which meant that Ollie and Will must be in bed already, and her granddad had probably dozed off in front of the fire.

She pushed the door to the living room open and held her breath. Her grandfather sat snoring on the sofa – that she had expected – with Ollie and Will curled up on either side of him, asleep in their pyjamas. A storybook lay open on her granddad's knees.

She tiptoed into the kitchen. Plates smeared with tomato sauce and enough cutlery for a dozen people were stacked in the sink. On the table were dirty glasses, a bottle of blackcurrant cordial, and a half-empty packet of custard cream biscuits, her granddad's favourites.

Cassie couldn't help but smile. Her granddad may have left a mess in the kitchen, but at least he had fed the boys, got them ready for bed and read them a story. Being at Patterdale was good for him. Feeling needed was good for him. Hadn't Rachel said that he had displayed no signs of confusion or forgetfulness since he'd been at the farm? Perhaps living at Bluebell Cottage didn't suit him any longer. After all, she worked most of the time and unless he went to the community centre for a game of cards or dominoes, he had no one to chat to during the day… except Doris's cat and Darren Morse.

She filled the kettle and flicked it on. As the water boiled, she gave the kitchen a quick tidy up, took a slab of cheese and some ham from the fridge, some sliced bread from the breadbin, and prepared a round of toasted sandwiches.

'Can I help?'

She gasped and looked towards the door. Stefan leant against the jamb and pointed to the knife in her hand.

'I'm sorry. I shouldn't have startled you when you're holding a knife.'

She put the knife on the worktop. 'I'm making sandwiches. Would you like some?'

'That would be nice.'

'I wanted to thank you again for being so kind, for taking me to the hospital, driving us back here… and generally helping me out this week at the clubhouse. I hope you don't think I took advantage of you.'

'I don't mind if you do.'

He looked at her – a deep, searching look that went straight to her heart. He didn't smile, didn't move from the doorway, and yet it felt that the air was shifting, thickening, and some kind of strange force connected them and pulled them closer. Her body tensed and tingled in awareness. She should speak, say something. Her lips parted but she couldn't utter a word.

He was the one who broke the silence. 'By the way, your granddad is helping Rachel put the boys to bed, but he said he wouldn't mind a tipple and Rachel sent me to get some brandy.'

She nodded and indicated one of the cupboards. 'There's a bottle in there.'

He seemed to fill in all the space as he walked in. Brushing past her, he opened the cupboard, took out a bottle of brandy and reached out for the liquor glasses. 'Shall I get a glass for you?'

'Why not?' She tilted her chin, gazed into his eyes, feeling altogether hot, weak and dizzy now he was within touching distance. A little brandy would steady her.

Stefan put four glasses on the worktop, filled a small measure of liquor in two of them and handed her a glass.

'Santé.'

They clinked their glasses together, and Cassie drank hers in one big gulp. Fire erupted in her throat, and trailed all the way down to her stomach. She coughed and tears burned her eyes.

'That was a mistake,' she croaked, before coughing again and gasping for air.

'Allow me.' He slipped her empty glass out of her fingers and put it down. Stepping closer, he encircled her in his arms, pulled her against his chest, and gently tapped the palm of his hands between her shoulder blades.

Her cough eased off, then stopped, but he didn't move. 'Better?' As usual, his deep voice gave her goosebumps.

'Much better,' she lied.

She wasn't better at all. Her heart thumped fast and wild and the heat from his body penetrated through her clothing. She tilted her face up, arched against him and lifted her hands on to his shoulders. He tensed under her touch, his arms tightened around her, and fire burned in his tawny lion eyes. How she wanted to stay right there... and how she yearned for his kiss...

He wasn't moving. He hardly appeared to be breathing. Would she dare? Standing on her tiptoes, she pressed her lips against his, breathing in his scent, and shivering as the stubble on his cheeks rasped against her skin, making her body tight and hot at the same time.

It only lasted one second. Two perhaps. He didn't respond but remained hard and still. Then he released her and stepped back.

Chapter Twenty-Four

Joseph Bell walked into the kitchen and pointed to the toaster. 'Something's burning. Are you two just going to stand there like lemons or are you going to do something about it?'

Stefan stared at the smoke billowing out of the sandwich maker, breathed in the acrid smell of burning bread and snapped out of his daze. 'I'll sort it...'

'Let me do it.' Cassie rushed past him and unplugged the toaster. She got hold of the knife, flipped the cover open and proceeded to scrape the charred bread and cheese off.

'What were you two doing? Did you not notice it was burning?' Joseph asked looking from Stefan to Cassie.

'Obviously not,' Cassie replied without turning round.

Joseph shrugged, poured a generous measure of brandy into a glass, drank a mouthful and let out a contented sigh. 'Are you not having a drink?'

'We had one already,' Cassie said, still without turning round. She threw the charred bread in the bin, and started chopping some cheese – hacking at it, would be a more accurate description.

Joseph frowned. 'What's the matter with you, Trifle? You're making a right mess with that cheese.'

Cassie stared at the mound of cheese crumbs in front of her. 'Nothing's the matter with me, and when I need advice on how to slice cheese I will make sure to ask you.'

The old man whistled between his teeth. 'When you're like that, you remind me of your grandma the time I forgot our wedding anniversary.'

Turning to Stefan, he added. 'We'd better retreat to the living room with this excellent brandy. I have no intention of getting in the way of an angry woman with a knife.'

'Good idea,' Cassie snapped and she stabbed at the cheese again.

Joseph arched his eyebrows and gestured for Stefan to follow him. 'Are you having another drink, son?' he asked once they were in the living room.

'I'll pass, thank you. I'm driving.'

'You're right, of course.' Joseph cocked his head to one side. 'You wouldn't have any idea why Cassie is in such a foul mood, by any chance? You two haven't argued or anything?'

Stefan's face heated. 'Hmm... No.'

The rattling of the front door opening saved him from Joseph's scrutiny.

'I'm home!' Tim called from the hallway, before popping his head into the living room. 'Hi, Stefan. Hi, Joseph. I'm glad to be back. Where are Rachel and the boys?'

Joseph replied that the two younger children were asleep and that Rachel was putting Louis to bed, and Tim said he'd check on him.

As Joseph finished his brandy, he seemed to have forgotten all about his question about Cassie, which was lucky because Stefan would have been hard-pressed to give him an answer.

He knew what *he* was feeling right now – a mix of regret, frustration, and the bitter satisfaction of having done the right thing by pulling away from her before he succumbed to the burning desire to kiss her. However, he had no idea what Cassie was thinking. She had been warm and soft in his arms as she snuggled against him, and the feel of her lips had almost tipped him over the edge. It had taken all his willpower to stop himself from giving in to the sweet madness he yearned for, kissing her, pulling her closer, touching her. Thank goodness he had remembered just in time that it would be a bad idea on so many different levels.

He was a mess, and he was only in Belthorn for a few weeks – the time to sort himself out. He had no right to get involved with her.

What's more it wasn't him she wanted. He remembered the longing on her face when she had looked at Hardman's photo in the interior design magazine, and the way her voice had mellowed as she said how talented and inspiring he was. *This* was the man she wanted. The man she was attracted to. Not him.

She only kissed him because she was grateful. She said so herself. She was grateful for his helping her in the clubhouse, and giving her cousins a lift back from hospital.

Tim and Rachel came back downstairs. Rachel made some tea and coffee, Cassie brought a dish piled high with toasted sandwiches, and they all sat down at the table to eat. She didn't look at him, her cheeks were red, and uncharacteristically for her, she wasn't smiling.

'The snow has caused accidents everywhere,' Tim said as he sipped the generous measure of brandy Joseph had poured to warm him up.

Stefan frowned. 'Then perhaps we should leave straight away.'

Cassie glanced at him, then at the grandfather clock. 'Let's have something to eat first. Half an hour shouldn't make much of a difference.'

He wasn't sure it was a good idea, but she sounded so annoyed so he didn't insist. The conversation around the table rolled around Louis's accident and Rachel's sister's forthcoming wedding, which prompted Joseph to regale them with a few risqué puns about Tarzan and Jane, and the odd policeman joke, then Rachel mentioned some gossip she'd overheard at school that morning.

'Another of your clients got burgled yesterday,' she told Cassie.

Cassie put her cup of tea down. 'Oh no! Who was it this time?'

'Tabitha Sweeney. All her jewellery and some cash were stolen when she was at her gym class. Her husband is mad at her because she didn't switch on the alarm, and now the insurance won't pay out.'

Cassie gasped. 'Tabitha always puts her alarm on. She must have been very distracted to forget it yesterday.'

'Or someone knew the code and disabled it,' Tim remarked.

'I don't think it's possible. Apart from her husband and herself, only her in-laws and I know it.'

'People are getting nervous,' Rachel remarked.

Cassie nodded. 'I'm not surprised. Nadine Hartley is a good friend of Tabitha's and she has tons of expensive jewellery. She's bound to review her security arrangements now.'

'At least, we don't risk anything here,' Rachel said. 'I don't have any jewellery worth stealing, and even if I had, nobody would get passed the dogs.'

'What do you mean, you have nothing worth stealing?' Tim protested. 'You have your engagement ring and the bracelet with the gold charms I bought you when the boys were born.'

Rachel leant against her husband's shoulder. 'How can I forget?' Turning to Stefan, she added. 'Do you know what charms my husband gave me to thank me for the hard time I had giving birth to his three sons?'

Tim's cheekbones flushed bright red. 'It was a joke, Rachel… and I'm a farmer after all.'

Oblivious, Rachel carried on, 'He bought me a sheep, a tractor and a cow! If he thinks that's an incentive for me to produce baby number four, he is seriously mistaken.'

Joseph laughed. 'Give the lad a break, Rachel. Tim loves you and the boys, and that matters more than any piece of jewellery. Anyway, I've been thinking about those burglaries. We've never had so much trouble in years. It's a shame Keith retired to Tenerife. He could have helped.'

He looked at Stefan and explained. 'Cassie's step-dad used to be a policeman. He would probably put those burglars in the nick in no time at all. Perhaps he could give us some idea about what's going on.'

'Keith is enjoying his retirement far too much to worry about burglaries in Red Moss, Granddad,' Cassie said, 'but I suppose I could always ask for his input next time I Skype Mum.'

Something had been niggling at Stefan's mind during the conversation. 'How many burglaries have there been so far?' he asked.

Cassie looked at him. 'That's the fifth one, and all the victims are my clients. People are going to believe that I bring bad luck.'

'Or that you're in league with the burglars,' Rachel said.

'Don't be silly,' Joseph retorted. 'No one who knows our Cassie would ever believe that.'

'I hope not, but you know what people are like...' Rachel stifled a yawn and started clearing the table. Joseph drank the last of his brandy. Whereas Stefan had stuck to coffee, Cassie's grandfather had been rather liberal with the liquor.

'Let's have one last joke before bedtime,' he insisted.

'I hope it's not another of your policeman's jokes,' Cassie remarked. 'We already had three tonight.'

Rachel chuckled. 'Or another naughty Tarzan and Jane one... I thought Stefan was going to choke on his sandwich because of your double-entendre about bananas.'

'Give over, Rachel! The lad's French, and everybody knows that the French are the masters of seduction. Stefan here isn't shocked by a few risqué puns, are you, son?' Joseph winked at Stefan, who forced a smile. Master of seduction? Had the old man taken a good look at him?

'Anyway,' Joseph added, 'your Kerry had better get used to hearing more naughty jokes. She's the one who wanted a Tarzan and Jane wedding reception after all. And who knows? That jungle theme may whip a bit of life into that stuffy fiancé of hers.'

He clasped his hand onto Stefan's shoulder. 'Are you ready for another joke, son? I promise there is nothing naughty about this one.'

Stefan seemed to have become the elderly man's guinea pig for testing his riddles. He hadn't been able to guess any answer so far, and was starting to feel rather stupid.

'Here it is. What do cows drive in Antarctica?'

Stefan sighed. Hell, why did Joseph always have to ask him for answers he didn't have? 'Hmm... Ice cream floats? Four-hoof-drives?'

He looked at Joseph. 'How am I doing?'

Joseph pulled a face. 'You're not even close.' He turned to Cassie, Tim and Rachel. 'Anybody else want to hazard a guess? No? Then here is the answer to my riddle. What do cows drive in Antarctica? Snow-moo-biles!'

Cassie smiled. 'That's very silly, Granddad, even by your standards.'

Silly or not, her grandfather's jokes seemed to have improved her mood.

Rachel got up and yawned. 'We'll need snowmobiles tomorrow morning if the weather doesn't improve! For now it's time to go to bed.' She looked at Cassie, then at Stefan. 'What are you two doing? Do you want to stop here for the night?'

'Thanks for the offer but I'll take my chances.' He glanced at Cassie. 'However, I'll understand if you'd rather stay here.'

Cassie shook her head. 'No. I'll go back with you. I'm sure we'll be fine.'

She kissed Rachel, Tim and her granddad goodnight, and put her coat and hat on.

Tim shook Stefan's hand as they were leaving. 'Thanks for picking Rachel and Louis up from the hospital. I really appreciate it. I'll call round at Belthorn in the morning. I'm on snow-ploughing duty with guys from neighbouring farms and the manor house is on my round.'

The goodbyes took a few more minutes, and then he was driving down the farm track with Cassie at his side.

It had only been one hour since Tim had come back but any tracks he might have left earlier were now covered with a mantle of snow so thick it was hard to see where the lane ended and the ditches on either side started. He could have done with one of the snowmobiles from Joseph's joke, he thought as he focussed on keeping the Range Rover on the road. Snowflakes danced in the beam of the headlights and stuck to the windscreen and wipers, enveloping the car in a white cocoon. Even the noise of the engine sounded muffled.

'What's happening over there?' Cassie pointed to blue and red lights flashing ahead. A police four-wheel drive was parked across the road, and two officers signalled for them to stop. Stefan wound his window down.

'There's been an accident, you can't get to Red Moss this way,' one of the policemen told Stefan. He explained that a twenty-mile diversion would take them back to the other side of the village, and the campsite where Cassie had left her van. 'But all the roads in the area are pretty bad, sir, and we can't guarantee that you won't get stuck further down.'

Stefan thanked him, and turned to Cassie. 'The best option is to take you back to the farm. You can always get your van tomorrow.'

'What about you?'

'I'll drive to Belthorn after dropping you off.'

She shook her head. 'Actually, it would be safer if we both went back to Belthorn together and I stayed overnight… that's if you don't mind.'

His heart skipped a beat, but he wasn't stupid enough to read anything into her suggestion. 'Are you sure?'

'I have been so focussed on the wedding reception that I've neglected my work for the past few days. If I stop over, at least I can spend some time in Belthorn first thing tomorrow morning before driving to Keswick for my meeting with Piers. Tim said he was coming up, so he can give me a lift back to the campsite on his tractor.'

Of course. The woman was as usual only thinking about her job.

'I don't keep timesheets, you know, and won't report you to Charlie or that estate manager of his if you miss a few days,' he said, not even trying to hide the temper in his voice.

She sighed. 'I know, but there's another reason I'd rather come with you.' She looked at him. 'I don't want you to be driving back on your own. It's not safe on a night like this. You could get lost or stuck on country lanes.'

He thought for a moment. She did have a point. Being alone on the road in a snowstorm was dangerous, but so would being alone at the manor house with Cassie...

'Are you sure that's what you want?' he asked nevertheless.

'It's the only sensible thing to do,' she replied.

He did a U-turn, and headed back towards the manor house.

If driving down from the farm had been difficult, it was even more treacherous to tackle the lane up to Belthorn. The wheels of the Range Rover kept spinning, and Stefan had to ease off the accelerator several times until the tyres bit into the snow again and the car sprung forward.

'I knew it would be bad, but I didn't think it would be this bad,' he muttered as the headlights swept over the lane, or what should be the lane.

Huge snowdrifts had accumulated on either side, reaching out almost to the top of the Sanctuary Stone. The car slid sideways. The steering wheel spun in his hands, light and unresponsive, and there was nothing he could do. The Range Rover bumped into the Sanctuary Stone with a dull thud, and the engine coughed and stalled.

'Damn. I don't believe this. Twice in the same place!' He turned to Cassie. 'Are you all right?' The impact hadn't been strong enough to deploy the airbags, but she may still be hurt, and he wouldn't be able to forgive himself if anything happened to her.

She nodded. 'I'm fine.'

He let out a sigh of relief, unbuckled his seat belt and took the key out of the ignition. 'There's no point trying to start the car again. We won't have enough traction to go any further, so I guess we're walking. Make sure you wrap up well.'

He switched off the lights, slipped the key in his coat pocket and jumped down. 'Wait. I'll help you get down.'

The snow reaching up to his knees, he walked around to her side, yanked the door open and held his arms out. 'Jump!'

She nodded and launched herself into his arms. Letting go of her once her boots touched the ground, he slammed the passenger door shut then stretched out his hand. With snow so deep, she would struggle to walk up the lane.

'Hold my hand and walk in my steps.'

Stefan trudged in the snow, and Cassie walked in his footsteps. He held onto her small, gloved hand, aware that she trembled and stumbled more and her breathing sounded more ragged and uneven with every step.

'Keep moving! Come on! Don't stop!' he urged every time he felt she was faltering.

He was focussing so much on taking her to the safety of the manor house that he ignored the telltale signs his own body was sending him. Ignored the increasing tightness across his shoulders, the sharpening ache in his lower back, and the burning in his legs. Stopping even for a minute was out of the question. With the snow falling thick and fast, and the icy gale howling from the fells, they needed to keep moving.

Cassie's hand gripped his more tightly as they neared the top of the lane. She didn't complain, didn't ask to stop and catch her breath. At last the house emerged from the shadows, its outline barely visible in the storm.

'Hang on a bit longer,' he shouted, pulling harder on her hand. 'We made it.'

He unlocked the front door, and they stumbled into the hallway, bringing the whirling blizzard in with them.

Having divested himself of his gloves and parka, he made a fire in record time and soon flames crackled and shot up in the fireplace. The wind blew into the chimney, wailing and lamenting, and making the fire hiss and pop. He let out a sigh of relief. At last they were safe.

He turned round and his chest tightened. Cassie had taken her boots off, and now stood in her stripy red and green socks, with her dungarees caked with snow from the knee down and her pom-pom hat still on. She looked like some Christmas elf the storm had blown in.

He wanted to smile. Tell her she could take her hat off now. But most of all he wanted to take her in his arms and hold her tight until she was warm and dry.

Instead, he stepped aside and gestured for her to come close to the fire.

'I'm sorry I put you through this. I should have been more careful driving up the lane. I should have…'

She looked up. She had stopped shaking, but her face was still very pink from the freezing wind. 'It could have been a lot nastier. You did well to get us back here safely.' She touched her shoulder and pulled a face. 'Although the way you dragged me up that lane it's a miracle I didn't dislocate my shoulder.'

'I'm sorry,' he said again, but she put her finger on his lips before he could say any more.

'Stop apologising. Without you, I would never have made it back here. I never thought I would one day say this, but I'm glad to be at Belthorn!'

He captured her hand in his. It was freezing cold, and he cursed himself again. 'I shouldn't have listened to you. You would have been far better staying at the farm with your family instead of being stuck here with me.'

There was something in her eyes now – something warm and soft and inviting that reminded him of the way she had looked at him in the kitchen at the farm earlier. His heart skipped a beat, as hope, caution and cynicism warred inside him.

'What if there was no one I'd rather be stuck with?' she asked.

Chapter Twenty-Five

He didn't reply. Didn't say anything. Perhaps she hadn't spoken loud enough. Or, and it was more likely, he was racking his brains to find words to let her down gently. Why had she even spoken? How stupid of her to throw herself at him again when he had turned her down once already that evening!

He let go of her hand, looked down. Shadows and flames danced in his eyes. 'What do you mean?'

Would she dare tell him what she felt?

She tilted her chin up. 'I'm glad to be snowed in with you, because I...' She should be brave for once, and come out with it. 'I am attracted to you.' There, she had said it!

She held her breath, but he still didn't speak. Her chest tightened, and a tidal wave of embarrassment flooded her.

'All right...' She sighed. She'd better make something up, slink away whilst her pride was still intact.

'I'll go to the kitchen and make some coffee. I'm sure you could do with some.'

She was about to turn away when he bent down, and pinned her to the spot with just one burning look.

'I don't want coffee.'

'Oh?' Her pulse picked up pace and she gazed at him in confusion. Was she misreading the heat and the longing in his eyes once again?

'I want to do this.' He lifted a hand to her face, and she tensed as he cupped her cheek and stroked the outline of her mouth with his thumb, making her shiver all over.

His eyes softened. He smiled, bent down further, and kissed her – a light, gentle touch of the lips, a barely there kiss, as if he was holding back to give her time to change her mind.

With a muffled cry, she lifted her hands to his shoulders, moulding her body to his and revelling in the feel of his

202

broad, hard chest. He cradled her against him, and kissed her again. She tasted the snow on his lips, and the cold wind on his skin. She shivered with pleasure as he trailed kisses down her throat, and revelled in the strength of his arms around her as he held her tight and lifted her off the ground.

'You're cold,' he said, putting her down lightly.

'My clothes are wet.'

His fingers slid up and down her back, tracing patterns that made her skin tingle.

'Mine are too. We should do something about it.'

'What do you have in mind?' She was getting dizzy and breathless now.

The hint of a smile flickered on his lips. 'Perhaps we should take them off. We don't want to catch a cold, do we?'

Did he really want her as badly as she wanted him, or was it all a dream? 'It's a wonderful idea.' Her voice husky with desire and emotion, she looked at him and smiled.

At once heat blazed in his eyes, and he held her more tightly.

'I love your smile, and I love those cute little dimples you have here...' He kissed the side of her mouth. 'And here.' He kissed the other side. 'It makes me crazy just to wonder if you have any in other places.'

Feeling wicked and naughty, and very much unlike her usual self, she let out a low chuckle. 'Then why don't you find out?'

He wanted her so much he ached, but he would take it slowly even if it killed him. Fire raged in his blood as he slid one hand at the back of her neck and stroked her soft, delicate skin. She shivered under his fingertips, and a rosy blush spread on her face.

The light from the fire painted sunny streaks in her hair as he combed his fingers through it. She threw her head back with a shaky sigh, offering her throat to his kisses.

Slowly still, he unzipped her fleece and slid it off her shoulders.

'How do you take these dungarees off?' he asked in a raspy voice as he fiddled with one of the metal clasps holding the garment up.

She deftly undid both buckles, the dungarees slipped down to her hips. Her grey top moulded her curves so perfectly he couldn't resist. He brushed his knuckles against her breasts, revelling in the feel of the tips hardening under his touch and the sounds of her breathing. Her fingers fluttered along his spine, tickled the back of his neck, and his body hardened further. This was torture – sweet, intolerable torture but he didn't want it to end.

He kissed her mouth again, slipped one hand under her top, and explored. Her skin was smooth and silky, her breasts so generous his mouth became dry and he let out a low moan. He wanted to see her – all of her. He wanted to touch, taste, and bury himself inside her. He lifted the T-shirt over her head, and let it drop to the floor. Next he pushed the dungarees past her hips. They pooled at her feet and she stepped out of them. With a muffled moan he bent down to kiss the hollow at the base of her throat. His fingers traced the contours of her face, trailed down her throat, her round shoulders and along her arms all the way to the inside of her wrists. He caressed the sides of her waist, cupped her breasts, and revelled in their weight and fullness in his hands.

'You are beautiful,' he whispered, circling the tips of her breasts with his fingers until they pebbled and darkened underneath the white bra. White heat flashed inside him, almost blinding him with desire. He wanted her naked and under him. He wanted her calling his name, touching him, surrendering. He buried his face in her hair, breathing in the fresh lemon fragrance he had come to associate with her. Combined with the feminine scent of her skin, it was the most potent elixir, and he felt almost drunk and lightheaded.

'I want to make love to you so much I'm going out of my mind,' he whispered.

'What are you waiting for?' She locked her fingers at the back of his neck, pressed her body closer and made a sexy, low humming sound that drove him even wilder. Her lips trailing tantalising soft kisses at the side of his neck, she slid her hands under his jumper, un-tucked his shirt from his jeans, and made contact with his bare skin.

He drew in a sharp breath as her fingers skimmed his chest, glided on his abs, ventured lower. It was her turn to touch and tease. It was fair enough, but he didn't know how long he could take it.

Stepping back, he got rid of his pullover, almost ripped the buttons off his shirt in his haste to undo them, and stood, shirt open to his bare chest, in front of her, every part of him aching for her.

'Wait a minute.' Still in her underwear, she crossed the room to close the curtains – as if anybody was likely to venture to Belthorn in the middle of a snowstorm, except perhaps that Grey Friar who was rumoured to haunt the grounds of the abbey – then walked up to the fireplace to switch the fairy lights on.

'I don't need fancy lights to make love to you.'

'No, but it's so much prettier, don't you think?' she asked with a shy smile.

And then reality hit him. A blast of freezing cold air spread into his heart, filled his chest, made him stumble back. What was he doing? He was a broken, ugly brute with a body covered with scars, and a grouchy temper, and she was the most delightful woman he'd ever laid his eyes on.

She couldn't want him. Not really. Hell, she just said she needed fairy lights to make the décor more appealing. She wanted a man like that designer whose photo she had sighed over – the sharp, handsome, dark-haired designer bloke who she said had inspired her. A hard lump formed in his gut.

He stood like a block of ice and let out a hollow laugh. 'It will take more than fairy lights to make me look pretty, you know.'

She came back to him and touched her lips to his chest, showering him with kisses as he stood still. 'I don't care for a pretty man. I care about you,' she said between kissing and teasing him. Her mouth, her hands glided over his bare skin, tormenting him.

He put his hands on her shoulders and pulled away slightly. 'Are you sure?'

She lifted her head up and laid her hand against his cheek. Her eyes were filled with heat and unfocussed, the grey irises clouded with arousal. Her lips were red and swollen, her face flushed.

She nodded, but didn't say anything. She didn't need to. Weak with relief, he enfolded her into his arms, enjoying the feel and the scent of her body, and the sounds of her breathing. She fitted so well against him, and nestled in his arms as if it was the most natural place to be. They didn't speak, didn't move. The fire crackled softly behind them, the flames painted shadows on the walls. Outside the howling of the wind had ceased, replaced by an eerie quiet.

It was the calm before the storm.

Cassie kissed the side of his mouth and slid the sides of his shirt off his shoulders, tugging on the sleeves until it dropped to the floor. Her lips kissed the jagged scars on his chest with such innocence and tenderness his heart expanded with pure joy.

A moment later innocence fizzled out when she stroked his chest with long, lingering, teasing touches. The mood changed, sizzled with tension and pleasure, and pulsed with dark, throbbing desires.

He brought his hands to her shoulders, slid the straps of her bra and yanked the triangles of fabric down to expose her breasts. Slowly he pushed her pants down, and took them off.

When she was naked, he enfolded her in his arms, lifted her up and brought her to the sofa where he lay her gently down, then he looked at her and held his breath. Her blonde hair draped over the cushions, and her bare skin glowed in the light of the fire. She looked wild, tantalising, and beautiful.

And when she reached out for him and called his name, his heart did something strange and powerful, something it had never done before. It roared and thundered and proclaimed that she was his.

Chapter Twenty-Six

'I'll never think about a feather duster in the same way ever again,' Stefan said, trailing Cassie's brand new blue feather duster along her leg, from her hip all the way down to the sole of her foot. She tried to roll away but the bed wasn't big enough to escape him, or the feather duster.

He had found a brand new duster in the kitchen cupboard as he fetched a bottle of wine and two glasses, and hadn't been able to resist taking one upstairs.

He kissed her bare shoulder. 'Who would have thought that this innocent looking fairy had such a naughty implement in her cleaning arsenal?'

Laughing, Cassie hid her leg under the duvet. 'There's nothing naughty about my feather duster, at least not when *I* use it. You're the one with the wicked mind.'

He dropped the feather duster to the floor, put a finger on her lips, and brushed her hair aside to kiss the curve of her neck. 'I didn't used to have a wicked mind. You worked your magic on me, *Mademoiselle la fée chasse-poussière*.'

'What does that mean?'

He smiled. 'It means "dust-busting fairy", but "*chasse-poussière*" is also the name given to a type of sandstorm in the Sahara Desert. They're little whirlwinds, just like you. I could also call you *chasse-tristesse* because you have worked wonders for my mood too.'

'Did I?' She didn't look convinced. '*Chasse-tristesse*,' she repeated. 'I like that.' She closed her eyes and relished the feel of his lips on her skin, the tenderness in his voice. 'I haven't quite finished working on you, actually. You are still terribly crabby and short-tempered at times.'

Dropping the feather duster to the floor, he rolled on top of her, lifted her arms on both sides of her head and intertwined his fingers with hers. The fire in his eyes was mesmerising. The heat and weight of his body took her breath away, his strength made her feel small and frail and very female, but it was the intimacy of their linked fingers that caused her heart to beat faster.

'Then perhaps you should perform a little more magic.'

His eyes darkened. He kissed her, and she was lost once again in a tumult of love and pleasure.

'I'm glad we came up to my room,' he said a while later, wrapping his arm around her waist, and pulling her on top of him. 'My bed is a lot more comfortable than the sofa downstairs.'

'I agree.' The sofa had spiky springs and hard lumps, and her back would probably sport bruises for days to come. She dare not imagine what it might have done to Stefan's back.

He pointed to one of the paintings opposite the bed. 'I believe that painting refers to a story about a hunchback and a swan.'

She glanced up, surprised. 'That's right. How do you know that?'

'André Vaillant mentions it in his diary. Can you tell me what it's about?'

'It's an old folk tale – a kind of Cumbrian *Beauty and the Beast* fairy tale.'

She expected him to laugh or make some kind of disparaging comment, but he said nothing. His fingers slowly stroked her waist. Perhaps he was falling asleep.

'Go on,' he said, his deep, rough voice reverberating inside her.

'Very well… There was once a hunchback who lived in a small cottage overlooking a lake. For years he went down to the lake every morning to feed a beautiful white swan, despite people making fun of him and children throwing stones at him. One morning, the hunchback didn't come. The swan waited all day, and the following day too, and the day after that, but still the hunchback didn't come. So the swan waddled to the cottage. It craned its neck to peer through the window, and saw the poor hunchback lying on his straw mattress. He wasn't moving. He didn't appear to be breathing. The swan broke the glass with its beak and managed to get inside the house, but it was too late. The hunchback was dead.'

His hand stilled. 'Is that it?'

'Not quite.' She kissed his chest, nestled closer and listened to the beating of his heart. 'The swan plucked her feathers with her beak and stuck them on the hunchback's arms, his shoulders, his chest, bit by bit covering all of his body with gleaming white feathers. And from that day on, there wasn't just one swan gliding on the lake, but two.'

'Some story,' Stefan said after a few moments.

'Why was the French soldier referring to this old story in his diary?'

'Ruth's parents were opposed to Vaillant courting their daughter. They wanted her to marry that rich farmer – Hardy – and laughed at her for being a hopeless romantic. Vaillant had been left a cripple when his plane was shot down, you see, and from what I gather Ruth was a pretty young woman.'

'That's true. She was stunning. My grandmother had old photos of her. I'll ask my granddad to dig them out if you want.'

'So it seems that Ruth was the swan and Vaillant the hunchback.' He let out a harsh laugh. 'A bit like you and me, now that I think about it. You're the beautiful swan and I'm the grumpy infirm.'

She refused to take the bait. He was no hunchback, no cripple. He was a strong, vibrant man, and if he wanted her to say otherwise then he could wait for a long time. She sat up, bent down to retrieve the feather duster from the side of the bed and tickled his chest.

'I am flattered to be compared to a swan, but you should know that the only feathers I am prepared to stick on you are these blue ones, and I don't think they'll help you glide gracefully on Wolf Tarn.'

She only got a few indulgent smiles for her efforts at tickling him before his hand shot up, his fingers encircled her wrist and he pulled her to him.

'Enough.' Desire flashed in his eyes.

'Or what?' she asked, licking her dry lips and straddling him.

He didn't answer but pulled her further towards him, and soon heat and pleasure spread inside her, and all she could think of was to show him how much she wanted him. How much she loved him.

Outside the night had grown silent. The storm must be over.

'You promised to tell me what was in the diary,' she said when she rested, content and fulfilled, in the crook of his arm.

So he told her about Vaillant's stay at Belthorn, about his love for Ruth and his fight with Gideon Hardy at Patterdale Farm. 'I still have a few pages left to read, but perhaps I could translate the diary for you.'

'Why don't you fetch it now so we can make a start?' She stifled a yawn.

Stefan chuckled and kissed the top of her head. 'Not now. You should sleep. It's late.'

'I'm not tired, and I don't want to sleep. I want to…' Her voice trailed off, her eyes closed. Her body slackened, and her thoughts drifted away like clouds pushed by the wind.

'It's been a long and exciting day,' she thought she heard him whisper just before she fell asleep, 'and this little fairy has to rest…'

Chapter Twenty-Seven

'Tim is here,' Cassie announced as she glanced out of the window to see her cousin's tractor pull up in front of the manor house.

Stefan wrapped his arms around her and she nestled against him. 'I was hoping we could stay snowed in a while longer.'

'So did I, all the more because I have that dreaded performance review with Piers this morning.' She stood on her tiptoes to kiss him. He slid his hands on her hips, drew her closer and kissed her until she was hot and breathless.

The sound of the tractor horn outside made them jump, and she tore herself from Stefan's embrace.

'I'll ask Tim in for breakfast, if you don't mind,' Cassie said. 'Knowing him, he must have been out clearing roads since dawn.'

'Good idea. I'll make some coffee.'

She opened the door as Tim was jumping from the cabin of the tractor. He opened his eyes wide when he saw her on the threshold.

'Cassie? What are you doing here, and where is your van?'

'I had to leave it at the campsite overnight. The road to Red Moss was blocked so I came back here with Stefan. We both thought it was the most sensible option, but it turned out that Stefan's Range Rover couldn't get up the lane and we had to walk back in the end.' She was aware of talking too fast, and too much, but she couldn't help herself.

Tim nodded. 'Yes, I saw it near the Sanctuary Stone. I'll pull it out of the ditch with my tractor on my way back. It shouldn't be too hard.' He frowned and looked at her. 'I hope you didn't have too many nightmares. I know how much you hate this place.'

She gave a casual shrug but it felt like her face was on fire.

'It wasn't too bad. I was tired and I slept like a dream. All night... in one of the guest rooms... on my own.' She stopped babbling and let out a forced giggle.

'Hmm... Did you, now?' Her cousin smiled slowly.

Her face must be bright red. She cleared her throat. 'Anyway, I'm sure you could do with a hot drink.'

'Great idea.' Tim frowned. 'Are you sure you're all right? You look a bit flustered.'

She let out a silly laugh. 'Of course I'm all right. Come in.'

Tim followed her into the kitchen where Stefan was making a pot of coffee. The two men shook hands and started talking about the weather and the state of the roads while Cassie tried to calm herself down by slicing up some bread. The last thing she wanted was for Tim to suspect that something had happened between Stefan and her and report back to Rachel, and her granddad.

Stefan poured coffee into three mugs and handed her one.

'It makes a change, me waiting on you,' he remarked.

'Thanks.' Their fingers brushed, causing her face to heat up again.

'My pleasure.' Stefan's voice had gone deeper. He smiled, and Tim frowned as he glanced from one to the other. He may not be the most perceptive of men, but if they carried on that way he would guess something was going on. She moved away from Stefan, put a pile of toasted bread, some jam and butter on the table and sat down.

'The Mountain Rescue Service is out training near Patterdale Farm later today,' Tim told Stefan as they ate breakfast. 'One of the new SAR helicopters is scheduled to take part. Why don't you come over so I can introduce you to the team? It's not every day we have an ace helicopter pilot at Red Moss.'

Interest flickered in Stefan's eyes, but almost immediately a bitter line appeared by the side of his mouth. 'I'm anything but an ace pilot.' He turned to the window, his face stony.

'Do come,' Tim insisted. 'You might like to compare notes with the pilot about rescue missions in different terrains and weather conditions. You're used to desert and sandstorms. He deals with mountains and snow blizzards. I'm sure you'll find it interesting.'

Stefan remained silent for a moment, then nodded. 'Well... all right, why not?'

'Great. Come to the farm after lunch, and we'll go together.' Tim got up. 'For now, we'd better pull your car out of the ditch.'

They finished their breakfast and piled up into the tractor's cabin to rescue Stefan's Range Rover. They towed it back onto the lane, and Stefan and Cassie were soon on their way to the campsite.

The roads were mostly clear by then and it didn't take long to get there. Stefan didn't talk much on the way. She wasn't even sure he listened to a word she said. He helped her out of the Range Rover but he didn't hold her in his arms as she had hoped. Instead he took a couple of steps back. A fist squeezed her heart until it hurt. Was he trying to tell her that he was having second thoughts about them?

He stood in front of her, and raked his fingers in his hair. 'Would you like to meet later today? We could go to the pub, or get a takeaway pizza and eat at Belthorn. That way, you could stop over tonight again, if you didn't want to drive back to the village, that is...'

He seemed so insecure suddenly that her chest filled with love. He wasn't letting her down at all. He was afraid that *she* had changed her mind! She would have to show him that she wanted him more than ever. Closing the gap between them, she linked her arms around his neck, and tilted her face right up to look into his eyes.

'I would like that very much. I'm meeting Kerry here at six, so I'll get the pizza afterwards and come to Belthorn to play with you and my feather duster. How does that sound?'

He didn't smile. Didn't say anything, but his eyes grew darker and he encircled her in his arms and lifted her up until she was almost at eye level with him. And whilst her feet dangled from the ground and she was pressed against his chest, he kissed her – a long, hot, leisurely kiss that made her heart dance and her soul fly.

When he finally put her down, she had trouble catching her breath. She loved him so much… She had to tell him, but not now. She would tell him later, when they were alone at Belthorn.

For now, she mumbled a feeble, 'See you tonight.'

She climbed into the van, waved him goodbye, and set off on her way home, with love and sunshine in her heart, blue sky in her eyes and a huge grin on her face. Was it possible to be so happy? She had been thoroughly loved and would be again, if Stefan made good on the hot promises he had whispered to her the night before and his parting kiss was anything to go by.

Gritting trucks and snowploughs had been out in force, and she was back at Bluebell Cottage in no time. She changed, gathered her files for her meeting with Piers, and was about to leave when her eyes fell on her design books. She recalled the article about Nathan in the design magazine. Perhaps she was indeed naïve, but she couldn't believe that the man she admired so much and had had such a massive crush on would be dishonest enough to use her work without giving her credit for it.

She had to get in touch with him, but it would take time and tact to write without appearing hysterical or vindictive, and right now she was in a rush. The email would have to wait.

Piers greeted her with a frown. 'You're late.'

'I'm sorry,' she said, hot and flustered from rushing across the town centre. 'It's market day, and the town centre is so busy I had to park on the lakeside.'

He didn't need to know that she had stopped at a stall of hand knitted woolly hats to buy Stefan a hat almost identical to her own, and a hardware shop for his very own feather duster. She couldn't stop grinning as she imagined him unwrapping his silly presents on Christmas Day...

Piers gestured for her to take a seat, and she sank into the leather armchair in front of his desk while he flicked open a thick file. After a couple of minutes, he looked up, his pale blue eyes filled with concern, and asked in a soft voice.

'How are you, Cassie?'

'I'm fine, thank you.'

He shook his head. 'No, really. How are you?'

'I told you. I'm—'

He lifted his hand to stop her. 'Coping with your clients, the holiday cottages and Belthorn on your own can't be easy now that Sophie has left.'

She shrugged. 'I am busy, that's true, but I have managed so far.'

He looked down, flicked through a few papers and pulled a sheet out. 'Are you sure about that? I regret to have to tell you that I've had some complaints about some of the holiday cottages.'

The blood drained from her face. 'Really?'

'I'm afraid so.' He started reading. '*We found a dirty dishcloth behind the television when we arrived at Lakeview Cottage, and one of the beds wasn't made although we had booked for four people.*'

'But...' She had made up the beds in both bedrooms, she was sure of it. As for the dishcloth, there was no way she would have misplaced it behind the television... Was there?

He lifted a hand. 'Let me finish.' He looked down again and carried on reading, '*The cottage was dusty and old-fashioned.*'

'I cleaned the cottage thoroughly as usual and can assure you that there wasn't a speck of dust when the guests arrived. And you can hardly blame me for the furniture and the wallpaper being old-fashioned! I did suggest a few changes to you to give the holiday cottages a fresh new look but you declined.'

He gave her a patronising smile. 'You're a cleaner, not a designer. It's not your job to give houses makeovers... Anyway, this wasn't the only complaint.'

He looked down. '*Very disappointed with our stay at The Brambles. We didn't like the biscuits on the welcome tray. We found spiders in the bath when we arrived, and the overpowering smell of lemon in the cottage made my wife sneeze all week.*'

'This couple is demanding compensation or they will write a bad review on a number of holiday internet sites,' Piers added.

Cassie blew a frustrated breath. 'I can't help it if people don't like Salomé's biscuits. I always buy the same ones – the ones you agreed to, if I remember correctly. And if this gentleman's wife was allergic to my cleaning products, they should have put the diffusers outside and told us about it immediately. I would have freshened up the house and cleaned with another product. As for spiders, this is the countryside and I can't do anything about them.'

She smiled. 'You know very well that some people will try anything to get a refund. Remember the woman who claimed there were too many Spaniards in Spain and the sand on the beach was too hot?'

Her smile faltered in front of Piers's stony face.

'What about all the lovely things people have written about the cottages?' She opened her file and showed him the printed photos of the guests' comments praising the clean, friendly feel of the cottages, and the delicious treats on the welcome tray.

Piers didn't even look down. 'Bad reviews count more than good ones, you know that. Besides, there is something else. Something a lot more serious.'

He pulled out another sheet, which looked like a list. 'I had an inventory made of a couple of cottages this week and found discrepancies between what should be there, and what was actually there. Several pieces of equipment appear to be missing. Cast your eyes down the list and tell me what you think is happening here.'

He pushed the paper towards her. She tried to make sense of what she was reading but her heart was beating too fast now, and the words and figures swam in front of her eyes. Was Piers accusing her of theft? It sounded like it. She urged herself to focus on the list of items missing from the cottage inventory: one digital radio, one hairdryer, a luxury blender and juicer, a Bluetooth speaker, and a pair of binoculars.

She frowned and looked up.

'And that's just for Riverside and Lakeview,' Piers said. 'Who knows how much is missing from the other cottages?'

She pushed the paper back and tried to straighten in the armchair, but it was very deep and she was too small, and it made her feel like a naughty pupil summoned to the head teacher's office.

'That is indeed worrying. From what I remember, these cottages haven't been rented since last October. I haven't been there for weeks.'

He arched his eyebrows, reclined on his chair and crossed his fingers on his stomach. 'Still. I would like to hear your views.'

She took a deep breath. 'What exactly do you want me to say, Piers? Perhaps the inventories weren't properly recorded after the last rentals.'

'Or perhaps someone has been helping themselves to the equipment and selling them off in pawn shops, hoping nobody would notice.'

She would not take the bait. If he wanted to accuse her of theft, then he would have to be straightforward about it. 'That sounds unlikely. I mean, this kind of stuff is hardly going to sell for much.'

He directed one of his innocent baby blue stares at her and arched his eyebrows. 'You tell me.'

Silence stretched between them.

'Anyway, we'll talk about this again in the New Year,' he said at last. 'By the way, I had an email from Charlie asking how you have been getting on with Lambert at Belthorn. Having seen the man myself the other day, I gather it can't be that easy to be around him every day. He is so ugly and battered I bet he gives you nightmares.' He chuckled.

Anger flashed inside her and she jumped to her feet. 'How dare you make fun of a brave man who nearly lost his life trying to save people?'

He arched his eyebrows and whistled between his teeth. 'I had no idea you had taken such a shine to the man.'

'Stefan is a wonderful man, and it is true that I do... like him very much.' She loved him, but she couldn't tell Piers that – couldn't tell anybody – perhaps not even Stefan.

'It is true that you seemed to get along quite nicely in the pub the other day.' Then he smiled and let out a loud breath. 'Of course, I get it. It's the bonus!'

'Sorry?'

'I should have thought of it before. You're cosying up to the guy to make sure you get your bonus at the end of January, aren't you?'

'What?' This time, shock rendered her speechless.

He checked his watch, and rose to his feet. 'I booked a table at the Troutbeck Hotel for one o'clock. We still have a few things to discuss, including the increase in the rent for Bluebell Cottage.'

Her chest tightened. 'You never mentioned any rent increase before.'

'Let's go for lunch. Talking business will be more pleasant in a less formal setting.'

'Formal is fine by me.'

'But you were late and I'm hungry. I can't talk business

219

on an empty stomach.' He gave her one of his boyish smiles, patted his belly, and said in a low voice, 'You know me. I'm a big boy, with a large appetite.'

'I'm not dressed smartly enough for the Troutbeck,' she objected, pointing to her dungarees and Doc Martens boots.

'You look fine. In fact, you've never looked more… appealing.' His gaze travelled from her face down to her boots and back up again, lingering a fraction of a few seconds longer than necessary on her chest.

'Shall we go?'

She didn't want to, but what choice did she have?

'Are you not taking your paperwork?' she asked.

'No need. I have all the facts in here.' He pointed to his forehead.

She pushed her own file back into her bag, slipped her duffle coat on and followed him into the street. The Troutbeck was an upmarket establishment overlooking the park. A waitress welcomed them, led them to a table tucked away in an alcove, and asked them what they wanted to drink.

'Two glasses of Mumm Champagne,' Piers told her, without consulting Cassie. 'Actually, sweetheart, make it a bottle.'

'I won't be drinking, Piers. I'm driving.'

'Nonsense. I bet you don't drink good champagne very often.' He sighed and looked around. 'It's nice here, isn't it?'

She nodded, but felt too preoccupied to appreciate her surroundings. 'Very nice. So, what were you saying about Bluebell Cottage?'

He laughed and raised his hands in front of him. 'Slow down, Cassie. Let's enjoy this meal, and each other's company, first. We have time to talk business.'

A solemn-looking waiter placed an ice bucket on the table and proceeded to uncork a bottle of champagne. There was a discreet popping sound, and he poured some wine into Piers's flute.

He nodded. 'Perfect.' And the waiter filled their glasses.

Piers raised his glass. 'Let's have a toast. To us and a long and enjoyable relationship.'

What was he playing at? One minute he had more or less accused her of theft and deception, and the next he was treating her to champagne. All through the meal, he was charming and attentive, and it was hard to determine if she was reading too much into his words and the way he looked at her, or if he was back to his old tricks and flirting with her again.

'Damn, the bottle is empty,' Piers said as he poured the last drop of champagne into his glass. 'Shall we have another?'

She shook her head. 'Not for me, thank you.' She'd only had a glass, but whether it was because she wasn't used to it or because Piers was making her uncomfortable, it tasted like acid and had given her stomach cramps.

Leaning across the table, he grabbed hold of her hand before she realised what he was doing and turned it over to stroke the inside of her wrist. 'Lovely, sexy Cassie.'

She pulled her hand back in shock. 'What are you doing?'

He sighed and combed his fingers into his mop of light blond hair, once again giving her his trademark boyish grin. 'You need to loosen up, darling. Nobody likes a girl who can't enjoy a bit of fun. In business, like in personal relationships, you have to be flexible to succeed. A little "give and take" goes a long way. Now about the small matter of Bluebell Cottage…'

He stopped talking as a waitress was bringing them coffee and chocolate truffles. 'Where were we? Ah yes, as you know Gabrielle Ashville is breathing down my neck about the estate not being as profitable as she had hoped, and I need to find extra sources of revenue. Bluebell would bring a lot more money as a holiday cottage, so I'm afraid I am going to have to terminate your grandfather's lease in the spring… unless he agrees to a substantial increase in rent.'

'How substantial?'

'With the cottage being on the large side and located in the centre of the village, I think I can ask for at least two thousand pounds a month.'

Cassie had been expecting it, but her disappointment was still acute. 'There's no way my grandfather can come up with that kind of money. It's almost triple what he's been paying so far.'

Piers shrugged. 'I'm afraid it's only what Charlie and Gabrielle would expect.'

'But my granddad has lived in that house for over forty years!'

'Perhaps it's time for him to move... and for you too. It can't be fun to live with the old man, however entertaining he is. However...' He popped a truffle in his mouth, leaving a dusting of cocoa on his lips. 'There is another possibility.'

'Oh?'

He licked the cocoa powder from his lips, and looked at her. 'It's no secret that I've always found you attractive. I booked a room here for the afternoon. Come up with me and we'll talk no more about the lease for your grandfather's house.'

Cassie recoiled in shock. She had been right to be wary... A wave of nausea rose inside her, but she took a few deep breaths and tried to remain calm. Her hands shaking, she folded her napkin on the table, picked up her handbag from the floor and stood up.

'You can stick your room and your champagne,' she said in a quiet but clear voice. 'I wonder what Gabrielle would think about your "give and take" approach to business. I bet she wouldn't take too kindly to her estate manager blackmailing women employees into sleeping with him.'

His grin froze and his eyes became hard. 'It's your word against mine, Cassie. You are making a big mistake by threatening me. Don't you know what is at stake here for you?'

'I do.' And it was making her sick with worry, but the

alternative was even worse. 'Goodbye, Piers.' Without warning he grabbed hold of her arm and pulled her towards him. He was a big man, and his fingers held her in an iron grip.

'You led me on,' he said between clenched teeth. 'All this time, you smiled and teased, and let me touch you, you little bitch.'

She swallowed hard, a feeling of guilt and self-loathing almost overwhelming her. He was right, in a way. She should have been more assertive, should have pushed him away before instead of tolerating his behaviour and hoping that he would stop by himself.

'You're hurting me,' she said in a stronger voice, although she felt anything but strong inside.

'Consider yourself fired,' he spat and let go of her so suddenly she stumbled backwards, attracting glances from people at nearby tables.

Holding her bag tightly, her eyes swimming with tears of shame and rage, she hurried across the restaurant to the lobby where she retrieved her duffle coat, and rushed out of the door.

Once outside, she ran into the deserted park, crying and gagging and heaving, bent double and was sick behind a bush.

Chapter Twenty-Eight

'Come in, my dear.' The woman peeled her gloves and beret off, patted her curly grey hair back into place, and gestured for him to follow her into the kitchen.

'You were very kind to give me a lift. I don't know what I would have done without you... You're that nice young man who is staying at Belthorn, aren't you?'

Stefan smiled. 'I am indeed staying at Belthorn, but it's a while since anyone called me young or nice.' Although thanks to Cassie, that morning he felt relaxed, happy and carefree for the first time in ages.

He pointed at the woman's shopping bags he was carrying. 'Where do you want these?'

'Put them on the table and sit down while I make us a drink. You must be hungry too. I have some shortbread biscuits from our village bakery. The girl may come from Spain, but she knows how to bake proper shortbread.'

He pulled out a chair and sat down as she busied herself making tea. He didn't dare tell her that he wasn't keen on tea. He'd just have to smile and drink up.

'Here you are,' she said a moment later as she placed a plate of biscuits and a mug of hot tea in front of him.

'I realise I didn't introduce myself. I'm Gwendolyn Parker.'

He stood up to shake her hand. 'Stefan Lambert.' Her name was familiar. 'Are you the primary school head teacher, by any chance?'

She took a shortbread finger and bit into it. 'Retired head teacher, thank heavens. I didn't realise my notoriety had spread all the way to France.'

He smiled. 'It hasn't, but Mason Austin mentioned your name a couple of weeks ago. He said you were a gold mine of information about the village.'

Stefan drank a sip of tea and repressed a grimace. It was strong and bitter, despite the milk the woman had poured in. 'I was hoping to talk to you one of these days about a diary I found at Belthorn.'

Curiosity shone in her eyes. 'A diary? Tell me about it.'

'It's the diary of a French pilot who stayed at Belthorn for a few months in 1919. His name was—'

'André Vaillant.' She looked at him. 'Am I right?'

He nodded. 'You heard about him.'

'Indeed. His love affair with a local girl created a scandal at the time, all the more when it ended in terrible tragedy.'

'Ruth Merriweather drowned at Wolf Tarn.'

'That's right. The poor girl died, and her unborn baby too, of course...'

He blinked in surprise. 'She was pregnant?'

'I'm afraid so.'

'How do you know?'

'My grandmother was the village midwife. She told me about Ruth's affair with her French sweetheart.'

'There are people who believe that Ruth's drowning was no accident, and that she wanted to die because Vaillant had abandoned her.' That was what Cassie believed.

'Suicide was indeed put forward at the time, but there were other rumours too.' She sighed. 'It's such a long time ago. It wouldn't do any good to raise the ugly ghosts of the past now.'

'I'm not sure it would do any good,' he said, 'but Ruth's family – and Vaillant's relatives if he still has any – might be interested to know what really happened.'

The woman munched on her shortbread, looking thoughtful. 'I shall think about it. There is another family to consider, you see, and I don't want to stir up bad feelings in the village.'

She was making him even more curious. Whom might she be talking about? It was however obvious she wouldn't say anything now, so he finished his tea and rose to his feet.

'If you change your mind, please let me know. Thanks for the tea and biscuits.'

She looked at him and chuckled. 'You don't like tea much, do you?'

He was about to shake his head in denial, but something told him that Miss Parker would see straight through him. He nodded. 'Not much. I prefer coffee. Black. No sugar.'

She didn't look in the least offended. 'I'll make sure I remember.'

Back in Red Moss, he wandered around the streets for a while. Nestling in the valley and surrounded by snowy peaks, the village looked pretty and welcoming. Christmas garlands dangled from lampposts, almost every door was adorned with festive wreaths, and posters stuck in shop windows announced the Christmas Fair. The cold breeze smelled of snow, wood smoke and pine trees. Children ran around laughing in the courtyard of the small primary school. Passersby smiled or nodded at him, some he'd seen in the pub and others he had never met before.

The warm, fuzzy feeling he'd had since waking up with Cassie in his arms returned, only stronger. It was as if the wind had blown away the thick, stifling grey fog that had weighed down on him for months and he could see clearly for the first time. Perhaps he could stay at Red Moss, find a house, and make the place his home?

He glanced at a few shop windows as he walked around the village. One of them offered an eclectic mix of clothing and jewellery, expensive stationery and artwork. A display of quirky necklaces in the window attracted his attention. Among them was a tiny, delicate white swan, carved in what looked like porcelain, hanging from a fine gold chain.

A swan... It was perfect for the woman who had rescued him from his black moods, and given him a reason to smile again, to hope again.

The door chimed when he pushed it open. A petite woman

with pink hair looked up from a book she was reading behind the counter and smiled.

'Hi! It's nice to see you. How are you doing?' she asked, as if she knew him.

He frowned. He was sure he'd never seen her before. 'Fine, thanks... I'd like the swan necklace in the window, please.'

Her smile widened. 'These necklaces are made by a local artist. She made several of the others, but only one swan,' she said as she bent down to reach out for the necklace in the window.

She brought the necklace to the counter and held it up to show him. 'Did you know that in Roman mythology, the swan was associated with Venus, the goddess of love?'

His face heated up. 'I didn't... but it sounds about right.'

She cocked her head to one side and gave him a wistful smile. 'There is also a local legend, a rather lovely one, I don't know if you heard of it. The Swan and—'

'The Hunchback,' he finished. 'Yes, I know of it.' Pity the artist hadn't made a porcelain hunchback. He could have bought it for himself...

Ten minutes later, with the necklace all wrapped up in pretty pink paper and safe in the breast pocket of his coat, he decided to call at the garage to ask Mason if he fancied a bite to eat at the Eagle and Child. The fact that he, who had come to Red Moss to be alone, was actively seeking someone else's company didn't hit him until he walked into the garage and smiled at Brenda in response to her enthusiastic wave from behind her office's glass window. What a difference a night filled with the love of a gorgeous woman made...

Mason welcomed his suggestion with eagerness. 'I've been up to my neck with breakdown calls since dawn. I need a beer and an hour of peace and quiet. Give me a minute to scrub my hands and make myself presentable.'

Fifteen minutes later, both men ordered pie and chips and

half a pint of beer, and sat down at a table near the window overlooking the main street.

'Ah... That's better.' Mason smacked his lips after drinking a long gulp of his beer. 'How did you get down from Belthorn? I would have thought the road impassable.'

'Tim cleared the snow with his tractor so that Cassie and I could drive down. Without him we would have been snowed in, especially as I had crashed the Range Rover on the lane last night.'

Mason looked up, an incredulous glint in his eyes. 'Again? It wasn't that Grey Friar or one of Belthorn's other ghosts that scared you off the road by any chance?'

'No. It was only the snow and my bad driving.'

'Don't worry about it, mate. The lane to Belthorn is notoriously treacherous. How did Cassie take it – having to spend the night at Belthorn? She loathes the place.'

'Well... no, she seemed completely... ahem... fine about it.' His ears and cheeks felt hot suddenly. Damn. He was blushing again...

Thankfully, Mason didn't appear to notice. 'Good,' he said. 'By the way, do you know how Cassie is getting on with her new tyres? I can't believe I didn't check what was wrong with her old ones. It turned out they weren't even punctured.'

Stefan put his pint down. 'They weren't?'

'No. They were only deflated. The valves must have been faulty or damaged.'

Could Morse have been fiddling with the valves that Saturday afternoon at Belthorn? And could he confide his suspicions to Mason and ask for his help, or should he keep them to himself and deal with Morse in his own way?

He looked out of the window, and watched people go in and out of the shops for a minute or two. Much of the snow had been cleared from the roads, and a narrow path had been dug out on the pavements, but the scene was still very wintry. It couldn't be a bigger contrast with where he had been the previous year. Then there had been only scorching heat, vast planes of red or golden sand, grit and rocks... and war. He knew and accepted the risks, even though he had never truly believed that anything would happen to him. He had got out unscathed from too many perilous situations before, and that had made him arrogant and over-confident.

His fingers tightened around his glass. Because of him people had died. Good, innocent people. Women, elderly people, children... and Isa, who would never have another Christmas.

If he had learned anything since, it was that he couldn't handle everything alone. He may have only just met Mason but there was a connection, and not just because they both knew about engines, cars and bikes. Mason was a good man, and he was a friend of Cassie's. He could trust him.

'Actually, there was something I wanted to talk to you about, although you may think I'm mad.'

Mason put his knife and fork down, leant back in his chair and smiled. 'Go on.'

In a few short sentences, Stefan related Morse's visit to Belthorn, and Cassie's encounter with him on the road moments after she found that her van's tyres were flat.

'It could be a coincidence, of course, although having faulty valves on two tyres at the same time is highly unusual,' Mason commented. 'Morse strikes me as an oddball, but as far as I know, people seem to like him. I can ask around, if you like.'

'I would appreciate it.'

Mason smiled. 'I'm glad Cassie has you to look out for her. She's a smashing girl and a good friend. She deserves... well... I suppose she deserves to be happy and well cared for.'

Once again, Stefan's face felt hot. He had no idea if he was the man who would make Cassie happy, but he would make sure he'd look out for her. He grunted a non-committal noise and drank up his beer.

Mason went back to work, leaving Stefan with a couple

of hours on his hands before meeting the Mountain Rescue Service at Patterdale. He ordered a coffee, took his phone out and googled Morse. Unsurprisingly he found that there were a lot of men called Morse.

It was time to narrow the search. Patrick had mentioned that Morse had worked in campsites around the country, and he remembered a couple of names – Wizard's Point in Devon and King's Forest in Yorkshire – which may be enough to triangulate information. He inputted several combinations but once again drew blanks. He put his phone down with a frustrated sigh. This was pointless. He didn't even know what he was looking for.

What if he tried Manchester? That's where Morse was from. Patrick had also mentioned a luxury retirement home there. He picked up the phone again. This time he got a hit, one link to the crime reports section in the *Manchester Herald*. He clicked on the newspaper link. It was an article dated three years before regarding the theft of cash and valuables at an old people's home in Prestwich. Police had interviewed all residents and members of staff but their enquiries had unfortunately been inconclusive. Several names were listed, among which was Darren Morse who worked there as a caretaker.

Stefan was about to look for more information when he glanced out of the pub's window and spotted Joseph Bell standing across the main street, looking at a piece of paper and frowning. Suddenly the old man staggered and sat down heavily on a nearby bench.

Stefan grabbed hold of his coat, waved goodbye to the waitress and rushed out. By the time he reached Bell, Joseph had slumped on the bench, his head in his hands.

Leaning down, Stefan put a hand on his shoulder. 'Is everything all right?'

Cassie's grandfather looked up. 'Ah, it's you, son.' He nodded. 'I'm having a rest. My knee is playing up.' He grimaced and rubbed his knee. 'Arthritis, you see. It must be the weather.'

The paper he was holding trembled between his fingers. It looked like a bank statement. When he saw Stefan looking at it, he stuffed it into his pocket and held his hand out. 'Help me up, son.'

Stefan heaved the old man to his feet. 'Do you need a lift back to Patterdale Farm?'

'It's kind of you to offer, son, but Rachel is taking me back later. Young Louis was feeling well enough to attend school this morning so she's gone to work, and I popped into the village for a few errands.'

He smiled. 'By the way, Tim said that our Cassie spent the night at Belthorn because the village road was blocked. It's lucky you were there to look after her.'

Stefan frantically tried to find something suitable to say. Telling Joseph that he had made love to his granddaughter most of the night was probably not what he had implied by him looking after Cassie. His face grew hot, again. Damn it, he was making a habit of this blushing business...

'I hope she was... ahem... comfortable enough,' he muttered.

'Good. Good.' Was there a twinkle in Joseph's eyes or was it just the sunlight?

'Actually, there's something I need from Bluebell Cottage. Would you mind coming with me, that's if you've nothing better to do, of course? With my bad knee and with the pavements being slippery, I could do with a steady arm to lean on. I don't want to fall and end up in Casualty with a broken bone, like Louis.'

'Sure.'

Once in front of the cottage, Joseph let go of Stefan's arm and fished a key out of his coat pocket. 'Let's hurry. I don't want Doris from across the road to see me. The woman scares me to death. She believes I'm trying to steal her cat when I can't abide the damned animal.'

Stefan repressed a smile at his panicked expression and the way he darted furtive glances across the street as if his neighbour was about to come out of her cottage and beat him with her walking stick.

'I have to agree with you that she is rather formidable. I met her on Tuesday when Cassie came back here to let the cat out.'

Joseph glanced up, a surprised look on his face. 'He came in again? I swear I'm going to start charging that cat rent soon.' He unlocked the front door and pulled a face. 'Come in, quick!'

Stefan did as he was told.

'Now, my lad, would you mind going upstairs and getting a file for me? I'm having a spot of bother with my bank and I need to check my papers, but I don't think I could manage the stairs just yet.'

He gave Stefan a description of the file he was after, and added, 'It's in the top drawer of the filing cabinet, in the back room. Second door on your left.'

He lowered himself onto a chair at the kitchen table, once again, looking old and forlorn. In fact, he hadn't cracked a single joke yet.

It didn't take long to find the file Joseph was after, all the more because it was sticking out of the drawer, preventing it from closing properly. As Stefan lifted it out, he spotted more files at the back, with stickers with names on, some of them he recognised. Hartley. Gasby. Sweeney. Bennett – wasn't that the vicar's name? Larger ones at the back read 'Ashville Cottages' and 'Belthorn'. The files must be Cassie's.

As he shut the drawer, something fell at the back of the cabinet with a hard thump. He bent down to retrieve it, and pulled out a chunky magazine he recognised straight away. It was a copy of the interior design magazine he had bought Cassie the day before at the hospital, the one with the photos of her hotel room designs, and the photo of her former boss.

He swallowed hard as the unpleasant sensation he had experienced in the hospital waiting room tightened his chest once more and left a bitter taste in his mouth. Jealousy – if that's what that nasty, gut-wrenching feeling was – wasn't something he cared for.

He put the magazine on top of the filing cabinet and was about to walk out when the radiator emitted a loud gurgling sound, and a damp patch spread on the carpet below.

He went back downstairs file in hand and put it on the kitchen table.

Joseph thanked him. 'I'd be grateful if you didn't mention my troubles to Cassie. I have been a little under the weather and have got sidetracked with my finances lately. Nothing serious, you understand, and I don't want her to worry over nothing. Can I count on you?'

What could Stefan say? He didn't like the idea of keeping secrets, but he nodded. 'By the way, your radiator is leaking.'

'Young Darren has been working on that radiator for weeks,' Joseph said. 'He said it was sorted last time he came.'

Stefan frowned. 'Do you want me to take a look? It shouldn't be too hard to fix.'

'It's nice of you to try. I have a few tools in a box under the sink. While you're up there, could you also get my arthritis medication from the bathroom cabinet? I've been fine without it until today, but I guess I'd better start taking it again.' He gave him the name of the medication and told him it was in a red and yellow box.

Back upstairs with the tool box in hand, it didn't take Stefan more than five minutes to identify the problem with the radiator, select the appropriate tool, and stop the leak, and a further five to lift the wet carpet and make sure there would be no lasting damage to the floorboards underneath.

Anyone with the most basic skills would have done the same, so what had taken Morse so long to *not* do the job?

What if he had just pretended to work? Stefan glanced at

the filing cabinet where Joseph stored his bank papers and Cassie some of her clients' files...

He rose to his feet, pulled the drawer towards him and grabbed the file named Gasby. From what he remembered, the woman had been burgled recently. Flicking through the papers, he found what he was looking for – a cleaning schedule for the past few months and notes detailing if Mrs Gasby had been in or out when Cassie had been cleaning at her house.

He put the file back and took another one out. Sweeney. The name had been mentioned at Patterdale Farm about yet another burglary. Once again, the file contained cleaning schedules with a snapshot of the woman's diary and weekly activities. Anyone studying the schedule would see a pattern emerge, and be able to select a day and time when the house was likely to be empty to commit a crime.

Anyone pretending to be fixing a radiator, that is...

Chapter Twenty-Nine

Kerry's car was already in the car park when Cassie arrived at the campsite. She unloaded the flip-flop flamingo that she had just collected from Cecilia's shop, taking care not to catch the long legs or the beak of the bird in the door, and locked the van. Cecilia had been very giddy – all twinkling blue eyes, lopsided smiles, and hints about Tarzan – but it hadn't been enough to restore the glorious mood of that morning...

Her body ached from scrubbing, dusting and polishing every inch of the holiday cottage Alastair had booked for the London friends who were coming to the wedding, and her eyes hurt from crying tears of rage and humiliation after the disaster of her lunch with Piers. More than anything, she was ashamed – ashamed to have let the situation with Piers run for so long; ashamed not to have told him before that she wasn't interested and not demanding that he stop groping her. It was her fault. She had been weak and pathetic, and now she was paying the price...

She had been so downhearted that she hadn't even tried any of the beautiful dresses Cecilia had selected for her. She would have to be careful about money from now on. Piers had terminated their arrangement, and without the Ashville holiday let contract, Bluebell Cleaning was as good as finished.

'Things are going to be a bit tight. I can't afford to buy a new dress,' she had confessed to her friend.

'Then I'll let you borrow one,' Cecilia had replied, before selecting a diaphanous knee-length grey dress that matched the colour of her eyes. 'I'm sure your French Tarzan will only have eyes for you in that dress.'

Cassie walked carefully on the gritted path to the clubhouse, her arms full of a pink flamingo taller than her. What else could go wrong today? Kerry might hate the jungle makeover, have one of her infamous tantrums and pop all the balloons Stefan had blown with her spiky heels, and demand real monkeys instead of the cardboard cut-outs Cassie had designed.

The door of the clubhouse swung open and Kerry walked out, a beaming smile on her pretty face.

'Cassie! I love it! It's beautiful *and* fun!' Her excited voice pierced through the night, followed by the clicking of heels as the young woman rushed down the steps. 'Here, let me help you with that... thing.'

'It's a flamingo made of recycled flip-flops, coming all the way from Kenya, via Cecilia's Studio,' Cassie explained as Kerry grabbed hold of the flamingo's feet and helped her carry it into the clubhouse.

They put the bird down and Kerry wrapped Cassie in a tight hug. 'Thank you so much. You've made my dream come true.' As the young woman pulled away, she was smiling but her eyes glistened with tears.

'You like it that much? Really?' Cassie gestured to the mock tropical forest, the paper flowers and animal masks peeping through the fake foliage, bathed in the golden glow of the fairy lights strung around the room.

'I told you. I *love* it!'

Cassie breathed a sigh of relief. The day wouldn't be a total disaster after all. 'Where do you want the flamingo? You're the bride, you decide,' she told Kerry, 'but I think it would look better here... or...'

Kerry nodded. 'Put it anywhere. I don't mind.'

The sounds of a car engine, of doors closing and men's voices outside interrupted her. Cassie glanced at Kerry. 'Is that Alastair? I thought you wanted to keep this a surprise for tomorrow.'

Rachel's sister blushed. 'I didn't think you would do such a great job. One of Alastair's friends is an interior designer... I asked him if he could join us and help with any last minute changes, but it turns out there's nothing to change,' she added quickly. 'It's just perfect as it is.'

The door creaked open, and Alastair strode in, looking very conservative as usual in his tailored navy blue coat, pinstriped suit and white shirt. He smiled at Kerry. 'Hello, darling. I heard on the grapevine that there was a Tarzan party. Is it true or was it all just a lot of bananas?'

Cassie shook her head in disbelief. Had prim, starchy Alastair just cracked a joke?

'I think you'd better stick to writing wills and powers of attorney,' a tall, dark-haired man said behind him.

Cassie blinked in surprise, and her mouth gaped open. Nathan Hardman, looking even more film star gorgeous than she remembered, glanced around the room and whistled between his teeth.

'Wow, that's brilliant. Kitsch, but brilliant nonetheless, especially since you only had a few days and a ridiculous budget to sort everything out.'

Kerry ran to her fiancé's side, snaked her arms around his neck and gave him a resounding kiss on the lips. 'Isn't it fab?'

Cassie stepped into the centre of the room. 'Hi, Nathan.'

It was Nathan's turn to be shocked. 'Cassie? Well, I never… How are you?'

She smiled. 'I'm fine. And you?'

'I'm good.' He frowned. 'So, the Bluebell Cleaning Fairy van parked outside is yours. I should have guessed.'

'I took over my mum's business when she retired, and made a few changes, including the name and the van.'

'I see you're still wearing dungarees.' He smiled and looked around again. 'So this is your doing. It's great.'

She couldn't help the glow of pleasure and pride inside her. 'Thanks but I can't take all the credit. A friend helped me. I wouldn't have been able to finish on time if it hadn't been for him.'

'I'm sorry I dragged you all the way here for nothing, old

chap, when you still have to drive to the holiday let, unpack your stuff and get ready for the stag do,' Alastair told Nathan. 'I should have trusted Cassie to do a great job and have everything under control.'

Nathan shrugged. 'Don't worry about it... Actually, I could murder a pint. Who is up for a drink at the pub?'

Kerry and Alastair replied that they were meeting the vicar for a last minute talk about the ceremony.

'What about you?' Nathan asked Cassie.

A drink with Nathan... Two years before she would have swooned at the idea. All she could think of now was that this was her chance to ask him about Hotel Maritel. 'I have a couple of things to sort out here, but why not?'

'Great. I'll meet you at the Eagle and Child.'

Once alone, Cassie forced herself to focus on putting the finishing touches to the décor and making sure everything was in order for the reception the following day, but she was shaking with nerves. She hated confrontations, especially after the ugly scene with Piers earlier on, and had no idea how to broach the subject of her hotel designs with Nathan.

Her fingers froze as she realised she was folding the petals of the same paper flower over and over again. She put the flower down. She was only wasting time... She should be brave and drive to the pub right now to ask Nathan for an explanation. As the horrid altercation with Piers had shown her that lunchtime, procrastinating only led to trouble.

Nathan was sipping a beer and chatting to Sadie at the bar when she walked in. She ordered an orange juice, and they took their drinks to a table near the fireplace.

Nathan glanced up at the paper snowflakes dangling from the ceiling, the lights flickering along the counter and the fireplace, and the tinsel draped around the Christmas tree, and pulled a face. 'In all the years I worked in Ambleside I've never been here at Christmas. The decorations are a bit over the top, aren't they?'

'Big Jim and his wife Ruby make everything themselves.'

'And doesn't it show?' he muttered before turning to look at her. 'I never thought I would ever bump into you again. I have known Alastair since school, but I had no idea his fiancée was related to you.'

'She is, in a roundabout way.' Now he was looking at her, his dark brown eyes soft as velvet, she could hardly speak. At least if she kept her sentences short there was less risk of stammering, or saying anything stupid. Her old feelings of inadequacy were springing back to the surface. It was as if she was the clueless young cleaner, and he the posh, handsome and talented designer all over again.

'I hope you weren't offended that Alastair called me to help with the clubhouse,' Nathan said. 'He was worried you couldn't pull it off, but you did a really good job, considering it was all very last minute.'

'Thank you.' She drank a sip of orange juice and wished she was less tongue-tied. Perhaps she should have asked Sadie to pour a slug of vodka or gin in her glass.

Nathan was smiling, but his fingers tapped against his pint glass, and he kept coughing to clear his throat. 'Is your cleaning business doing well?'

'I manage.' Or she did, before the fiasco with Piers. She would have to work really hard to get new clients if – when – Piers terminated her contract.

'Good. Good. Have you... ahem... thought any more about working in interior design?'

She nodded. 'Every single day.' Now would be the time to mention that she read the professional press, and had seen the article in *Great Designs* about Maritel.

'Ah...' He drank a sip of beer. 'Have you worked on any design project since I moved to London?'

'A few.' This wasn't strictly a lie. Mason's house, Salomé's living room and Cecilia's shop refurbishment counted as proper interior design projects after all, albeit on a small scale. She couldn't however mention her sketches for Belthorn or the holiday cottages since she had no intention of ever submitting them.

He fiddled with his beer mat and appeared engrossed in reading the slogan printed at the front. 'Good... Actually it's lucky I bumped into you because I have something rather interesting to tell you.'

He cleared his throat again. 'It's about the hotel refurbishment competition I worked on two years ago. Do you remember?'

'Of course.' Did he expect her to have forgotten that he had branded her sketches as amateurish, and broken her heart in the process?

'Well, the thing is I found your portfolio when I unpacked my stuff in my London studio and realised that some of your ideas were actually quite good – for an amateur, that is.' He looked at her and smiled, probably expecting her to jump up with joy.

When she didn't say anything, he carried on. 'Of course, your sketches needed a lot of redrafting but they provided me with an initial idea. I reworked some of them and submitted them to Maritel. And guess what?'

'You won the competition, and now you have the contract to refurbish their whole chain,' she answered.

He glared at her. 'You know?'

'I saw the article and the photos in *Great Designs* magazine.'

'Ah. Yes.' He gave her a tight smile. 'I should have told you, shouldn't I, that I was using some of your ideas, but I... I didn't know how to get in touch.'

This was the biggest, most ridiculous lie she'd ever heard, and all of a sudden her shyness and confusion fell away. 'I've had the same phone number for years – the same you texted me on every week to arrange my cleaning days. And even if you'd lost it, you could have checked the internet, or asked any of your friends or former business contacts who lived locally.'

He looked down, and sighed. It was so strange, sitting opposite this man she had once had a massive crush on – a man she always believed was completely out of her league, being more intelligent, more talented, and altogether more worthy than her – and feel nothing but contempt.

'Why didn't you tell Maritel your designs were my ideas?'

He drained what was left of his beer and gave her a quizzical look before putting his glass down. 'Do you really not understand?' He sounded haughty and patronising now. 'They wanted a designer with a good track record and wouldn't have taken the proposal seriously if I had told them it came from a cleaning lady who only had one A-Level and a distance-learning diploma.'

She shook her head. 'What mattered was the work, not my CV, and at the end of the day, you used my ideas.'

'Believe me, there's a lot of snobbism in the field of interior design, and Maritel would have scrunched the papers into a ball and thrown them in the bin without even glancing at them if they'd had your name on them. Anyway, like I said, I did have to rework and refine the whole concept and sell it to them.'

She opened her mouth to protest. Rework the whole concept? As far as she had been able to see from the magazine photo, the designs, colours, inspiration were hers – all hers.

'However,' Nathan carried on, 'I want to make things right and I have a proposal for you. Maritel has two hotels in the North of England, one in Manchester and another in Leeds – both five star. I am prepared to take you on as a trainee to oversee both refurbishments. It would mean you being involved full-time, so you would have to give up your cleaning business or hire a manager.'

Cassie's heart skipped a beat. 'You would take me on? You would *really* offer me a job?' She couldn't help her voice from squeaking with surprise and excitement. Could her dreams be finally about to become reality?

'On one, non-negotiable condition: you must never tell anyone that the London designs were yours.' He drew in a breath. 'I mean, partly yours. I don't want to risk Maritel cancelling everything, since I have little doubt that the manager of the chain would change his mind if he knew that someone like you had a hand in them.'

'Someone like me...'

He made a dismissive gesture with his hand. 'You know what I mean.' He looked more like the old Nathan now, confident and self-assured – all smooth, velvety dark eyes and sexy smile.

'If you agree, I'll have a non-disclosure agreement drawn up before I go back to London and you can start in the New Year. So, what do you say?'

She would be mad to refuse. It was the chance of a lifetime, the chance she had been hoping for. She couldn't let it slip through her fingers. So what if she didn't get the credit for the hotel design? After all, she had created good designs once, she could do it again.

She was about to accept when her grandfather's voice rang in her mind. *'Never sell yourself cheap, Trifle.'* He had said that when she was fixing her cleaning prices after taking over from her mum and she wanted to give generous discounts to clients.

She took a deep breath and kept her tone calm and cool. 'Thank you, Nathan. It's a great offer, but I need to think about it. Can I take a few days to make my mind up?'

He frowned, and annoyance tightened his mouth. 'You need to think about it?' Suddenly he relaxed and smiled. 'Oh, I see. You need time to wind up your little business, tell your clients and your family, and put your sponges, mops and feather dusters in the bin...'

Leaning forward, he put his hand on her arm. 'I'm here

242

all week. Let me know what you decide by next Saturday…'
He lowered his voice and added, 'You are a very attractive woman, Cassie. I can't believe I never realised that before today. I guess that's because I never saw beyond your rubber gloves and your mop and cleaning spray. I would like it very much if we could go out, and spend some time together this week, so that we can get to know each other better.'

His voice became low and cajoling. 'And I would like it even more if you wore a pinny like that cute Bluebell fairy painted on your van. What do you think?' He flashed his sexy smile again.

Nathan found her attractive and hinted at a possible romance between them? She should pinch herself to make sure she wasn't dreaming, yet it left her indifferent, and even slightly queasy.

She rose to her feet. 'I think I would look completely ridiculous if I went out wearing a pinny. I need to think about your offer – your work offer, that is. For now it's getting late, I have things to do, and you probably need to get ready for Alastair's stag do. I shall see you tomorrow at the wedding.'

As they walked out of the pub, Sadie winked at her from behind the bar and gave her the thumbs up. Cassie had better tell her she had got it all wrong. She had to think hard about Nathan's work offer, but she had no intention of starting any personal relationship with him.

He was too late. She loved another.

Chapter Thirty

'I thought you had changed your mind.' Stefan pulled her into his arms as soon as she put the pizza boxes on the hall table and dropped her overnight bag to the floor. She tilted her face up, and received the full blast of his warm, golden gaze.

She couldn't wait to tell him about seeing Nathan, about his reluctant acknowledgement that he had indeed used her ideas for his hotel project, and about his surprise job offer... and the mixed feelings it aroused inside her.

'I had to stop at the cottage to get my bag, and then there was a queue at the pizza place, but guess what happened. I bumped into—' He didn't let her finish her sentence but lifted her up and kissed her with an intensity that left her breathless.

When he finally put her down, she knotted her fingers behind his neck, revelling in the feel of his hard, strong body against hers, and the texture of his skin, of his hair under her touch. All the worries and events of the day faded into nothingness. All that mattered was being in Stefan's arms, and melting into his embrace.

He must have felt the same because he pulled away a little, rested his forehead against hers and whispered. 'Are you hungry? Because all I want is to take you upstairs and get you out of those clothes—'

She kissed the corner of his mouth. 'What about the pizzas?'

'They can be reheated.'

Laughing and kissing, they made their way upstairs, under the stern, disapproving glare of the Ashville portraits lining the wall.

'Should we try that big four-poster bed?' Stefan asked as they reached the master bedroom.

She shook her head. 'I hate that room. It's dark and gloomy, and it overlooks Wolf Tarn and the abbey.'

She shuddered and her breath caught in her throat, but immediately Stefan encircled her into his arms. 'You said once that talking made everything better. Perhaps if you tell me what happened here, it will make the ghosts go away.'

She looked into his eyes and stroked his cheek. His beard felt rough and bristly against her touch.

'You should talk to me about your ghosts too. I can see them lurking in your eyes, sometimes even when you smile.'

He drew in a breath. 'Perhaps one day. Let's forget about the past for now.'

It wasn't hard to forget about everything but his touch, his warmth, the infinitely tender look in his eyes as he slowly peeled her clothes away and led her to bed – and the definitely more dangerous and primitive glow in his eyes as he undressed quickly and stood over her in the manner of a man about to claim his woman, and savouring every second of the conquest.

Would she ever get used to Stefan's feverish kisses; to the power she had to make him tremble with desire and whisper heated words; to the waves of dark, hot, blinding pleasure he aroused inside her; and the erratic beating of his heart as he pulled her on top of him after having thoroughly loved her?

For the first time she felt the joy and the magic of loving and being loved. She loved him. Loved the way his eyes went from bright to burnished gold. Loved the curve of his lips when he smiled, the sound of his broken voice, and the solid feel of his body against hers. But it was more than that. She loved his strength and vulnerability, and his kindness. She may not know the facts, the details, but it was obvious he was a man who had been hurt, and almost destroyed in terrible events.

What if it was different for him and their lovemaking was just a pleasant but meaningless interlude? He couldn't stay at Belthorn forever. He hadn't made any plans or any promises. What would she do when he left and returned to France, or travelled to whichever country the army posted him?

She wouldn't think about it for now. She nestled closer against him, and stroked his chest, smiling when she heard his breathing quicken and felt his body harden under her touch.

The pizzas were stone cold when they finally made their way downstairs. She had slipped a pair of leggings and one of Stefan's sweatshirts on, and he was wearing his army jogging pants and a shirt. He went to the drawing room to poke the fire he had made before back to life, and she carried the pizzas to the kitchen.

As she put them into the oven, she made a mental note to write on the receipt that one of the pizzas was for her and pay it back. Even if Stefan had insisted he repay all the groceries she bought for him, she still had to send detailed receipts to Piers at the end of each week. After the ugly scene at the restaurant, the last thing she needed was for him to accuse her of fraud as well as theft, even if it was only the price of a pizza.

Stefan glanced at her as he walked in. 'Is there anything wrong? You look preoccupied.'

She shrugged. 'It's nothing.' Mentioning her troubles with Piers would spoil the evening, but it was as if a black cloud had suddenly filled her heart.

'By the way, how did your meeting go?' Stefan asked, as if he was reading her mind.

'It was... all right.'

She looked away immediately, opened the oven and pretended to check on the pizzas. She couldn't tell him about Piers – about the accusations, the customer complaints, and, most of all, about the horrid scene at the restaurant and the way he had fired her. Guilt and shame churned inside her. She should have told Piers to stop pestering her instead of hoping that he would get the message. He said she led him on, and perhaps he had a point.

'Are you sure you're all right?' Stefan asked from behind her.

She turned round and forced a smile. 'Yes, of course.'

Frowning as if he didn't quite believe her, he took a bottle of wine and two glasses out of the cupboard. 'Shall we eat in the drawing room? I got the fire going again.'

She smiled. 'Good idea.'

'Did Kerry like the clubhouse?' he asked as they sat on the rug in front of the fireplace to eat.

'She loved it and Alastair too. He even cracked a joke, which is a first.'

'That's your grandfather's influence, no doubt.'

She licked the tomato off her fingers, extended her legs in front of her and leaned back against the sofa. She was about to tell him about Nathan when Stefan spoke.

'Actually... I met your grandfather in the village today.'

'Was he all right?'

Was it her imagination or did he hesitate before answering?

'He was a bit preoccupied.'

Immediately alarm tightened her chest. 'What was the matter with him? Was he ill?'

'No. He said his knee was playing up, and he asked me to walk home with him because he wanted to check... ahem... something.'

Why did she have the feeling that he wasn't telling her everything? 'There was something else, wasn't there?'

Stefan sighed and combed his fingers in his hair. 'I'm sorry, Cassie. I promised him I wouldn't tell. He said you would only worry for nothing. But I can tell you that I fixed the radiator in the upstairs room.'

'Oh, I see.' He had gone to the back room. That's where the filing cabinet was, where her granddad kept his bank papers.

'Was my granddad's preoccupation to do with money, by any chance?'

The look in Stefan's eyes told her she was right.

She sighed. 'I've been worried about my granddad for a while. He's been tired, distracted and forgetful for weeks now.'

'Perhaps he's just getting old.' He rose to his feet and held out his hand. 'Come on. It's late. Let's go to bed.'

He had winced as he got up, but as usual, and even though he might be in pain, he didn't complain. She had seen the scars slashing his chest, his back. Her fingers had stroked their cruel grooves, and her lips left soft, tender kisses along them. Love such as she had never felt before swelled inside her, almost choking her.

Could she tell him how she felt? Or was it too soon?

'Stefan,' she said, extending her hand.

He reached out for her and pulled her to his feet. 'Yes?'

But she couldn't say the words. Not yet. 'I'm glad I'm here, with you,' she said instead.

He cupped her face between his hands and gave her a kiss as light as the caress of a butterfly. In the light of the dying fire, his gaze was so tender her heart ached. 'So am I, little bluebell. So am I.'

She snuggled against him, her body soft and warm. Her fingers lingered on his chest, and she half-heartedly attempted to tickle him again. She may not succeed in making him squirm and giggle but she aroused a whole host of other sensations. He looked down and smiled. Strands of blonde hair caressed his neck as she now moved to kiss his chest.

She didn't smile back but held his gaze, her eyes a light, cloudy grey. 'Tell me about your ghosts and I'll tell you about mine,' she said.

His heart grew heavy. 'Why do you want to know?'

'Because it makes you sad, and I don't want you to be sad.'

Would he ever dare tell her about Mali? About the catastrophic failings that had led to so many deaths – *his* catastrophic failings?

Would it make him feel better? More to the point, did he have the right to feel better? The guilt and nightmares were his purgatory. His punishment.

At the same time, it was dishonest and cowardly to keep that massive chunk of his past from her.

'Very well.'

He took a moment to gather his thoughts. 'My regiment was deployed in Mali five years ago. Things went well at first and the situation was under control, but after a couple of years terrorist attacks on civilians increased with suicide bombers blowing themselves up in markets or in the makeshift camps set up by humanitarian organisations like Inter Medics.'

'Is that where you met Charles Ashville?'

Stefan nodded. 'We were assigned to the protection of the medical staff and local civilians, and we followed Charlie and his staff around the country, airlifting sick or injured people to the nearest base. Charlie and I became friends.'

He closed his eyes. 'Last summer my helicopter was targeted by extremists. We were rescuing women and children from a dispensary that had almost been completely destroyed by a mortar attack in the south of the country. We knew that the men responsible were still in the area, waiting to finish the job, but I thought…' He swallowed hard. 'I thought I had time to evacuate everybody safely.'

He took a deep breath, almost expecting the foul smells of blood, burning flesh and death. But there was only the lemony scent of Cassie's skin.

'I was wrong. The terrorists waited until the last women and children were on board, and then launched a rocket attack as I was taking off.'

He closed his eyes. 'Charlie and I were the lucky ones, I managed to pull him and two children out of the wreckage, and went back to help the others, but the helicopter burst into flames in front of me.

'I don't remember much after that. I was repatriated to the Val-de-Grâce Hospital in Paris – that's the military hospital. I've been on sick leave ever since.'

He opened his eyes, glad for the young woman's warmth

against him, and for her soothing touch. Could he speak about it – the memories that wrenched his heart, and ripped him apart more than any other? His throat tight, his eyes stinging, he added, 'There was a little girl. She must have been only seven or eight. She didn't want to get into the helicopter. She was scared. I told her everything would be all right, so she climbed on board, looked at me and smiled… She was one of the two kids I pulled free of the wreckage.'

'So you saved them.'

He let out a shaky breath. 'Neither of them made it. Their injuries were too severe.'

His voice broke, as if it was possible for it to break even further, but he had to carry on. Now he had started, he wanted to tell her everything.

'I lost someone else that day, someone who was very dear to me. Isa, my co-pilot.'

'The woman in the photo on your phone.'

He nodded. 'She was a good friend as well as a colleague. She trusted me. I let her down.' And this time his voice broke.

'I'm so sorry,' Cassie said, rubbing her hand along his arm in a sweet but futile attempt to comfort him. Nothing would ever erase the pain, the guilt, the remorse.

He took a deep breath. 'Her parents, her fiancé hate me, and with good reason. She was supposed to spend Christmas at home with them. It would have been the first in three years. She was a bit like you. She loved Christmas, and she was over the moon when her leave of absence was approved… Now she's dead, and instead of celebrating her family are going to mourn her.'

He sighed. 'They've been emailing me constantly these past few weeks – with insults and reproaches, no doubt…'

She propped herself up on one elbow to look at him. 'What do you mean – no doubt? You haven't read any of their messages?'

He shook his head. 'I'm a coward, aren't I? The thing is,

they can't tell me anything I'm not telling myself already, and they can't hate me any more than I hate myself.'

'Oh, Stefan!' She threw her arms around him and buried her face in his chest. 'Did you have anyone to confide in – your parents, or close friends?'

He took a deep breath. 'We've never talked much, my parents and I. My mother means well but she was relieved when I announced I was going away for a while. As for my dad, he's ashamed of me and I don't expect him to welcome me home with open arms.'

'Ashamed? Why? You only did your best and—'

'But I didn't, did I?' he cut in. 'I failed, and my father doesn't deal well with failure. Self-doubt and emotional breakdown never featured in his career path, and shouldn't have featured in mine. Anyway,' he carried on, stroking her hair, her shoulders, slowly, lightly, tentatively. Did she still want him now she knew what he'd done? 'My army days are likely to be over, and I don't have a clue what I'm going to do.'

Actually, that wasn't completely true. His meeting with the SAR helicopter pilot and the Mountain Rescue Service team that afternoon had been surprisingly positive, and, even though he hadn't been able to bring himself to climb into the helicopter, the pilot had stepped down and talked about his own experience in the Royal Navy. It seemed that he had known some gruelling times too and nevertheless managed to pull through. Perhaps there was hope for Stefan and he could still put his skills to good use.

'Is that why you came here?' Cassie asked. 'To work things out?'

He looked down into her clear and clever grey eyes. 'That was the plan.'

It sounded less pathetic than to say that he had run away to a place far enough for no one to be able to reach him at Christmas time. Of course, he hadn't banked on getting involved with anyone... or to be rescued from his doom and gloom and his self-imposed exile by a kind and cheerful housekeeping fairy, her joker grandfather, and their welcoming friends and family.

Dread filled his heart, cold and heavy like a stone. What had he been thinking of, taking Cassie to bed, making love to her? It had been wrong of him to take advantage of her. He was a damaged man. He had failed with catastrophic consequences. He had nothing to offer her.

He pushed the thought out of his mind and forced a smile.

'Your turn. I told you about my ghosts, now you tell me about yours.'

Immediately her face closed up. 'It's late, and I'm tired.'

He frowned and cupped her cheek with his hand. 'Hey. We had a deal.'

'You're going to think I'm crazy, or stupid, or both, or that I drank too much that night,' she said. 'Everybody thinks that.'

'Come here.' He wrapped his arms around her waist, pulled her down and held her tightly against him. Her hair tickled his chest. Her breath on his skin aroused delicious sensations, making his body tighten and pulse once more. But now wasn't the time.

'Tell me what happened.'

She shuddered against him. 'Ten years ago, my friends and I had a Christmas Eve bonfire on the banks of Wolf Tarn. We packed food and drinks, a couple of disposable barbecues and a CD player and we all piled up in a big old Land Rover that belonged to someone's dad. We knew that Lord Ashville was spending Christmas in London and that Belthorn would be empty so we drove into the estate through a broken gate, unloaded all our stuff, and made a fire on the lakeshore. It was a cold, clear night. I remember looking up at the sky and thinking how magical it was, with the stars reflecting onto the surface of the lake, making it sparkle in the moonlight.'

'It sounds like a good night out.'

'It was... at first. A few of us were in a band so we sang

and danced until well after midnight. Then the girls retreated into the Land Rover with their boyfriends because they were cold and... well, they wanted a bit of privacy, if you can call privacy being cooped up in a car with two other couples. I was left on my own on the shore with the dying fire, the remains of our picnic and the CD player.' She sighed. 'After a while, I got bored and walked along the shore.'

She tensed and her voice became a whisper. 'That's when I saw them.'

'Them?'

'There was a big man carrying a woman. She wasn't moving. Her body looked all floppy, her head tipped backwards and her hair was so long it almost touched the ground. Another man stood back, as if he only wanted to watch from a distance, and he was, like me, a spectator. He was partly concealed behind the ruins of the abbey but I could see that he was tall and wore a kind of long robe, like a priest or a...'

Stefan frowned. 'A monk?' he finished, trying to tone down the incredulity in his voice. 'You think you saw that Grey Friar your family was talking about, don't you?'

She nodded. 'I know what you're thinking. That I was drunk, or deluded, or again sleepwalking, and you know something? I really wish I was any of those things, but I was sober and fully awake, and that terrifies me...'

He cursed himself for doubting and upsetting her. Kissing the top of her head, he tightened his embrace. 'Carry on.'

She sighed. 'The whole thing was like a nightmare, or a scene from a horror film.'

He looked down. 'What exactly *was* happening?'

She took a deep breath. 'The big man walked into the lake with the woman in his arms, and held her down underwater for what felt like an eternity. I couldn't move, couldn't speak, and couldn't stop what was happening. It was horrible. Finally he let go of her, her body floated, on the moonlit tarn... and it was as if the spell was broken and I could move again. I started screaming but he just vanished and so did the body of the woman. It was as if I had dreamt the whole thing.'

'What about the… other man you said you saw?' The more she told him about the scene she said she had witnessed, the more he was convinced she had had some kind of hallucination.

'He disappeared too. One second he was standing near the ruins of the abbey. The next he was gone. What scared me so much about him was that he had no face. No face at all…'

She wouldn't like it, but he had to ask. 'Could it have been shadows of trees or clouds passing in front of the moon?'

She shook her head. 'I saw people, Stefan, not moon shadows.'

'All right… Sorry. What did you do?'

'I ran back to the car in a total panic. I was hysterical, and told the others I had just witnessed a murder. They ran back with me but couldn't see anything, so we drove back to my house in a hurry. My step-dad being a policeman, we thought he would know what to do. We woke him up, blurted the whole story out and he immediately called in mountain rescue and his colleagues from Keswick for backup. They went up to Wolf Tarn that night but didn't find anything. The following day – Christmas Day – divers searched the lake whilst police and sniffer dogs patrolled the shore, the abbey and the hillside. Once again, they found nothing. I was castigated for wasting police time. They said I must have been drinking, or taking drugs, or again that I was attention seeking. Only my grandma believed me…'

She was silent for a few seconds then added. 'After that night, I only went back to Belthorn with my mother. It was Sophie who was supposed to take care of you, but she quit, leaving me no choice but to come back on my own.'

He flipped her body until she was under him, lifted her arms on the pillow and intertwined his fingers with hers. 'Well, I'm glad she did or we may have never met.'

And he meant it, with every fibre of his being.

Chapter Thirty-One

'And this, ladies and gentlemen, is what you get when you cross a parrot with a centipede... a walkie-talkie!'

There was a chorus of applause and laughter, and Joseph Bell, his face flushed and his hair ruffled, bowed his head in salute as he sat down. He loosened his tie as he waited for the noise to quieten down. 'That will be all for tonight, folks. I haven't had much time to make up many after-dinner jokes suitable for this Tarzan and Jane extravaganza since our lovely Kerry decided to go ape for her wedding only a week ago.'

People clapped again as he sat down. A few shouted that they wanted more jungle jokes, so Joseph stood up again. 'All right. Just one more, since you're asking so nicely.'

Despite his protests, it was obvious he relished every minute of being the centre of attention. 'Here it is... What kind of key do you need to open a banana?' He looked around the room. A few people shouted answers, he shook his head and his face creased into a smile. 'A monkey, of course!'

Once the whistles had died down, the music resumed, and Stefan looked at Cassie across the room. She was sitting next to Rachel, Tim and the boys, with her grandfather at the head of the table, like a patriarch.

'Isn't the old fellow a hoot?' the man next to him said. 'I mean, not that any of his jokes are funny, just the opposite. They're so rubbish you just have to laugh! I was told he's competing in the local pub comedy night next Friday.' The man gulped the rest of his wine, and let out a horsy laugh. 'That should be a blast. I can't wait.'

'Are you here for the week?' Stefan asked politely, although his impatience at the man was getting stronger with every smug and superior word he uttered.

'We came up from London for Alastair's wedding and booked an "adventure week" – hiking, abseiling, quad biking, air rifle shooting, you name it. I'd rather be partying in Tijuana or Patong, but the others are keen on that kind of outdoor stuff.'

The DJ announced that it was time for the newlyweds' first dance. The main lights dimmed as the groom helped his bride to the dance floor, and the couple stood in the golden beam of a single spotlight, with the fairy lights hidden in the foliage around the room creating the illusion of an enchanted forest. The music started with soft piano chords then a well-known English singer sang about love and magic, peace and harmony. Stefan wasn't one for sentimental music, but there was something sweet about the way the couple swirled slowly, gazing adoringly into each other's eyes that made his chest ache, as if there was a bruise on his heart.

He looked across the room to where Cassie was talking to a dark-haired man whose features he couldn't distinguish in the dim lighting.

'That scoundrel Nathan's already chatting up some girl,' the man next to him said, pointing to Cassie's table. 'He's been in a foul mood since we arrived last night. Almost didn't come to the reception, but it looks like it will be his lucky night after all... not that he needs luck. The man is a babe-magnet, and that chick over there doesn't look too bad for a country girl.'

Stefan's fingers tightened on his glass. Nathan. Wasn't that the name of the designer who had appropriated Cassie's designs for himself? 'Is Nathan an interior designer, by any chance?' he asked.

The man looked surprised. 'You've heard of him, then? I didn't think he was that famous. Mind you, he's doing all right for himself at the moment. He just signed a huge contract for a chain of posh hotels.'

So it was indeed Nathan who was talking to Cassie. Had

she confronted him about using her designs? And if so, what was he going to do about it? They were talking and smiling, so it was fair to assume that they must have found a way to solve their differences.

The slow music was followed by a lively pop song, and adults and children alike rushed to the dance floor. The music was now too loud to talk to the men next to him – not that their conversation had been riveting anyway. They were all friends of the groom, most of them high flyers from London, working for media companies, law firms or in the City.

He scanned the room again, recognised a few faces. There was exotic looking Salomé, whose pastries he had taken a liking to, chatting to the petite, pink-haired woman who worked in the village gift shop. Piers Hardy, Charlie's estate manager, was talking to a glamorous blonde woman – slobbering all over her, would be more exact. He must have sensed that Stefan was looking at him because he glanced his way, smirked and waved his flute of champagne at him. Stefan reluctantly nodded back.

He hadn't liked the possessive way Hardy had clasped his hand on Cassie's shoulder when they had met him in the pub and the lecherous look in his eyes when he'd kissed her goodbye. Of course, knowing that he was related to the bully who'd given André Vaillant a serious beating did nothing to improve his opinion of the man.

Stefan sighed. Seeing Hardy reminded him that he should have probed harder about how Cassie's meeting with him in Keswick had gone. She had looked unsettled, worried even, the night before, and perhaps it had something to do with Charlie's estate manager. He also wanted to tell her his theory about Darren Morse even if it was only a hunch and he didn't have any proof.

He sat back and sipped his glass of water. The meal had been nice enough, and he'd enjoyed listening to Joseph Bell's silly jokes, but now he longed to be back at Belthorn and enjoy the peace and silence of the manor house that had become his haven.

The weather had been bright, and after Cassie had left to get ready for the wedding ceremony at the village church, and then the lunch at a nearby exclusive hotel, he had walked around Wolf Tarn and the abbey, all the time thinking about the story she had told him. What had really happened that Christmas Eve? Cassie may claim otherwise, but it must have been some kind of dream or the police divers and mountain rescue teams would have found a body in the tarn.

As he walked around the ruins, he tried to imagine Belthorn as it had been in its heyday, before Henry the Eighth ordered it to be destroyed.

The abbey was on a small scale, and not much of it was still standing – the church's north and south transept walls with their arched windows, parts of the cloister and what must have been the dormitory and living quarters. From there, it took him less than two minutes to walk to Wolf Tarn, and he stood on the pebbly shore, looking at the water that mirrored the blue sky and the snowy mountains around. It was a perfect setting on a perfect day, yet he hadn't exaggerated when he'd told Cassie that he found the small, round lake eerie. Finding out that Ruth Merriweather had drowned there made it even more sinister.

In fact, he wouldn't be surprised if her great-great-aunt's death hadn't preyed on Cassie's mind as she stood on the shore that fateful Christmas Eve. Miss Parker's words about the story behind the young woman's drowning came back to him. He needed to pay the retired headmistress another visit, and ask her about the abbey and Belthorn... and about Ruth's death, and if she was willing to reveal what she knew.

'Stefan! The DJ is playing one of my favourite songs. Come and dance with me.' Cassie tapped him on the shoulder, her beaming smile as usual filling him with joy and that primal, elusive feeling that threatened to turn him into a gormless ape man every time he was near her, and that he was trying hard, but unsuccessfully, to fight. He wished he could go all Tarzan on her, throw her over his shoulder and take her back to Belthorn to make love to her all night, not shuffle his big feet on a dance floor like the clumsy oaf he was and make a spectacle of himself.

'I'm not much of a dancer,' he objected.

'Who cares? Come on,' she urged, pulling on his hand.

So he rose to his feet and let her lead him to the dance floor. The song was another slow dance, so he wrapped his arms around her waist, and she knotted her fingers behind his neck. She looked lovely, with her hair loose and shiny on her shoulders, and wearing a dress the same pale grey as her eyes. The silky shift glided under his fingertips, reminding him of the texture of her skin. Then again, he liked her in her dungarees too... but he liked her best when she wore nothing at all.

They didn't talk as they slowly swirled to the music. Her face nestled against his chest, her hair tickled his chin, her body moved in his arms. It was bliss, and it felt like his heart sang along with the music.

'I wanted to be with you all evening,' she said as the music ended, 'but I had to talk to family members I hadn't seen in ages, then Rachel asked me to mind the boys... and then you'll never guess what happened.'

The music merged into another slow dance. 'Let's go out for a minute,' she said, dragging him towards the exit. 'I have something exciting to tell you. I wanted to tell you yesterday but somehow didn't get round to it.'

A bulky figure stood in their way. 'Not so fast,' Piers Hardy said in a loud, slurred voice. 'Can I have a dance, Cassie, or do you keep them exclusively for your punters?'

Hardy staggered and grabbed Cassie's bare arm.

Stefan stepped forward. 'Let go, Hardy.'

The man's face turned a violent shade of beetroot, a mean

smile twisted his mouth, but he released Cassie, who stepped back and came to stand right next to Stefan, close enough for her hip to brush against his.

Hardy sneered. 'Poor sod. You really have no idea, do you?'

Stefan frowned. 'No idea about what?'

'About being Charlie's charity case. Cassie is only sucking up to you to make sure you give her a good report. You can't blame a girl for wanting her bonus. Two thousand pounds isn't something to be sniffed at. I'm sure Cassie is working her butt off for it – literally.'

Stefan clenched his fists, and turned to Cassie. 'Bonus? What bonus?'

Hardy laughed – a slow, slimy laugh. 'Hasn't the minx told you? You see, your mate Charlie promised Cassie a bonus if you were satisfied with her services and wrote a good report at the end of your stay. He must know that with the way you look, you need to pay to get laid, and he asked our Bluebell fairy to come to your rescue, and bring a smile to your ugly face with a bit of dusting, a bit of cooking and a bit of f—!'

Cassie slapped Hardy's cheek, hard. He brought his hand to his face, and narrowed his eyes. 'You'll pay for that.'

Stefan stepped in front of Cassie and scowled at Hardy. 'You'd better leave us now,' he said between clenched teeth, 'because I'm going to carry on what Cassie started, and I promise you won't be standing when I finish with you.'

Hardy took a step back and spat, 'Ah... You think she gives you jokes to cheer you up, you poor bastard. You don't even realise *you're* the joke.'

With a last snicker he tottered away, and Stefan turned to Cassie. 'Let's get out of here.'

She followed him into the lobby of the clubhouse, which thankfully was empty. He crossed his arms, looked down into her face. 'Is that true?'

Cassie smiled, but it wasn't her usual smile. It was reticent and timid, and he knew then that Hardy had spoken the truth.

'Charlie promised you a bonus for looking after me,' he said in flat voice.

'Yes, but I don't see why it makes any difference between us. I mean, it's not like Piers says at all, I didn't...'

It was like a fist slamming into Stefan's chest. How was it possible to go from feeling on top of the world happy to cut into shreds in less than five minutes?

'It makes all the difference to me,' he said in a low voice.

'Don't tell me that you believe that I slept with you only for that bonus Charles promised! What do you take me for?'

Hardy's words had hit a raw nerve, opened an abyss of doubt inside him, and now he didn't know what to believe. He couldn't even think straight.

The door to the clubhouse opened and Nathan Hardman walked in. 'Cassie! I was looking for you. Are you ready to leave? I've cleared it with the boys. They're staying a while longer, so we should have the cottage to ourselves for a while.'

Cassie's face coloured. 'Give me five minutes, Nathan. I need to talk to Stefan first.'

The designer arched his eyebrows and gave Stefan a puzzled look. 'Okay. I'll go back to the cottage now and pour us a glass of wine while I wait for you.'

The moment he had left, Cassie turned to him. 'This isn't what it sounds like. I was just about to tell you that Nathan offered me a job as a trainee designer yesterday, and he now wants to discuss the terms of our contract.'

It was as if a light was being switched off in his heart. 'You saw him yesterday.'

'Yes... I didn't know he was coming but he is a friend of Alastair's, and anyway, we went to the Eagle and Child for a drink and I—'

'You went to the pub with him?'

'Yes. He explained why he used some of my ideas for the hotel project and more or less promised me a job. Now he wants to discuss the terms of the contract... I won't be long, I promise.' She smiled.

She had kept such a big piece of news from him the night before – hadn't even mentioned seeing the designer as they made love and ate and talked. But of course, why would she? She didn't have to tell him anything of her personal life. He was the one who had got everything wrong. All along, he had only been a job for her. A job that would yield a bonus if she did it well...

He took his car keys out of his trouser pocket. 'You can be as long as you want. Congratulations on the job offer. That's great, and I hope you enjoy your evening with your new boss. I'll see you around.'

Chapter Thirty-Two

How could Stefan storm out without giving her the chance to explain? Worse still, how could he even for one second believe that she would sleep with him for the sake of a bonus? Should she run after him, explain that he'd got it all wrong, and apologise for not telling him about Nathan the night before? Or was it better to leave him alone to think things through? Surely he would realise that Piers was a bitter and nasty drunk who had lied in the hope of wrecking their relationship.

Anger grew and twisted inside her, before giving way to a feeling of total devastation. Tears streaming down her face, she ran to the ladies toilets and locked herself into one of the cubicles.

She pulled down the top of the toilet seat, sat down and cried until her eyes burned and her throat and chest hurt, and she'd used up all the toilet roll to blow her nose. The music changed from pop to a slow dance, from rock to country. A steady stream of women came in, and Cassie listened to their excited chattering about make-up or outfits, or the attributes of their various dance partners.

She waited until the toilets were empty before coming out of the cubicle. Turning the tap on, she splashed her face with cold water and stared at her reflection in the mirror. Heavens, she looked a sight. She felt even worse.

The door creaked open, and Salomé came in, holding a glass of red wine as dark as her lipstick. Her eyes widened as she looked at Cassie.

'So that's where you've been hiding. We thought you had gone home! What's up?'

Cassie burst into fresh tears. 'Oh, Salomé. What am I going to do?'

'What happened, darling?' Salomé put her glass down on

the sink and took her in her arms, hugging her tightly whilst Cassie sobbed that everything was ruined.

'Shh...' Salomé patted her back. 'Is this to do with that hunky French guy you seem so keen on?'

Cassie nodded. 'Stefan thinks... he thinks I only slept with him because of Charles Ashville's bonus. That's what Piers said, and he believed him.'

'What bonus?'

'Charles promised me a bonus if I looked after Stefan well and if he was happy at Belthorn. Piers told him that was the only reason I slept with him.'

'And he believed him? That's a bit much!' Salomé brushed a strand of hair from Cassie's face. 'Anyway, why did Piers Hardy tell him about the bonus? What is it to him?'

Cassie heaved a shaky sigh. 'He is angry because I wouldn't sleep with him yesterday.'

'What?'

'After my performance review, he took me for lunch to that posh hotel in Keswick, and after...' Cassie shuddered. 'He wanted me to go up to a room with him.'

Salomé's eyes opened wide in shock. 'He didn't, did he? The disgusting pig!' She shook her head. 'Right, I'll tell you what we'll do. There's no way you can go back in there, and I'm not letting you drive home on your own when you're in that state. I'll get Cecilia and we'll go back to mine. We'll talk it over, watch a film, play Scrabble – you choose. But whatever you decide, we'll definitely drink wine and eat cake. Does that sound like a plan to you?'

Cassie had cried so much she felt drained, and her mind was in a fuddle. 'Can you tell Rachel and my granddad that I'm leaving early because I have a headache – but try not to worry them?'

Salomé nodded. 'Sure. I'll be back in five minutes. Wait in the lobby.'

A few minutes later, Salomé came back with Cassie's handbag

and duffle coat. Cecilia was already wrapped up against the cold. She gave Cassie a comforting hug and a kiss on the cheek.

'I'm sorry to spoil your evening,' Cassie told her. 'You were so kind to lend me this gorgeous dress, and now it's all wrinkled and it's got tear-stains all over the front. You did my hair and make-up too, and look at me now, I ruined everything.'

'Rubbish! The one who ruined everything is Stefan Lambert who believed Piers over you,' Salomé remarked in a serious voice. 'Then again, what else could you expect from a friend of Charles Ashville's? Come on, girls, let's go and eat cake. Cake makes everything better.'

Salomé's house was only a couple of miles down the road and Cassie felt well enough to drive, especially with her friends in the van with her, squashed together on the passenger seat with a seat belt round them both. Luckily it only took five minutes and once there, Salomé lit the stove, opened a bottle of red wine, laid out a selection of tapas, breadsticks and dips on a brightly coloured platter, and cut thick slabs of chocolate and ginger cake.

'Now, start the story again, from the beginning this time,' Salomé instructed as she put the food on the table and the three women snuggled on the sofa.

Cassie told them about her meeting with Piers, and how he had more or less accused her of not doing her job and stealing items from the holiday cottages, and how he had used the lease on Bluebell Cottage to try to blackmail her into sleeping with him, and told her she was fired when she refused.

'The man is vile.' Cecilia clenched her fists in anger. 'You must expose his disgusting blackmail.'

'Who can I complain to? Charles Ashville is somewhere in the Sahara Desert. Gabrielle is busy with her theatre in London, and whatever Stefan says about her, I never found her to be the most approachable and friendly of women. I told you how she treated poor Mason years ago...'

Her friends muttered disagreeable comments about

Charles's sister, and she carried on, 'It's the lease on Bluebell Cottage I'm worried about too.'

'Perhaps it is time for your granddad to move,' Cecilia remarked. 'Would he be happy to live at the farm with Rachel, Tim and the boys? You always say that he loves it up there.'

Cassie nodded. 'He might be. The farm is certainly big enough, and I think he is a bit lonely at the cottage.'

'What about you? Where would you go?' Salomé asked.

She lifted her shoulders in a weak shrug. 'I'll have to move too... which brings me to the other thing I wanted to tell you.' Cassie told her friends about Nathan submitting her sketches to the hotel design competition, and about him offering her a trainee position in his practice to make it up to her.

'He is waiting for me right now, actually. I must text him and tell him I won't be coming. He wanted us to talk, but I was a bit uncomfortable with being on my own with him in his holiday cottage anyway.'

'Hang on a minute.' Salomé frowned. 'Were you actually going to accept his offer even if it meant not getting any credit for your own designs?'

'You think I'm being a pushover, don't you?' Cassie put her plate with her half-finished piece of cake on the coffee table. 'You would be right, of course, but this is the chance to do the job I've always dreamed of, the chance to prove to myself, and others, that I can be more than just a cleaner.'

'You already did that when you took over from your mum and set up Bluebell Cleaning,' Salomé said. 'I understand what you're saying, about snatching the chance to work for an established interior design practice, but you don't need to accept Nathan Hardman's measly trainee position, and even less his non-disclosure agreement. You are incredibly talented. Look at the great job you did for me in here. This room, the colour, the artefacts... it's so me it's uncanny!'

She gestured to the South American tapestries hanging on the terracotta walls that contrasted with the dramatic black and white photos of iconic Flamenco dancer Antonia La Singla who Salomé idolised, and the quirky pieces of pottery dotted around the room. Cassie had had lots of fun designing the room and sourcing artwork for her friend.

'You helped me redesign my aunt's shop and turn it into a terrific, bright and modern space,' Cecilia added.

Salomé dipped her breadstick into some salsa sauce and munched on it for a while. 'Perhaps it's not too late to claim credit for the hotel competition. You must have some drawings that prove the designs were your original ideas.'

Cassie nodded. 'I gave Nathan the final sketches, but I kept most of my drafts. They're somewhere in the loft at the cottage.'

'Then go to London and show them to the manager of the hotel company,' Salomé said. 'And stuff Nathan and his trainee position!'

'I wouldn't trust him anyway,' Cecilia said as she picked up a handful of green olives from the tapas platter. 'Who's to say he wouldn't steal more of your ideas, or even fire you in the next few months?'

'Why did he need to see you on your own at the holiday cottage tonight anyway?' Salomé asked. 'It sounds like a trap to me. From what I saw of him earlier, he is a very smooth and slick guy – the type who thinks he can charm a girl into doing or saying anything.'

'I used to have such a massive crush on him, but that was before... before I met Stefan, and before I realised Nathan used me,' Cassie said. 'Now not only does Stefan think I faked everything between us because I was after Charles Ashville's money...' Her voice broke, and she wiped the tears that had started falling again. 'But he probably believes that I was going to sleep with Nathan to make sure he gave me a job.'

'If he believes that of you, then I'm sorry, but he doesn't deserve you,' Cecilia said in a pensive voice. 'Yet after yesterday, I was sure he had feelings for you – very strong feelings.' She shrugged.

'What do you mean?' Cassie asked, but before Cecilia could reply, she hiccupped and poured the last of the wine into her glass. 'Oops, it looks like the bottle is empty.'

'I'll get another one,' Salomé said. 'I agree with Cecilia. If he truly loves you, your Tarzan will realise he's got it all wrong and he'll come back to you, swinging from tree branches... even if he'd be better crawling on his knees and asking you for forgiveness.'

Cassie slumped on the sofa and closed her eyes. 'I want to sleep for a hundred years and forget about cleaning and interior design and Tarzan...' She hiccupped again. 'Especially about Tarzan... and love.'

'No problem,' Salomé said. 'I'll make up the futon in the spare room for you.'

Did the sun have to shine so brightly, and did Salomé have to bang about the house so much? Cassie's mouth was parched. Her stomach was doing somersaults, and her back ached from sleeping on the futon's thin mattress. And her head! Heavens, her head hurt so much...

She put the pillow over her head with a groan. The pounding came from inside her skull, not from the house. Why did she drink so much wine the night before?

The door creaked open. 'Good afternoon, sleepyhead,' Salomé called in a voice far too loud and cheerful. 'I'm bringing tea and fresh croissants, even if it's a bit late for breakfast.'

'What time is it?' Cassie asked from under the pillow.

'Just after two...'

She groaned. 'Already? I promised Patrick I would clear the clubhouse today. Stefan was going to help me.' She moaned again. 'I feel terrible. There's no way I can get up.'

'You certainly won't be able to get up with that pillow on your head. Come on. Sit up and have something to drink. It'll help you feel better.'

Cassie lifted the pillow off and sat up, and winced as shards of light pierced her skull. 'I am sorry to have spoilt your and Cecilia's evening... and most of your Sunday, by the looks of it.'

'You didn't spoil anything. You were having a terrible time and needed your friends around you. As for today, I left the bakery in the capable hands of my new baker whose croissants you are just about to sample.'

'What new baker? I didn't know you were hiring staff.'

Salomé gave her a mischievous look. 'I couldn't cope with baking, running the shop and making deliveries on my own any longer. His name is Max – or Maximilien, to use his full name – and he is absolutely gorgeous. He arrived yesterday morning and I put him to work straight away.'

Cassie drank the hot, sweet tea, but could only grimace at the plump, golden croissants, the pot of strawberry jam and the curls of butter in the small white dish. 'I'll pass on the croissants, if you don't mind.'

'Don't worry. I won't tell Max.'

Two cups of tea later, and Cassie felt strong enough to get up. As she had taken off the dress Cecilia had lent her before going to sleep, and was only wearing her underwear, Salomé lent her a jumper and some leggings, so that she could at least go home, shower and change before going to the clubhouse.

Her heart hammered in her chest and she felt sick as she drove to the campsite one hour later, but this time it had nothing to do with having a hangover. Would Stefan be there? Would he still be angry with her? And how was she going to convince him that her feelings for him were sincere?

But Stefan wasn't at the campsite. The only vehicle in the car park was Darren's white Fiesta. A light was on in the office, so she went in to get the key to the clubhouse, and found Darren sitting in Patrick's chair, his booted feet on the desk, with a cigarette in one hand and his mobile in the other.

Darren's eyes widened when she walked in. He immediately took his feet off the desk, shuffled a few papers, and slipped his phone into his pocket.

'Hi, Cassie. I wasn't expecting you today.'

He looked embarrassed, as if he'd been caught doing something he shouldn't, but Cassie couldn't see anything amiss – apart from perhaps the cigarette, since there was a big 'No Smoking' sign on the wall.

Standing up, he slid the window open and threw the cigarette outside.

'Is there anything I can help you with?'

She told him she had come to get the keys to the clubhouse and tidy the room up.

'You're too late. The French guy already did it. He took everything down and boxed everything up. It took him all morning. All the stuff is now in the stockroom. He said you would decide what to do with it all.'

'Stefan was here?'

'He banged on the door of my caravan at eight o'clock. He looked rough. Really rough. Mind you, he looked even rougher after working for four hours solid.'

Cassie's heart tightened. Things were going from bad to worse. Stefan must have expected her to come and help, and when she didn't, he must have thought that's because she had been too busy cavorting with Nathan.

'Didn't you offer to help?' she asked in a choked voice.

Darren shrugged. 'I couldn't. I was on duty here all day. I've been busy.'

From the way he had been sitting when she came in, she very much doubted he'd been that busy, but who was she to talk? She should have been there. Tidying up the clubhouse after the wedding was her responsibility, not Stefan's.

'I'll pick up the boxes another day,' she said, 'but I'd like to take the flamingo now.'

'No worries. I'll take it out of the store room for you.'

As he opened the door, a draft of cold air blew into the office and lifted the papers off the desk.

'Watch it!' she called. 'All your papers are flying away.'

Darren started towards the desk but Cassie was closer and she caught them before they scattered on the floor. She looked down. It was a CV, with Darren's name on it.

She glanced at him. 'Are you thinking of leaving?'

'I'm not sure.' He didn't look at her, and his usually impassive face looked flushed as he grabbed hold of the papers and quickly put them back on the desk. It was cold in the office, but Darren's forehead seemed damp with perspiration. She looked at the angry red marks slashing the back of his hand. She was no doctor, but the scratches looked infected, and his hand appeared swollen too.

He stretched his fingers in front of him and flinched. It was on the tip of her tongue to tell him he should put some disinfectant on his hand or even perhaps see the GP, but she remembered how curt he had been when she'd suggested that at Barbara's house a few days before.

'I'll get the bird out of the store room now,' he said.

'Thanks.'

Once the flamingo was safely loaded into the van, Cassie drove to Cecilia's house. 'Thanks for returning it,' Cecilia said. 'Do you want to come in for a drink? Although I drank enough wine yesterday to put me off for at least a full month,' she added quickly.

'Make it a full year,' Cassie retorted. She promised to get the grey dress dry-cleaned, and said she was going home to sleep.

But first she had to see Stefan, and tell him she didn't care about the bonus – in fact, she would email Charles Ashville this very evening and tell him she didn't want it any more. She would also tell Stefan she didn't care about Nathan's job offer. More importantly, she wanted to tell him what she should have told him before – that she loved him.

But Belthorn was cold, dark and empty, and on the kitchen table was a handwritten note. She didn't need to read it to guess what was written. Stefan had left. Perhaps for good...

Chapter Thirty-Three

He pulled the collar of his parka up against the blowing gale, dug his hands into his pockets and made his way back to the car. Wizard Point's in Devon stood windblown and deserted in the bleak winter's afternoon. His was the only car in the car park. No lights shone at the windows of the chalets and static caravans.

The shop and restaurant were boarded up, and padlocks and chains hung from the doors to the shower blocks and launderette. There was no sign of life in the office either. All that was needed to complete the desolate décor was tumbleweed blowing about and whining harmonica of a Spaghetti Western soundtrack.

The advert claimed that the site was open all year round, but it was obviously not the case. It looked like he wouldn't find out any information about Morse in Devon after all, but he only had himself to blame. He should have phoned ahead.

He went back to the car and started the engine. Hopefully, he wouldn't waste his time when he stopped in Yorkshire and Manchester to check out the places where Morse had worked before coming to Red Moss.

He had spotted a teashop in a nearby village on his way to the campsite. He would call there for some food and a hot drink since he hadn't had anything to eat since leaving London. A tractor trundled along in front and the winding road was too narrow for him to overtake, so he reclined against the headrest and crawled behind.

It had been a frantic few days, but he had to keep busy after Saturday night's debacle. His mind, and his heart, needed space and time away from Red Moss – and away from Cassie. He was done with hiding. It was time he took control of his life once more...

After clearing the clubhouse on Sunday morning, he had driven down to London where he had spent the night in Charlie's flat, before flying to Paris first thing on Monday for a medical at the army headquarters, and a review of his case with the officer in charge of Human Resources. Old habits die hard, and he couldn't bring himself to report at the army headquarters looking like some 'damned hippy', as his father had called him, so he'd had his hair trimmed and his beard shaved. When he gave his name to the sentry on duty, he looked, and felt, more like his former self than he'd done in months...

'The results of your medical are encouraging,' the officer had said, flicking through Stefan's various test results. He had looked stunned when Stefan said that he was planning on leaving. 'You could stay on as an instructor or work in the control room and manage operations from the ground.' His insistence had surprised Stefan. After the fiasco of his last mission, he would have thought that the army would be glad to be rid of him.

However, nothing the man said could change his mind. He would finish work on the training manual, as promised, but there would be no going back. He was ready for something new, even if he wasn't sure yet what it was, or where it was.

He had stopped running away from Isa's parents too. Having finally summoned the courage to read their texts and emails, he had been humbled to find that instead of the accusations he deserved, they only expressed kindness and concern. He had mustered the courage to phone them and they had invited him to visit. It had been an emotionally charged evening, but however much he blamed himself for Isa's death, her parents didn't and they had begged him to keep in touch. He was a precious link to their daughter, and would always be welcome at their house.

There was something else he wanted to do whilst in Paris – find out what had happened to André Vaillant. He had spent so long reading the man's diary that he felt he knew him and he couldn't believe that Vaillant had abandoned Ruth. He had a contact in the army archives and asked him to dig out Vaillant's service record and any information he could find on the man. His friend had scanned and emailed the documents to Stefan as he was waiting to board his plane back to London that very morning. The papers confirmed what he'd thought all along. Vaillant was no heartless, cowardly seducer. Something *had* happened that had prevented him from going back to Red Moss...

Being busy and on the move had stopped him from brooding too much about Cassie, but every time he was alone, images of her tormented him. Her smile and luminous grey eyes; her body stretching on the bed or nestling in his arms; her smile and her kindness...

Cassie... Once the black mist of self-doubt and jealousy had cleared, it had been too late to make amends. Would she ever forgive him for what he'd said to her and how he'd behaved at the wedding reception? He hadn't truly believed Hardy's slimy accusations that she'd only been after Charlie's bonus – he knew her better than that. She was fun, loyal, and kind, and she cared about him, that much he knew.

It was her kindness that had pushed her into his arms, and it was his fault if he had been too quick to believe that there was something between them – that the story of the beautiful swan in love with a hunchback wasn't just an old folk tale. It was obvious Cassie was still smitten with her swanky interior designer, so smitten in fact that she was ready to forgive him for stealing her ideas and accept his offer of a job.

He owed it to her to help her live her dream, so whilst in London, he had met Gabrielle for a coffee and told her about Cassie's design ideas for Belthorn and the holiday cottages. Charlie's sister planned to get more involved in the estate in the New Year, and said she wanted to see her work. Whether Cassie now followed through would be up to her... Even though Cassie hadn't complained about Hardy, Stefan had also told Gabrielle about the estate manager's bullish attitude. 'I did pick up a few bad vibes about him,' Gabrielle had said before promising to drive up to Red Moss in the next few weeks and meet up with him.

The tractor turned into a dirt road at last and Stefan was able to step on the accelerator. Driving into the village, he was relieved to see the OPEN sign in the teashop window.

He may have wandered the streets of Paris and London without anyone paying him any attention, but there mustn't be many strangers in December in Wizard's Point, and as soon as he walked into the teashop, ten heads turned towards him, all conversations stopped and curious female eyes stared at him, from his army boots to his now shorter hair that the sea breeze had ruffled.

'Ladies.' He nodded and chose a table near the window, repressing a groan of pain as he sat down. The hours spent driving hadn't done his back any favours.

A young woman took his order, and he killed time by reading through the local gazette, which a previous customer had left behind. The conversations resumed around him, and from what he could make out, a certain Tony Snell, whose funeral had taken place in the morning, provided the main topic of discussion.

'He was a mess in the end, poor Tony, and that's not surprising since he'd been drinking himself silly every single day for the past six months,' one woman was saying.

'The poor man was depressed,' another objected, 'and who could blame him? He lost everything. Not only did the police think he was involved in the burglaries in and around the village, but his father went doolally and squandered all their money... And then Sandra left him.'

'Squandered?' Somebody chipped in. 'He always said he had no idea where the money went, and if old Will Snell did indeed lose his marbles, it was all very sudden. My niece used to work at the campsite and she said there was nothing wrong with him until she went on holidays last May. When she returned two weeks later, he was confused, forgetful – and a completely different person.'

'Perhaps it was his medication. It can happen.'

'Poor man... he buried his only son today, the campsite that had been in his family for fifty years is in ruin, and now he's on his own at the nursing home.'

The waitress came back with Stefan's coffee and the pie and chips he had ordered. Something the women said made him pay attention again. 'What happened to that young man you used to go out with last spring, Bryony, the one who was so helpful? Nothing was ever too much trouble for him.'

The waitress was gathering dirty cups. She paused. 'Darren? He went back to Manchester, I think.'

'You were upset when he left the campsite, weren't you, love?'

The girl nodded, and sighed. 'I was, but I knew he would leave sooner or later. To be fair, my nan missed him as much as I did. He was always at her house, fixing one thing or another.'

'He helped a lot of old folks out with their shopping and things. He was Tony Snell's right hand man for a while.'

'Oh yes?' another woman said. 'And look where that got poor Tony! Despite all the good things people said about him, there was something I didn't trust about that Darren. He was a shady character.'

He had heard enough. When the waitress came to his table and asked him if he would like anything else, he smiled.

'I was wondering if I could have a word with you.'

276

Chapter Thirty-Four

'I'm sorry, Cassie, but I don't need you any more,' Sylvia Gasby said in lieu of greeting. 'There's only me here, and a cleaner was a luxury I can't afford.'

'I'm sorry to hear that.' Cassie smiled to hide her disappointment. Sylvia was the third client that week to finish with Bluebell Cleaning. 'Would it help if I came less often – every other week, for example?' she asked in a hopeful voice.

Sylvia shook her head. 'No, I don't want you to come at all. Tell me how much I owe you for this month and I'll pay you now.'

She sounded nervous, on edge. Poor Sylvia. The burglary must have taken its toll on her.

'Don't worry about it now. I'll pop my invoice in your letterbox later this week.'

The woman nodded. 'All right, but I want my spare set of keys back straight away.'

She extended her hand and Cassie frowned. Sylvia had never been so rude before.

'Of course,' she mumbled, pulling a bunch of keys out of her bag, together with a Post-it note. 'Here is your joke for the week. It's one of Granddad's latest. I hope you like it.'

Sylvia stuffed the keys in the pocket of her cardigan and read the note aloud. 'Why was the podiatrist angry at the traffic warden? Because his car was towed away.' She frowned. 'I don't get it... Ah yes, towed, as in toe.' A smile shivered on the corners of her mouth, and she slipped the paper into her pocket. 'Your granddad is a dear, dear man.'

Suddenly she looked about to burst into tears and Cassie stepped forward to comfort her. 'Whatever is the matter, Sylvia? Can I help at all? You seem upset.'

Sylvia recoiled with a gasp. 'It's nothing. Nothing at all. Goodbye.'

She slammed the door shut, leaving Cassie standing in the cold, with her feather duster sticking out of her cleaning bag and an overwhelming urge to cry.

She drove back to Red Moss, parked at the vicarage and gave herself a pep talk. Losing clients was bound to happen some time. It was part of running a business, and she shouldn't take it personally. Then why did she have the feeling that it *was* personal? Sylvia had behaved as if she actually disliked her, and she had no idea what she had done.

She wiped her tears, pulled the visor down and rubbed the smudged mascara with a tissue. She even put a bit of lip gloss on and forced a smile. There, that was better. She couldn't get out of the van looking like an angel of doom when she was supposed to be the good mood fairy! Yet doom was all she felt now Stefan had left...

One of her elderly customers – one of the few she had left – had remarked on how downcast she was. 'What's the matter with you, love? You didn't smile at your granddad's joke although it was a really good one this week... and you didn't even finish your cinnamon twist.'

The woman was right. The days merged into one another, bleak, grey and lonely. It hadn't even been a week since Stefan had left, and yet time seemed to stretch endlessly.

Reverend Bennett greeted her with her usual calm, friendly manner. As Cassie was early, she asked if she wouldn't mind giving the community centre a tidy up before coming back to the vicarage. 'The children made Christmas decorations last night and I'm afraid they left the place in a bit of a mess.'

A bit of a mess? Cassie thought when she walked into the community centre. The place looked like a tornado had swept through it – twice! As Cassie picked up plastic cups, empty bottles of cordial and packets of crisps that had been left on the tables, she recalled what Stefan told her about the whirlwinds that blew through the Sahara Desert. They were called '*chasse-poussière*'. How loving he had been when he had said she deserved to be called '*chasse tristesse*' too because she made his sadness disappear...

She let out a shaky sigh and swept up bits of tinsel, cardboard, felt and cotton wool from the floor, as well as glitter and white dust from the plaster of Paris. She was tipping the contents of her dustpan into a bin bag when three elderly women tottered in, with Doris Pearson leading the way.

Cassie looked at her and smiled. 'Good morning.'

The women didn't reply but gave her a harsh look before hanging their coats up. As Doris took her gloves off, Cassie noticed a large bandage on the back of her hand.

'What's wrong with your hand, Doris?' she asked. 'Isn't that where Fluffy scratched you the other day?'

Doris nodded curtly. 'The doctor said it was infected and gave me antibiotics. Fluffy would never have scratched me if he hadn't been upset about you locking him up in your house.'

'I did say I was sorry, but it wasn't my fault.'

Doris's eyes flashed in anger. 'What about this morning? It wasn't your fault again, I presume! I'm in a mind to call the RSPCA and report you for animal cruelty.'

Cassie put the rubbish bag down. 'What are you talking about?'

Doris waved her walking stick at her. 'Don't play the innocent with me, Cassie Bell. Not only did you take my Fluffy into your house again, but you used him as a guinea pig for your fancy smelling oils. He came home smeared in some disgusting lemon stuff.'

'I don't understand... Are you saying that he was in my house this morning?'

'That's exactly what I'm saying.'

'That's impossible. I checked every single window and door before leaving.' But she knew it was pointless. If Doris had decided she was guilty, nothing she could say would change her mind. It wasn't her fault Fluffy preferred Bluebell Cottage to his own house. It was however worrying that the cat had managed to sneak in again.

She carried on tidying up and tried to ignore Doris and the two other ladies who were whispering and staring at her as she wiped all the tables clean with a damp cloth.

'Are you going to be long?' Doris asked. 'Our meeting starts in ten minutes and we have important things to discuss in private.'

Reverend Bennett walked in and smiled. 'You do exaggerate, Doris. We're only talking about the rota for the cake stall at tomorrow's Christmas Fair. It's hardly top-secret business! Actually, would you mind getting the tea and coffee ready? The others won't be long.'

Doris cast Cassie one last begrudging look before disappearing into the small kitchen, and the vicar turned to Cassie. 'I left the vicarage back door open for you.'

'Thanks.' Cassie gathered her cleaning things and went into the hallway to put her coat on.

'You're far too trusting, vicar, leaving *her* alone in your house,' one of Doris's friends, a woman called Elspeth, said. 'I hope you locked your cash and jewellery away.'

Cassie's blood froze, and her heart started thumping so hard it hurt.

'Nonsense!' Julie Bennett's terse reply shot out.

'Nadine Hartley and Tabitha Sweeney were talking about *her* in the bakery yesterday and they said it was very odd that all her clients got burgled in the past few weeks.'

'From what I heard, it's not all Cassie's clients, but only a few of them,' Julie Bennett corrected, 'and it doesn't prove anything at all.'

'Still, they said—'

'I'm not interested in what these women have to say,' Julie Bennett's voice was sharper this time, 'and I suggest you ladies concentrate on preparing for the meeting instead of spreading malicious rumours.'

'You can't ignore what happened to poor Barbara,' Elspeth remarked. 'She said that after Cassie's last visit, her engagement ring – the one with the big ruby – disappeared, along with some money from her savings jar that she always keeps in the kitchen.'

'I always thought she was a bit odd,' Doris agreed. 'Remember that hoo-ha she made when she claimed she saw a murder up at Wolf Tarn and got the police involved? And all this carry-on with my Fluffy... The girl is trouble, I'm telling you. It's her granddad I feel sorry for. He'll be devastated when he finds out what she's been up to.'

So that was why Doris and her friends had looked at her in that way. They thought she was a thief – not just a cat snatcher, but a burglar too. Cassie exhaled slowly, but anger and shock made her whole body shake. Now the way Nadine had followed her around as she was cleaning her house earlier in the week made sense, as did Tabitha's last minute cancellation the day before, and the three clients who had decided not to employ her any longer.

And what about Barbara? How could the old lady believe that she would steal her favourite ring and help herself to her savings?

Well, she wouldn't have it. Nobody would call her a thief!

She squared her shoulders and marched right back into the community centre, right up to Elspeth who was placing cups and saucers on a table.

'How dare you accuse me of stealing from my clients?'

The woman jerked back with a startled cry. 'Cassie... You heard... Ahem... I was just...'

'All of you have known me and all my family for... like, forever, and you think me capable of stealing from my customers? Worse still, stealing from the very people I care for?' She stopped abruptly. Tears blurred her vision, and she wiped her eyes. Suddenly all her anger was spent and she stumbled against the table.

A calming hand patted her shoulder, and Julie said, 'It's not worth you getting upset about these ridiculous gossips, my darling. Come with me.'

Once in the vicarage kitchen, Julie pulled a chair out. 'Sit down. I'll make you a cup of tea.' She boiled a kettle, and put two cups on the table. 'I wouldn't take too much notice of Doris or Elspeth if I were you.'

'It's not just them, though, is it? I can't believe that neighbours, clients, and people I have known most of my life think I had something to do with the burglaries.' Cassie's voice broke.

Julie Bennett shrugged. 'It's only a few people, and they will soon see sense. Now, drink your tea and go home.'

Cassie drank her tea and stood up. 'Thanks, Julie, but you are one of the few customers I have left, and I will do my job here as planned.'

After Reverend Bennett left, Cassie poured some of her homemade lemon and vinegar cleaning fluid into a bucket, slipped her gloves on and scrubbed, wiped and polished until the kitchen taps and the sink glistened, the cupboards reflected the sunlight outside and there wasn't a single stain left on the tiled floor. The vicarage's bathrooms received the same treatment. Next she dusted and polished the furniture, vacuumed every room, and tackled the windows.

The mindless, repetitive gestures soothed her. Perhaps the burglaries would stop and the whole thing would blow over. But then people might say that she had stopped her criminal activities because she had been afraid of being caught. It was far better if the police arrested the culprit so she could clear her name. This really had to be one of the most horrid weeks of her life. Every day had brought more heartache and bad news.

She went home a couple of hours later. Something puzzled

her… How had Fluffy managed to sneak in and out of Bluebell Cottage that morning? As for the cat being covered in lemon-scented oil, she understood how that had happened the moment she opened the front door.

The diffuser bottle she kept on the hall table had smashed to the ground, and a puddle of scented oil slicked the floor, with ginger cat hairs sticking to the tiles… Fluffy must have knocked the bottle over and decided it was a good idea to roll about in the oil. Sighing, she stepped over it and followed the paw prints to the kitchen. They shot across the floor, all the way to the back door…

But the door was locked, she had made sure of that before leaving that morning! Just to make sure, she rattled the handle.

For a moment, she stared at the paw prints, unable to understand how it was possible that they seemed to go right to the door. It wasn't as if the cat could have gone through it, was it? No, of course not. Someone must have opened the door to let it out.

Her granddad must have called home that day.

She took her phone out of her bag and rang him at the farm.

'I didn't go home today, Trifle,' he said.

'Did you lend Rachel or Tim your keys by any chance?'

'Nope. Why do you ask?'

Now wasn't the moment to worry him about Fluffy or the back door, and even less about the nasty rumours some residents from Red Moss were spreading about her. Tonight was Comedy Night at the Eagle and Child, one of the most important events of the year for her grandfather. Kerry's and Alastair's wedding had given him his confidence back.

'It's nothing. Forget it. How are you feeling? Are you ready for tonight?'

He sighed. 'I'm trying to go over my jokes one last time but my knee is playing up and I can't concentrate.'

It was a good job then that she had copied all the jokes he was planning to perform that evening onto Post-it notes as backup in case his memory failed him.

'You have your medication, don't you? Why don't you take a couple of tablets for the pain?'

'Good idea. I'll do it right now.'

There was a knock on the front door. Frowning, she made her way to the front door. What if Doris had come to have another rant about her beloved cat?

'I have to go. There's someone at the door. I'll see you tonight.'

'See you tonight, Trifle.'

It wasn't Doris, but two police officers, a man and a woman, who stood on the doorstep.

The policeman smiled. 'Cassie Bell?'

She nodded.

'Could we have a word?'

She gasped, and rested her hand on the doorjamb for support. 'Has something happened to a member of my family? My mum or my step-dad in Tenerife?'

The man shook his head. 'No, it's nothing like that. Don't worry.'

She let out a sigh of relief and moved aside. 'Please come in. I'm sorry for the broken glass and the smell. My neighbour's cat knocked over a bottle of some essential lemon oil this morning,' she said as she led them into the kitchen. 'I've only just come back and haven't had time to mop it up.'

She should stop babbling, or they would think she was nervous... But she *was* nervous, even though she had no idea why.

'Please sit down.' She gestured to the chairs around the table.

'Nice cottage.' The policeman smiled.

Cassie smiled back. 'Thank you.'

The woman took out a notebook and a pen. 'I understand you live here with your grandfather, Joseph Bell.'

'That's right, but he isn't here at the moment. He is staying at Patterdale Farm with relatives.'

'And you are a cleaner by trade, aren't you? That's your van, parked outside.'

Cassie nodded. 'All my papers, my road tax and insurance, are in order, and I don't think I drove through any red lights. Did I?'

She smiled but the policewoman's face remained stony. 'Your name was mentioned in connection with a series of burglaries that were committed in and around Red Moss recently.'

'What?' Cassie's ears started buzzing, her body felt cold and clammy at the same time, and a wave of nausea made her heave. She gripped the back of a chair for support. 'I think I'm going to be sick.'

The policeman stood up and pulled the chair out for her. 'Please sit down, Miss Bell. I'll get you some water.'

He poured some tap water into a glass and handed it to her.

'Thank you.' She took the glass with a trembling hand.

'Better?' he asked. When she nodded, he carried on. 'Would you mind telling us where you were on the following days?' And he listed several recent dates.

Once her head had stopped spinning and her breathing was under control, Cassie pulled her diary out of her handbag and flicked through the pages to find the first date the policewoman had mentioned. 'I write down all my appointments with clients.'

The policewoman wrote everything down, then snapped her notebook shut and rose to her feet, followed by her colleague.

'We will check all this with your clients. Thank you for cooperating with us this morning. We'll be in touch.'

Chapter Thirty-Five

When Cassie walked into the Eagle and Child that evening most tables were occupied. It was standing room only at the bar, and from what she could see the back room was packed too. Red Moss's residents had turned out in force to support their local comedians and enjoy Big Jim's famous mulled wine.

She scanned the room and her heart sank. Stefan wasn't there. She hadn't really expected him to be, even if he had promised her granddad he'd attend – not after the way they had parted at Kerry's wedding reception. She didn't have his mobile number so she couldn't even reach him on his mobile. Perhaps it was for the best... What would she tell him anyway? He had made it crystal clear what he thought of her.

She glanced at the tiny stage that Big Jim had, like every year, erected next to the Christmas tree, and checked her handbag once again for the Post-it notes with her grandfather's jokes she had bundled together in preparation for the evening. His memory seemed fine these days, but it was better to be prepared.

From the table Big Jim had reserved for her family, she waved at Mason and Brenda, and at Salomé and Cecilia on the other side of the room. Behind the bar Sadie was chatting up Salomé's new employee. Her friend had been right about Max – or Maximilien, as he apparently preferred to be called. The man was indeed gorgeous. Tall, with green eyes and dark brown hair, he had a winning smile and the talent to create the most delicious pastries, which Salomé had forced on her all week under the guise of doing quality control. It was a shame her stomach was so knotted she hadn't been able to enjoy them...

She had attended Comedy Night every year since she was

a child, but it felt different this time, and not only because it was her granddad's last ever performance. She felt restless, and worry and sadness weighed heavily on her chest. Every time the door opened her heart stopped, then bumped to a start again. She forced a deep breath in. It was useless. She'd better accept once and for all that Stefan wasn't coming back.

Big Jim brought over a cup of mulled wine. The worried look on his face contrasted with the bright and cheerful red and green cowboy shirt he was sporting that evening. 'Hi, Cassie. Where's your granddad? The show starts in less than half an hour.'

Cassie frowned. 'He should be here by now... He's coming with Tim and Rachel. Perhaps their babysitter was running late. Let me check my phone.'

As 'reigning comedy king', her granddad would be last on stage but he needed to be there to open the competition and introduce the first contestant.

'There's a text from Rachel.' She read it out, '"Small problem with Joseph but on our way now." I wonder what could be the matter.'

'Never mind. I'll ask Sadie to hand out more mulled wine while we're waiting.' Big Jim hesitated. 'Actually, Cassie, I wanted to tell you that Ruby and I don't believe a word of these stupid rumours flying about in the village... you know, about the burglaries.'

Her smile crumpled as a toxic mix of shame and anxiety churned inside her, making her want to cry all over again. 'Thanks, Jim. It's sweet of you to say so.'

'I believe the police came to see you today.'

'Nothing stays a secret for long around here, does it?' She sighed. 'Yes, that's true. Two police officers came to see me this afternoon. I can't wait for them to catch that burglar, whoever they are.'

He put his big hand on her shoulder and gave her a comforting squeeze. 'We all do, love. The truth will come out eventually, don't worry. Let me get you more mulled wine to cheer you up.'

He pushed his way through the crowd at the bar, and she checked her phone again. There was no new text from Rachel.

Tom Hays, one of her grandfather's friends sitting at a nearby table, pointed at his watch and called out, 'Where's your granddad? I bet the old rascal chickened out when he heard there were people from London in the audience. The old "What did the policeman say..." or "Doctor, doctor" jokes won't cut it with them!'

People from London? Her fingers toying nervously with her phone, she glanced around the room, and spotted several of Alastair's friends standing near the bar. She couldn't see Nathan but perhaps he was in the back room. If he was here, she would tell him she would not take up his offer. He had given her until the following morning, but her mind was made up and there was no point in delaying their conversation.

She turned to look at Tom. 'He's on his way right now,' she replied with more assurance than she felt.

It was almost half-past eight when Tim, Rachel and her grandfather finally arrived. Tim walked ahead to carve a passage through the crowd, and Rachel linked arms with her granddad to support him. Cassie couldn't repress a gasp when she saw how ill and frail he looked. His shoulders were hunched, he looked pale and old, and his hand was shaking when he took his tweed cap off and put it on the table.

Cassie put her hand on his arm, worry gnawing at her chest. 'What's wrong? You look awful.'

'Nothing's wrong, Trifle,' he answered with a shrug. 'I got a bit confused with my arthritis medication this afternoon, that's all. I'm all right now.'

'What do you mean, you got confused?'

Rachel shook her head. 'He took a couple of sleeping tablets instead of his arthritis pills. We only realised something was wrong when he didn't come down to eat his tea, and when even the boys jumping on his bed didn't disturb him. It took us hours to wake him up, that's why we're so late.'

Cassie gasped. 'Granddad! Did you not look at the box?'

'I did, pet, but I couldn't find my glasses. The pills were all mixed up and they looked the same to me.'

'He's right,' Rachel said. 'The sleeping tablets were inside the box of arthritis medication.' She looked at him sternly. 'I don't know how this could have happened. It could have been extremely serious, Joseph, you realise that.'

'Aye. I'm sorry, darling.' He clasped his shaking fingers together on the table, and Cassie felt a rush of love and tenderness for him.

'I only picked up the box of medication from the cottage last week. In fact, it was Lambert who fetched it from the bathroom cabinet for me. I must have mixed up the tablets ages ago, but didn't realise as I haven't needed them for a while.'

Rachel frowned. 'It was last Friday, the day after our Louis broke his arm. Your knee was aching that day too, and that evening you went to bed straight after tea, and didn't even read the boys their story. You must have taken a sleeping tablet then too and we didn't realise. Who knows how long you've been doing that.'

Cassie's grandfather nodded. 'I suppose it explains why I was falling asleep during the day when you were out at work and waking up all befuddled to find that it was already evening.'

Tim came back with three cups of mulled wine and a pint of orange juice that he placed in front of her grandfather. 'That's all you'll be drinking tonight, Joseph.' He winked. 'Mixing alcohol with sleeping pills isn't a good idea, especially when you have your act to get through.'

'I suppose you're right.' Joseph shook his head but the look of utter dejection on his face made Cassie laugh, and she pecked a kiss on his cheek.

'You can have a drink tomorrow evening, after the fair,' she said to cheer him up.

The noise level in the pub suddenly increased as Big Jim made his way to the stage. 'Ladies and gentlemen, thank you for being here tonight for our annual Christmas Comedy Night. The reputation of our comedians draws crowds from the whole of Cumbria, and tonight again our contestants have come from far and wide and represent the best of comic genius our region has to offer, from Windermere to Keswick, from Troutbeck to Arnside.'

People laughed, but Jim soldiered on. 'As you know, our very own Joseph Bell has for the past fifteen years been our comedy champion. He is defending his title tonight and we cannot wait for him to regale us with his witty puns and unique jokes.'

He gestured for Cassie's grandfather to come forward. 'Ladies and gentlemen, I give you Joseph Bell!'

He passed the mike to Cassie's granddad, who smiled and waited for the clapping to die down. Colour had come back to his cheeks, and he was standing tall and straight again.

'Once again our friend Big Jim has set up the stage next to the Christmas tree, even though I tell him every single year that it's a bad idea, because it gives us "pines and needles".'

People jeered but he carried on. 'He never listens to me. It was the same the other day, when he was stuffing himself with chocolate log. "Slow down, Jim," I said, "or *Yule* get indigestion!" But like I said Big Jim always does exactly as he pleases – his sense of style, for example, is unique.'

He grimaced and pointed to Jim's cowboy shirt. 'He went to town to buy a camouflage shirt the other day, but as he couldn't find any, he came back with that instead.'

Big Jim shook his head, clapped his hand on his shoulder and handed him a piece of paper that Cassie's granddad read out loud. 'I am pleased to announce our first contestant of the evening, Rob Quince, who has come all the way from sunny Walney. Come here, son, don't be shy!'

A tall, gangly young man, with a face as red as a tomato climbed onto the stage. Cassie's granddad whispered something to him and they both laughed, then he wished him good luck and came back to sit down.

Cassie couldn't resist giving her grandfather another kiss. 'Well done,' she said as she leant against his arm, breathing in his familiar, reassuring scent.

'You're a good girl, Trifle.' He looked around the crowd, frowned, and turned back to her. 'I thought Lambert would be here tonight.'

Her eyes filled with tears at the mere mention of Stefan's name. She blinked and looked away. 'He left after Kerry's wedding. I haven't seen him since.'

'Have you two had a falling out?'

Her throat too tight to speak, she gave a little nod.

'He'll be back. He promised, didn't he?' He gave her hand a comforting pat.

There were seven contestants in total, and each with a very different kind of humour. Some told traditional jokes, others more risqué puns. There were even two female mimes.

'What was that all about?' her grandfather asked, shaking his head in dismay as the young women pirouetted off the stage, waving their black bowler hats and squirting water at the audience. 'They didn't even say a word! Jokes are meant to be spoken. It's a comedy night, not a flamin' circus.'

'They were funny, though, you have to admit,' Tim said, bright red from laughing.

Cassie nudged her grandfather. 'It looks like it's your turn. How are you feeling?'

'Never better.' But he struggled to get up from his chair, and Tim had to help him climb onto the stage.

'Why don't you go to bed and sleep it off, Granddad?' a man with a London accent shouted from the bar.

How rude! Cassie swung back to scan the crowd to see who had shouted. This time she spotted Nathan. He was chatting to his friends and laughing. She shot them an angry look and turned back to give her granddad an encouraging smile.

His face pale and drawn, he swayed on his feet before taking hold of the mike to start his act. To be on the safe side, she took the Post-it notes out of her bag and put them on the table in front of her.

Chapter Thirty-Six

Stefan had left Manchester well before the Friday evening rush hour, but there had been a string of incidents on the motorway and the journey that should have taken a couple of hours turned out to take twice as long. He would go straight to the Eagle and Child. With luck, he could still watch Joseph's act.

He could hear the laughter and the clapping as soon as he got out of the car. There were other sounds too – sounds of heckling and booing that he hadn't expected. He pushed the door to the pub open as Joseph launched into a joke.

Stefan's first thought was that the man looked ill. His features were pinched, his skin more lined than usual and he appeared to sway on his feet as if he was drunk. He scanned the audience and spotted Tim, Rachel... and Cassie, but she was far too busy flicking through a bundle of Post-it notes to take any notice of him.

'I went into our lovely village bakery the other day,' Joseph was saying, hesitation creeping into his voice, 'and the shop assistant said... ahem... she said that she could hear noises coming from the back room... at night. Ahem...'

He paused, took a handkerchief out of the pocket of his corduroy trousers to wipe his forehead and looked at Cassie. She immediately glanced down at one of the Post-it notes before mouthing a few words.

Joseph nodded, and resumed speaking. '"Someone's hiding in there," she said, "but who could be hiding in a bakery at Christmas?" "Well, that's obvious," I replied, "it can only be a mince spy!"'

He smiled as the audience cheered. Cassie put the note down on the table and leant against the back of her chair but she still looked tense as her fingers flicked restlessly through her notes.

He had expected to see her there, of course, but what he hadn't expected was the way his heartbeat picked up and his throat tightened, so much he felt he couldn't breathe.

'That mince spy could have been in trouble with the police had he been caught,' Joseph carried on. 'I love my policemen jokes, as you well know. Here is a brand new one for you, folks. What did the policeman say to the naughty jacket potato?' Joseph paused. 'He said, "You're under a vest..."'

Joseph took a few steps on the stage, paused and frowned as he pulled on his ear, a puzzled look on his face. 'Can you hear that, folks?'

People in the audience shouted that they couldn't hear anything, but one man exclaimed, 'Get your hearing aid fixed if you're hearing voices, old man!'

Ignoring him, Joseph carried on. 'I can definitely hear something. It sounds like... a Christmas Quacker! Do you know what that is?'

'It's a bad joke, like the ones you've been feeding us for the past half an hour!' the same man shouted again.

It was the stocky man with the horsy face he had sat next to at the wedding reception. Next to him, Nathan Hardman threw his head back to laugh.

Why was he laughing with his friend instead of sitting with Cassie and supporting her grandfather? After all, she said she was going to work for him, and more importantly they had spent the night together the evening of the wedding... and what a night it must have been for Cassie to forget that the wedding decorations at the clubhouse needed to be taken down.

He had tried, and failed, so many times over the past few days not to think about her in Hardman's arms – in Hardman's bed. Tried, and failed, not to picture her kissing him, smiling at him with that sunny smile of hers, looking at him with eyes clouded with pleasure... the way she had looked at him.

He realised that his fists were clenched, so he took a deep breath and made a conscious effort to uncurl his fingers.

'So, any idea what a Christmas Quacker is?' Joseph quizzed the audience once more.

'Festive Porridge oats?' a man's voice shouted out.

Joseph shook his head. 'Nope.'

'A rubbish doctor?' Cassie's pink-haired friend suggested.

Joseph smiled. 'I might as well give you the answer. A Christmas Quacker, folks, is what you get when you cross Santa with a duck.'

There were whistles and hooting as Stefan pushed his way through the crowd towards the bar. At least if he stood near Hardman and his pals he could perhaps stop them from shouting any more nasty comments.

He cut through the crowd and managed to reach the bar just as applause died down and Joseph was speaking again. He made a few more jokes about Father Christmas and elves, some of which Stefan remembered because they were on the Post-it notes Cassie had given him when she came to Belthorn.

'Last one from me, folks,' Joseph said. 'What do you call an impolite elf riding a reindeer? A Rud-elf!' He slotted the mike back into the stand. 'That's all for tonight. Thanks for listening.'

Big Jim climbed onto the stage and gave Joseph's back a pat. 'Our distinguished panel of judges will now proceed to the voting and I'll announce the results shortly.'

'Thank goodness that's over!' Hardman's friend shouted. 'I never heard so much rubbish in my life.'

Stefan came right up to him. 'I think you should show more respect,' he said in a low voice.

The man opened his eyes wide. 'Hey, I recognise you. You were at the wedding reception. What's up? Don't tell me you enjoyed the old man's performance. It was awful.'

He guffawed and put his pint glass on the counter. His blue

eyes were bloodshot, his face flushed. It didn't take much to see that he was drunk… and full of himself.

'Nobody was forcing you to stay,' Stefan said, 'so get out or shut up. Which will it be?'

Hardman tilted his chin and stared at him. 'Hey! It's a free country. The old man's completely hopeless. Everybody thinks so but nobody has the guts to say it aloud.'

Stefan narrowed his eyes. 'It's Cassie's grandfather you're talking about.'

Hardman shrugged. 'So what?'

The urge to punch the guy was suddenly so overwhelming Stefan had to shove his clenched fists into his pocket. Hardman must have seen something in his eyes, unless it was the set of his jaw, because he stumbled back against the bar and knocked his friend's pint over, spilling beer all over his trousers.

He swore and looked down at his trouser legs. 'Look at what you made me do… and all that for an old man who can't even crack a stupid joke without forgetting his lines!'

Stefan pushed a deep breath down and forced his fingers to uncurl. He had never been a violent man but right now he could easily do something he might regret… or not.

'What's going on, Nathan? Is there a problem?' Cassie asked behind him.

Stefan turned to face her. 'Good evening, Cassie.'

She gasped, her face became even paler and her eyes opened wide in shock. No wonder she was surprised. She hadn't seen him without a beard and with short hair before.

'Stefan? I didn't see you come in. You look… different.' She looked from him to Hardman. 'What's happening?'

Hardman's friend pointed at Stefan. 'Your *friend* insulted us.'

Cassie frowned. 'Did you?' she asked him. 'Why?'

'I…' Stefan swallowed hard, finding it impossible to repeat the nasty comments Hardman had said about Joseph. 'We had a minor disagreement.'

He smiled a contrite smile. He couldn't stop gazing at her, and taking in her tousled blonde hair, her beautiful grey eyes and the pretty pink lips set into a pout he wanted to kiss, and kiss again. How he wanted to pull her into his arms, bury his face into her hair and breathe in her sunny scent, and never let her go. He had missed her so much it was almost like physical pain.

Hardman cast him a venomous glare. 'A minor disagreement? I could have you done for affray,' he sputtered.

Big Jim made his way behind the bar. 'Affray? Give over!' He laughed, and his belly shook under his colourful cowboy shirt. 'You had too much to drink and stumbled against the counter, that's all. You should go home and change into dry trousers.'

Looking at Stefan, he broke into a smile. 'I've been itching to shut these two up most of the evening.'

Hardman's mouth gaped open. 'I have just been assaulted and I'm the one who has to get out? I could have your licence revoked, do you hear me?'

Big Jim wasn't smiling any longer. 'Why don't you try? I don't think you'll find anyone here to back you up.'

Hardman surveyed the crowed and sneered. 'I'm not surprised, actually. It's full of peasants who stink of sheep dung.'

Big Jim leaned over the counter. 'Now you're really asking for trouble. Get out and don't bother coming back.'

Cassie gasped. 'Jim... Nathan... Please don't argue. It's Comedy Night. We should be happy, not shouting at one another.'

'Comedy Night? That's the best joke I heard all night,' Hardman sneered before looking at Cassie. 'Actually, I only endured the evening because I wanted to talk to you, but I guess it's going to have to wait until tomorrow. I've given you enough time to decide if you want my job or not. I'll be at the holiday cottage until ten a.m. tomorrow. Don't be late.'

He turned to his friend and gestured for him to follow. 'Come on, let's get out of this dive.'

Stefan gave Cassie a tentative smile. Hardman wasn't the only one who wanted to talk. He had a lot to say, and an awful lot to apologise about.

He cleared his throat, which did nothing to make his voice any smoother. 'How have you been?'

She tilted her chin up. 'Fine. And you?'

'I'm all right.' He leant forward. 'Listen, I am sorry I left so suddenly. I had to take care of a few things…'

She shrugged. 'You don't have to explain anything to me. After all, I'm only the scheming woman who slept with you for the sake of a measly bonus. At least, that's what you believe.' She drew in a shaky breath. 'So that you know, I emailed Charles Ashville that he could keep his bonus.' Her voice wobbled, and suddenly tears swam in her eyes.

He reached out to touch her arm then thought better of it and let his hand drop by his side and cursed himself for the umpteenth time. He had to apologise, and tell her he had spoken in anger, but to do so he wanted to be alone with her, not surrounded by noise and people.

'Could we go somewhere quiet for a few minutes? I really need to talk to you.'

She cast him an angry glare and shook her head. 'What makes you think I want to talk to you? You said more than enough the other night…' She turned on her heels and pushed her way through the crowd to the ladies' toilets.

He deserved that, but he didn't like this feeling of helplessness, this sensation of having rusty nails pushed slowly into his heart. He had hurt her, and if he could never take his words back, at least he had to apologise properly.

Big Jim tapped him on the shoulder and handed him a cup of mulled wine. 'I wouldn't take too much notice if Cassie is a bit cranky tonight. She's had a bad day. The police came to see her about the burglaries around the village. There have been nasty rumours circulating about her, and she lost a few clients.'

'What rumours?'

'Some people said that she was involved in the burglaries,' Big Jim said.

Stefan's fingers contracted on his glass. 'She's done nothing wrong,' he said in a gruff voice.

'I know that, but you know what some people are like.'

'Thanks for telling me. And thanks for the drink.' Stefan took his mulled wine and walked over to Joseph's table. He had to tell him about Morse. Then he'd drive to the campsite and confront the man himself. Talking to Cassie would have to wait…

Chapter Thirty-Seven

She wasn't ready to face her family, not when her heart beat so hard and her whole being was in turmoil... Stefan was back. He said he wanted to talk, but what was the point? She knew what he thought of her. And yet despite it all, she couldn't stop her feelings for him. Couldn't stop wanting him. Couldn't stop loving him.

It had been hard enough going to Belthorn every day – her footsteps echoing in the empty house, her fingers trailing on the clothes he'd left behind that carried his fresh, masculine scent, and her thoughts flowing back to the tender and passionate moments they had shared in his bed, on the sofa, in front of the fire in the drawing room downstairs; her body remembering his heated whispers and caresses, and the way his eyes darkened and his body tensed and hardened as he moved above her, inside her; and her heart remembering his sweet goodnight kisses. He had trusted her with his most traumatic memories. She had told him about her nightmarish events at Wolf Tarn. They had shared more than hot kisses and intimate embraces.

Or so she thought... How could he believe, even for a second, that she had faked all that for the sake of a few thousand pounds?

She let out a resigned sigh. Whatever he had to say could wait until she went to Belthorn the following day.

Big Jim's booming voice was announcing the results of the comedy contest as she walked out of the toilets. She held her breath and crossed her fingers but she already knew that her granddad wouldn't win tonight. He hadn't been his usual sparkling self. He had been hesitant, had forgotten a few lines. He had even resorted to standard Christmas cracker jokes, even though that was against the competition rules.

Thank goodness she'd had the good idea to bring her notes to prompt him when he faltered.

'Ladies and gentlemen,' Big Jim started, 'I am delighted to crown our new Comedy Queens – yes, you heard me right, Comedy Queens, the wonderfully talented mimes Chantelle and Neve. Girls, if you care to come on the stage to receive your prize…'

Cassie's heart sank. She knew it would be hard for her granddad to win again this year, but it was still a shock and she dare not look at him for fear of seeing the sadness and disappointment on his face.

Clapping and cheering erupted as the mimes, still in costume and with their face paint on, hopped on stage, smiling and giggling to receive a bottle of champagne each.

Big Jim waited until the noise had died down. 'But that's not all. This year, we are awarding a lifetime achievement prize to a very dear and very special friend – Joseph Bell, our comedy king for the past fifteen years.'

This time the noise inside the pub was deafening, and Cassie's eyes filled with tears as her grandfather climbed on the stage, helped by Tim and Rachel. Big Jim gave him a bottle of special ale that he clutched against his chest as he took the microphone again.

'What can I say, folks? Thank you, from the bottom of my heart.' His voice shook and his eyes were shiny. 'It has been an honour to perform here every year for so long, but it's time to bow out.' He pulled a comical face. 'I'm getting on in years, and I'm losing my marbles.'

'Tell us something we don't know!' one of his old friends shouted.

Nodding to the two mimes, he added. 'Ladies, you were brilliant, but you look awfully young to me. Do your parents know you're mimes, or have you kept that quiet?'

Everybody laughed. He didn't seem upset by the judges' decision in the slightest, quite the opposite in fact.

'Look everybody, I can do miming too,' he said, making a kind of wiping gesture as if he was cleaning a window.

'What are you doing, you muppet?' another of his friends shouted.

'I'm cleaning windows,' he replied, 'which reminds me of a bloke who told me the other day that his wife had left him for the window cleaner. He was a bit upset, as you can imagine, but I told him not to worry. "She'll be back", I said, "when she realises that the glass isn't always cleaner on the other side."'

He bowed to the applauding audience, and, still clutching his large bottle of real ale, sat back at the table.

'Well done, Granddad!' She bent down to kiss his cheek. 'Are you not too disappointed to have lost your crown?'

He gave her a smile. 'I'm not disappointed at all, Trifle. Those two girls were funny, even if they didn't say a word. It was high time I passed the baton on. And to tell the truth, I like real ale better than champagne.' He frowned. 'Although I may need to drink something stronger than beer after what Lambert told us.'

Immediately, her heartbeat picked up again. Frowning, she looked around, but Stefan was nowhere to be seen. 'Why? What did he say?'

'It was about young Darren, and you'll never guess. Apparently, the scoundrel has been fleecing old folks all over the country.'

'What do you mean?'

'He makes himself useful to old people, pretending to fix stuff whilst all the time taking money or bank details from them to rob them. Lambert said that he believes Morse even interferes with their medication to make them confused.'

He shook his head. 'That's what he must have done to me too, and I never suspected anything. I thought there was something wrong with me for dozing off during the day and not remembering things.'

'How does Stefan know all this?'

'He went to places where Darren worked and talked to people.'

'I see.' So many things fell into place suddenly.

Her granddad frowned. 'You don't seem overly surprised, Trifle.'

'I am... but everything makes sense now.' Her grandfather's money problems, the radiator that leaked no matter how many times Darren came to 'fix' it, Fluffy who kept coming in and his paw prints leading to the back door... Darren must have drugged her granddad and snooped through their personal papers for his bank details, for her cleaning logbook, as well as the code for the alarm to Tabitha Sweeney's house which she had foolishly written down. He must also have kept a key when he fitted a new lock to sneak in and out of Bluebell Cottage when they weren't there.

She gasped. What about Barbara? Darren had fitted a new lock to her back door too. He must have slipped back into her house too, taken her ring and stolen her money.

And what about the stuff that had gone missing from the holiday lets? Did Darren steal them after making copies of the keys to the holiday cottages?

She glanced around the room. 'Where is Stefan?' That was probably what he had wanted to talk to her about before she stormed off to the toilets.

'He went to the campsite to talk to Darren,' Rachel replied.

Cassie got up and grabbed her handbag. 'Then I'll go too.'

Tim scrambled to his feet. 'I'm coming with you. It could be dangerous.'

Cassie's grandfather shook his head. 'Sit down, Tim, and finish your pint. Lambert won't let anything happen to Cassie. He cares far too much about her.'

'No he doesn't!' Cassie retorted.

Rachel chuckled. 'Don't be daft. It's obvious he does, from the way he looks at you, and the way he talks about you.'

Both her grandfather and Tim gave her a knowing smile, and Cassie's chest tightened. If only they knew... Whatever Stefan might have once felt for her was gone, replaced with scorn and anger.

She slipped her coat on and grabbed hold of her handbag. 'I wish you were right. I'll be in touch as soon as there is news.'

As she drove to the campsite, fingers clamped on the steering wheel, she recalled her last meeting with Darren. He had been writing his CV, and said he was thinking of leaving Red Moss. Perhaps he was already on his way to a new place where he could con people and play havoc with their health by mixing up their medication.

To think that she had defended him when Stefan accused him of fiddling with her tyres! Now she was sure he wasn't stalking her or interested in her personally. He certainly wasn't in love with her. He only wanted information about her clients. And when he drove to Belthorn to bring the bottle of wine he claimed she'd forgotten, insisted he wanted to help, and asked for a tour of the manor house, he probably only wanted to locate items worth stealing...

There were only a few cars at the campsite, but Darren's white Fiesta wasn't among them. She parked next to Stefan's four-wheel drive and dashed into the manager's office, which was lit up.

Stefan and Patrick were riffling through a stash of papers on the desk and both turned round as she came in. Stefan put the papers down and arched his eyebrows. 'Cassie? What are you doing here?'

He looked so different now he had shaved his beard and with his brown hair shorter that she felt shy and awkward. 'My granddad told me about Darren. Where is he? Have you spoken to him yet?'

Patrick's shoulders sagged and he shook his head. 'He's done a runner. I left him in charge today and when I returned, the office was a complete mess. He took all the cash he could find, here and in the clubhouse. He even took the office laptop and printer. Stefan told me what he's done, not only in Red Moss but in other places too. I can't believe I never suspected anything.'

'I didn't either,' Cassie said, 'and he was at my house several times a week, pretending to help my granddad with DIY. So what happens now?'

Patrick sighed. 'I phoned the police. They're looking for him.'

Stefan put his hand on Patrick's shoulder. 'They'll catch up with him. In the meantime, I'll help you sort things out in here.'

'I'll help too,' Cassie decided, taking her coat off and draping it on the back of a chair.

Patrick smiled weakly. 'That's kind of you. Thanks. While you two sort things out here, I'll make a start on the clubhouse.'

He closed the door behind him, and they were alone in the office.

Cassie picked up a stash of pens and pencils from the floor and stuck them into a drawer at random whilst Stefan arranged papers in neat piles on the desk. Neither of them seemed eager to talk, and for a minute or two the silence fizzed with tension and awkwardness.

Stefan cleared his throat. 'Big Jim said the police questioned you about the burglaries. At least now they'll know you had nothing to do with them.'

She looked at him. 'That's thanks to you. What made you suspect Darren?'

'The fact it took me ten minutes to fix the radiator in the room where you keep all your papers; that your neighbour's cat kept sneaking into your house even though you were adamant you hadn't let him in; and the fact most of your clients were getting burgled.'

'The cat!' she exclaimed suddenly. 'Of course, Darren has been sporting nasty scratches on his hand for the past few days – the same as Doris. Perhaps Fluffy scratched him one day when he sneaked into Bluebell Cottage with him.'

She hesitated. 'Actually, there's something else I need to thank you for. I'm sorry I didn't help you tidy up the clubhouse last Sunday. I did come but you had already left by the time I arrived.'

His eyes turned cold. 'I suppose you were too busy finalising your job description with Hardman.'

Her breath caught in her throat. 'Is that what you believe? That I was with Nathan and couldn't be bothered to come here?'

He arched his eyebrows. 'Isn't that what happened?'

'You really have a poor opinion of me, don't you?' Hurt made her voice tremble and clenched a cruel fist around her heart.

She swallowed hard and tilted her face. 'If you must know, I stayed at Salomé's with Cecilia. We cursed men, drank too much wine and ate cake all night... well, until I collapsed. I couldn't get up in the morning, and by the time I made it here, it was too late and you had already packed everything up.'

He closed his eyes, let out a deep, long breath.

'And for the record,' she carried on, 'I won't be accepting Nathan's job offer. If I'm ever to become a designer, I will do it on my own terms and not with someone who stole my ideas and blackmailed me into keeping quiet, and who insulted me by saying nobody would ever look at designs made by a lowly cleaner. Besides, it annoys me the way he thinks he's irresistible and I'm stupid, and he can get me to agree to anything he wants... I may have had a crush on him years ago, but it's over now.'

'Are you saying that you won't be leaving Red Moss to be with him, to work for him?'

'That's exactly what I'm saying.' She tilted her head up defiantly. 'I suppose you weren't expecting that, were you? After all, you thought I would do anything for money.'

He shook his head. 'No, I never believed that of you, and I regretted my stupid, nasty words the second I spoke them. It's just that... Hardy got to me, played on all my insecurities –

not that it makes it right, of course. And when I saw you with Hardman...'

He let out a long, shaky breath. 'I suppose I was jealous. I'm sorry I hurt you, and sorry I messed things up between us. I was an idiot, and I wouldn't blame you if you wanted nothing to do with me but...'

His face softened as he took a step towards her, and a deep, golden fire glowed in his eyes. 'Whatever you decide, whatever happens now, I want you to know that I'm sorry I caused you pain. I hope you can forgive me one day... and I love you.' He paused and repeated, 'I love you, Cassie Bell.'

She held her breath. 'You do?'

He nodded, extended his hand and stroked the tips of her fingers in a timid and heart-warming caress. Happiness bubbled inside her. With a shriek of delight, she closed the gap between them, and linked her arms around his neck. 'Of course, I forgive you!'

He wrapped his arms around her waist. 'Just like that?'

She laughed. 'Just like that! I was never able to hold a grudge, even if that makes me a complete pushover.'

His eyes softened and a slow, tender smile formed on his lips. 'It doesn't make you a pushover at all. It makes you a beautiful person – and the most wonderful woman I've ever met.'

This time she had nothing to say. She could only look at him. Her eyes filled with tears, and her heart felt almost too full of love, hope and joy as she took in the intense heat in his eyes, the line of his lips, the broken nose and fine scars lining his now clean-shaven face. How could this strong, brave and selfless man believe he was inferior to the likes of Piers or Nathan?

He pulled her closer. 'I want to kiss you.'

'Then why don't you?' she asked.

Holding her tightly she could hardly breathe, and covered her mouth with his.

Chapter Thirty-Eight

How he had missed her! Missed holding her, kissing her. Missed the feel of her body in his arms, the taste of her lips, and her scent surrounding him and warming him like sunshine. More than anything else, he had missed the joy, the fun, and the kindness she radiated onto everyone she touched. When she said she hadn't spent the night with Hardman and had no intention of leaving Red Moss with him, something in his chest had loosened and expanded – like a window opening onto glorious blue sky.

'Will you ever forgive me for doubting you, for believing even for one second Hardy's slimy lies?' His throat tightened. 'The thing is that I couldn't see how you could ever fancy someone like me.'

She looked up. 'I don't just *fancy* you, Stefan. I love you.'

His hands stilled. 'But I let everybody down. People died because of me.'

Her fingers stroked the back of his neck in a soft, feathery caress. 'It wasn't you who trapped these poor people in the dispensary. It wasn't you who launched the rocket attack on the helicopter. You did your best, and it's about time you forgave yourself.'

She rose on her tiptoes, and looked into his eyes. 'I love you, Stefan, and nothing you can say will change how I feel. When you left I felt like I was dying inside, and I never, ever, want to feel like that again.'

He looked into her eyes, and his heart felt too big for his chest. He was about to kiss her again when the door to the office slammed open, and Patrick walked in, holding three glasses.

He froze in the doorway. 'Ah. Sorry. I didn't mean to interrupt anything.'

Cassie blushed and pulled away from Stefan's embrace, but still held on to his hand.

'I got us a tipple to keep us going,' Patrick said, putting three glasses on the desk. 'By the way, the police just phoned. They haven't located Darren yet but got a search warrant for his father's house in Manchester and found pieces of jewellery that match the description of several stolen items. It looks like Morse senior was helping sell off the stuff his son had stolen.'

'What I don't understand is why he made such a mess of this place,' Stefan remarked. 'He must have known you would alert the police straight away... Why didn't he just hand in his notice and slip away quietly? He didn't know I was about to expose him, so why attract attention on himself like this?'

He gestured to the mess in the room. 'This looks like the action of somebody irrational and in a panic – someone who's lost their grip on things.'

'He was a little odd yesterday, now that you mention it,' Patrick said. 'His hand was swollen and seemed to be causing him pain, and he looked feverish. I even asked him if he needed to see the doctor.'

Cassie gasped. 'He said he'd been scratched by a cat... Doris had to have antibiotics when Fluffy scratched her hand the other day. Fluffy must have scratched him too. He does have a bit of a temper.'

'Like its owner,' Stefan remarked. He sighed. 'Right, we'd better make a move or we'll never get this place tidied up.'

An hour later, the office was almost back to normal.

'You two should go home now,' Patrick said. 'I can manage on my own.'

'Are you sure?' Stefan asked.

'Positive. Off you go.'

As soon as they were outside and Patrick closed the door, Stefan took Cassie in his arms. 'It's late. Do you want to go back to the pub? It may still be open. Or would you rather go home, to Bluebell Cottage?'

She put her hands on his shoulders and looked into his eyes.

'I'd rather go back to Belthorn with you,' she replied.

He tightened his grip around her waist and bent down to kiss her again, and again. 'That's the answer I was hoping for.'

She drove ahead and Stefan followed, and it wasn't long before they arrived at Belthorn.

'Shall I make a fire?' he asked as they walked into the drawing room.

She switched on the fairy lights along the mantelpiece. 'Good idea. I'll get us a hot drink and warm up some stew for you. I made a batch last week and froze it and—'

He grabbed hold of her, and pulled her to him. 'Will you stop this?'

'Stop what?'

A smile tugged at the corner of his mouth. 'Stop your Bluebell Cleaning Fairy antics. I don't need food, or drink. I only need you.'

He cupped her face between his hands, and bent down, teasing her mouth until her lips parted, and kissed her. She let out a muffled whimper, and curled her fingers in the lapels of his parka.

'I missed you,' he said, in a hoarse whisper before raking his fingers in her hair, and taking a deep breath. 'God, I missed you.'

It was very late when she snuggled in his arms with a contented sigh. They had made it to bed eventually, feasted on toast dripping with jam and a mug of tea for her and a couple of ham and cheese sandwiches and black coffee for him.

'I didn't even ask you if your granddad retained his Comedy King title at the pub,' he asked.

'He didn't, but he seemed all right about it. I think he was relieved to find out that the reason why he was so drowsy and confused all the time these past few weeks was that Darren mixed his medicine with sleeping tablets.'

'In the places I visited, people told me how the elderly

people Morse seemingly helped with DIY became suddenly ill and confused.'

'Probably in order to make them easier to steal from.'

He nodded. 'I hope the police catch him soon. He has done a lot of harm, and not only to your granddad.' He pulled her on top of him, his arms tense like steel bands around her, his heartbeat reverberating inside her, and his eyes dark with desire. 'But enough about Darren Morse.'

'You're doing *what*?' Cassie looked at Stefan, trying very hard not to burst out laughing.

He put his mobile back into his pocket and pulled a face. 'Big Jim said his wife needed help behind the counter because one of their barmaids had called in sick and he couldn't spend all afternoon dressed up as Santa in the grotto... What else could I do?' A faint and endearing blush crept onto his cheeks, which made her want to knot her arms around his neck and give him a long, tender kiss.

'Besides,' he added, 'it's for a good cause. I'm pretty sure no one will guess I'm the one in the Father Christmas outfit, so it will be more money for the Mountain Rescue Service.' He looked at her, and there was a trace of vulnerability in his eyes. 'You don't think I'm going to scare all the children away, do you?'

'Of course not, but they're going to wonder why Father Christmas speaks with a French accent this year.'

'I could always say I have been holidaying on the Côte d'Azur.'

She smiled. 'When I think that a few weeks ago you didn't even want a Christmas tree, and today you're dressing up as Father Christmas!'

She checked her watch. She'd better hurry if she didn't want to miss Nathan at the holiday cottage. 'I'll see you later. Who knows, I may even pay you a visit in your grotto so I can sit on your knee and give you a cuddle.'

He grinned back. 'I would like that very much.' His face became serious again. 'Are you sure you don't want me to come with you? I'm not happy about you meeting Hardman on your own.'

'I'm only going to tell him I don't want his job.' She planned to tell Nathan more, but Stefan didn't need to know. He would only insist on coming with her, and this was something she wanted to do on her own. Her days of feeling inferior and insecure and of being scared to speak out were over.

'I still don't like it,' Stefan said.

'Don't worry. I'll be fine.'

He sighed, and there was suddenly an air of mild panic on his face. 'Then I'd better go. Big Jim said I could change in his flat above the pub, which means I'm going to have to walk down the streets dressed like Father Christmas and make a right fool out of myself.'

This time she didn't hesitate. Never mind that they were in the main street and half of Red Moss would see them. She stepped closer to him, rose on her tiptoes and put her hands on either side of his face. 'You'll be great.' And she gave him a long, leisurely kiss.

They agreed to meet at the Fair in the afternoon and Cassie drove to Nathan's holiday cottage. Despite her earlier show of confidence, the knot of anxiety in her stomach was growing bigger and tighter by the second, and when she rang the bell, she felt sick.

Nathan opened the door and squinted against the bright sunlight. He was unshaven, his skin was pale and blotchy and his eyes red-rimmed. 'It's about time.'

He gestured for her to go in and she reluctantly followed him into the kitchen. 'The others left for London an hour ago,' he said, plonking himself on a stool at the kitchen bar in front of a steaming mug of coffee.

There were dirty plates and glasses, takeaway boxes, and empty bottles of beer, vodka and whisky strewn everywhere.

'I see nobody bothered to tidy up,' she remarked.

He arched his eyebrows. 'That's what the cleaner gets paid for... And that would be you, unless you accept my offer, which frankly you would be stupid not to.'

'Then you can call me stupid,' she replied with a cold voice. 'And for your information, holidaymakers are supposed to leave their cottage reasonably clean, so I will take photos of the mess you've made and you and your friends will be charged for the extra cleaning.'

To make her point, she took her phone out of her bag.

He stared at her in shock. 'Hang on a minute. Did you just say that you don't want the internship?'

She nodded. 'That's right.'

'Do you have any idea how lucky you were to get such an offer?'

'Lucky?'

'You're hardly qualified and have no experience. You should be bloody grateful I was ready to take you on.'

Her fingers gripped her phone more tightly. Suddenly she knew that she was doing the right thing. Nathan would always try to wriggle out of giving her the recognition she deserved, and she would never be able to prove anything against him. Unless... She glanced down at her phone, pressed on the recording button and slipped the phone back into her bag.

'So that you know,' she said, 'I won't be signing your non-disclosure agreement either. I intend to go to London and show Maritel's general manager the draft sketches I have left.'

Nathan slammed his mug on the bar, jumped down from his stool and walked towards her, his mouth twisted into a nasty, menacing scowl, and a cruel glint shone in his dark brown eyes. 'You bitch. You won't spoil things for me, do you hear? I won't let you. I need this contract.'

She took a step back. 'You should have thought of that

before, Nathan. You should have been honest and told Maritel you were using my designs.'

She tried to keep her voice calm even though her heart drummed fast and her throat was tight. Surely he wouldn't harm her?

'You said you had other sketches,' Nathan said. 'Where are they? I'll buy them from you.'

She backed off again. 'They're not for sale.'

He frowned then his face softened, and the charming, cajoling smile she remembered so well played on his lips. 'Don't be like that. I'm sure we can come to some agreement. What if I gave you some of the money Maritel paid for the London refurbishment... on the condition you sign that non-disclosure agreement, of course?'

She shook her head. 'I want them to know you used my ideas.'

The soft look vanished from his eyes. 'Go on then. Try it. They'll only laugh. You're a cleaner, for Pete's sake! What do you know about interior design?'

'I know enough to have won the competition.'

'It will be your word against mine. I'll say you stole the designs from my office when you were cleaning, that you wanted revenge because you had the hots for me... That bit is true, isn't?' His lips stretched into a mean smile.

So he had known how she felt about him? Her face felt warm, but she didn't deny it. 'That was years ago, Nathan. I was young and impressionable.'

'Ah! I knew it. You were always looking at me with big, puppy eyes...' He shook his head, and carried on, 'You'll be made to pay a massive amount in damages and you'll lose your pathetic little cleaning company, all the way down to your last feather duster.'

He must have thought she would quake in her shoes, but she wasn't afraid. Even if nothing came out of it, and if the Maritel executives did laugh at her like Nathan predicted, she would still take her portfolio to London and prove that it was her ideas Nathan had copied. And now, she also had the recording of their conversation…

'We'll see about that. Leave the keys to the cottage in the key box when you go, and don't forget to clean up your mess.'

This time he didn't try to stop her.

Her hands were shaking as she drove back to Bluebell Cottage. She may have looked calm in front of Nathan, but now it was over she was overwhelmed by the sheer unpleasantness of it all. She needed a moment alone and a cup of tea at home.

A strong smell of lemon essential oil still floated in the hallway when she walked in and hung her coat. There may be no sign that Darren or Fluffy had sneaked in again, but she couldn't help feeling restless. She would never feel safe at Bluebell Cottage until she had all the locks changed.

The idea of talking to Piers may make her physically sick, but she needed his approval to change the locks. She also needed to clarify her position regarding the holiday lets contract… and Belthorn.

'Hardy,' Piers barked down the phone. She could hear men shouting in the background. He must be watching a rugby match.

'I don't mind if you're paying for it,' he said a moment later, when she had explained about fitting new locks at Bluebell Cottage. After their last encounter, she was expecting angry words, insults even, but he sounded strangely subdued, probably because there were people around.

She took a deep breath. 'Actually, there was something else. According to my contract I get one week's notice, and even though I haven't received any official confirmation it is now over a week since you fired me. I am therefore no longer your employee and you need to find a new cleaner and a housekeeper for Belthorn.'

There was a short silence, and Piers mumbled a series of

inaudible words. 'Now you're being hasty... I can't find a cleaner at such short notice... I'm sure we can extend... You must stay on... I'll make it worth your while.'

She drew in a shocked breath. 'Are you serious? Even if you hadn't fired me, I would have left after what you did at the restaurant. I will drop the holiday lets keys and paperwork at your house this afternoon and transfer whatever money I owe back into Charles Ashville's bank account with details of everything I spent so far so you can't accuse me of any wrongdoing.'

There was another silence. 'I'm not at home today. I'll come round to Bluebell Cottage.'

'No!' The thought of being alone with Piers made her skin crawl. 'If you come to Belthorn this evening, I'll have everything ready for you.' And at least Piers wouldn't try anything with Stefan there.

He mumbled that he would be there by seven, and she put the phone down. Everything was changing... Soon she would move out of Bluebell Cottage, and with the loss of the Ashville contract and the clients who had deserted her, Bluebell Cleaning was as good as finished. On the plus side, these may be the incentives she needed to change her life around.

She could contact Maritel, show them her designs, and even play the recording of her meeting with Nathan...

Or she could draw a line on the past, forget Nathan and Maritel, and start afresh. There was no reason why she couldn't offer both cleaning and designing services. She could even tweak her slogan into 'When dust and grime get to you, or you fancy a home that's new... call Bluebell to the Rescue!' She pouted. Perhaps she could get her granddad to work on that one...

The most important thing was that Stefan was back and that he loved her. She put the kettle on, dropped a tea bag into a mug and sat down. Taking her mobile out of her bag, she saw that she had a voicemail message from Patrick.

'Hi, Cassie. I thought you might like to know that Darren was arrested this morning in Manchester. He was found asleep in his car at the side of the road, and taken to hospital with suspected sepsis. The police found a lot of stuff he'd stolen in the boot of his car, including my office printer and computer, so it looks like the folks he robbed in Red Moss will get their things back soon. I'll let you know when I find out more. Bye for now.'

Cassie sat down and heaved a sigh of relief. With Darren being arrested, no one would ever call her a thief again.

She could plan Christmas properly now...

Chapter Thirty-Nine

'There you are, young man,' Miss Parker said as she tottered into the small room in the community centre that had been allocated to serve as Santa's grotto. 'A couple of homemade mince pies, and one coffee, black, no sugar.' She smiled as she handed him the mug and the small cake. 'See? I remembered.'

Stefan stood up from the armchair where he had just spent a few uncomfortable hours and took the plate of cakes and the hot drink. 'Thank you. I need these.'

She smiled. 'The fair is winding down, and I was wondering if I could have a word about that old story we discussed the other day.'

'You mean, Ruth and André?'

She nodded. 'I decided that you were right. Their families need to know what was rumoured at the time. But please don't let my talking stop you from eating. You look exhausted, if you don't mind me saying.'

'Shell-shocked would be more accurate. I'm not used to dealing with children.' Stefan pulled his fake beard to drink a sip of hot coffee. The wig stuck to his scalp and tickled his neck. His head ached from the squeals of overexcited boys and girls who had bounced on his knees and from the Christmas music blearing out of speakers. And his back felt stiff, rusty and creaky from sitting down all afternoon.

Miss Parker laughed. 'At least the day is almost over… Now, about Ruth… My grandmother told me that there was a lot of speculation at the time that Ruth's former fiancé, Gideon Hardy, had something to do with her death.'

Stefan put his coffee down. 'Ruth was scared of him.'

'It looks like she had good reason to be. Gideon had a fearsome reputation for being a brute and a bully. On Christmas Eve – the night Ruth died – he drank heavily at the pub before driving his cart back to his farm. Two farm labourers saw him stop at a crossroads to harangue Ruth who was walking back to the rectory.'

Miss Parker paused, and explained, 'The vicar had taken her in after her parents threw her out of Patterdale Farm. The witnesses said that Gideon shouted at her then jumped down from his cart, grabbed hold of her and slapped her around the head, and before they could do anything to help, he threw her in the back of the cart and drove off. That was the last time Ruth was seen alive.'

'Why didn't they come forward when her body was recovered from Wolf Tarn?'

'Perhaps they did and nobody believed them, or Hardy threatened them or paid them off to avoid being convicted. Of course, there may not have been a crime... Nobody will ever know for sure what happened to Ruth.'

Thinking back to what Cassie had seen near Wolf Tarn on Christmas Eve ten years before, Stefan drew in a long breath and whispered, 'Perhaps you're wrong.'

Miss Parker looked up at him. 'Sorry?'

He shook his head. 'It's nothing. Just an idea I had.' A far-fetched and completely ridiculous idea, no doubt, and one he wasn't prepared to share with Miss Parker. He could however share what he'd found out about André Vaillant during his trip to Paris.

'What a tragic story,' Miss Parker commented when he had finished. 'Poor young man and poor Ruth.'

'At least now I know that André Vaillant did not abandon the woman he loved and meant to come back to Belthorn, which I suspected all along.'

He finished the coffee, gulped down the mince pies and handed her the empty mug and plate before slapping his false beard back on and patting the pillow stuffed in his costume. 'I'd better get ready for more visitors...'

Thankfully, Miss Parker was right about the fair winding

down. He welcomed a few more excited children into the grotto, then the music stopped and one of the organisers told him that he could call it a day. He decided to wait for Cassie at the pub since she hadn't paid him a visit as promised. She must have a good reason, but he couldn't help the uneasy feeling weighing down on his chest, and which had nothing to do with the fat pillow stuck under his tunic.

Back at the pub Tim, Mason and a couple of their friends from the mountain rescue team cheered when he walked in. They all clapped his shoulder in turn and Mason pushed a pint of bitter in front of him. 'Here, mate, get that down you. You've earned it. Nobody guessed you were Santa, and the charity gets to keep all the money collected this year.'

That was great news. At least he hadn't suffered all afternoon for nothing.

'You look shattered,' Tim said. 'There's nothing more tiring than dealing with little kids. I should know. I have three!' He grinned. 'They may be hard work but they're worth it. I can't wait to see their faces when they open their presents Christmas morning. By the way, I don't know if Cassie told you, but you're invited for Christmas dinner.'

'Am I?' Stefan put his pint down.

Tim's phone let out a loud jingling sound, and he smiled as he took it out of his pocket. 'Talking of which… it's Rachel.' His smile vanished the moment he put the phone to his ear.

'You're sure you looked everywhere? In the loft, and the barn? What about the tractor? He likes to climb in there, even though he's not allowed.' He nodded. 'I'm on my way. Try not to worry, love. We'll find him. He can't have gone very far – not with his broken arm.'

'Any problems?' Stefan asked as Tim held his phone, a frown creasing his forehead.

'It's Louis. He's nowhere to be found… The thing is, he had a temperature this morning and was left behind at the farm while Rachel took his brothers shopping, but it appears he sneaked out when Joseph was having a nap in front of the TV. Rachel said they've looked everywhere but they can't find him.'

'I'll get my car keys from Jim's flat and meet you back at the farm,' Stefan offered.

Tim nodded. 'Thanks. I'll set off now and wait for you there.'

Stefan ran upstairs, wrenched the pillow from under his top but didn't bother to get changed. Slipping his parka on, he shoved his fake beard, wig and red hat into the pockets. He had his sturdy army boots on and a pair of jeans under the red nylon trousers, so he would be all right if he had to walk on the hillside looking for Louis.

Tim had already left by the time he came down. Mason and his friends said they would be on standby to help with the search for the boy, and he promised to give them updates as soon as he could. He was held up by a few people wanting to congratulate him for raising funds for the mountain rescue charity, and then he was stuck in a traffic jam and was delayed another twenty minutes.

The dogs barked and jumped at him when he got out of the car in the muddy farmyard. Rachel opened the front door, and her face fell as she saw him.

'Oh... I thought it was Tim coming back.'

'Is there any news?'

She shook her head. 'Tim drove up to the sheepfold on his quad bike. Louis often goes there when he's sulking.'

'Have you tried the old quarry?'

She shook her head. 'Why would Louis go up there when he knows he's not allowed?'

Stefan was no expert on young boys' minds but that probably made the quarry even more attractive. 'I'll check it out anyway.' He took a torch out of the glove box and flicked the switch on to make sure it worked.

'By the way, have you heard from Cassie?'

'Her mobile is switched off, and she hasn't replied to my texts. She said she was going shopping this afternoon. Please hurry...'

The path climbed steeply up the hill and stones rolled underfoot, making progress tricky, but he swept the ground with his torchlight to make sure he didn't veer off the track and quickly got into a rhythm. He soon came across the rusty machinery he had seen before, and took care not to slip on the broken slate or trip on the massive cables discarded by the side of the path.

Finally he reached the fence and paused in front of the 'Keep Out' sign. There was nobody around, and no light shone from inside the quarry.

Stefan called and held his breath whilst he waited for a reply.

He called again, and this time a weak voice called back – Louis's voice!

'Louis? It's Stefan. Are you all right?'

'I slipped and I hurt my leg. Help me, please. It's dark and it's cold in here,' Louis's voice trailed off, weak and whimpering.

'Don't worry. I'm coming. Keep talking so I can locate you.'

'Hurry, please. I'm scared.'

Stefan remembered the place where the grillage was broken. He lifted the rusty metal up, and crouched down to get to the other side. He kept calling out random questions to keep Louis talking as he scrambled down a narrow path littered with debris and broken slate and entered a cave. He hissed a shocked breath as his boots splashed in freezing cold water that reached up to his shins and shone his light into the back of the cave, where Louis sat, hugging his knees.

'Don't move. I'm coming to get you.'

'I'm so glad you found me.' Louis's teeth chattered with cold and in the torchlight's harsh glare his little face was gaunt, his eyes huge and scared and his lips had a bluish tinge.

Stefan took off his parka and wrapped it around the boy's shoulders. 'Show me where you're hurt.'

Louis pointed to his ripped jeans and the bloodied knee peeping through the tear in the fabric.

'I knew it was wrong to come here, but I was annoyed with Mum because she didn't want to take me to town and it just wasn't fair. So I took my metal detector to go treasure hunting... but instead I fell and I hurt myself. Now Father Christmas will be angry and I won't get any presents, will I?' His voice wobbled with sobs.

Stefan gave him a reassuring smile. 'I'm sure everything will be fine. Can you move your leg at all?'

The boy shook his head. 'It hurts. I think it's broken.'

'Then I'll carry you out of here. Hang on.' He carefully lifted the shivering boy into his arms. 'Hold the torch so I can find the way out,' he instructed as he started out of the cave.

As soon as they were out into the open, he readjusted his hold on Louis so that he could hold him with one arm whilst pulling his phone out of his jeans pocket and dialling the emergency services number. Luckily he got through straight away, and the operator said that airlifting Louis would be the safest way to get him to hospital.

'A helicopter will be with you in five minutes,' she said.

Stefan ended the call and smiled at the boy. 'It looks like you are going on a helicopter ride.' Despite his best efforts to keep him awake, Louis became quiet, and his head soon lolled and flopped against Stefan's shoulder. The five minutes felt like an eternity, but at last the pulsing noise of a chopper's rotary blades sliced through the night. The noise got louder and red and white lights flickered in the night as the craft approached. Stefan held out his mobile and waved it above his head so that the glow from the screen would alert the pilot as to his position without blinding them as his torch light would have done.

Soon the helicopter shone a bright white light beam onto the hillside. The noise now made Stefan's ears ache, and the gusts of freezing wind churned by the rotors as the helicopter landed almost knocked the breath out of him, but Louis didn't even open his eyes. The paramedics – a man and a woman – jumped down. They were carrying a stretcher and a medical kit, and ran towards him.

'What's the status of the casualty?' the woman asked when she reached him.

Stefan mentioned the boy's injured leg and his broken arm. 'I think he's got hypothermia too. He's become drowsy in the past few minutes,' Stefan added as he lowered a sleepy Louis onto the stretcher. The paramedics checked Louis's breathing, examined his arm and his injured leg, and covered him with a blanket.

'You're coming too,' the medic told him, as he gave Stefan his parka back and gestured to the helicopter.

Stefan recoiled. 'I'd rather make my way back to the farm. I must tell Louis's parents that he is safe and on his way to hospital.' He hadn't flown in a helicopter since the crash in Mali, and he'd rather walk miles on his own in the dark than climb on board.

He took another step back but the medic shook his head. 'There's no need. We'll radio the emergency services and they'll let them know. We don't want you getting lost or injured on your way back down and having to respond to another emergency tonight. Get in.'

Every second he delayed getting in the chopper put Louis at risk, and this time he had no choice other than to comply. The noise and vibrations of the craft reverberated inside him, all the way to his core. His heart thumped, his stomach churned and cold sweat pearled on his forehead, and his hands shook as he clipped his belt on.

The pilot turned round and gave him the thumbs up, and Stefan nodded back. A few months before, he had been in the piloting seat, and now the thought of a ten-minute flight gave him a panic attack...

He had to get a hold on himself. He focussed his attention on the medics as they checked Louis's vitals, and when the helicopter lifted off and took to the sky, he shoved his hands in his pocket and fiddled with the wig and the fake beard, but he was so tense it felt like he was about to snap.

They were a few minutes into the flight when Louis opened his eyes and looked around, fear and confusion in his eyes as he took in his surroundings.

'Where am I? What's going on? Where's my mum?' His voice wobbled as he moved restlessly on the stretcher.

'We're taking you to hospital so the doctors can take a look at you,' the female medic said, shouting over the noise of the engine.

'I want my mummy. Now!' Louis's eyes filled with tears and his face twisted in pain. He needed something to distract him until they landed.

Stefan leaned over. 'Listen, pal, your mum and dad will be at the hospital soon after we get there. In the meantime, I'm here with you... and if you're a good boy I'll let you in on a secret. Can you keep a secret?'

Louis looked at him and nodded. Stefan took his wig, hat and beard out of his pocket and slipped them on, and Louis's eyes almost popped out in shock. 'You're... Santa?'

'Not the real one but Santa couldn't come to the fair today and asked me to stand in for him. It was me today in the grotto, but you mustn't tell anyone – not even your brothers.'

'The real Santa let your borrow his clothes?' Louis's eyes filled with wonder.

'He did.' He wasn't *exactly* lying... and if he was, it was for a good cause.

Opposite him, the medics smiled.

'Can I let you in on another secret? I haven't been in a helicopter for a while and I'm feeling a bit nervous.' Terrified would be a more accurate description of his state of mind right now.

'Are you scared you'll have another accident, like the one you had in Africa?' Louis looked at him with concern. How mature and concerned he sounded.

Stefan nodded.

'Then I'll hold your hand. Don't be afraid. Everything will be all right.' And the little boy sneaked his hand in his and gripped his fingers tight.

The medic tapped on his arm and smiled. 'Are you all right?'

'Yeah, I am now.' Still holding Louis's hand, Stefan smiled back and reclined against the seat. His fear about flying slowly subsided. It would be fine. This wasn't Mali. No armed thugs lay in ambush, waiting to shoot them down. They were on their way to the hospital, and he would soon be with Cassie.

Chapter Forty

Cassie smiled as she admired the feast laid out on the kitchen table. There was fresh bread and a pot of that pâté Salomé said French people were crazy about, a platter of king prawns and smoked salmon, three kinds of French cheese and a mixed salad. A bottle of champagne chilled in the fridge together with a deluxe Yule log from Salomé's bakery. She had decorated the kitchen with fresh sprigs of pine and holly, lit a fire and the fairy lights in the drawing room, and plumped up all the cushions she had made in the past few weeks.

There may be no tree, tinsel or baubles, but Belthorn was ready for Christmas... And so was she. She had taken a bath, washed her hair and put make-up on, before slipping on a slinky black satin dress with a low-cut front that Cecilia had lent her and her black pumps. There would be no dungarees, Doc Martens boots or bandanas that evening, only softness and seduction. At least that was the plan.

Cassie checked the clock. Seven already. Where was Stefan? She should have called at the fair to remind him not to be late, but she'd had too much fun shopping and chatting to her friends at The Studio that she had left it too late and the community centre was closing when she drove past. And then she had driven back to Belthorn in a hurry to get everything ready.

The sound of a car engine broke the silence. At last, he was back! She rushed to the hallway to open the front door, and her spirits plummeted. It wasn't Stefan's Range Rover that stood in front of the house but Piers's SUV.

She may not want to see him on her own, but they had unfinished business, and it was too late to pretend she wasn't in, so she stood on the threshold in the freezing cold.

'Hello, gorgeous.' He smiled his usual boyish smile as he climbed out of his car, combed his fingers in his mop of light-blond hair and gave her a long, slow stare.

'You're a sight for sore eyes,' he added in a hoarse voice as he took a few unsteady steps forward. He reeked of beer. How could he even drive when he'd been drinking?

She had no intention of letting him come into the house. 'Stay here while I get the paperwork and the keys,' she said, retreating into the hallway and pushing the door closed.

Ignoring her, he pushed the door aside and strode straight in. 'Not so fast. Don't you think you should ask me in and offer me a drink so we can talk?'

She shook her head. 'I think you've had enough to drink already, and I don't want to talk. I only want to give you the files and the keys.'

'Well, I want to talk. You are causing me a lot of problems, Cassie.' He glared at her, all pretence of joviality gone from his face or his voice. 'There's no way I can find a new cleaner so fast. You can't quit... Be reasonable.'

She hissed a shocked breath as if she'd been stung. 'Reasonable? You do have a short memory! You fired me, remember? What's more, you questioned the quality of my work, accused me of stealing from the cottages, and then tried to blackmail me into sleeping with you. The only reasonable thing to do, as far as I'm concerned, is to keep as far away from you as I can.'

He tightened his mouth and a twitch appeared by the side of his left eye. 'What if I increased your fees – if I forgot about the rent at Bluebell Cottage?'

She crossed her arms. 'I still wouldn't stay on. It's over, Piers.'

He let out a long sigh. 'That bitch Gabrielle is mithering me, asking me for audits, accounts and all kinds of reports, *and* this morning she called to demand I hire you to refurbish this place and the cottages.'

She stood still. 'Gabrielle wants me to renovate the cottages?'

He nodded. 'And Belthorn too... She wants to see your proposals and your budget as soon as possible.'

'How does she know about my designs?'

He sneered. 'Don't play the innocent with me. She knows because you complained about me, probably threatened to sue me for sexual harassment. And you pushed that refurbishing scheme of yours at the same time... Put a bit of pressure on her that way. It was very clever, really.'

'I didn't tell Gabrielle anything. In fact, I haven't spoken to her for months.'

'So who did? How does she know my management style is inappropriate?' He made gestures with his fingers to indicate speech marks. 'And who told her about your so-called skills as a designer?'

'I did,' Stefan said as he walked into the hallway, his face red from the cold. He smiled at her. 'I knew she would love your ideas. I hope you don't mind.'

He narrowed his eyes to stare at Piers. 'I also told her that I didn't think much of the way you behaved with Cassie.'

'Stefan!' Heaving a sigh of relief, Cassie rushed to his side. He enclosed her in his arms with a deep sigh and kissed her forehead, before pulling away and glancing from her to Piers and back to her again, a quizzical look on his face. 'What's going on? Are you all right?'

She nodded. 'Piers came to collect the paperwork for the holiday lets. I quit working for the Ashville Estate.'

Piers gave her a sheepish look and made a gesture with his hands. 'Cassie, come on. There's no need to be so hasty. Can we not come to some kind of arrangement? What am I going to do if I can't find a cleaner at such short notice?'

She smiled. 'Buy a pair of rubber gloves, a packet of sponges and some cleaning fluid and do it yourself. I'm sure you'll manage.'

She went into the drawing room, and collected the bag with the logbooks, paperwork and keys she had gathered, and she handed it to him. 'Good luck, Piers, and have a Merry Christmas.'

He snatched the bag from her, cast a murderous glance in her direction and stormed out. Seconds later, the revving of his engine resounded outside.

'I'm so glad you're here.' She nestled in Stefan's arms, her nose brushed against the red Father Christmas nylon tunic and she looked up in surprise. 'Why are you still dressed as Santa? And where have you been all this time? I was getting worried, especially when Piers showed up and I was on my own.'

He let out a long sigh. 'It's been quite a day, but before I tell you all about it, I need to sit down and have a bite to eat.'

As he demolished the pâté and the bread, the salmon and the cheese, he told her about Louis's misadventure in the old quarry and the helicopter flight to the hospital. 'He'll be fine but he had to stay in overnight for observation,' he said. 'I left when Tim and Rachel arrived.'

'Poor little boy.' She looked at him, eyes full of concern, and touched her fingers to the sleeve of his red tunic. 'What about you? What was it like to be in a helicopter again?'

How well she knew him already. He met her tender gaze, and covered her hand with his. 'I was terrified at first. I couldn't even climb into the chopper... but I did, and now I think I'll be all right. It may take me a while to get there, but I think I can fly again.'

'That's great news!' She laughed and clapped her hands. Her beaming smile dug those cute dimples in her cheeks again, filling his heart with sunshine and joy, and he couldn't help but smile back.

'We must celebrate!' she added. 'We'll take the bottle of champagne to the drawing room and drink it in front of the fire.'

'Before that, I'd like to talk to you.' He rose to his feet, took her hands and pulled her up. He'd thought about it whilst waiting for Tim and Rachel to arrive at the hospital, and in the taxi back to Red Moss.

'Put your boots on, wrap up in your coat and your hat. We're going outside.'

Her happy smile faded, her face paled and her fingers tensed in his grip. 'But...'

He looked down. 'It will be all right, Cassie. Come with me. If this afternoon taught me anything, if *you* taught me anything over the past few weeks, it's that sometimes you need to face your fears or you get stuck – stuck in the past, stuck in misery and regrets, with darkness and ghosts crowding your heart and your mind, and stopping you from moving on. Come outside with me. I'd like to tell you a story.'

'Why can't you tell me your story here?'

Without leaving her any more time to protest, he led her into the hallway, took her coat off the rack and handed it to her before shrugging his parka on.

'I can't do this,' she whispered, her eyes huge with worry.

'Yes, you can.' He put his index finger under her chin, tilted her face up and kissed her lips, before grabbing hold of her pom-pom hat and pulling it on her head. He opened the front door as she swapped her shoes for her snow boots and wrapped a scarf around her neck. 'Come on.'

The moonlight carved haunting shadows in the landscape but was bright enough to light the way to the lake. The night was quiet, only disturbed by sounds of their breathing and their boots crunching the icy snow. A silver ray caught the tip of a collapsed wall of the ruined abbey. Shadows seemed to move and thicken as they walked past. Cassie's hand tensed and trembled, but he pushed on until they reached the shores of the lake.

Wolf Tarn stood still and peaceful in front of them. Standing behind Cassie, Stefan enfolded her into his arms.

'I wanted to tell you what I found out about Ruth and André.'

'We didn't need to come here. You could have told me in Belthorn... Let's go back, before...' She shuddered and he held her more tightly.

'Nothing's going to happen, Cassie. I do believe that you saw something here, ten years ago – that somehow the memory of a terrible event was etched onto the fabric of that night. I'm not sure what exactly it was, but I don't want you to be scared any more.

'When I was in Paris I asked a friend who works in the army records to do a bit of digging for me. André didn't abandon Ruth. He died of tuberculosis in 1922, in a sanatorium in Haute-Savoie.'

Cassie turned round to face him, slid her hands on his forearms, and looked up. Her eyes reflected the starry sky, and silver moonlight bathed her face. 'In his last letter to Ruth, he mentioned being ill with the influenza,' she said. 'Perhaps it wasn't the flu he was suffering from, but TB, that's probably why he asked his sister to write to Ruth to break the relationship off.'

'He knew there was little hope for him to recover, and he didn't want to risk exposing Ruth to the deadly disease if she came over to France to nurse him.'

Cassie's eyes shone with tears. 'He knew she would have come for him, so he pretended to be a cad and not to care for her. This is so sad... He must have died thinking she hated him for abandoning her. Do you think he knew she drowned herself because of him?'

'I don't think Ruth committed suicide,' Stefan said then. 'I think Gideon Hardy killed her.' He told her what Miss Parker had related at the fair that afternoon.

Cassie gasped in shock and started trembling in his arms again. 'Do you think that's what I saw that night? That somehow I witnessed Gideon Hardy murder Ruth... all those years ago?'

He slid his hands up and down her back to keep her warm and stop her from shaking. 'A few weeks ago, I would have said that it was nonsense. Now, knowing what we know about Ruth's death, I'm not sure.'

'What about *the other one*?' she whispered. 'The man hiding in the ruins of the abbey?'

He shrugged. 'It's up to you to decide if it was a shadow, a trick of the moonlight, or...'

'The Grey Friar,' she finished, drawing in a shaky breath, and snuggling in his arms.

'Let's go back,' he said after a while. 'I think I'm ready for that champagne you promised earlier.'

'There's chocolate log for dessert,' she said.

He gave her a long, hot, leisurely kiss. 'Forget about dessert. I have a much better idea.'

Chapter Forty-One

'Surprise!'

'Mum! Keith! What are you doing here?' Cassie dropped the bag full of Christmas presents to the floor and hurried across the living room and into her mother's open arms.

'Merry Christmas, my darling,' her mother said, enclosing her in a tight hug. 'We thought we'd spend Christmas back here with you this year. Tim and Rachel knew we were coming, of course, but they were sworn to secrecy.'

'I can't believe you're here. This is the best surprise ever... the best Christmas ever!' Cassie's voice broke and her eyes filled with tears. 'I don't even know why I'm crying. It must be because I'm so happy.' She gave her mother another hug, then snuggled in her step-dad's arms, enjoying the feel of his solid, comforting embrace.

'Merry Christmas, Cassie,' he said. 'I believe there's been quite a lot of drama lately at Red Moss, but that it's all ended well and the thief was arrested in the end.'

'Yes, he was, and I am relieved it's finally over. Patrick called earlier. He said that Darren was still in the hospital but was responding to treatment and should be all right... and when he comes out, he'll be taken into custody. Most of the stuff recovered from the boot of his car was traced back to their legitimate owners... But best of all, I called at Bluebell Cottage before coming here and there were cards from Doris, Sylvia Gasby and Tabitha Sweeney wishing me a Merry Christmas and apologising for upsetting me. Sylvia even wrote that she would like me to clean for her again.'

She let out a long sigh. 'I am so glad people won't be gossiping about me any longer... But enough about all that! When did you arrive?'

'Yesterday evening,' her mother replied.

Turning to Stefan, she smiled. 'I assume you're Stefan – Louis's hero?'

He arched an eyebrow. 'Hero?'

She laughed. 'Oh yes! If he is to be believed, Batman, Superman and all the superheroes from Avengers are nothing compared to you. He's been full of your exploits and told us in great detail about your rescuing him from the cave. I am very pleased to meet you at last.'

Sitting down on the sofa, she patted the seat next to her and gestured to Cassie. 'Come here, my darling, we need a good catch up. Rachel said she had everything under control in the kitchen. Your granddad is setting up the boys' new train track upstairs, and Tim is seeing to the animals. Farming doesn't stop because it's Christmas Day.'

'I'll ask him if he needs a hand,' Stefan said, probably eager to escape any further enquiries from her mother.

'I'll come with you,' Keith said, and the two men walked out into the yard. Cassie couldn't help but pull a face. Keith always took his step-dad's duties very seriously. No doubt he now intended to quiz Stefan about his plans for the future...

Her mother wrapped her arm around her shoulder. 'So, my darling, tell me everything that's been happening around here, and, more importantly, tell me all about Stefan. I don't see any trace of the miserable Grinch in him at all, especially when he looks at you.'

It was a bright and clear winter's day. A bright and wonderful Christmas Day, filled with love and surprises, with family and fun, singing and laughter, and magnificent food. Cassie had feared that it might be too much for Stefan – for the man who had come to Belthorn to forget all about Christmas, the man who didn't even want a Christmas tree. The man who had opened her silly presents that morning with a stunned expression on his face, followed by a naughty grin. He had put on the silly hat, and brandished his feather duster and given chase to her throughout the bedroom, before catching her, throwing her on the bed and making love to her. Again, and again. He hadn't given her a Christmas present, but then she hadn't expected one. The only present she wanted was him – to paraphrase a well-known Christmas song – for however long he was planning to stay.

'Since it is Stefan's first English Christmas Day,' Rachel announced as she came out of the kitchen with an enormous glass bowl filled with layers of sponge biscuits, jelly and custard, topped with whipped cream, 'I made a very special pudding. I figured it was time he tried some trifle.'

All eyes were on Stefan as he sampled the dessert and declared it delicious. Cassie's granddad regaled them with several dessert related jokes, and produced a bottle of sherry he said he was saving for a special occasion, and pudding was followed by a game of Monopoly that had everybody arguing and laughing. All the time, Stefan looked at her across the table, his tawny eyes in turns warm or serious, making her cheeks grow hot and her heart beat harder. After the game, they said their goodbyes, promised to call again the following day to help finish the leftovers, and Stefan drove back to Belthorn.

'Do you fancy a walk?' Stefan asked when he stopped in front of the manor house. She said she did and he took her hand and led her to Wolf Tarn as daylight faded into the blue grey dusk and the fells slowly disappeared in shadows.

How strange that her fears had vanished, that she was able to walk on the lakeshore without the pangs of anxiety and the terror she used to experience every time Belthorn was mentioned. She had no idea what she had really seen ten years before, no idea if it had been a memory, a hallucination, or a trick of the moonlight, but thanks to Stefan she wasn't afraid any longer.

She turned to face him, looked up. 'Thank you...'

'I want to thank you...' he said at the same time.

He smiled, traced the outline of her lips with his finger then cupped her cheek in the palm of his hand. 'We're doing this again... Go on, you first.'

She cocked her head to one side, enjoying the warmth of his hand against her cold skin. 'Thank you for coming with me to Patterdale Farm today. It meant a lot to me. I know you're not keen on Christmas, so I am very grateful that you agreed to spend the day with my family. All together, they can be quite overwhelming.' She held his hand. 'And thank you for talking to Gabrielle about my ideas, and giving me the chance and the confidence to prove myself as a designer.'

He stroked her cheek slowly, bent down and kissed her lips. 'You have already proved yourself as a designer... and more importantly as someone who touches and changes people's lives... You have a gift, Cassie. You have your smile, and your kindness, and your courage.' He punctuated almost every word with a kiss. 'God knows I was a miserable, self-centred, grouchy man when I arrived here, wallowing in self-pity and despair.'

'You had good reason to be!' she protested. 'You'd been through war, the death of your friend and of the people you cared for. You were injured and in pain, lonely and...'

He interrupted her with another kiss. 'And you changed all that. With your kindness, your cushions, your smiles and that lemon scent your granddad says you spray around to improve people's mood... You gave me the greatest gift I could ever have wished for. The greatest gift a man can ever want. Your love.'

His voice became rough, and in the dim light of dusk, his eyes were a soft and mellow gold. Her heart was close to bursting with love, and she wasn't even trying to stop the tears from falling.

He cleared his throat, and pulled something out of his pocket. A small pink box she recognised as being a gift box from The Studio.

'I should have given you this earlier,' he said. 'I was waiting for the right moment. The right place. The right words. And this is it.' He gestured to Wolf Tarn, to the stars that had started to twinkle in the darkening skies, and the shiny moon peeping over the line of the mountains.

He gave her the box. Her fingers were clumsy as she opened it and pulled the beautiful necklace out. It was a tiny, beautiful, delicately carved swan, hanging from a fine gold chain. A work of art.

'You changed me, Cassie. You are that beautiful white swan from the story, the one that saves the ugly hunchback by giving him her love. You rescued me from myself, showed me that I could have a present, and a future. I love you more than I ever, ever thought I could love anyone, and I hope you'll want me by your side forever.'

He pointed to the necklace nestling in the palm of her hand. 'It's not much, I know,' he said quickly. 'But I promise I'll do better next Christmas, and the Christmas after that... and every Christmas for the rest of our lives.'

And as he enfolded her in his arms, and touched his lips to hers, her heart felt as big as the moon rising above the snowy peaks, as big as the sky filling with stars.

Thank You

Dear Reader,

Thank you so much for reading *Bluebell's Christmas Magic*. I loved writing Cassie and Stefan's story, and I hope you enjoyed spending some time with them and their friends in the little Cumbrian village of Red Moss. The story was inspired by a family holiday in Coniston, which is one of my all times favourite places, and I hope my writing did this wonderful place justice.

If you did enjoy the story, then I would be very grateful if you could take a few minutes to leave a review. It is a wonderful feeling for an author when readers let you know that they loved your story and your characters. Reviews are invaluable, not only to raise a book's profile, but also to encourage the author to keep writing, especially when self-doubt creeps in.

Please feel free to contact me using the information at the bottom of my 'About the Author' page.

Marie

About the Author

Originally from Lyon in France, Marie now lives in Lancashire with her family. She works full-time as a modern languages teacher, and in her spare time loves writing romance and dreaming about romantic heroes. She writes both historical and contemporary romance, and best-selling *Little Pink Taxi* was her debut romantic comedy novel with Choc Lit. She is a member of the Romantic Novelists' Association and the Society of Authors. Her native France, as well as her passion for history and research, very much influences her writing, and all her novels have what she likes to call 'a French twist'!

For more on Marie visit:
www.twitter.com/MarieLaval1
www.facebook.com/marielavalauthor/
https://www.pinterest.co.uk/laval0232/

More Choc Lit

From Marie Laval

Little Pink Taxi

Take a ride with Love Taxis, the cab company with a Heart …

Rosalie Heart is a well-known face in Irlwick – well, if you drive a bright pink taxi and your signature style is a pink anorak, you're going to draw a bit of attention! But Rosalie's company Love Taxis is more than just a gimmick – for many people in the remote Scottish village, it's a lifeline.

Which is something that Marc Petersen will never understand. Marc's ruthless approach to business doesn't extend to pink taxi companies running at a loss. When he arrives in Irlwick to see to a new acquisition – Raventhorn, a rundown castle – it's apparent he poses a threat to Rosalie's entire existence; not just her business, but her childhood home too.

On the face of it Marc and Rosalie should loathe each other, but what they didn't count on was somebody playing cupid …

Escape to the Little Chateau

Will Amy's dreams of a Provençal escape come true?

There are many reasons Amy Carter is determined to make Bellefontaine, her farmhouse hotel in the French countryside, a success. Of course, there's the time and money she's put in to making it beautiful, but she also has something to prove – particularly to people like Fabien Coste.

Fabien is the owner of the nearby château, and he might just be the most arrogant, patronising man Amy has ever met … unfortunately, he's also the most handsome.

But as rumours circulate in the local community and secrets about the old farmhouse begin to reveal themselves, Amy quickly sees the less idyllic side of life at Bellefontaine. Could Fabien be the man to help prevent her Provençal dream from turning into a nightmare?

A Paris Fairy Tale

Is Paris the city of happily ever afters?

Workaholic art historian Aurora Black doesn't have time for fairy tales or Prince Charmings, even in the most romantic city in the world. She has recently been hired by a Parisian auction house for a job that could make or break her career. Unfortunately, daredevil journalist Cédric Castel seems intent on disrupting Aurora's routine.

As Aurora and Cédric embark on a journey across France, they get more than they bargained for as they find themselves battling rogue antiques dealers and personal demons, not to mention a growing attraction to each other.

But with the help of a fairy godmother or two, could they both find their happily ever afters?

Visit www.choc-lit.com for details.

Angel of the Lost Treasure

An ancient secret hidden within a mother's song …

When young widow, Marie-Ange Norton is invited to Beauregard in France by the mysterious Monsieur Malleval to collect an inheritance, she has no choice but to accept.

But when she embarks on the voyage with her fiery-tempered travelling companion Capitaine Hugo Saintclair, little does she know what waits for her across the sea in turbulent nineteenth-century France on the eve of Napoleon's return from exile. When she arrives, she is taken aback by Malleval's fascination with her family – seemingly inspired by his belief they are connected to a sacred relic he's read about in coded manuscripts by the Knights Templar.

As it becomes clear that Malleval's obsession has driven him to madness, Marie-Ange is horrified to realise she is more the man's prisoner than his guest. Not only that, but Hugo is the only person who might be able to help her, and he could represent a different kind of danger …

Happy Dreams at Mermaid Cove

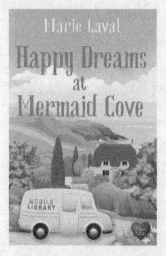

From the big city to a little yellow mobile library on the Isle of Skye …

Workaholic art historian Aurora When Jenna Palmer agrees to the new position of mobile librarian on the tiny Arrandale peninsular of the Isle of Skye, she knows she's signing up for difficult working conditions and mediocre wages. But Jenna needs to get away, and a little yellow mobile library called Buttercup could be her escape to happier dreams …

However, whilst Jenna can get to grips with foggy island roads, local mermaid legends and even big purple monsters, she never expected to have to contend with a boss as grumpy as Daniel McGregor, or a young book lover as enthusiastic as his niece, Katrina.

Arrandale might represent Jenna's safe port in a storm, but could she and Buttercup also become a beacon of hope to Daniel, Katrina and the entire island community?

Visit www.choc-lit.com for details.

Introducing Choc Lit

We're an independent publisher creating
a delicious selection of fiction.
Where heroes are like chocolate – irresistible!
Quality stories with a romance at the heart.

See our selection here:
www.choc-lit.com

We'd love to hear how you enjoyed *Bluebell's Christmas
Magic*. Please visit **www.choc-lit.com** and give your feedback
or leave a review where you purchased this novel.

Choc Lit novels are selected by genuine readers like yourself.
We only publish stories our Choc Lit Tasting Panel want to
see in print. Our reviews and awards speak for themselves.

Could you be a Star Selector and join our Tasting Panel?
Would you like to play a role in choosing which novels
we decide to publish? Do you enjoy reading women's
fiction? Then you could be perfect for our Tasting Panel.

Visit here for more details…
www.choc-lit.com/join-the-choc-lit-tasting-panel

Keep in touch:
Sign up for our monthly newsletter Spread for all the latest
news and offers: www.spread.choc-lit.com. Follow us
on Twitter: @ChocLituk and Facebook: Choc Lit.

Where heroes are like chocolate – irresistible!